In the Crosshairs: The Body on Leffis Key

by

M. S. Spencer

Dedication

To Gary, My Love & the Voice of Reason in My Head

Chapter One

Diddle diddle dumpling, my son John
Went to bed with his britches on.
One shoe off, and one shoe on.
Diddle diddle dumpling, my son John.

Leffis Key, Tuesday, May 16

"Okay, let me see…" Palmer, from her perch at the top of a small hill, looked out over the choppy water, then down at her map. "That's the Intracoastal Waterway, and across the way is Cortez. *Hmm.* Note says it's a historic fishing village. I'll have to check it out." Her gaze swung north. "The Cortez bridge and the town of Bradenton Beach." Behind her rose the dunes of Leffis Key and behind them, across the road, was Coquina Beach. Due south lay the Longboat Pass inlet, Land's End, and Jewfish Key. Everywhere she turned, she faced deep blue sky, white, white sand, and undulating palm trees. "Breathtaking." A movement below caught her eye. "Oh, look! It's a flock of ibis!" The pure white birds meandered among the mangroves, their long, curved bills dipping in and out of the muck.

Once they moved on and were lost to sight among the trees, she raised her binoculars to the shoreline. *What's that big bird, the one flapping his wings? A great blue heron? No…too small.* She flipped through the pages of her guide. There—dark blue with a rufous head and neck. Bigger than a little blue heron. *Could it be a reddish egret?* Her skin tingled with excitement. If it were, it would be a life bird for her. Her gaze swept the lagoon. "Damn, it's gone."

A tremor of disappointment passed through her. So far she hadn't seen a bird in Florida that she hadn't already observed on Chincoteague or Hatteras. *Shouldn't come as a surprise, Palmer. This is the Atlantic Flyway, after all.* Most eastern birds migrated along the same path every year, resting at the same spots along the coast from Florida to Canada. *Still, it would be nice to see something different.*

She glanced at her watch. Eleven thirty. *I'll break for lunch in a few minutes.* The sun was hot on her shoulders. The slight breeze here on the hummock that dominated the Coquina Bay nature trail wasn't enough to cool her down. *Think I'll ramble through the mangroves one more time, then go up to that little village center for something to eat.*

She stumbled down the rocky path to a wooden bridge that crossed a weed-choked creek. Beyond it lay a boardwalk that wound its way through the swamp. She'd gone a few feet when the trail took a sharp turn, revealing a clearing in the thicket of mangroves. Something pink fluttered on the ground. She had started toward it when a whoop of laughter came from the water. *Uh oh, I hope it isn't a party boat—they'll scare away the wildlife.* Palmer stepped up her pace.

She rounded a clump of black mangrove. The pink patch had grown larger. She slowed, treading softly on the warped boards. *Aha.* A roseate spoonbill perched at the spot where the bank sloped into the bay, its flat bill—rounded like a soup spoon at the end—poised over the water. With lightning swiftness it speared a minnow, but before Palmer could snap a photo, the bird took off in a flurry of ruffled wings. Even though it dropped the fish, it didn't pause, flapping away over the water and honking loudly.

Something must have flushed it. It couldn't have been her—she was too far away. She kept going.

An observation platform had been built at the end of the walkway, affording a view of the channel. She bent over the rail. About ten yards out, what looked like a big mound of black seaweed pulsed and eddied on the surface. Patches of yellow peeked through the mass. Suddenly part of the mound broke away and raised its wings. *That's a bird!* A black vulture clutched something in its talon. She adjusted her lens. A cylindrical object about four inches long, pale white. *Fish?* No. Crab leg? She focused the binoculars back on the mound. More yellow was visible. *It looks like fabric.* "Wait—that isn't seaweed. It's a whole mob of vultures. They're feeding on something." She raised her arm. "Shoo!"

The birds ignored her. *It's probably just a dead fish.* She was about to give up when the *chug-chug* of a motor approaching made her pause. A loud report rang out. *A rifle shot?* The birds swarmed up into the air, emitting angry squawks and catcalls.

A man's voice boomed. "Get away from there. Beat it! Scram!"

At first she thought he was yelling at her. *Hello? Who the hell do you think you are?* She shaded her eyes. A tall, thin man stood in the stern of his bass boat, a long gun tucked in the crook of his arm. As she watched, he laid it down and picked up a small landing net. He leaned over the stern and swished the net around. Suddenly he went still, then reared back and sat down. Wiping his forehead with a bandanna, he stared into the water.

Curiosity won out and she cried, "Can you tell what it is?"

He squinted into the sun.

She called again. "You there! What is it?"

Instead of answering, he moved back to the stern and revved the motor. He turned the boat so the bow faced the object and gently propelled it toward the land. Palmer stepped off the boardwalk and followed a faint track of pounded mud that led through the undergrowth to a sliver of beach. When he was close enough, the man shouted, "Do you have a phone?"

"Yes. Why?"

"Because you'd better call 9-1-1." At that instant, the thing he was pushing rolled onto the sand.

Palmer screamed.

The man cut the engine. "Why the devil are you screaming, lady?"

She stopped abruptly and pointed. "That's a…a…"

"Corpse. Yes. And your squealing like an egret in heat isn't going to do him any good now. I recommend calling the police as a more practical course of action."

His calm voice brought her back to reality. "Egrets do not have estrus cycles," she stated with dignity.

"Oh, yeah? Did *not* know that." He hopped out of the boat and dragged it up on the beach.

The body lay on its stomach, its head facing away. From the sparse gray hairs covering his crown, Palmer guessed him to be an older man. He was dressed in a

4

loud yellow plaid jacket and chinos. One bare foot and one tasseled loafer. *No socks.*

The eclectic ensemble practically shouted Goodwill. Palmer was trying to discern what was awry with his hand when the fisherman prodded the thing's shoulder with the barrel of his gun. She heard a popping sound, and a horrible stench rose from the corpse.

The man pinched his nose. "He must have been in the water a few days. Vultures only started on him when he rose to the surface." He bent down and looked at the face. "Hold on…Oh God. It's—" He straightened. "Are you going to make that call or should I leave you here with him while I go get help?"

"Oh, oh. Sorry." She punched in the numbers. "Hi. Hi. This is Palmer Lind and…what's that? Yes, I'm on…um…Anna Maria Island and—"

Her companion held up his hand. "Tell them we're on Leffis Key—the Coquina Bay Walk. The…object is on the beach at the end of the boardwalk."

She repeated the directions to the dispatcher. "We've found a dead body…Yes, washed up here…I don't know…Could the police? The marine patrol? Yes…thank you." She hung up. "They're coming."

He snorted. "Thanks for the update." He leaned against the bow of the boat and folded his arms.

She retreated up the path as far from the scene as possible.

"You leaving?"

"I thought…er…I'd direct the cops when they get here."

"They won't come that way."

"What do you mean?" When the man didn't explain, she stamped a foot. "Who are you, anyway?"

"Me? I'm just a drifter." He winked. "Out mullet fishing. Heard you cry out and came to investigate."

"You don't have a name?"

He looked for a minute as though he wouldn't answer, then blurted, "Hooper. Sonny Hooper."

She surveyed his denim shorts, flip-flops, and a torn T-shirt that read Star Market: Free Beer on Thursdays. "You must be a local."

He gave her a strange grin. "You could say that." A siren rent the quiet air. It seemed to be coming across the water. "Here they are."

Payback time. "What was your first clue?"

He didn't answer. A green-and-white Carolina skiff with the Manatee County emblem and Marine Patrol emblazoned on its side came into view. Hooper waved his hat over his head, and they steered closer. A cheerful, portly man in a dark green uniform called from the bow. "We got a report of a floater?"

"Right here, Officer."

The man addressed his colleague in the stern. "Hold the boat steady, Rory." He jumped to shore. "Whew, what a stink." He pulled a phone from his belt. "Maggie? Sid here. Got a stiff, partial decomposition. Call an ambulance. Have 'em meet us at the post. We'll bring him down in the boat. Oh, and alert Manatee sheriff's office." He chewed his lip. "Might as well call Bradenton Beach and Longboat Key cops too." He snapped it off and pulled out a notebook. "Now, who found the body?"

Hooper seemed to debate with himself before reluctantly stating, "I did."

"Was it on the beach?"

"No, it was in the water."

6

"And you two were cruising by and saw it?"

Palmer gasped. "No, no. I don't know this man. I was up there"—she pointed at the sandy bluff that marked the highest elevation in Bradenton Beach— "and saw a spoonbill, and then some vultures, and…and…"

Hooper broke in. "I noticed the vultures, too. It was kind of unusual to see them so low on the water, so I ventured over."

Without thinking, Palmer offered, "He shot at the birds to scare them off."

Sid cocked an eyebrow. "Shot?"

Hooper grinned and went to his boat. He came back with his gun. "My trusty potato shooter. It did the trick."

Sid chuckled. "Too bad you didn't have a slingshot."

"It's in my other boat."

The patrolman gestured at Rory. "Throw me a tarp." He turned back to Palmer and Hooper. "Better come on back to the rescue facility with me. We'll meet the police there." He took out a notebook. "Names?" He looked at Palmer.

"Palmer Lind."

"Address?"

"I'm visiting from Virginia and renting a condo on Gulf of Mexico Drive. I don't remember the address. Fifty-eight something."

"Phone where we can reach you?"

"703-555-4914."

"Okay, and you?" Sid held his pencil poised.

Hooper hesitated a fraction of a second. "Sonny…er…Hooper. I live in the Village."

"Longbeach Village?"

"Yeah. Seven-eighty Bayou Hammock Road. My cell is 202-555-8304."

Sid returned his notebook to his chest pocket. "All right, why don't you follow me in your boat."

Palmer took a step back. "I have a car."

"Oh? Where is it?"

"I parked it over in the Coquina Beach lot."

The officer shook his head. "Tell you what—you come along with your friend here, and you can retrieve your car when we're finished with you."

"He's not my—" Palmer caught Sid's expression and settled for "Okay."

"Here, Hooper, give me a hand."

The two men rolled the corpse onto the tarp, taking care not to touch it, and lifted the bundle into the patrol boat.

Palmer climbed into the bass boat, and Hooper pushed it back in the water. They motored after the skiff. Hooper gazed over Palmer's head, his expression unreadable. She studied him. Dusty blond hair cut short, but not short enough to lose the wave. Luminescent gray eyes whose brooding depths reminded her of a sea captain far from home or a world-weary traveler. His gnarly hands plus the five o'clock shadow on his chin attested to his beach bum status. She checked out the filthy shorts and ragged shirt barely concealing the tanned chest. *He must live alone.* The thought had a curious effect on her. A kind of warmish, softish feeling, a feeling she was not in the habit of having, at least not since Peter died.

His eyes dropped to hers. "Like what you see?"

Her momentary embarrassment was swiftly

replaced by irritation. "You could use a wash and brush up."

His cheeks tightened. "Last I checked you weren't my mother."

"True. I'm not your wife either, but one or the other should take a hand with you."

A spasm crossed his face. Then he attempted a wry grin. "Since I currently have neither, perhaps you could do the honors."

She sucked in a breath. "Sorry, just passing through." *Yikes. Did he think I was flirting with him?*

"Oh. Well, then." They had reached the dock. He cranked the engine down. "Hop out and I'll tie up."

Palmer ran over their conversation, trying to tease out any misleading statements she had made. *How to explain that I'm not in the market—not so soon after Peter…* She regarded the man at the tiller. Something about him… *Am I attracted to him?* No, it was something else, something enigmatic about him… He looked startled when he saw the dead man's face. And he had hesitated when the patrolman asked his name. *He also acted cagey when I called him a native.* Why? *Could he be a fugitive from justice?* She sized him up. "So…what's your real name and who are you really?"

Chapter Two

A sailor went to sea you see
To see what he could see you see
But all that he could see you see
Was the bottom of the deep blue sea you see.
Anna Maria Island Marine Rescue Facility

Tuesday, May 16

Hooper switched off the motor. "Who am I? I could ask the same thing of you."

"I've got nothing to hide. My legal name is Palmer Lind. I'm from Virginia, and I'm on a birding trip."

"Huh. Where in Virginia?"

"Alexandria."

He looked her up and down. "You a swamp creature?"

She sniffed. "If you mean am I employed by the federal government, the short answer is yes...and no."

"Huh."

When it became clear he was disinclined to pursue the subject, she stifled her annoyance. *If he's going to play that game, so will I.*

Hooper tied the boat to a pylon and clambered out onto the dock. The marine rescue facility stood by itself in the dunes. Patrol boats crowded the marina. "Let's go round to the front."

An ambulance idled at the entrance, its light rotating slowly. Next to it stood a gurney on which lay the body. The tarp had been removed, and Palmer was distressed to see the dead man's bloated face for the first time. Two EMTs were talking to Sid. Palmer strode up to them, Hooper shuffling behind. "Did you find any identification on the man?"

Sid turned to her. "I'm sorry, I didn't realize you were law enforcement."

"Oh, er, I'm not. I was just—"

"Miss Lind feels she has a vested interest, since we discovered the body." Hooper managed to sound both gruff and diffident.

"*Humph.*" Sid gave him a frosty look. "I've only made a cursory examination so far. We're waiting for Criminal Investigations. Since the body's been exposed for so long, it will require a full forensic analysis."

"Is he…it…staying here?"

"No. They'll take him to the District 12 morgue in Bradenton to be autopsied. Sheriff gave the case to Captain Thrasher of the Longboat Key police, and he wants the county crime scene unit to go over the nature trail for clues." He beetled his brows at Palmer. "He'll want to talk to you two as well."

Palmer bit her lip. "I don't think he came from the key, Officer. He was in the water when we spotted him."

"Right, which means he could have floated from anywhere. It's going to take a while to figure out where he went into the intracoastal."

"You mean where he died."

"Yeah. Could be Cortez, could be Jewfish Key, or anywhere along the channel." He scratched his temple.

11

"A-course, he could have been killed elsewhere and transported to the bay." He stared at the body, musing.

Palmer tried not to inhale. " 'Killed'? You think he was…he was…"

"Murdered? Not sure yet. That'll be for the pathologist to determine."

Hooper wrinkled his nose. "From the state of…er…deterioration, I'd say he'd been…er…soaking for several days."

"Thus widening the search perimeter." Sid rubbed his hands together gleefully. "I'd better advise the Coast Guard." He went inside.

Palmer and Hooper looked at each other. "Now what?"

"I guess I'll walk back to my car." Palmer started toward the main road.

She was halfway across when she heard a shout. "Miss Lind! Come back!"

Hooper was waving at her, a visibly angry Sid beside him. When she drew near enough, the officer bawled, "Where the hell are you going?"

"I thought you were finished with us."

"Not by a long shot, missy. Perhaps you didn't hear me. Police are on their way. Ah, here's the crime unit."

A van marked Manatee County Criminal Investigations Division—Crime Scene Unit turned in at the entrance and stopped beside them. A stern-faced, swarthy man leaned out the window. "Where?"

"Hey, John. End of the nature walk."

John turned to his partner, a slight, pasty-faced blond in a polo shirt and khakis. "Give the vic a once-over before I check the area, will you, Phil?" The two men got out, shrugging on jackets marked Sheriff—

CSU. John pulled some gear from the van and waited while Phil walked over to the ambulance. Starting at the head, he circled the gurney, eyeballing the corpse. He called out, "Male, fifties, overweight... From the spider veins on his nose, I'd wager he drank to excess." He lifted the lapel of the sodden jacket. "Polyester suit. Frayed cuffs. One shoe—expensive leather."

"Identification?"

He checked the pockets. "Nada."

Palmer piped up. "Could he have been a homeless man?"

"A bum? Mebbe."

Beside her, Hooper stirred. She glanced at him. "What is it?"

His face blank, he breathed out, "Nothing."

John barked, "Cause of death?"

Phil shook his head. "Hard to tell considering his condition. I see a patch of what may be blood on his chest. We'll have to wait for the ME to look him over."

"All right—go on inside and collect the paperwork. The ambulance can take him to the morgue." John hoisted his satchel to his shoulder. He said to Hooper, "Show me where you found him."

The entrance to the nature walk was only a few hundred yards from the station. The three of them trooped down the winding path. The sun was now directly overhead, and despite the lack of humidity, Palmer felt herself overheating. She was grateful for the shade of the mangroves. The agent trod ahead of them, his eyes darting back and forth over the ground. He took photographs every few feet. At one point he paused to pull on latex gloves. Just before they reached the little bridge, he stooped and picked an object up, only to toss it away.

When they reached the end of the walkway, he had Palmer and then Hooper describe what they had seen. He spent some time examining the little beach. Finally, he stood up, hands on hips. "I don't see any evidence that the vic came from the trail. You found him in the water, right?"

"Yes."

John pulled out a tablet. "*Hmm.* Might as well wait to hear the medical examiner's results before we start searching the area."

"How come?"

"I need to know how long he was dead and how long he was in the water. Then we can check tide tables and currents for likely spots where he may have gone in."

Palmer understood. "I see. So you could retrace potential routes."

"Correct."

By the time they returned to the marine rescue facility, squad cars from Longboat Key and Bradenton Beach filled the little lot. The two crime scene investigators went off to their van to confer. A couple of uniformed officers lolled by the cars, watching a man in a dark suit stride into the building.

Hooper pointed at him. "I'll bet he's the detective we're supposed to report to."

As Palmer and Hooper approached him, he turned and held up a restraining hand. "Who are *you*?"

Sid intervened. "They found the body."

"You get their particulars?"

He nodded.

"Okay. You can go. We'll be in touch."

Thus summarily dismissed, the two stood awkwardly in the parking lot. Finally Hooper said, "Uh...I'll be getting back to my boat. Nice meeting you."

She almost giggled. "Yes, um, me too. Bye." She sprinted across the road to her car. She was about to make the right turn toward Longboat Key and home when a disembodied voice thundered from the radio. "News and traffic next at one o'clock." *No wonder my tummy's growling. Might as well get some lunch before I head back to the condo.*

She drove into the little town of Bradenton Beach and took the first exit off the miniature rotary. The sign said Welcome to Historic Bridge Street. Only four blocks long, the road ended at the town pier. She was in luck—a car was vacating the only parking spot left. Country music spilled from loudspeakers in an open-air bar on the corner. The Bridge Tender Inn ~ $2 Draft 4-6 Every Day was scrawled across a chalkboard. *It looks inviting.* She chose a table under the trees by the marina and sat perusing the menu.

"I highly recommend the chicken livers. They are especially succulent."

She dropped the menu. "Mr. Hooper? What are you doing here?"

"Just Hooper." He spread his hands. "Um, it's lunchtime and this is a restaurant?"

"I mean...you know what I mean."

He gestured at the bass boat tied to a pylon. "There was a slip free." He put a hand on the back of her chair. "Mind if I join you?"

"I guess not."

"Wow, curb your enthusiasm, ma'am."

"I'll do my best." Palmer was secretly glad to see him. It would be comforting to have company while she stewed over recent events. *Besides, his gray eyes are awfully nice. And I like the way his nose kind of turns up at the end. But really, it's only that it's not much fun to eat alone.*

"You're pretty, too. I have a soft spot for redheads."

"I beg your pardon?" *Shit.*

"That's what you were thinking, wasn't it? That I'm cute." His face was deadly serious, but as she gazed at him, unable to come up with a clever reply, his mouth twitched. "I hope so anyway." He picked up the menu. "Like I said, Fred's chicken livers are a masterpiece. I'm ordering them. What about you?"

"Chicken livers? It's not exactly beach fare, is it?"

"Trust me. Once you've tasted them, whenever you want to conjure up your fabulous seaside vacation, the smell of Fred's chicken livers will waft across your nostrils and you'll sigh happily."

"Huh. Okay."

They gave the waitress their orders. While waiting, they watched the boats in the river—bow riders, pontoons, jet skis—zip past them. Palmer recalled what she'd read about it. "This is the Intracoastal Waterway, right?"

"Yup. Beginning in Boston, it runs 3,000 miles along the Atlantic coast, then north up the Gulf of Mexico to Brownsville, Texas."

"Is it man-made? Like a canal?"

"Some sections are. Most of it is natural, although it's all dredged and maintained by the Army Corps of Engineers." He pointed south. "Right below us it flows into Sarasota Bay."

A wedge of brown pelicans swooped under the Cortez bridge and landed in front of them, shaking their wings and stretching their necks. The light breeze blowing off the choppy water was most welcome. Palmer tossed a crumb to the house sparrow hopping around on the gravel. "Did you know there are between fifty and four hundred billion birds on the planet?"

"I did not."

"And nearly all those billions belong to only four species."

"Four species out of how many?"

"Ten thousand nine hundred. And counting."

He whistled. "And who are the lucky four species who need not worry about extinction?"

"House sparrows, ring-billed gulls, European starlings, and barn swallows."

"What about chickens? There have got to be a lot more of *them*."

"Yeah, but they don't count. They're domestic." She said it with a slightly curled lip.

"Well, I'll be. Is that merely a bit of trivia you save for cocktail conversation, or are you an ornithologist?"

Palmer was saved from replying by the arrival of their drinks.

Hooper picked up his mug. "Cheers." When she'd taken a sip of her beer, he said, "Well?"

"Well, what?"

"Before we get into the mystery of the corpse, tell me about yourself. I mean, other than that your auburn tresses and smashing emerald eyes must have attracted hordes of admirers—all of whom you fought off knowing that someday you would meet me." He looked her over. "They were doubtless also awestruck by those Betty Grable legs."

"Huh?"

"I'll take that as a rhetorical statement."

Palmer never liked talking about herself. It made her uncomfortable. She thought about deflecting, but a glimpse of his cool smoky eyes gave her courage. "What do you want to know?"

"Where you're from. If you have any interests besides birding. What you've been doing the last—let me guess, twenty-eight?—years?"

"I told you—I'm from Virginia. Or at least I have been for the past five years."

"And before that?"

"Oh, I moved around a lot—lived abroad and in Boston. Chicago."

"Chasing after boyfriends?"

"Excuse me?" *So he's the kind who assumes women are only interested in romance. Jerk.* "No. After college I went to graduate school."

He raised a brow. "Couldn't wrench yourself away from the ivory tower?"

"I was a doctoral candidate." She hoped she didn't sound too huffy.

He tossed a crumb to the sparrow. "Ornithology?"

"No, no, that's just a hobby of mine."

"Ah, so…a perennial student. I know the type. Living in your parents' basement, subsisting on Kit-Kats and apples. Maybe a cat or two. Not to eat; to pet." He peered at her. "Am I right?"

Palmer felt unaccountably defensive. "I did nothing of the sort. In between degrees I picked up short-term jobs that gave me a chance to travel. I ran a student hostel in Paris for a while." She laughed.

"What's so funny?"

"Oh, it turned out the American who'd made the arrangements didn't bother to check the current room rates. He was charging the students twice what the hotel itself charged. It was not a success."

"But you got free room and board in the heart of Paris."

"True."

He gulped his beer. "In that case, I'm guessing the first time you ever wore heels was the day you walked into the office at the department of...which federal agency did you burrow into?"

The waitress slid soup bowls filled with brown chunks in gravy onto the table. "Fred's chicken livers. Enjoy."

Palmer speared a lump. It melted in her mouth. *"Oh golly."*

"Didn't I tell you?" He smiled at her.

She hadn't noticed the rows of even white teeth before. She was glad he didn't have a beard. *That square chin should be displayed with pride.*

"So...agency?"

"Interior. I worked for an assistant secretary. Took some marvelous junkets." She closed her eyes, a mistake, since Peter's image rose before her. He was waving her off at the airport, joking that she'd better come back. *Don't get hooked on moose meat or some Alaskan mountain man and abandon me.*

"Miss Lind?"

The gentle voice roused her. She was mortified to feel tears streaming down her cheeks. "I'm...I'm all right." She wiped her face with a napkin. "Please, call me Palmer."

"All right. Palmer. You want to tell me about it?"

She took a swallow of beer. "My…my husband Peter. He died while I was away on business in Alaska."

"How long ago?"

"Two years. It was…very sudden, and it took me a year to get his affairs in order."

"You quit your job?"

"I took a leave of absence. Once you work for the feds, they can't fire you, so I'm keeping my options open."

"That's what you meant by yes and no." He nodded. She wondered what that signaled— understanding? Or lack of interest? "What brings you to the Sunshine State?"

Now she was on firmer ground. "I love bird-watching. I used to volunteer at the Atlantic Birding Association on the weekends. After…after Peter died, the president urged me to take a road trip down the east coast. Bury myself in birding. Get away from it all."

"Ah. So you're on a birding quest? What's that they call it? A Big Year?"

"Not officially, although I'm reporting back to Mr. Pochard along the way. It's been great fun. I spent a week in Chincoteague and drove down through North and South Carolina via the barrier islands. And now I'm exploring Florida."

"I take it no children."

She felt the tears well up again. "We hadn't gotten around to it."

He patted her shoulder awkwardly. "Again, I'm very sorry. I shouldn't have pried—" His phone buzzed.

"Hello? Yes, this is Sonny Hooper... I guess so. Who? Oh, yeah. She's right here. Pardon me? No, we just happened to pick the same restaurant. No, we've only just met." He listened for a few minutes, then angrily shouted, "What are you insinuating? Look, I... Okay. We'll be there in half an hour. Yes, we're going to finish our lunch first...Well, tough." He slammed the phone down on the table.

Palmer's eyes were wide. "Was that the police?"

"Yes. The Longboat Key police. They just had a call from the medical examiner. Our friendly neighborhood corpse? He was murdered."

Chapter Three

Who killed Cock Robin?
I, said the Sparrow,
With my bow and arrow,
I killed Cock Robin.

Longboat Key police station, Tuesday, May 16

"Again, Captain Thrasher, Miss Lind and I only met this morning. We happened on the dead man at the same time. She by land and me by sea."

The police detective kept the suspicious look on his face, somewhat obscured by the thick, black-framed glasses he wore. "Did you touch the corpse?"

"I gave it a slight poke, yes." Hooper's face turned slightly green. "That was enough. You are aware it was ripe enough to entice hungry vultures, right?"

Thrasher nodded. He skimmed a form on his desk. "ME says it took a while to sift through the damage to find the cause of death."

"Drowning?" Palmer's tone was hopeful.

"No. He'd been stabbed in the heart." He ran his pencil down the page. "He was also missing the index finger on his left hand." He shot Palmer a look from under his brows. "You didn't happen to come across it, did you?"

She recalled a whitish object in a bird's talon.

"I...er...believe one of the vultures may have bitten it off."

"Ah." He studied the autopsy report. "Dr. Conure collected splinters of wood lodged in the skin, and also minute bronze filings inside the wound. He's pretty sure the latter came from an arrow."

"An arrow?"

Hooper echoed Palmer's question, a catch in his voice. "A *bronze* arrow?"

"Yes. A specific type of arrow. The kind they use in crossbows. He says the splinters came from the bow, and the filings from the arrow."

"Crossbow you say?"

"Yeah. Weird, huh. Don't see too much crossbow hunting around here."

Palmer, who had been watching Hooper, nudged him. "You have something to add?"

Hooper made a gurgling sound in his throat. "Um, yeah. Modern crossbows are made of steel, not wood. The projectiles are called bolts, which are aluminum, not bronze."

"Well, well. How come you know so much?"

"I, uh, was thinking of taking up archery. Been reading up on it."

"Really?" Thrasher was unimpressed. "Lemme take a wild guess. You've done a bit more than read up on it. Wanna come clean?" When Hooper didn't answer immediately, he added, "This is something we can easily ascertain."

Hooper's shoulders sagged. "All right. I have dabbled in archery. I have used a crossbow."

The detective closed the report. "You say crossbows are made of metal? So where do you think the bits of wood came from?"

"I've no idea. Look, can we go now?"

"Will you be at your house? He checked his clipboard again. "In the Village?"

"You mean, do I plan to skip town while the gumshoes are breathing down my neck? No, I don't. Plan to."

"Okay." The detective's dark brows beetled. "I think...I *know*...we'll have more questions for you."

Hooper and Palmer parted at the Gulf of Mexico Drive, the highway that spanned the length of the island. "How will you get home?"

"My boat's tied up behind the station. How about you?"

"I left my car at my place and walked. The Palapa Inn is only half a mile away." She pointed up the road. "I rented a suite there."

"Oh, okay. Then I guess I'll see you around. Um...bye."

The Palapa Inn was a small, cozy resort, its cheerful yellow walls reflecting the Florida sunshine. Palmer had the second floor of the building to herself, presenting an apartment-wide view of the Gulf. Though tempted to drop onto the bed and sleep away the late unpleasantness, she decided to hike the beach. *I need to clear my head.*

The shimmering heat waves floated parallel to the waves on the water. It was siesta time, and most people were indoors. They would trickle back out to watch the sunset before worming their way into the bumper-to-bumper traffic heading to an "Early Bird" supper. Palmer was alone except for the occasional skimmer gliding along the ebbing tide and a herd or two of sanderlings skittering along the water line. When she reached the first seawall, she turned around, almost tripping over a ghost crab. "Oops! Sorry, fellah." The crab angrily twiddled his eyestalks at her before retreating into his hole.

Once back at home, she took a shower and changed her clothes. As the sun dipped below the sea, it lobbed flaming gouts of yellow and crimson and salmon into the clouds. She sat on her balcony, a vodka gimlet at her elbow, and contemplated the day.

She went over the discovery of the body and the bizarre cause of death. She dwelt rather longer on Hooper's face. *Perhaps it won't be the last time I see him, since this thing is far from over. On the other hand, I'm only here for a week or two.* The detective had seemed—*what's the word I'm looking for?*—distrustful of Hooper, but she herself didn't have much more to offer the police. *So they might not contact me again. In which case, Sonny Hooper—or whatever his name is—will become an interesting memory.*

His true identity… *He never did reveal it, did he? What could he be hiding?* He had recoiled at his first sight of the dead man's face. Was it merely shock at seeing a corpse, or did he recognize him? He was so—how to describe it?—self-assured. Competent. *Could he be a contract killer?* She mustered up his image. Chiseled jaw. Firm chin. Manly chest…but she was getting off track. *The murder is top priority, Palmer, not the color of his eyes.* If not a professional assassin, then what? A jealous husband? *He wouldn't have been startled to see the victim then.* And anyway, he said he wasn't married. Palmer quickly stifled the ping of pleasure that fact gave her.

She finished her drink. Perhaps they were business partners and had a falling out. *No—the victim wore thrift-store hand-me-downs.* Of course, Hooper's attire was hardly Fifth Avenue.

At any rate, until he explained himself, she had to treat him as a potential suspect. Who knows? Maybe the next time she confronted him she'd be in the witness stand facing the defendant, Mr. X, alias Sonny Hooper. *So maybe I* don't *want to see him again.*

She fixed herself a sandwich and then checked the TV listings. She decided against the Perry Mason marathon, opting for a rerun of *Love Boat*. *I've had enough murder for one day.*

****

Durante Park, Friday evening

Palmer didn't hear from either the police or Hooper the next day or the next. She'd settled into a routine of visiting nature preserves in the morning and sitting on the beach in the afternoon. *Maybe I'll extend my stay here. There's no real hurry.* With Peter gone, she had nothing to return to. Sure, she was officially on leave, but Human Relations said that could be as long or as short as she liked. "If it's more than a year, you may have to fill out some forms, and we'll have to find a spot at your grade level somewhere. Just give us a heads-up." She'd inherited Peter's pension, which meant she was unencumbered by financial worries—at least for now.

No, I don't have to go back anytime soon. The weather was nice, and the birdlife plentiful. The idea that she was waiting for something—hoping to run across a gray-eyed fisherman—didn't cross her mind more than once or twice.

It was early evening on the Friday after the awful events. Palmer thought she'd stroll the couple of blocks down to Durante Park. The park—a lovely bayside preserve covered in lush natural plantings—was empty of people. She took the boardwalk trail that wound among the mangroves along the edge of the bay. Several observation platforms had been built out over the water. She walked out to one and surveyed the vast Sarasota Bay. *Didn't the book say white pelicans often congregate here?* Snowy white and huge, they dwarfed the ubiquitous brown pelicans. She had trained her binoculars on a distant blob of white when she heard an outboard motor. A familiar bass boat passed out of the mangroves and came into view.

"Well, hello there, Palmer!"

"Hooper!"

He bent down in the boat. When he rose, he held a wriggling, silvery fish in each hand. "Lookee what I caught!"

"What are they?"

"Mullet."

"Oh? A man on the beach told me mullet weren't edible."

"Did he now?" He shook his head in disapproval. "Undoubtedly some Yankee greenhorn. Here in Florida they're relished—especially smoked. In St. Augustine, when someone yells, 'Mullet on the beach!' every Minorcan within earshot drops what he's doing and goes fishing. No, these babies are great." He put them back in the cooler. "Say, would you like to sample them and make up your own mind? I'm going to grill tonight."

"Sure! I guess I can…um…change my plans." *The*

ones I don't have.

"Do you want to meet me at my place? Or come with me?"

Oh my God, should I? What if he's a...a... She looked down into friendly eyes the color of goose down and decided to trust her instincts. *Besides, as Peter always said, never miss an opportunity to take a boat ride.* "I'll come with you."

Hooper maneuvered the boat to the sandbank next to the platform, and she stepped over the gunwale. "Grab that life vest, and sit in the bow." They motored up the bay. On her right was a series of small mangrove islets. He pointed them out. "Those are the Sister Keys—they're protected from development."

The white blob she'd seen from the park turned out to be a piece of cloth hanging from a tree. *Darn it—I can't cross white pelican off my list just yet.*

A few minutes later, Hooper turned into a bayou that led to a canal. Brightly painted houses lined the shore, each with its own dock. He tied the boat up at one and helped Palmer out. "Here we are."

She beheld a single-story house, painted a bright primrose trimmed with aqua, sitting on piles a foot off the ground. The high roof was steeply pitched, providing shade to the porch that ran the length of the front. A large bougainvillea climbed up a trellis by the front door. Scattered among the crushed white shell mulch were plants she recognized from her guide to tropical plants. "Let me see. Areca palms. Autograph trees. Coontie. Oh, and the blue flowers are Mexican petunias."

"A perfect score. Bravo." Hooper stood facing the building, hands on hips. "It was originally a cracker house."

"Oh? What's a cracker?"

"That's what they called the settlers who came from the Carolinas and Georgia to run cattle. The nickname referred to the sound their bullwhips made, or so I've been told. The houses were raised to allow air circulation when it's ninety-five degrees in the shade." He chuckled. "It also keeps the snakes out." He picked up the cooler and poured his catch onto a wooden table on the dock. "Tell you what, you go inside while I clean the fish. There's a liquor cabinet in the study. Make us some gin and tonics?"

She pretended to roll up her sleeves. "Coming right up." She found the bottle and took it into the kitchen, noting with interest how spotless the room was. *Either his mother was a tough taskmistress, or he's anal-retentive.* She opted for dictatorial mother and filled two glasses with ice, gin, tonic, and lime slices.

Through the window she glimpsed a stone patio, where Hooper was firing up a large grill. She went out through the sliding glass doors and handed him a glass.

He took a long gulp. "Ah. Hits the spot. Thanks." He moved the fish around on the grate. "I'll cook these two and smoke the other four."

They sat in folding beach chairs and watched a great egret nosing around the cooler. Palmer decided it was a perfect opportunity to clear up the little matter of Hooper's identity. "You were telling me your real name."

"I was? Oh, back when... Yes. Well, I suppose it wouldn't do any harm, although I must say I've become rather attached to Sonny Hooper. Makes me feel like a famous actor."

She clapped her hand to her mouth. "*That's* why it was so familiar! Wasn't it a movie about a stuntman?"

"Yes. 'Burt Reynolds at his rollicking best,' according to the reviews." He grinned. "I like to think I'd have made a great stand-in if I could only grow a moustache." He set his glass on a side table. "I'm—"

The doorbell rang. Two seconds later, someone knocked loudly on the front door. "Mr. Hooper!"

Hooper went through the house, Palmer behind him. "Who is it?"

"The police."

He opened the door. "What can I do for you, Officer?"

A big, burly man in uniform showed his badge. "Sergeant Jaeger, Longboat Key police. Are you Sonny Hooper?"

Hooper glanced quickly at Palmer. "Yes."

"You're wanted for questioning in the murder of Theodore Swallow. Please come with me."

Palmer gawked at the policeman, but Hooper didn't blink an eye. He walked obediently out the door. She stood uncertainly on the threshold. "What about me?"

The cop turned. "Who are you?"

"Palmer Lind."

He turned a page of his notebook. "I have you down as a renter in the Palapa Inn, 5854 Gulf of Mexico Drive. Is that correct? Or do you live here with Mr. Hooper?"

"No! I mean, I was just visiting. We came by boat."

"Well, you were next on my list."

"Am I under arrest?"

"No, ma'am. Captain Thrasher just wants clarification on some particulars. Come along, please."

Her heart pounding, Palmer collected her shoulder bag and binoculars and got in the squad car next to Hooper. She took a deep breath and whispered to him, "Now you're going to *have* to confess your real name."

He grimaced. "That's what I'm afraid of."

Chapter Four

There was a crooked man,
And he walked a crooked mile.
He found a crooked sixpence
Against a crooked stile;
He bought a crooked cat,
Which caught a crooked mouse,
And they all lived together
In a little crooked house.

Longboat Key police station, Friday, May 19

Captain Thrasher ushered Palmer and Hooper into a well-appointed office. A top-of-the-line red-dot optic sight lay next to what looked like a very fancy body camera. A bulletproof vest hung from the hat tree, its thousand-dollar price tag still attached. At Hooper's raised eyebrow, Thrasher remarked, "We got a grant from the State to upgrade our equipment." He sniggered. "There's some really cool stuff in the police supply catalogue. Have a seat."

The chairs did not live up to the plush space. Hooper squirmed on his seat. "I'm guessing your furniture comes from the Lord's Warehouse, though. Am I right?"

"Chief's a member of the congregation, so we get a discount."

At Palmer's blank look, Hooper whispered, "Local chapel's white elephant barn."

The detective sat down behind the desk and steepled his fingers. A tense silence descended, broken finally by the irrepressible Thrasher. "You're probably wondering why I asked you both here."

Hooper cleared his throat. "Officer Jaeger said you had questions about the dead man, but we've already told you everything we know."

The detective inclined his head. "Um, no, I don't think so. Nope, you haven't told me everything, Mr. Carson Hawk."

Hooper flinched, and Palmer felt a tiny thrill of satisfaction. *I knew it.*

"I see you've uncovered my secret identity. Sonny Hooper is my version of Clark Kent, but without the glasses. I use it to shield my superpowers from the masses. So what?"

Thrasher read his notes. "So what, you ask? It kind of bears on this here case we're investigating. First off, you were acquainted with the deceased, Mr. Theodore Swallow. In fact, you had several very public altercations with him back in Washington, DC."

Carson wiped his forehead with a grubby bandanna. "Yes, but they meant nothing. I work...worked on Capitol Hill. He was a very tenacious lobbyist. Some of those guys are relentless. They try to grind you down until you give in and agree to their position. I had no idea he was down here in Florida. We...lost touch after I left DC."

"You mean after your boss, Senator Atticus Wren, was found dead in your apartment on April 14."

Palmer gasped. Carson said quietly, "It was ruled a

suicide. I—for self-evident reasons—was not at home at the time."

"No, naturally you weren't." Thrasher was suspiciously soothing. "And after the inquest, you packed your little Gladstone bag and hippety-hopped to sunnier climes. Says here you missed the funeral."

Carson stared at his lap. "I couldn't face Joanna."

"Wren's wife?"

"Yes. She blamed me for Atticus's death, even though I had no inkling he was planning to kill himself. I'd gone out to pick up some food. We were expecting to pull an all-nighter to work on his statement regarding Senate Bill 219."

"You were his speechwriter, correct?"

"Yes. The bill is very controversial. He was getting a lot of pressure to withdraw it. Nevertheless, he was planning to announce his support in a speech on the Senate floor. The wording had to be very diplomatic. It would have been a long night, and we both needed sustenance."

"So you drove to the Peking Inn and picked up…" The detective consulted his notes. "Kung pao chicken, moo shu pork, two orders of dragon and phoenix—no garlic—and a six-pack of Tsingtao beer. When you returned, you found him hanging from the chandelier."

"Yes."

Thrasher turned a page. "There was no note."

"No. Look, Captain, this is old news. Why are we here?"

"Ah. See, this man Swallow worked for Wilfred Vogel, one of Wren's biggest donors."

"Common knowledge. So?"

"So, Vogel is based in San Francisco. What would

bring a member of his Washington lobbying office to little old Longboat Key?" He didn't let Carson answer. "Unless it was to see you?"

"How would he know I was here? I'm out of a job, since my boss has, shall we say, left the company. I came to Longboat Key for a well-deserved vacation." He kept his eyes riveted on Thrasher.

Palmer watched Carson. *Is he looking for a sign that Thrasher believes him? Or is he afraid the detective's holding back a damning piece of information?*

Carson continued deliberately. "Vogel is a billionaire, with enterprises all over the country. Swallow did a lot of jobs for him besides lobbying the Senate. Could be he's looking to pick up some Florida swampland." He rose. "Can we go now?"

The detective's lip wobbled. Palmer guessed that's how he showed frustration. "Yes. I'll be in touch."

They stood outside on the sidewalk. The sky by now was pitch black. There were few cars on the road. Palmer peered back at the station. "How do they expect us to get home?"

Carson shrugged. "My house is three miles away. Did I hear you mention you were staying at the Palapa?"

"Uh-huh. It's a few blocks from here. My car's there. I can give you a lift." Palmer secretly hoped he wouldn't want to go home. *I know it's silly, but I'm not ready for the evening to end just yet.*

"Thanks, that would be great."

At that moment Sergeant Jaeger appeared. "I can drop Miss Lind at her condo and drive you home, Mr. Hawk."

Palmer had opened her mouth to accept when Carson shyly touched her arm. "I still owe you that fish dinner. Why don't you come along with me?"

Whew. "Sure."

The sergeant left them at the cracker house. Carson rekindled the smoldering coals and put the fish back on the grill. At his direction, Palmer found glasses and a bottle of Muscadet and brought them outside. They sat and gazed at the stars for a precious few serene minutes before he broke the stillness. "I suppose you have a few questions."

Palmer wasn't sure how much she wanted to know. Carson had a past—*but then doesn't everybody? Yeah, but...a boss who committed suicide? In his apartment no less?* "Did you run away?"

He grunted. "I guess you could call it that." He flipped the fish. "I didn't kill Atticus."

"That's good."

"But I think he was murdered."

She choked on her wine. "Do you have proof?"

Carson rose. "How about if we have some dinner, and then I'll explain."

"Okay. What can I do?"

"Set the table. Dishes and cutlery are in the pantry. There's a salad chilling in the refrigerator." He took a warm baguette out of the oven and wrapped it in a dish towel. When she was settled, he slid a golden fish onto her plate and took the remaining one. "Lemon?"

"Yes, please." He squeezed half a lemon over her fish and the other half over his own. Palmer took a bite. "You were right: the mullet is excellent."

"Told you so. The trick is to rub the fish with butter, then dust on a smidgen of flour. Makes for a nice crispy skin." He pulled a bone from between his teeth. "The other trick is catching the bones before you swallow them."

She tried the salad. "*Mmm*. Basil? And"—she chewed thoughtfully—"thyme?"

He nodded. "The rest are microgreens, dressed with lemon juice and olive oil. I have a little garden behind the shed, with a few vegetables and herbs. Albert—my, uh, landlord—is allowing me to put in some tropical fruit plants as well. Passionfruit, Surinam cherry, maybe a Natal plum. That's if the coppers are through with me."

When she'd finished, Carson took their plates to the kitchen. "Let's go outside."

They sat in the beach chairs. She filled his glass. "You were explaining."

"Yes." He thought a minute. "Let me back up some. Senate Bill 219 would restrict the amount of US land that can be purchased by foreign investors. The Chinese have recently been amassing significant acreage here in the form of foreclosed farms and ranches. Meanwhile, Wilfred Vogel has been buying up whole swaths encircling cities like Tampa, Houston, and Nashville. He now owns some 250,000 acres—more than any other single entity."

"Vogel…isn't he the dead man's employer?"

"Yes. Depending on his audience, he claims it's to ensure space for affordable housing is available, or alternately"—he curled fingers in the air to indicate quotation marks—"it's for 'environmental' reasons. The theory on the street is that's code for taking farmland out of production."

"Why would anyone do that?"

"The usual bogeyman: climate change. Of course, now that we know it's hardly a 'crisis,' they've taken to calling it 'severe weather threats.' " He rolled his eyes.

Palmer frowned. "How would the bill stop Vogel?"

"It also prohibits international conglomerates from acquiring property. Vogel Enterprises is based in Geneva and San Francisco. That's why he's opposed to the bill."

"Okay, so environmentalists want to limit agriculture and thereby reduce greenhouse gases, but which faction is Vogel courting with the affordable housing line?"

"The cities he's been targeting. The high-growth metro areas need room to expand."

"Shouldn't we applaud him for preserving the properties so they're available when the cities need them?"

"The fear is once Vogel acquires enough adjacent land, he'll jack up the price. He could put a chokehold on the ability of a municipality to thrive."

She cocked her head. "Meanwhile making money hand over fist. It's becoming clear that Mr. Vogel's intentions aren't entirely transparent, and they're certainly not benevolent."

"Indeed. As you can imagine, his activities have met with opposition in Congress. Hence S. 219."

"He lobbied hard against it?"

" 'Hard' is the operative word. He assigned lobbyists in his shop to every single fence-sitter in the Senate. Atticus was gifted Tipsy Swallow."

"Tipsy?"

"Theodore Swallow. In the land of heavy tipplers called K Street, Tipsy was a legend."

She giggled. "His last name is just a lucky accident?" She sobered at his grim expression. "You recognized him when we first pulled him out of the water, didn't you?"

Carson avoided her glance. "Yes, but I knew if I identified him to the police, all hell would break loose."

"In the end they smoked out your connection anyway."

"My mantra from now on: never underestimate the police."

She finished her wine and licked the rim. "I've been thinking. If the bill is about to be considered, Tipsy would surely stay near the corridors of power. What would bring him to Florida?"

"Like I told Thrasher, Tipsy did other kinds of work for Vogel." He winked.

"Meaning shady stuff?"

"Possibly." He went inside, returning with a second bottle of Muscadet. "More wine?"

She held out her glass. "Could he have been undercover? You know…the polyester suit and all?"

"Who knows? Anyway, Vogel told Tipsy to go easy on Wren. Vogel wasn't too nervous about the senator's decision, since he was Wren's most generous donor. He expected Atticus would eventually toe the line."

"I take it he didn't know Wren was writing a speech in favor of the bill?"

"Now that's a good question." He sipped his wine. The stars blinked on and off above them. A whip-poor-will hooted in the mangroves.

When it became clear he had no answer, she asked, "Have they replaced Senator Wren?"

"Not yet. The governor set a special election for July." He refilled her glass. "The new guy will have no seniority, so the chairmanship of the committee goes to Hugh Bunting of Iowa and he opposes S. 219. He also happens to be another grateful recipient of Vogel's largesse."

Palmer considered what she knew of Senate rules. Committee staffs were fairly stable, while the personal staffs of members were dependent on the whims of the electorate. "Were you committee staff?"

"Yes."

"Then why didn't you keep your job?"

"Bunting's legislative assistant took over my issues, and the senator doesn't need another speechwriter." He checked the cooler. "Four more fish. I can grill another one if you're still hungry."

"No, thanks."

"Okay. I'll set these aside and wait for the coals to cool down. Then we'll smoke 'em." He closed the lid just as the egret snatched at one of the fish. "Get out of here, Oscar." He turned to Palmer. "Will you pour me some wine?"

Palmer obliged. "You said you believe your boss was murdered. Could Tipsy have done it?"

"I don't know. Atticus was having second thoughts due to Tipsy's persistence, but at the last minute he decided to keep S. 219 on the agenda."

"Agenda?"

"The committee agenda. Wren was chair of Environment and Public Works, which has jurisdiction."

"Not Commerce?"

He glowered. "Don't get me started. There was a

lot of wrangling over who got it—Ag wanted it; Commerce wanted it too. Atticus persuaded the parliamentarian to give it to us. He planned to hold a series of hearings on the bill, but the week before he died, he decided to go directly to a vote."

"How come?"

"He had his staff run the table. There were enough yea votes to approve. It would have been in markup the Wednesday after he died, after which it would go to the Floor. Majority Leader Murre is a big promoter of 219, so he'd likely bring it up at the first opportunity."

"What happened?"

Carson pressed his lips together. "Like an idiot, Atticus felt it was incumbent on him to give Vogel a heads-up. So, rather than have him find out from the news media, Wren sent him an email on Monday. On Tuesday night he called me and said he wanted to make some changes to his opening statement. I was headed to the Russell building when he called again and said he preferred to meet at my apartment instead." He gulped his wine. "He sounded…odd."

"Odd?"

"It could have been worry; it could have been fear. It could have been alcohol. When he got to my place, it was clear he'd been drinking."

"Did he tell you what was wrong?"

"No. He just told me to make myself scarce, that he had a couple of private calls to make. I said I'd go buy some sandwiches." He shook his head. "I figured I'd get the scoop when I returned, but…"

"Did you see anyone entering or leaving the building?"

"Uh-uh. And before you ask, they found no record

of any calls from his phone."

"How long were you gone?"

"A little over an hour. Long enough anyway," he said bitterly. "The sub place was closed, so I had to order Chinese and wait for it."

Palmer was silent, thinking over Carson's tale. "Did the police accuse you of killing him?"

"They made noises about it, but I had witnesses from the Peking Inn as well as the doorman. Oh, and my neighbor reported he heard crashing sounds during the period I was out. Police surmised that was when Atticus jumped off the chair."

"It could have been he and his killer fighting."

"That's my theory."

"So why didn't you stay and press the police to investigate further? Why did you flee?"

Carson got up and checked the coals. "They've died down enough." He put the other four mullet on the grate and shut the lid. "They'll smoke all night, and in the morning we can have Florida kippers."

Palmer—although she was too intelligent not to be aware of the direction the evening was taking—wanted the answer to her question first. "If the police didn't suspect you, why did you bug out?"

"Because," he said without turning around, "I'd received death threats myself."

Chapter Five

Row, row, row your boat gently down the stream
Merrily, merrily, merrily, merrily, life is but a dream.

Carson's house, Friday, May 19

"You know something? I'm not going to ask. Not until tomorrow, anyway." Palmer smiled at Carson.

He gazed at her. "I guess murder really does bring people together." He reached out a hand. She took it. "Are you tired?"

Tired of being alone. "No. Shall we?"

As they walked down the hall, she was visited by a frisson of doubt. "Tell me: is a cracker bed stuffed with crackers?"

He laughed. "I have a water bed. Don't worry. It's comfortable, although since I filled it with salt water, it does give off the aroma of the sea. A nice, briny smell, like a fresh oyster."

"Well, that's a relief. I do love oysters."

****

Carson's house, Saturday morning

Palmer woke up wondering if they'd gone out on Carson's boat in the middle of the night. "Where am I?"

He rolled over, causing the mattress to ebb and flow. "Don't you remember?"

"Oh!" She put a hand to her mouth. "I can't believe

I'm here."

"Thanks a lot."

"No. I mean—yes, it was wonderful." She snuggled under his arm. "What I can't believe is that I did this. It's only been two years since Peter... My heavens, I never asked you. Are you...er...alone?"

"Not now." He kissed her nose. "I was divorced thirteen years ago. I've been waiting for you ever since."

She let her eyelids close down. "I think I'll rest a little."

He slid out from under her. "I'll see about breakfast."

She opened one eye. "And then we need to talk."

"Scariest words in the English language."

****

Carson's house, Saturday late morning

It turned out that they didn't have a chance to talk that Saturday. Palmer got a call from the secretary of a local birding group, reminding her that the hike she'd signed up for started at nine a.m. The woman fluted in a tremulous soprano, "We've received a report of a nest of burrowing owls next to the boardwalk in Robinson Preserve! They only live in Florida, you know. We're meeting at Mr. Bantam's house on Perico Island. Can you make it?"

"Oh, yes, Hortense. I'll be there with bells on!" Palmer was so excited she grabbed her purse and trotted out to the driveway, only to see an unfamiliar pickup truck taking up the space. "Where's my car?"

Carson came out, still holding his mug of coffee. "You left it back at your place, remember? Sergeant Jaeger brought us here."

"Oh dear, I must still be fuzzy from all that wine." She gestured at the truck. "Can you drive me home?"

"Not in the pickup. Lenny needs a new distributor cap. I've been waiting a week for the part to come in." He peered at her. "I do have other means of transportation."

"The bass boat?"

"That and…a motorcycle. You game?"

Palmer rose on her toes. "I *love* motorcycles!"

"Let me get the keys." Carson went back inside, then led her to a shed behind the garage. Inside was an ancient yellow Peugeot station wagon and an imposing motorcycle. He pointed at the car. "That's Daisy and"—he patted the bike's seat—"this is Nellie. She's a 1991 Dyna-frame FXDB Sturgis Harley-Davidson."

Palmer was momentarily speechless.

As he pulled helmets off wall hooks, she looked around. "So, you own a bass boat, a hog, a pickup, and a station wagon. Your choice of speeds. Did I also see a kayak overturned by the dock?"

"You did." He handed her a helmet. "I like vehicles. I choose one or the other according to my mood or requirements."

"One if by land and two if by water—what about the air?"

"The Cessna's in a hangar a few miles from here."

She pretended to take this in stride. "Ah, and what is *her* name?"

"Queenie. Why do you ask?"

"You seem to have named all your pets—by which I mean modes of transportation. So the question arises: how did you get all of them down here from DC? And does your landlord know you keep a flotilla of vehicles at his house?"

"That's two questions."

"Uh-huh. And?"

"Okay. I had most of them transported. I drove the Bugatti." He tapped his lip. "Should've driven the station wagon. More room. But I don't trust Isadora to anyone else. And yes, Albert—my landlord—is perfectly fine with it."

Palmer jumped on the pillion behind Carson, and they rode down Gulf of Mexico Drive to the Palapa Inn. She shyly handed him a piece of paper. "My phone number, if you…if you—"

His eyes lit up. "You're in luck! I wrote mine down too." He gave her a wadded scrap of napkin. When she held it up by a corner with a puzzled air, he said with some chagrin, "I lost my nerve a couple of times."

She kissed him on the cheek. "I'll be home this evening."

"Me too, but I have a conference call. See you tomorrow?"

"A conference call! I thought you were retired."

"No, just lying low. I'm working with a DC think tank."

"Oh?" His remark about her being a swamp creature came to mind. "So you're one of those slippery K Street 'consultants.' "

"Not at all. The group is a judicial watchdog. They contacted me a couple of days after Atticus's death because they're not convinced it was suicide either. They're sure there's some hanky-panky going on and the FBI is compromised. I set them to digging up evidence."

He didn't elaborate, and in a decision Palmer

would later regret, she didn't press him. "Be careful."

"Why, thank you!" He grinned and revved the engine.

As he roared off, she realized she'd never asked him about the death threats.

****

The Palapa Inn, Sunday, early morning

"Carson! It's me, Palmer. Are you busy?"

A sleepy voice answered. "If by busy you mean asleep, yes. I was up late last night. What's the matter?"

"I was out with the birding club yesterday."

"I know."

"We were hunting for the owl's nest and came across something. A boat."

"Wow—aren't many of those in Florida."

"Ha-ha. My point is: it looked abandoned."

"The nest?"

"No, the boat."

"Where is it?"

"On one of the Sister Keys."

"I thought you were going to Robinson Preserve?"

"We were, but Hortense went on this internet chatroom for birders. According to a guy named Zack, the burrowing owls aren't at the preserve; they're on one of the Sister Keys."

"You do know the islands are only accessible by boat, right?"

"We do now. That's why we went to Cannons Marina and rented one."

"And you abandoned it?"

"No! Let me finish. Carson?"

"What?"

"In the bow? There was a big blob of…Carson, it

looked like blood." She heard a crash and a yelp. "What happened? Are you all right? Have you been attacked? Get off the phone. I'm going to call 9-1-1!"

"Huh? No! Stop! I hit my head on the fan. It's these damned low ceilings. Native Floridians must all be under four feet tall."

"I think it's because of hurricanes."

"Yeah, well, it means we're that much closer to sea level when it floods. Which it does."

"*Anyway*. Do you want to go see it?"

"See what?"

"The *boat*." Her patience was thinning.

"Why would I want to see it?"

"Because of the blood, dummy. I'm thinking maybe that's where the fellow—Swallow—was killed."

"Wait a minute. The blood—it's not in your boat?"

"No, of course not. Why would you think that? We wouldn't have gotten in it if there was a big puddle of dried blood in the bottom. Even if Cannons said it was from fish or bait or something I still don't think—"

"All right, we've established that the blood is not in your rented boat."

"Well? Do you want to come see it or not?"

"Yes. Yes I do." She was about to hang up when he said, "Why did you wait until now to tell me about it?"

This was the tricky part. "It just came to me. I was lying in bed. I couldn't sleep"—*because I was thinking of you, but that's neither here nor there*—"and it came to me that Swallow could have been killed in a boat and not on land."

"In other words, he was dumped from a boat and not from shore? *Hmm*. Worth giving it a look-see. And while we're doing that, I'll update you on my conversations with the think tank yesterday."

Palmer wasn't going to forget again. "And the death threats."

"Oh yeah, them. They were probably bogus. A copycat."

"Why would someone threaten you about a suicide?"

"Good question. Shall I pick you up?"

"Depends. Which transport were you planning to use?"

"I suggest we take the boat today. Otherwise we'd have to swim."

"There's a dock on the canal where the Palapa annex is."

"Is that off Harris Bayou?"

"No idea. It's south of Cannons. The manatees come there a lot."

"I know it."

"I'll wait for you there."

****

Sister Keys, Sunday late morning

"There. See that inlet?"

Carson guided the skiff into a narrow estuary. Red mangroves had spread out into the shallow water, their walking-stick roots bowed like an old cowhand's legs. A snowy egret stepped carefully among the tangled branches, its bright yellow feet flashing in the dappled light. It snapped at a fiddler crab, gobbling it up. High-pitched squeals told them a pair of raccoons were engaged in a family squabble. "Duck your head."

Palmer bent down just in time to avoid being smacked in the face by a vast spider web. Its owner raced to protect its outer defenses. She pointed at the bizarrely patterned arachnid with scarlet spikes and a white-and-black polka-dot body. "What the heck is that?"

"A mangrove spider. Isn't she pretty?" He slowed the motor. "So how far in was the boat?"

Palmer surveyed the underbrush. "This is it. We ditched the pontoon here and went down that little path."

"You never said if you caught a glimpse of the burrowing owls."

"No, we didn't." Palmer scowled. "Raven—she's the group leader's teenage daughter—went crashing through the thickets and scared everything away. She was the one who found the boat." She continued to grumble. "Not sure why she came—she didn't seem all that interested in bird-watching. Talked incessantly about racing."

"NASCAR?"

"No—something called karting?"

"Ah—the old-time kids' go-karts. It's coming back as a sport. I have one. It's stored in the garage with the Bugatti."

"I expected no less." She jumped out of the boat. "Isn't a Bugatti one of those incredibly pricy sports cars?"

"When new, yes, but I discovered Isadora in a junkyard. She had been totaled, and the owner couldn't be bothered to deal with her. I hear he's driving a Corvette now."

"If it was totaled, why did you want it?"

"So I could rebuild her. She'll never be the same, but she clocks at two hundred miles per hour. Drives the ladies wild."

"That's nice." *Wait.* "Isadora Duncan, the dancer. Wasn't she killed when her scarf caught in the spokes of her car's wheel? A rather inauspicious nickname, eh?"

"It would be, but my Isadora is named after my grandmother."

"Oh." Palmer filed the information in her mental cubby marked Carson's Toys. "How come we took the Harley instead of the Bugatti the other day?"

"I'm waiting on new plates for the car. We'll take her for a spin soon. You were saying about the boat?"

"No, I was talking about Raven. She hasn't come on our other expeditions, and Hardy kept saying he wanted me to meet her."

"Hardy?"

"Hardy Bantam. The club president. He was sure she and I would hit it off, so he brought her along."

Carson's eyes narrowed. "Oh, he did."

She went on obliviously. "He's been so welcoming—he even waived the membership fee since I'm only here for a short time."

"Oh, he did."

"Yes, wasn't that sweet? He invited me to their club potluck next week too. The group has its share of eccentrics, but he seems pretty normal."

"Oh, he does."

Carson's tone finally penetrated. "Is something bothering you?"

"Nope. Nothing. I'm fine. Is that the boat?" He pointed. The edge of a blue-painted stern showed through a knot of buttonwood and air potato.

"Yes."

He brushed aside the vines and branches. The little

aluminum jon boat was pulled up on the bank, half out of the water. Carson dragged it all the way up and checked the side. "No name; just a number. Most likely a rental." He swiped a finger through the dark splotch of dried gunk in the bottom and smelled it. "You were right. It's blood." He framed the stain with his fingers. "A lot of it."

She stood a few feet back, not keen to revisit the grisly goo. "Do you see anything else?"

"Nothing except an old life preserver. The starter cord for the trolling motor has been snipped, and the oars are gone. Somebody must have lugged them out of here."

"Or they were lost when Swallow was killed." Palmer turned around. "I'm going to search the area." It was tough going through the mangroves, but as the ground grew more solid she only had to push through palmetto and nickerbean. "Wait!" She reached down into a shallow depression. "There's something here!"

"Let me." Carson tugged. The object came loose so quickly he fell backward with it. "Damn." He staggered up and brushed ineffectually at his muddy pants. "Here."

Palmer held up the piece of wood. "It looks like a toy airplane's wing."

Carson took it. "Not a wing. See here: these small notches? This is part of the bowstave of a crossbow." He plucked out a piece of string that was stuck in one notch. "The string is strung through both ends, then pulled taut and cocked on the barrel's sear. I'm going to take a wild guess that this is part of the murder weapon and it was broken off during a tussle."

"Didn't you tell Captain Thrasher that crossbows

were made of steel?"

"Modern crossbows, yes. Medieval crossbows were wooden—usually ash or yew."

Palmer pointed at the blood. "Tipsy must have been murdered in the boat, then thrown overboard."

"And the killer beached the boat here." He looked up. "But how did he get off the key?"

Palmer put a hand on the gunwale. "He had to have had help. Someone picked him up."

"Damn. There's no way of knowing where they went."

She shook her head. "Plus it rained this morning, so any fingerprints have washed off."

Carson tapped the stave on his knee. "We'd best take this to Thrasher. I think it's time the police did some of their own legwork."

"Yes, I really think you should put it like that to him."

Chapter Six

Little Miss Muffet sat on a tuffet
Eating her curds and whey.
Along came a spider and sat down beside her
And frightened Miss Muffet away.

Longboat Key police station, Sunday, May 21

The sergeant at the desk directed them to Captain Thrasher's office.

"Come in."

Carson said heartily, "Glad to see you're in today."

The policeman's smile was wry. "Turns out the chief expects us peons to work overtime when there's a murder investigation going on. Who knew?" He gestured at the bag in Carson's hand. "What have you got there?"

"A present." Carson handed it to him.

With a gloved hand, Thrasher pulled the piece of wood and the bit of string out and laid them on the desk. It took Palmer a minute to realize he had no idea what he was looking at.

She nudged Carson, who spoke loudly. "It's the prod—the crosspiece—of a crossbow. We found it on one of the Sister Keys. Near a rented jon boat. A boat with blood in it." He handed the detective a sheet torn from Palmer's notebook. "Here's the registration number." He indicated the prod. "It's got to be the murder weapon."

"Huh." Thrasher nudged it. "How did you happen to come across it?"

Palmer told him about the birders.

"Why didn't they come to me?"

"I…uh…didn't tell them about the murder. I thought it would upset the girl who found the boat."

"All right, then why didn't *you* come directly to me?"

Palmer's mouth opened and shut. "I…uh…"

"I see." He turned his gaze to Carson. "Your timing couldn't be better. We just learned something of interest."

"Oh?"

"Yes." He clicked on a screen and read aloud, "Carson Hawk, thirty-five, of Washington, DC, holds marksmanship trophies for archery from competitions in New York and Virginia. Hawk is proficient in both longbow and crossbow, as well as in sporting clays. He will be participating in next year's Florida Circuit Championship to be held in Lakeland, Florida." He looked up. "Would you be that Carson Hawk?"

Carson closed his eyes. "Yes."

"Now…" Thrasher lifted his legs to the desk and crossed them at the ankles. He leaned back in his chair and said cheerfully, "Is it just possible that you already knew where the boat was? And the crossbow?"

"Don't be absurd. Why would I intentionally go back to the place I hid it? Let alone let Palmer find it?"

"You've just told me that Miss Lind and her friends found it. You had no choice but to play along."

Carson's only response to this was a snort.

After a minute, the detective lowered his feet to the floor. "Yeah, well. We're going to pursue these leads."

Carson said grudgingly, "You might want to find out who rented the boat."

"Won't be hard now that we've got a description and registration number."

"I mean the other boat."

"What other boat?"

"The one that picked up the killer after he grounded the first one."

Thrasher squinted at Carson. "You're saying the culprit had an accomplice?"

"He must have. How else would he get off the island?"

The detective pushed away from his desk. "We'll look into it. Meanwhile…"

Carson said it for him. "Stay put."

****

The Palapa Inn, Monday morning

"Do you have to go?"

Palmer cradled the phone under her ear while she pulled a denim skirt up over her hips. "Yes, of course I do. I told Hardy I'd meet the gang at Chubby's for a drink."

"You spent all Saturday with them. Isn't that enough for a while?"

Palmer couldn't understand why Carson sounded so fretful. "I'm here on a birding trip, Carson. The club is holding a rap session on which migratory birds generally pass through Longboat Key in the spring. I don't want to miss it."

He was quiet. "Too bad. I had something to tell you."

"Oh?"

"It can wait. I suppose Thrasher should hear it first anyway."

Oh, for Pete's sake. "I'll come over, but I have to leave by six."

"That's okay. I have…a date too."

"A what?" But he'd hung up.

She pulled the aqua shirt printed with magenta flamingos over her head, twisted her long chestnut hair into a knot at her neck, and grabbed her keys and phone.

Carson was in the backyard hovering over the grill. "I made some snacks for you. Chubby's still doesn't have a working kitchen."

She accepted the small platter of grilled baby vegetables on skewers. "I can't stay, Carson."

"I know. Here, try this. It's called *cacık*—made with yogurt and cucumber and mint. You'll find it goes very well with the veggies. Drink?" He held up a tall glass filled with pink liquid. "My own version of planter's punch." He dropped a paper umbrella in it and handed it to her.

She took a sip. "Very tasty. Not too sweet." She put the glass down. "I can't stay long."

"I know. Just let me tee up some more tidbits. Then we'll talk. I wanted to tell you about the death threats."

She knew he was bribing her, but her curiosity was too intense to ignore. "All right." She sat down on one of the rickety lawn chairs to wait. A black cat raced across the yard chasing a lizard. *I swear there are more anoles than ants here.*

Carson brought out a tray and set it on the table. "Let me see…" He pointed at one row. "Tomatillo paste with chorizo and shaved Manchego cheese." His finger moved to the next row of bite-sized, open-faced sandwiches. "Smashed scallop seviche with lime and cilantro. And the last is *muhammara*—that's a roasted red pepper dip—with feta and black olives." He slid grilled fig halves onto another platter. "I've been experimenting with recipes for fresh figs. Most dishes call for the dried variety." He indicated a large bush with the familiar five-fingered leaves, bursting with brown fruit.

Palmer—busy tasting and smelling and oohing and aahing—forgot both her purpose for coming and the time. Twenty minutes later, she emerged from a cloud of ecstasy to find Carson watching her raptly. His shadowy eyes bored into hers. She caught her breath. "What is it?"

"Do you know how beautiful you are, Palmer?"

The shock cut through her haze and brought her back to reality. "Thank you. Death threats?"

"I love green eyes, you know. They're my favorite. Feline. They remind me of my cat."

"Oh?" She indicated the sleek mouser currently licking lizard orts off its paws. "Is that him?"

"No. That one's a stray. Fitz is with my ex-wife. I used to get him weekends, but he's too old to travel now."

"Sorry." She shifted in her chair.

He ignored her discomfort. "And your hair—that amazing color—like cordovan shoes or the deep red rust on an old fishing trawler."

"That doesn't sound very pretty."

"It is, though." He raised his eyes to the sky. "The trawler—we'll call her the *Angeliki*—has done yeoman's work for decades, riding the high seas and hauling in netfuls of cod and menhaden." He lowered his gaze. "Its captain—an old Greek named…let's see…Yiannis, has long since passed, and the ship has lain idle in a corner of the docks, slowly rusting away. In the evenings, the old salts sit in the local tavern and swap yarns of her adventures: of the storms she survived, of the pirates she fought off, of the flying fish that leapt in the bow waves when Cap'n Yiannis cranked her up to twenty knots." Carson touched an auburn curl that had escaped the bun. "Rust is the color of seafaring dreams."

She said crossly, "I still don't see it as a compliment. You're comparing me to a dirty, smelly, dilapidated fishing boat."

"And I haven't even started on your cheekbones." He grinned. "Did you want to know about the threats?"

She couldn't keep the laugh down. After another sip of punch, she folded her arms. "Spill."

"It was after they'd ruled Atticus's death a suicide. I refused to believe it and wrote online about the lack of evidence. Even penned an op-ed in the *DC Exposé* lambasting the police for conducting a shoddy investigation. I insinuated they were covering up for someone."

"Vogel?"

"I avoided naming names. Vogel is a very powerful man."

"But you suspect he was implicated in the senator's death?"

Carson shrugged. "As I told you, Atticus emailed Vogel the night before he died, informing him he was going to add 219 to the markup agenda. Atticus didn't mention to me that he'd responded, so it's unclear whether or not Wilfred received it."

"You're positing that he *did* receive the email and took action? Surely a man of his position wouldn't go around knocking people off? Did Vogel get in touch with you after the senator's death?"

"No, but Joanna did, and she was—shall we say—close to Wilfred Vogel."

"Joanna?"

"Joanna Wren."

"The senator's wife?"

"Yes. I got a call from her asking me to cease and desist. Claimed she didn't want to open up old wounds."

"Did she say she believed the suicide verdict?"

"Not in so many words, but she talked vaguely about family problems and hinted Atticus was depressed. I was noncommittal."

"And the threats came after that? Phone calls?"

"Messages on the machine. Texts on my phone."

"Did you report them?"

He popped a fig in his mouth. "No."

"But that's stupid!"

"After what I said about the DC police in my op-ed? No, sir. I took the safer route—I went AWOL."

Palmer was silent, considering Carson's tale. Finally she said slowly, "The dead man—Tipsy Swallow. Could he have been sent here to kill you?"

"I don't know. At first I thought his presence might have been sheer serendipity—I covered my tracks pretty well. I flew to Seattle and then to Denver before taking the train to Chicago to pick up the Bugatti. I closed all my bank and utility accounts. My cousin

Albert rented the house to me."

"Couldn't someone trace you through him?"

"To do that, they'd have to go through one of those genealogy sites that tests your DNA. He's my third cousin, once removed. His name's Pigeon."

"Albert *Pigeon*?"

He smirked. "We're a large, extended family. The Pigeons and the Hawks go all the way back to Noah."

Palmer decided to move on. "What about social media? Your phone? Doesn't it track you?"

"Tracking's turned off. Access to my social media is restricted to a very small group of friends."

"*Hmm.*" She finished the drink with a final glug. "Do you have any more of this?"

He refilled her glass from a pitcher. "Have another canape."

She was still feeling rather peckish. *I'll just have one more*. "I can't stay long."

"Right."

She chewed and swallowed and reached for another one. "These melt in your mouth! I taste the feta and roasted peppers, but what's the crust?"

"Secret recipe." His eyes twinkled. "I'll just say it involves lots of butter and fresh filo dough."

She ate a third. "Go on. You were saying… Wait a minute! You said 'at first' you assumed Tipsy's presence was fortuitous. What made you change your mind?"

"I found something in the boat."

"The rowboat?" She gazed in consternation at him. "Something you didn't tell the detective about?"

"Yes."

"Or me?"

"I'm telling you now." He dug his fingers into the back pocket of his jeans. "Here." He handed her a rectangle of white cardboard.

It felt damp and one corner was dog-eared. She read the words. " 'Carson Hawk.' This is your business card." She looked up. "Do you think it was in the killer's pocket? Are you his next target?"

"No, I'm betting Tipsy had it. See the brown spot? That's blood. If the card were in his breast pocket when he was shot, it would have blood spatter on it."

"Then why is it wet?"

He took the card and put it on the table between them. "I found it in the bottom of the boat. It must have fallen out when the killer heaved Tipsy's body overboard."

Palmer pulled the umbrella out of her drink and twirled it thoughtfully. "Okay. Tipsy worked for Vogel, right? Number one suspect for the murder of the senator."

"Tipsy or Vogel?"

"Well, the boss would be the one ordering the hit, so he's technically the murderer."

Carson frowned. "I don't think that's how it works. If he didn't pull the trigger, he'd only be an accessory."

Palmer tapped the card. "Well, the killer wouldn't have killed unless he were ordered to. So the responsibility has to lie with the one in charge, no?"

Carson slipped another tomatillo toast onto her plate. "Hold on a minute. I think we're getting over our skis here. We don't know that *either* Tipsy *or* Vogel had anything to do with Wren's death."

"Then why did Tipsy have your card?"

"I'm stumped." He topped up her drink. "Say, I

have a heavenly Niçoise salad in the fridge. Care to join me?"

"What? Oh, no. I can't stay—remember? I'm supposed to meet Hardy at six—" She caught sight of the outdoor clock set in the belly of a sultry mermaid. "Oh dear, it's seven o'clock already!"

Carson hid the smile. "You'd be more than an hour late. I'm sure they've given up on you by now."

She rooted through her purse for her phone. "Damn, it's out of juice. May I borrow yours?"

He shook his head. "I don't have Bantam's number. You can call and apologize tomorrow. Tell them you were...uh...caught in traffic."

Palmer hoped she hadn't lost track of time on purpose. *Still, I've got to admit, this mystery is way more engrossing than the mating habits of semipalmated plovers.* "I...suppose I could stay for a little longer."

Chapter Seven

Froggie went a-courting and he did ride, m-hum!
Froggie went a-courting and he did ride, m-hum!
Froggie went a-courting and he did ride
A sword and a pistol by his side, m-hum!

Carson's house, Monday, May 22

"I could get used to this." Palmer put down her fork. A few crumbs were all that remained of the freshly baked strudel Carson had presented her with. She gave the tray to Carson but tucked the frangipani blossom behind her ear. "What is that yummy citrusy filling?"

"Beautyberry jelly." He gestured at a gangly shrub in the side yard with clusters of bright mauve berries. "It's a native plant. Good insect repellent as well."

"How do you know so much about Florida flora? You've only been here a month or so."

He indicated a book that lay on the bedside table. The romantic cover featuring two people kissing in front of a lurid sunset bore the title *Whirlwind Romance*. "Found this on the bookshelf. The author opens every chapter with a recipe for jelly made from some native fruit. I decided to try one."

"So it's not the bawdy prose, it's the recipes? Huh."

He laughed. "Something like that. More coffee?"

"Thanks." He sat on the bed. "While you were sleeping, I got in touch with my friends at the think tank."

"It's based in DC, right? Which one is it?"

"It's best I keep their name a secret."

"Why?" She peered at his face. "I'm not in danger, am I?"

He didn't answer for a minute. "They know Tipsy traveled to Longboat Key and that he died here."

"Do they also know you're here?"

"They do now. I had to tell them."

"Have they found evidence Tipsy was stalking you?"

"Not yet. They're exploring leads on his activities before he arrived here."

"Are they prepared to defend you if the police charge you?"

He shook his head. "They're a think tank, not a law firm. They told me Senate Bill 219 was pulled from the markup after Atticus's death, but the new chairman, Senator Bunting, has scheduled a hearing. I think he's just flexing his new authority, since he plans to vote against the bill. He's requesting that Vogel testify. Wilfred has refused."

"No surprise there."

"I disagree. He's vehemently opposed to the bill. Why wouldn't he take the opportunity to get his position in the record?"

Palmer chewed on a slice of mango. "Because there's a good chance his ulterior motives would be exposed?"

"What ulterior motives?"

"Didn't you say he's going to take farmland out of production?"

"Not me—it's a theory in some circles that he wants to shrink the food supply to decrease the population."

"He wants to *starve* people to death?"

Carson's lip curled. "Hey! It's for a good cause: to save the planet. *Publicly* Vogel insists he's securing territory for expanding cities."

"Still, there must be more to his agenda, if he was willing to send an assassin after you."

"There's no proof of that." He rubbed his chin. "And it doesn't answer the question of who killed Tipsy. Friend or foe?"

"You mean of yours or his?"

"Of mine. Murdering a person hardly denotes amicable feelings."

Palmer shivered involuntarily. "Let's hope Thrasher comes up with something."

He stood up. "But that's not all."

"What?" Palmer put down her cup.

"They've also invited Joanna Wren to testify."

"Really? The senator's wife? What expertise does she have?"

"She's been involved in environmental causes for years. She worked as an unpaid assistant to the director of the EPA before Atticus was elected to the Senate."

"What does S. 219 have to do with the environment?"

Carson picked up the tray. "To a fanatic, *everything* has to do with the environment. At the very least, they might be expecting her to shed light on Atticus's position. If the two talked about the issue at all."

Palmer sipped her coffee. "Were they happy?"

"Atticus and Joanna? I suppose. They were like any number of inside-the-Beltway power couples. They lived a life in the public eye." His eyes softened. "It began as a real love affair, though. Atticus swept Joanna off her feet, despite her coming from a family whose Democrat roots go back to Andrew Jackson." He chuckled. "Her aunt offered her ten thousand dollars not to marry him."

"God forbid she should be 'indoctrinated' by a member of the party of Teddy Roosevelt."

"Right. The constant pressure from her family may have affected their marriage. Atticus never spoke about it."

"So has Mrs. Wren agreed to testify?"

"Yes. Before she quit her job, her specialty was suburban land use and ecology." He rose. "Let me go wash up these things." He took the tray to the kitchen and came back with the coffee pot. "More coffee?"

She held her cup out. "The committee considers her an expert?"

"Dunno. It's been twenty years since she worked in government. Atticus—"

The conversation was interrupted by Carson's phone. "Hi, Detective. Really? Sure, I can. See you in fifteen. You do? Um…I think I know where she is… Yes, I'll let her know." He clicked Off.

"The police want to see you again?"

"And you."

She suppressed the giggle. "I gather you didn't think it appropriate to tell him I was here."

He was serious. "I don't want him to suspect we're

an item, or even communicating. What if he decides we're in this together?"

"Oh." She plucked at the old shirt of his she was wearing. "I'd better get dressed. Can you drop me at my place?"

"Only for a minute. They want us there by ten thirty."

****

Longboat Key police station, Monday late morning

Thrasher rose from his desk and opened the glass door to his office for Palmer and Carson. "Welcome, welcome!"

Palmer determined not to be daunted by his sudden bonhomie. *At least not yet.* "Why did you want to see us?"

"Well, first to let you know we traced the boat you found to Sara Bay Marina on Tamiami Trail."

"So it *was* rented."

"Yes, *but*"—he held up a palm—"before you ask, the transaction was online. When the boat wasn't returned, the agency tried to get in touch with the customer and discovered he'd given them a false name and number."

"What about the credit card? Couldn't they trace that?"

Thrasher shook his head. "Stolen."

Palmer held up a finger. "I don't understand. Why would they let him take a boat out if his card was declined?"

"They don't run it until the rental is returned."

"So the marina wasn't ever paid?" She was indignant.

The detective made a wry face. "I daresay a person

intent on murder is not going to balk at a little fraud."

Carson clucked his tongue. "Someone must have come to pick up the boat in the first place."

"The renter had arranged to have the keys left in an envelope on the door after the office closed." He shook his head. "They told me it's not unusual for people to come and go outside of office hours."

"Bummer." Carson harrumphed. He started to rise.

"But that's not why I called you here." The detective pulled a large flat box from under his desk. "This is the crossbow fragment you two found on the key." He signaled to a man standing in the lobby. "Edward? Could you come in?" When the man entered, he offered him his desk. "Please sit down." He looked at Carson. "Edward Dunlin is a weapons expert with the Tampa division of the ATF. Edward?"

Dunlin picked up the piece of splintered wood with gloved hands. "This is yew. It was used in Europe until the late Middle Ages to make crossbow limbs." He lifted a fragment of fiber out with a pair of tweezers. "And this is hemp, commonly used for the string during the same period. I'd wager these items come from an Italian crossbow, fashioned in the late twelfth or early thirteenth century in Genoa."

Palmer was intrigued. "You got all that from a chunk of wood? How can you pinpoint the place of manufacture so precisely?"

Suddenly abashed, Edward stammered, "Most medieval crossbows were made in Genoa. It's a pretty safe guess."

Thrasher lifted a hand. "Thank you, Edward."

When the expert had left, Thrasher reclaimed his desk. "Okay, Hawk. We've already ascertained that you are a crack shot with a crossbow. Know anything about antique armaments?"

Something about the detective's body language signaled to Palmer that he already knew the answer. Carson must have sensed the same thing, for he nodded. "I am a collector."

"Not only that, but you reported a robbery the day after Senator Wren was found dead."

Carson straightened, his expression wary. "So?"

"Among other items, an antique crossbow and a set of bronze bolts were stolen from your apartment. Unfortunately, you could not provide paperwork for the crossbow, hindering the investigation."

"I gave the police the serial number, but the sales receipt is back at my house in Illinois. I keep all my important papers there, since I only rent a loft in DC."

"Lucky for you they accepted your explanation. Were any of the other things recovered?"

"No. Well, they found my watch in a garbage can a block away." His lip curled. "I guess they couldn't be bothered with a Timex."

Thrasher turned a page in his file. "I had them check for any crimes committed with an uncommon weapon in the last two months. Turns out criminals are just as set in their ways as other folks. Unwilling to try out some newfangled toy, they all stuck with their illegal Smith and Wessons. So." He closed the file and locked his eyes on Carson. "I've been exploring a new hypothesis. That you were never robbed."

Palmer gasped.

"You mean, that I brought the crossbow with me to Florida and used it to kill Tipsy Swallow?" Carson's voice was taut and low.

Thrasher shrugged. "Let's say he traced you here. You discovered he was on your trail and waited for your opportunity. I've been reading up on crossbows. They're not good for close quarters—not like, say, a blunderbuss. You could hit a target from some distance."

"They have a range of up to a thousand feet," said Carson wearily.

"Right." Thrasher beamed at him. "So you shot him—likely from your bass boat. Then you motored to one of the Sisters, extracted the arrow—excuse me, *bolt*—dragged the jon boat into the brush, and went your merry way."

"Why didn't I simply leave him to drift? That way there wouldn't be any clues that I'd been in the vicinity."

"According to the autopsy, the metal filings in Swallow's heart indicated the bolt had been ripped from the body, which means you must have had contact with your victim after he was dead. I asked myself, why would you do that? Why not split before you were caught?"

"Because the bolt could be traced back to me."

"Bingo."

"Okay, how did I manage two boats?"

"Tied a line to his bow and towed him." Thrasher sat back with a self-satisfied air.

Carson leaned forward. "When I got out of my boat to retrieve the bolt, why didn't I leave the crossbow behind? Why lug it along?"

"*Hmm.* Maybe you wanted to be sure he was dead?" He peered at Carson, who sat rigid in his chair, his face a mask. "Have I left anything out?"

Carson exhaled. "Motive?"

"That's the easy part. Swallow worked for Wilfred Vogel. Vogel is a key supporter of Senator Wren. Vogel is not pleased that you've killed his golden boy. He sends Swallow to bring you back to face justice."

Carson's eyes were troubled. "It doesn't make sense."

"Does to me."

"I mean, aside from the fact that I didn't kill either Wren or Swallow, why would Vogel be upset that Wren died? The senator was sponsoring a bill that Vogel adamantly opposes. I'd say the timing of Atticus's demise worked in his favor."

"Only for that particular bill. As I understand it, Wren and Vogel agreed on ninety-nine percent of the issues. Vogel is one of the richest men in the world. He's used to getting his own way. Your disposing of a fellow traveler and source of his power over Congress would stick in his craw. He wouldn't think twice about taking the law into his own hands."

Carson muttered something about watching too many *Godfather* flicks.

Palmer put a placating hand on his arm. "What are you going to do, Captain?"

Thrasher opened his door. "Officer?" Sergeant Jaeger came in. The captain faced Carson. "Carson Hawk, I'm arresting you for the murder of Tipsy Swallow. Ollie, read him his rights."

Palmer slumped in her chair. Her mind was in turmoil. She wanted to shout, to howl that Carson was innocent, that this was all a misunderstanding, that Thrasher was an idiot. Her mouth opened and shut again. She watched the policeman take Carson away, unable to move.

Chapter Eight

Jack Sprat could eat no fat;
His wife could eat no lean,
And so betwixt them both you see,
They licked the platter clean.

The Palapa Inn, Monday, May 22

Palmer gazed out at the Gulf of Mexico, chin in hand. The phone sat on the little wicker table by her side. The only man she knew on Longboat Key—other than Carson—was on his way over. Hardy had been soothing, although Palmer detected a subdued eagerness in his voice. *It's nice that he's willing to be supportive, even though he doesn't know Carson.* The doorbell rang.

Hardy Bantam—only an inch or so taller than she, with a shock of brown hair and royal blue eyes, stood on the threshold. He held up a paper bag. "I brought wine and whiskey. I wasn't sure how strong a drink you were in need of."

"Whiskey'll do." She took the bag. "Come in. Where's Raven? I thought she'd come with you."

"Raven?" He looked momentarily disconcerted. "She went out with some friends. You said you had disturbing news. I took that to mean you wanted a sympathetic shoulder."

"Oh. Yes." *How sweet*. She set two tumblers on the sideboard.

He held up the wine bottle. "Mind if I stick with my Gavi di Gavi?"

"Not at all." She handed him a corkscrew and balloon glass, then splashed bourbon in her tumbler. "Let's go out to the balcony."

"I'll bring the bottles."

They sat watching the sun disappear below the choppy waves. "The gulf is busy today."

Hardy nodded. "A storm off Yucatan is churning the water all the way to Tampa."

"I see. It's turtle nesting season, isn't it? Does the rough weather make it harder for them to make it to the beach?"

"According to my reading, they actually prefer a light chop. The females ride the surf all the way to land."

Palmer laughed. "The original surfer dudettes."

"Their greatest obstacles are bright lights and beach furniture. Not to mention the holes to China the kids dig."

She surveyed the water line with the faint hope that she'd see a giant mama turtle dragging her egg-laden body over the sand. "Do you get a lot of nests here?"

Hardy nodded. "Several hundred a season—mostly loggerheads, but once in a while a green or a Kemp's ridley."

"Are they endangered?"

"Three of the five species we have in Florida—the leatherback, hawksbill, and Kemp's ridley—are classified as endangered under the Endangered Species Act. The other two—the loggerhead and the green—are only threatened. The green turtles have come a long way. Until recently, they were nearly extinct." He set his lips in a tight line. "Due I fear to the fact that they're the ones that make the best soup."

If he thought Palmer would be shocked, he was disappointed. "I read that it's delicious. I'd love to have tasted it."

"Oh, dear!" His eyes filled with horror. "Well, luckily they're protected now."

She could almost hear the unspoken words "from monsters like you."

He went on, his voice prim. "I myself believe humans should practice a plant-based diet. We don't have the right to kill innocent animals just to eat them."

"I suppose Soylent Green is okay though?"

"Soylent Green? You mean…" Hardy stopped, then growled, "It's not funny, Palmer."

She tittered. "I'm just yanking your chain, Hardy. More wine?"

He cautiously held his glass out.

An osprey shot through the air just above their heads, dangling a mackerel from its beak. It left a trail of fish scent behind.

Hardy pointed. "You can tell the female osprey by the golden necklace adorning her breast. Males are solid white."

"I'll remember that."

Hardy seemed content to sit and enjoy the atmosphere, but Palmer was itching to get the day's events off her chest.

"I'd better tell you why I asked you over. You remember the boat Raven showed us on the Sister key?"

"*Mm-hmm.* Find 'em all the time in the little mangrove islets around here. They get loose from their moorings and drift with the tide."

"I—we—went back to it. Guess what we found?"

"Who's we?"

"Me and Carson Hawk. Do you know him?"

"No." Hardy bit the word off. "I've heard of a Hawk who rents a house in the Village. Friend of mine saw him at Chubby's the other day. He's rumored to be a lush." His glance was penetrating. "How did you hook up with him?"

"Serendipity." For some reason, she felt the need to defend Carson. "I think if he had a drinking problem, I would have noticed. Anyway, he helped me with the body."

There was dead silence for a minute. Finally, Hardy said brokenly, "Body?"

"Oh dear, I forgot to mention it to you. I was on the Coquina Bay Walk a week ago—you know, the nature trail on Leffis Key? Well, I saw a body floating in the water. Carson happened to come by in a boat and pushed it to shore. We called the police, and they took it to the marine rescue facility."

"I…see."

Palmer tried to marshal her words. "The police identified him. He was from Washington, DC. Hardy? He was murdered. The medical examiner says with a crossbow."

"Oh? What does that have to do with the boat Raven found?"

"I didn't say anything to you at the time because she was there, but I suspected the red stain in it was blood. I asked Carson to go with me to check it out, and

I was right! It *was* blood. *And* we found pieces of a crossbow nearby."

His eyes widened. "What did the police do?"

This was the touchy part. "It…uh…turns out Carson knows about crossbows and archery and stuff, so they think he did it and arrested him. But he didn't. Do it. See?"

Hardy stood. "I think I *will* have that whiskey. I'm going to get a glass and more ice. You?"

"Yes, please."

He went inside. Palmer watched a pair of dolphins circling a school of fish who were leaping and splashing in an effort to escape, their silver scales reflected in the waning light. Hardy returned. He plunked ice into her glass and poured more bourbon. He seemed to have calmed somewhat. "So what is it you'd like me to do?"

"Do? I don't know." All of a sudden Palmer was at a loss as to why she'd called him. *I've just roped him into this mess without thinking.* "I'm so sorry. You're my only friend here, and Carson's in a jam and I had to tell someone."

He heaved a big sigh. "Tell you what. I'll take you to dinner and we'll talk."

She was about to say no when her stomach grumbled. *When did I last eat? Oh, yes, the strudel. After…* She tried not to blush. "Okay."

He pulled out his keys. "We'll go to Harry's, and on the way, you can tell me why your new best buddy Carson Hawk murdered a man."

****

Harry's Restaurant, Monday evening

"We'd like a table in the garden room, Drago."

The waiter led the way to a booth in the corner. The back wall of the room was all glass, exposing to view a miniature tropical garden. "Oh, it's glorious!" cried Palmer. "What are those white flowers with the speckled burgundy throats?"

The waiter started to answer, but Hardy held up a hand. "I can manage, Drago. It's a vine called pandora. And the bush with the yellow-and-pink blossoms is lantana. Over there is a clump of bird-of-paradise."

Palmer admired the tall plant with an orange-and-blue flower resembling a pelican's bill. She pointed at a cascade of red-and-yellow blooms. "And that?"

"Heliconia."

"They look like little Russian Cossack pants. And those"—she indicated a large yellow-and-green-leafed plant with a panicle of tubular flowers—"are exactly like shrimp."

"It's a shell ginger plant."

"Oh? So you can eat it? The root part I mean?"

"No, no, although it's a relative of the edible kind. Now over—"

The waiter raised his voice. "May I get you all something to drink? Water?"

Palmer felt slightly giddy after the whiskey but kind of liked the feeling. It took her mind off her troubles. "I'll have a whiskey sour, please."

"Just seltzer for me. With a slice of lime." Hardy took her hand. "Feeling more relaxed?"

He had to let go when the waiter set a basket with assorted rolls and a silver cup of butter curls on the table. Before Hardy could speak, Drago plopped their drinks down.

Palmer eyed him. *I get the feeling he's not a fan of*

my escort.

Hardy waited until Drago had moved to another table. "So…you okay?"

Palmer swallowed half her drink. "Yes, although I feel so helpless. I can't believe Carson killed anyone."

"Tell me about him. He's not a local?"

"No. He's from…*hmm.* I'm not sure. He worked for that senator from Illinois who was found dead last month."

"Atticus Wren? The one who committed suicide?"

"Carson doesn't think he did. He thinks he was murdered."

"*Another* murder?" Hardy pretended to wipe his brow. "You run in perilous circles, m'lady."

"Well, I don't really know him that well." *No reason to go into a night of floating passion on a cracker-house water bed.* "See, he left DC right after the senator died. He didn't tell anyone where he was going, so the police think he fled the scene of the crime."

"And came here to Florida." He bit his lip. "Where he killed someone else?"

"No, I'm sure he didn't." Palmer hoped Drago would come back so they could order. Hardy's face was growing fuzzy. She gulped some water.

Hardy mumbled something she didn't hear. Then he remarked, "You say this Hawk fellow is an archery enthusiast?"

"Uh-huh. Bows and…crossbows."

"So when the remnants of a crossbow were discovered near Raven's boat the police naturally thought of him? Seems a stretch."

"I think the fact that he was the one who found it

made them suspicious. And there's more. The blood we found? The lab says it matches the dead man's."

Hardy took a sip of his seltzer. "The victim was from DC too, right?"

"Yes. Tipsy—Theodore—Swallow. He was a lobbyist."

"Did Hawk and Swallow know each other?"

She nodded miserably.

"I see." He put his glass down. "Let me get this straight. The man Hawk works for kills himself. Hawk splits immediately after and secretly moves to Florida. An acquaintance of his trails him from Washington to Florida and is also found dead. Yup. That kinda clinches the case."

She sighed. "It does sound bad when you put it like that."

"Are you ready to order?"

She jumped. "Oh! I didn't see you there, Drago."

The waiter grinned. "Harry trains us to walk softly and carry a big tray. What'll it be?"

She scanned the list of specials. "I'd like the gulf shrimp cocktail and the veal medallions, please."

Hardy closed his menu. "I'll just have a small salad."

"Dressing?"

"Oil and vinegar. On the side." His expression exuded virtue. "I may have mentioned I'm a vegetarian. It's so much better for your digestion—and the earth, don't you think?"

Palmer thought it safer not to reply.

Hardy handed his glass back to the waiter. "We'll have a bottle of Christophe-et-fils premier cru Chablis 2018. Thanks."

At least he doesn't stint on the wine.

He patted Palmer's hand again. "To be honest, I have no palate. Raven just cooks something and sets it in front of me and tells me to eat it. She swears I wouldn't know if it's animal, vegetable, or mineral half the time, but I'm sure she wouldn't trick me into eating something…improper."

Palmer had a feeling he wanted to say "wicked." She also couldn't imagine being indifferent to food. The infinite variety, tastes, and textures—it made life so much more interesting. "Well, I hope you enjoy your salad."

"I'm sure I will. Now, you were saying you didn't think Hawk was the killer. Why not? It sounds pretty cut and dried. Finding a former colleague dead so near his hideout can't be coincidental."

"Naturally they're related…but he has no idea what Mr. Swallow was doing here—whether it was to warn him or bring him back to DC…or worse."

The waiter displayed the bottle for Hardy, then opened it with a flourish. After Hardy had pronounced it acceptable, Drago poured for both of them. "I'll be right back with your food."

Palmer tasted her wine. "I'd better not have much of this, but it's delicious."

"The only comestible I know something about. Palmer?"

"*Mmm?*"

"Can we change the subject? I have some news."

She felt unexpectedly relieved. *I thought I wanted to vent about Carson with Hardy, but somehow I don't feel any more at ease.* He seemed inexplicably to take the side of the police. *He's supposed to agree with* me, *not them.* "I'm listening."

"I came across the report of a credible sighting of a red-cockaded woodpecker. It has almost entirely disappeared from the eastern seaboard. According to Audubon, its habitat is restricted to old growth, long-leaf pine forests, which Florida has in abundance."

"Where was it observed?"

"In Myakka River State Park. Would you like to go tomorrow—see if we can catch a glimpse?"

"Absolutely! Oh, wait—" She clasped a hand to her mouth. "Maybe I should stick around in case Carson needs help—bail or something."

Hardy's eyes glinted with displeasure. "I'm sure he has relatives or other sources to turn to. Didn't you say you just met him? The court may be reluctant to allow anyone but a licensed bail bondsman to bail out a convict...I mean a detainee."

"I believe he's only been on Longboat Key for a month. I don't think he knows anyone here." She cast her mind back. *Did he mention any relatives? A cousin, I think. And something about an ex-wife?*

Drago set a tray down and placed Palmer's shrimp cocktail lovingly before her. He picked up the salad. "Do you want this now or when I bring the lady's entrée?"

"Now, please." Hardy sprinkled oil and vinegar over the bowl and speared a single piece of lettuce. He chewed pensively. Palmer had just swallowed a large shrimp when he said abruptly, "If Carson has your phone number, he can call you. I'd hate to have you miss out on a chance to see the woodpecker—possibly one of the last of its kind."

She put down her fork. "You're right. I'm being

silly. I…I just feel like he needs a friend."

Hardy gave a forced laugh. "I could use one too! Now eat up and I'll take you home. You need to get some stuff together for our trek tomorrow. Pick you up at five a.m.?"

As a birder, Palmer was used to early hours, but the recent stress had taken its toll and the idea did not appeal. She reluctantly agreed. "Tomorrow at five."

Chapter Nine

Georgie Porgie puddin' and pie,
Kissed the girls and made them cry.

The Palapa Inn, Tuesday, May 23

The doorbell sounded precisely at five. Palmer stuffed everything in her backpack and walked out to the stairwell. Hardy still had his hand on the buzzer. "Wow, you're quick. Sure we don't have time for a cup of coffee?"

"I'm up and ready to go. Why don't we get some on the way?"

He cast a wistful look over her shoulder into her apartment and shrugged. "Okey doke. It takes about forty-five minutes to get there." He led the way to his van. Palmer noted the empty interior. "Where's Raven?"

"Oh, she didn't want to come."

"Will the rest of the group meet us there?"

"They were all busy." He started up the car. "There's a minimart on Clark Road. We can get some breakfast there."

They drove south on Tamiami Trail. Inside a dusty garage-turned-bodega, they bought coffees and a couple of honey buns that could have dated from the Jurassic period. Once they'd passed under Interstate 75, the landscape changed to open fields and megachurches, interspersed with a few large housing communities under construction. Hardy remarked, "More and more people are moving to Florida. Not so long ago the whole interior of the state—excluding Orlando—was empty except for citrus groves and cattle ranches."

Palmer admired the massive live oaks dripping with Spanish moss and the fields dotted with cattle egrets, their gilded manes glimmering in the rising sun. "I've been reading about the history of Florida. Colorful, to say the least."

"Yes." He slowed and pointed out his window. "Crested caracara on that fence post."

The large raptor, its curved orange beak dominating its profile, stood like a statue gazing over its domain. "He's magnificent! Are they rare?"

"Used to be threatened, but they're making a comeback. They're mainly found in Mexico and Texas, but they're becoming more common in central Florida. We're lucky to see one."

Palmer turned to the index section of her National Geographic *Birds of America* and checked off *Caracara cheriway* with a satisfying swipe.

Another couple of miles brought them to the state park. Hardy paid the entrance fee, and they entered a wetland of palmetto and slash pine scrub. Just before a bridge over a marshy stream, he pulled onto the verge. "This is a tributary of the Myakka River. Good spot for anhingas and little blue herons. With luck, we might see an American avocet or a black-necked stilt."

There didn't seem to be much happening except for a large volt of vultures clustered on the other side of the road. The sight gave Palmer a reminiscent judder.

Hardy trained his binoculars on the jostling pack. "Sure are a lot of them. I don't see any roadkill though."

Palmer turned away. "Let's not talk about roadkill, shall we?"

"Oops, sorry." He was quiet for a second, then, apparently unable to resist, remarked, "They're a real nuisance in the park, vultures. They do tremendous damage to cars."

"Really? How?"

"Their talons scratch the roofs and ruin the finish. Also, they poop on the hoods."

She dropped back against the seat and closed her eyes. "To tell the truth, I've had enough of vultures for a lifetime."

"Oh? How so?"

"Never mind." She had deliberately skipped over the part the birds played in her story and saw no reason to insert it now. "Where was the woodpecker observed?"

"In a stand of pine bordering Big Flats Marsh. Come on." They drove up the road to another parking area. "We'll leave the car here and walk along the river bank. Watch out for alligators."

The bank had eroded into a cliff some six feet high. Trees crowded the edge, forcing Palmer and Hardy to skirt around them. In the slow-moving creek below, a king rail stepped gingerly through the arrowhead and pickerelweed. At one point, Palmer thought she heard the telltale knocking of a woodpecker, but it was too far away to identify. A large, white-speckled brown bird with a curved bill landed on a fallen pine with a flurry of feathers. "What's that?"

Hardy swung his binoculars up. "Limpkin. Their diet consists of a single item—apple snails."

Palmer was enjoying herself. *This is what I came to Florida for*. She bent down to look across to the other bank. Something was scrabbling among the bushes. A small, black animal. "Oh my God! Is that a pig?"

"Uh-huh. I think the Spaniards brought them. Feral pigs have gone hog wild around here." He grinned. "If you see bacon on special in the local Publix, it means someone caught a little feller rooting in his garden."

Concentrating on the pig, she almost missed the rippling movement in the water. She stepped back—just in time. An alligator surfaced right beneath her. She yelped in fear and slipped. As she started to slide down the mud wall, Hardy yanked her back. She spun around to face him, and he wrapped his arms around her. "S'okay. I've got you," he whispered huskily.

She tried to stop trembling. "It was so close."

"It's easy to forget this park is crawling with gators. Come and sit down on this log."

She sat, gulping air. Hardy kept his arm around her. At one point he squeezed her shoulders. "Better?"

"I…I think so. We should keep going."

His arm tightened. "Palmer? I'm going to kiss you."

She couldn't believe his timing. *Really? Now?* "I don't…Hardy, I—" Her phone tinkled. *Thank you God*. "I have to get this." She stood up quickly, knocking him off the log. She ignored him as he scrambled back up. "Hello?"

It was Carson. She mouthed his name at Hardy.

His eyes burning, Hardy stood stiffly while she listened. "That's good news. I'm about an hour away.

We'll be back as soon as we can…What? Hardy's with me…Bird-watching. What did you think we were doing?" Her face darkened. "I'll thank you to watch your language. We'll be there when we get there." She gave the phone a ferocious click.

Hardy blinked. "What's going on?"

"Carson's been released from jail. The think tank he's associated with put up collateral for the bond. He needs a ride home."

"He's free until the arraignment?"

"He didn't say. I guess so."

"And he expects you to drop everything and race to his side?"

"So it seems." She picked up her binoculars. "Now, let's see if we can spot that woodpecker."

Hardy allowed the trace of a smile to cross his features. "All right."

Two hours later, he dropped her at the inn. He hadn't touched her since the inartful attempt at the river, but when he walked her to her door he kissed her forehead. "I'm thinking I took things a little too fast this morning."

Palmer was still angry at Carson and so was less sure of her feelings about the episode. *Still, best not to encourage him.* She smiled. "Perhaps. Thanks for the excursion."

"Yes, next time we'll find the woodpecker for sure. The day was not a total loss, though." His hopeful expression made her feel guilty.

"No indeed." She went inside.

Down the hall, glass doors opened on the balcony that faced the Gulf. Through them she saw a figure hunched on the chair. *Carson?* She thought about backing up and making a run for it, but at that moment the man turned. *Who in hell is that?*

A strange little creature in an impeccably tailored linen suit rose and walked toward her. What was left of his hair clung to his temples like a stranded cliff climber. His flattened nose might have been the result of a previous career as a prize fighter or maybe as a peeping Tom. He wore wire-rimmed bifocals, enhancing the resemblance to Benjamin Franklin. Extending a manicured hand, he lilted, "Palmer Lind? I'm Wilfred Vogel."

"Wilfred Vogel! Oh dear."

He permitted himself a small smile. "That's not how I'm usually greeted."

She found her voice. "How did you get in here?"

He retained the smile, albeit a bit stilted now. "Your key is under the mat. Unoriginal, but convenient." At her expression, he added, "It was very hot in the parking lot, and there is a balmy breeze off the Gulf up here. Do forgive me—I'm not used to the humidity."

Palmer had no idea how to respond. She thought furiously. *I can't remember: did Carson believe he had a hand in Senator Wren's death or not?* He was surely not going to do anything to her—not here. *But how did he know who I am? And where to find me?*

"May I sit down?"

"Um, okay." She indicated the sofa but pulled a kitchen chair out and sat near the front door in case she needed to make a quick exit. "What do you want?"

"I need your help."

"Me?"

The smile was completely gone now. "Perhaps I

should explain, although you appear to know at least something about me. I am a financier, chairman of the board of Vogel Enterprises. I have long been active in politics—in a financial capacity. The late lamented Atticus Wren was a protégé of mine. I was his biggest donor. It was a terrible blow to hear of his death."

Don't give anything away, Palmer.

"I learned recently that it occurred in Carson Hawk's apartment and that Hawk had disappeared. The police had been searching for him, but they closed the case this past week. They determined that Wren committed suicide and that Hawk had no part in it."

Still Palmer said nothing. Vogel shifted in his seat a little. "A few days ago, I received a call from the Longboat Key police that an employee of mine, a Theodore Swallow, had been found dead—murdered. They asked me to come down to confirm his identity and arrange for the disposal of his remains."

Startled, she peered at him. "Why you?"

His glance whipped around, his eyes furtive. "Theodore has—had—no family. He's been in my service for seventeen years. We were…close. When I arrived, I discovered that Hawk was the one who found the body. Naturally, I was curious."

"Naturally." *There's something off about him. He's too slick. I don't trust him.* She resolved to keep giving answers that were brief and uninformative.

He shot her a perceptive look. "I do not suspect Hawk of foul play, if that's what you're thinking. I simply want to talk to him."

"What about?"

"He and Senator Wren were working on a statement about a bill that is important to me. At the time of Atticus's death, he was on the fence whether to withdraw it or support it. When I last spoke with him, he was leaning toward approval, but with significant amendments. I would like to know if he told Carson what he finally decided."

He's lying. He knew from Wren's email what the senator's decision was. What's his ploy? "What does this have to do with me?"

"I understand from the police that you are in contact with Carson. Can you arrange for us to meet? Again, I only have a few questions."

Oh dear. What do I say? Do I pretend I don't know Carson? She peeked at Vogel. He didn't seem the kind of man who would put up with any prevarications. "I can try."

He rose. "That's all I ask. I appreciate your help." He handed her a card. "I'm staying at the Zota Beach Resort. Call me when you've set a time and place."

She noticed he didn't make it a request.

He touched his wristwatch. "I'm ready to go." He looked up at Palmer, his face bland. "Goodbye, Miss Lind." He walked out the door.

Palmer ran to the back bedroom in time to see a long white limousine pull into the parking lot. Vogel slipped into the back seat.

She dropped down on the sofa and mulled over the conversation. If he knew how Wren was going to vote, why come all this way to ask Carson? *Wait—Carson said there was no confirmation that Vogel had received the email.* Nonetheless, she was certain Mr. Wilfred Vogel was not being straightforward.

She waited ten minutes, then hopped in her car and drove the two miles to Carson's house at top speed.

She found him in the backyard trimming a six-foot-tall Spanish bayonet. When he heard her step, he turned around, but suddenly screeched. "Ouch!"

"What is it?"

"A spine went right through my glove." He showed her a vicious-looking thorn sticking out of the leather. "Don't know what possesses people to plant these monsters." He regarded it. "I'd cut it down, but I'm afraid it would grow back in the night and kill me in my bed. They'd find me—a human pincushion—speared to the mattress."

"Well, speared to the frame. The mattress would be empty and the water would be sloshing around the floor ruining what's left of your bedroom. I say, leave the fellow alone."

He carefully pulled the glove off and, with his other hand, yanked the spine out. "Well, here you are."

"Here I am. I came to tell you—"

"How sorry you are that you left me hanging around a den of thieves—by which I mean the police station—for an hour before the kindliest of sergeants gave me a lift home?"

"No." *And I'm not sorry.* "Wilfred Vogel is in town."

"I presume to take possession of his lackey's effects."

"He came to see me."

Carson stumbled and almost fell on the Spanish bayonet. "*What*?"

Chapter Ten

Oh, the grand old Duke of York, he had ten thousand men.
He marched them up to the top of the hill, and he marched them down again.
And when they were up they were up, and when they were down they were down.
And when they were only halfway up, they were neither up nor down.

Carson's house, Tuesday, May 23

Palmer said calmly, "Vogel wanted my help to find you."

Carson had recovered from his surprise. "Why didn't the police give him my address?"

"I don't think they're allowed to."

"*Hmm.*" Carson pulled off the second glove and put the pair on the picnic table. "So what does he want with me?"

"He claims he doesn't know what Senator Wren's final decision on 219 was. He's lying, though, isn't he?"

"He may not be. Atticus sent him the email, yes. But he never replied. Perhaps he never saw it. Other than that, I was the only one Atticus told. That's why he came to my apartment instead of writing the statement in his office or at his home." He stopped abruptly. "At his home. I wonder…"

"What?"

"Nothing." He peered at her. "So how come you didn't pick me up?"

Her resentment flared. "I'm not at your beck and call, Carson."

He threw his hands up. "Nobody said you were. It was a simple request—a favor to a friend. That's all. I guess you couldn't tear yourself away from *Hardy*. Where did the group go today?"

She wasn't in the mood to cushion his feelings. "The *group* didn't go anywhere. While we were at dinner, Hardy mentioned that a red cockaded woodpecker had been sighted in Myakka State Park, so he and I went to look for it this morning."

"You had dinner with him?"

Palmer felt defensive, which galled her. "Hardy feared I was…unnerved by the events at the police station. He took me to Harry's to take my mind off them."

"You mean you were upset that they arrested me and went to him for comfort." His voice was ominously cold.

She didn't want to give him the satisfaction. "Not at all. I missed lunch, and I was hungry."

Carson's eyes flickered, but he evidently decided to hold his fire. "So you two went alone to Myakka? Is that allowed?"

Now she *was* pissed. "Allowed by whom? I'm an adult, Carson. Hardy's an adult. We can go anywhere we want, any time we want. I don't need permission from some…some birding oversight board." Her eyes shot tiny needles. "Or you."

He backed off. "Sorry." After a minute, he ventured, "So did you see the woodpecker?"

"No." She curbed her anger. "We saw feral pigs though. And an alligator almost had me for breakfast."

"An alligator attacked you? That's weird."

"You don't think I'm tasty enough?"

He ogled her. "Oh, you're tasty all right." He waited for the laugh that didn't come. "No, alligators feed at night. Most of the day is spent sunning or floating. Were you perchance swimming?"

"No! I was standing on the bank, and he surfaced near me. Suddenly." It sounded rather lame now that she said it aloud.

Carson was on a tangent. "And Hardy told you it was about to grab you. So he grabbed you first. Quick thinking, motherf—twit."

The trouble with scolding him for being jealous was that he was right. Palmer opted to change the subject. "What are you going to do about Vogel?"

Instead of answering, he said abruptly, "I need some water. Coming?"

"Okay." He retrieved two bottles from the refrigerator and handed her one.

She waited, but he didn't seem inclined to talk. Finally she said, "Vogel?"

"Right. You said he came to Florida to deal with Tipsy?"

"Yes, among other things."

"Did he say how he found out about the murder?"

"The police called him. Swallow had no family, so they went to his place of employment."

"Didn't it seem strange to them that the chairman

of the board came down himself?"

"I doubt if they thought about it much."

Carson sipped his water. "Everyone inside the Beltway knew Tipsy. He'd been a lobbyist for Vogel Enterprises for years. We took it for granted he was a favorite of the boss, but there was no indication they were on intimate terms."

Palmer thought of the dapper little man who had visited her. *Was he…?* "What do you mean, intimate?"

He whistled. "Boy, do *you* have a dirty mind. No, I meant that he might have been Wilfred's enforcer. Vogel isn't exactly a mobster, but he is powerful enough to employ people to…er…take care of things when he needs something done." He scratched his chin. "Think I'll put out some feelers. See if anyone knows what, if any, extracurricular work Tipsy did for Wilfred."

"That's great." Palmer put down her bottle. "I've got to go."

"Why?" Suspicion clouded his face. "Are you meeting someone?"

"I'm going home to take a shower. Or didn't you notice the mud splatters on my face?"

"Ah yes, from the abortive reptile mugging. They can be grumpy when roused from their nap."

She shut her mouth and stalked out to her car. As she made the left onto Gulf of Mexico Drive, a white stretch limousine turned onto Broadway. The rear windows were tinted, but she could make out a man in a chauffeur's hat at the wheel and a bald head in the rear. *Vogel.*

****

The Palapa Inn, Wednesday, 3:30 am

Palmer was happily ensconced in a dream about sailing the Spanish Main with a gentle pirate and a crew of singing walruses when the tapping woke her. She rose and picked up a broom, preparing to scare the woodpecker away from her gutter.

"Palmer?"

The rather hoarse shout came from the balcony. She peered through the glass doors. All she could make out were two hands clinging tightly to the railing. "Who's there?"

"Carson. Can you help me?"

She slid the door open and walked outside. "What the hell are you doing?"

"What do you *think* I'm doing?"

"I'm not sure." She tried unsuccessfully to pry up one of his fingers. "Are you trying to climb up or drop down?"

He made an unpleasant sound in his throat. "Guess."

She couldn't delay much longer, although she was thoroughly enjoying the sight of his legs swinging wildly in the breeze. She took hold of his arms and tried to haul him up. "Whew, you're heavy. I can't—"

"Stop. That's enough to let me get a foothold." He slipped over the railing and dropped in a heap on the floor, winded. "Whew! Thanks." He looked her up and down. "Nice nightgown."

She realized that the light from the living room was shining right through the sheer silk negligée. She ran back inside and shimmied on her bathrobe. When she returned, he'd pulled himself onto a chair, and his breathing had returned to normal. She handed him a bottle of water. "How long have you been hanging around?"

"Ha-ha. Only a few minutes. Thank God no one is in the apartment below you."

"What time is it?"

"Must be at least two a.m."

Palmer checked the clock. "It's three thirty." She remembered seeing the limousine near his house. "Are you fleeing from Vogel?"

"How did you guess?"

"I saw the car go down Broadway as I was leaving. What did he want?"

"Well, apparently he had discovered my whereabouts without your assistance. He caught me off guard."

She recalled the man's air of latent aggression. "Did he take a swing at you?"

He cocked an eyebrow. "You've seen him. Do *you* think he's capable of hand-to-hand combat?"

"I guess not."

"No, he only wanted to talk. He had a rather dismaying tale to tell."

"Oh?"

"He had been under the impression that Atticus was planning to support S. 219."

"He told me that. So he must have received the email after all."

"He says not. However"—Carson looked at her gravely—"he informed me that someone *else* had learned of Atticus's decision, and that that someone was *extremely* displeased."

"Displeased that the bill would go forward?"

"Uh-huh."

"Thus implying that Vogel agrees the senator was

murdered?" She frowned. "That's not what he told me. He was quite clear that the police determined it was suicide and had closed the case."

"Well, they may have done so, but he's still pursuing it."

"Does he think *you* did it?"

Carson shook his head. "On the contrary, he says rumors are flying that *I'm* in danger. The killer having disposed of Atticus, he—or she—wants to silence me."

"Why?"

"Because I insisted—publicly—that Atticus's death was a homicide. Wilfred sent Swallow down to warn me. When he didn't hear back from him, he contacted the police, and they told him he was dead. But that's not all."

"Oh?"

"He has narrowed down his list of suspects in Wren's death to one name."

"This mysterious person who didn't want him to sponsor the bill?" Palmer thought this over. "Okay, the bill would make US land off-limits to both foreign and corporate buyers."

"Yes, and that would ordinarily suit someone close to the environmental movement. But not in this case."

"I give up."

"Joanna Wren."

Palmer's hand flew to her mouth. "The senator's *wife*?" She scrutinized Carson's face. "That makes no sense. Why would she be unhappy about 219?"

"I don't know, and Vogel wouldn't elaborate. There's more going on here than meets the eye." He sipped his water. "Could we be overthinking this? Could it be merely a personal matter?"

"Between the senator and his wife? How likely is that?"

Carson didn't answer.

Palmer got up and poured herself a glass of juice. When she returned, she asked, "Question: why is Vogel telling *you* all this?"

"In case the police arrest me for Atticus's murder. He said he would provide for my defense if it came to that."

"Would he betray Joanna?"

"Unlikely he'd go that far." His brow creased. "He's convinced I'm in danger, though."

"I don't understand." Palmer finished her juice. "What's in it for him? Why does he care about your well-being?"

"Well, it's not because of my good looks or charming disposition as you might suspect. No, I think it's because I have all the materials on the bill. He kept asking about them."

"Why would he want the files?"

"Not a clue."

"There must be something damning—or at least disadvantageous in them. Did you look them over?"

"No. I shoved them in a folder and stuck it in Wren's briefcase."

"Wren's briefcase?"

Carson began to fidget. "Look, do you have a cookie or something I can munch on? I'm starving."

"I might have a granola bar."

He curled his lip. "Did you know that ice cream is actually better for you than granola?"

"I did not know that. Are you rejecting my offer?"

He held out his hand reluctantly. "No. I guess not."

Palmer rummaged through her bread box and picked out her least favorite flavor. She handed it to him.

"*Hmm*. Coconut almond. Is that the only kind you—" He stopped at the look on her face. "Thanks." He unwrapped it and took a bite, his face crinkled with distaste.

"You were saying about Atticus's briefcase?"

"Yes. When Atticus came to the apartment, he had a briefcase with him. He asked me to keep it. To be precise, he asked me to hide it."

"Did he say why?"

"No, and he wouldn't tell me what the contents were."

"You're sure it's the files and not the briefcase Vogel is after?"

"I think so. I don't know. This is all getting muddled. Is Vogel right or wrong? Lying or not?" Carson rubbed his temples. "I just want out. Look, can I stay here for a while?"

"You're no safer here. Vogel knows where I live, too."

"I know, but if *he's* the bad guy, he won't make a move until he has the documents in his hot little hands. On the other hand, if it's Joanna—or someone else we haven't thought of—then I'm better off here."

Palmer warmed to the idea. *It would clarify things with Hardy if he finds Carson here.* She regarded the man who was gazing hungrily toward the kitchen. *But would I be trading one can of worms for another?*

"Do you have anything else to eat? I left the house right after I got rid of Vogel and couldn't find an open restaurant."

She pointed at the refrigerator. "Help yourself. I'm going back to bed."

He brightened. "I'll be right in."

"No, you won't. You have a choice: the sofa or the floor. I'll provide a pillow and blanket."

"I am your slave." He kissed her cheek.

Chapter Eleven

Girls and boys come out to play
The moon doth shine as bright as day
Leave your supper, and leave your sleep
And join your playfellows in the street.

The Palapa Inn, Wednesday, May 24

The phone shook her out of a fitful doze at five a.m. *Hello? When did I join the army?* It was Hardy. "Did I wake you?"

"Sadly, no."

"Oh good. I forgot to tell you. The whole crew is heading to Oscar Scherer Park this morning. When Raven heard it's a good spot to see gopher tortoises, she was ga-ga to come. Care to join us?"

Sigh. Palmer was torn. Birding was the whole reason she was here. She knew Oscar Scherer was a good spot to view the elusive Florida scrub jay. *Can I leave Carson here? Can I trust him?*

A voice in her other ear whispered, "Good idea. I'll tag along too. Safety in numbers."

Palmer experienced the first of many sinking feelings but couldn't think of an excuse to deny him. "Hardy? Sure, I'd love to come. I can be ready in an hour. Oh, and my…sister's husband is here on business but had the day off. Do you mind if I bring him?"

"That's fine."

The whisper came again. "Tell him you'll take your own car."

"Can we hitch a ride with you?"

"No problem. I've got the minivan. We'll be at your door around seven."

She hung up, sensing disgruntled eyes boring into the back of her head. She trilled merrily to the air, "Well, I'd better get ready."

Palmer expected Carson to leave, but he remained sitting on the bed. "So, I'm to meet the redoubtable Hardy. *Humph.*"

"Won't it be fun?" She laid out a black skort, then chose a dark teal cotton gauze shirt that matched her eyes.

As she was heading to the bathroom, he said something under his breath.

"What was that?"

"Why do I have to be your brother-in-law? To allay his suspicions? To keep him on the hook? Well?"

She replied with dignity. "How else do I explain your presence here? Hardy is bringing his daughter. I do not want to traumatize the child."

"*Humph.*"

"You should work on your vocabulary."

****

The Palapa Inn, Wednesday morning

Carson and Palmer were standing on the gravel near the entrance to the inn when a gray minivan arrived. Hardy got out. "This must be your brother-in-law. Are you going to introduce us, Palmer?"

"Of course. Hardy, this is Car…" Palmer suddenly realized she couldn't give Carson's real name. She floundered, panicked. "Um…"

Carson took the reins and said smoothly, "Sonny Hooper. Pleased to meet you."

Hardy made a show of seating Palmer in front. He nudged her to look to the rear where a young girl sat. "Say hello to Miss Lind, Raven."

The girl gave Palmer a half-hearted smile, then slumped down in the seat and stared glumly out the window. Her tight braids and long T-shirt made her appear younger than her thirteen years, and the baby fat filling out her cheeks and torso only exacerbated the effect. *Hardy said she was thrilled to be coming. Wishful thinking?*

Carson climbed in and sat beside Raven.

Hardy looked him over critically. "Palmer tells me you're here on business. What kind of business?"

"I sell toys." He grinned.

Raven perked up. "Toys?"

"Not Barbies or GI Joes. I mean rich men's toys. Single engine planes. Fast cars."

"Oh." With an effort, she added, "Cool." She eyed Carson. "Are you rich too?"

"Raven!" Hardy's face flushed.

She ignored him. "Well, are you?"

"Not as rich as I'd like to be."

She giggled. "You're funny."

Hardy slid behind the wheel. "We'll meet the others there." He turned on the AC. "It's going to be a hot one."

The park was ten miles south, just off the Tamiami Trail. They stopped at the visitor center first, then pulled in at the trail head next to a second, identical gray minivan. A plump, fortyish woman in a flowered tunic and capri pants got out of the driver seat. "Hellooo, fellow birders!"

Palmer nudged Carson. "That's Hortense. She's the group's secretary. Very devoted to…the cause."

The woman came over and sidled up to Hardy. "We're all here and ready for adventure, Hardy. The Fish and Wildlife Service bulletin says a pair of great crested flycatchers are nesting in the park. I *do* hope we spy them! Isn't it a beautiful day for birding?" She gazed at him with adoring eyes.

A tall man in his seventies ambled toward the group. He wore a plaid flannel beret and a hiking vest bulging with optical paraphernalia. In a rich BBC accent, he boomed heartily, "Morning, ducks. I am optimistic this is the day we shall be vouchsafed an encounter with the elusive smooth-billed ani. They are almost extinct in south Florida, but my Oxford birding guide asserts they have been observed on the Gulf coast." He bobbed his head in Carson's direction. "Gareth Petrel at your service."

Palmer tried not to laugh. Only Gareth could use the word "vouchsafe" without batting an eye.

A shrill, high voice came from behind him. "Will you move your big behind, Gareth? I want to meet the newbies." He stepped aside, revealing a diminutive woman—Palmer guessed her to be at least eighty-five—in a madras camp shirt and pedal pushers. Her short, curly white hair framed an angular face set in a vast plain of wrinkles. Two chipmunk-like brown eyes zeroed in on Palmer. "You must be Palmer. Hardy has talked nonstop about you since you arrived. I'm afraid I've been under the weather and missed our last two outings." She held out a bony hand. "I'm Opal. Opal

Godwit. Who's your friend?"

Palmer held back the titter. "How do you do. This is my brother-in-law, Sonny Hooper. He came along for the ride."

"Not for the birds?" Opal whinnied. "So...Hardy? Shall we?"

Hardy jumped. "Everybody have water? Wipes?"

"Yup."

"Yes."

"Yes, indeedy." Gareth held up an expensive-looking pair of binoculars. "I shall lead the way with my new Zeiss 20x60mm Porro Prism image-stabilizing binoculars. Arrived from Hammacher-Schlemmer only yesterday." He beamed like a fond parent.

Carson nodded in appreciation, then his face fell. "I'm so sorry. I forgot to pack my binoculars. May I borrow a pair?"

When no one responded, Palmer turned to Hardy. "You usually keep a second pair in your glove compartment, don't you? Can Car...er...Sonny use them?"

Hardy blinked. "Um, no. Darn it, left 'em at home."

"No, you didn't, Daddy!" Raven touched his arm. "I saw you put them in the car this morning. I'll go get them." She ran to the minivan and returned with a small folding case. Blushing, she said to Carson, "They're not great, but since it's mostly open fields, you won't need fancy-dancy glasses here." She tossed Gareth an arch look.

They set out on a path that only allowed two abreast. Hardy took Palmer's elbow and led the way.

Raven snuggled up to Carson. She simpered, "I'll

be your guide…Mr. Hooper."

"Sonny, please." Carson smiled at her.

The park was mainly fallow farmland—treeless and grassy. They had barely reached the first turn in the path when Gareth hissed, "Scrub jay, one o'clock."

Everyone dutifully trained their binoculars on the large gray-blue bird perched on the top of an abandoned telephone pole. Raven handed Carson the case, but he waved it away. "I'm more interested in that big turtle over there."

She turned. "Where? Is it a gopher tortoise? Yippee!" She took off toward the creek. Carson went after her. The others stood uncertainly.

Finally Palmer strolled over to the bank. Sure enough, a brown tortoise about a foot long was making its slow way through the muddy turf. It paused a moment to examine the humans. Palmer yanked a guide to North American wildlife from her backpack. "It's a gopher tortoise all right. They're not endangered, but they only live in Florida and tiny pockets of the southeastern United States."

Carson slipped a folded paper from his pocket and skimmed it. "Huh. Can anyone guess why they're called gopher tortoises?"

Raven raised her hand and cried, "I know, I know!"

He bowed. "Yes, you in the front row."

"It's because—like gophers—they actually dig these burrows underground. The burrows can be as long as a city block and ten feet wide."

"Right. They use them for protection and to brumate."

Raven tugged his sleeve. "What's 'brumate' mean? Like, poop?" She sniggered.

"Nope. Brumation is what reptiles like turtles and snakes do in the winter. Animals that hibernate go into a deep slumber. For cold-blooded creatures, it's more of a catnap. If the weather warms up enough, they revive." He read on. "Gopher tortoises are also very hospitable creatures. Says here they welcome other animals into the burrow—at last count up to four hundred species take refuge in the tunnels."

"Is it a sym...symbi..."

"Symbiotic relationship? No, it's called 'commensal.' I think it means they just like the company."

Raven, enthralled, gazed at the turtle, then aimed her veneration at Carson. "Jeepers, you know a lot."

He held up the park brochure. "I know how to navigate a visitors' center anyway." He and Palmer started back toward the others, Raven trotting behind them. When they reached the group, Palmer expected her to gabble to her father about the turtle, but instead she stuck close to Carson.

Hardy gave her a speculative look. He took Palmer aside. "Might we have a crush developing?"

"I don't know. I hope not."

"Ditto."

****

Oscar Scherer Park, Wednesday afternoon

To the distress of both Palmer and Hardy (and possibly Carson), Raven did indeed spend the rest of the day hanging on Carson's every word. He was very patient. It occurred to Palmer that, though she knew he was divorced, he hadn't mentioned children. *He seems awfully good with her*.

When the group at last returned to their cars, Raven

scrambled joyfully into the back seat of her father's minivan. "Coming, Sonny?"

Hardy coughed. "He's Mr. Hooper to you, Raven."

"No, Daddy! He asked me to call him Sonny. Didn't you...Sonny?" She glowed at him.

"It's all right." Carson seemed only slightly uncomfortable.

"He says he's going to show me his sports car and his motorcycle. And guess what, Daddy? He has a go-kart! It's a Voodoo VR-1—just like the one Sebastian Vettel raced when he was first starting out!"

"Great."

Raven didn't notice the tone and chattered happily all the way back to Longboat Key.

Hardy said over his shoulder, "Where can I drop you, Hooper? Are you staying at the Longboat Key Club?"

"Um, no. A...business associate lent me his place in Longbeach Village. It's okay to leave me at Palmer's if that's easier."

Hardy was *more* than happy to take Carson home.

They drove down Bayou Hammock Road and stopped before the pink house. Hardy peered at it. "Wait a minute, doesn't an Albert Pigeon live here? I know for a fact he's out of town."

Might as well confess. "We weren't being exactly square with you, Hardy. Hooper is really Carson Hawk—the friend I told you about. Albert is his cousin. He's renting the place from him."

Hardy slowed the car. "Hawk...You're the one who was arrested?"

Carson nodded. "Released on my own recognizance."

"But you're still charged? Will there be an arraignment?" Hardy's voice held a note of hope.

"There have been some further developments in the case. The police have rescinded the charge for now."

"For now." Hardy inspected Carson. "*Hmm.*"

Raven tapped her father on the shoulder. "Daddy, could we go in and see Mr. Hooper's—I mean Mr. Hawk's—go-kart?"

Hardy shook his head violently, then glanced at Palmer and gulped air. "No, dear. It's too late today. Another time."

Carson patted the girl's shoulder. "I have some work to do this afternoon, Raven. We'll set a date when we can spend some quality time together." At her aggrieved expression, he said kindly, "I'll even let you take her out for a spin."

Raven slouched back on the seat in a funk. She waved dully as Carson plodded up his front walk, although Palmer saw her write something on her wrist. *His address?*

Hardy said, "Fancy some lunch? We could hit Lazy Lobster."

Palmer looked at her watch. Two o'clock. *I've been up for over ten hours.* "I think I'll just go home and take a nap. It's been a very long day already."

Hardy's jaw rolled as though he were grinding his teeth. "It has, hasn't it? I'll take you back to the Palapa." He turned around in Carson's driveway and drove back down Gulf of Mexico Drive to Palmer's condo. As they left, Raven gave her an apathetic thumbs-up.

Once inside her condo, Palmer peeled off her skort, tore off her sweaty shirt, and flopped on the bed. She was sound asleep in an instant.

The incessant ringing woke her up. It was pitch black in the room. She fumbled first for the light and then for the phone. "Hello?"

"It's Carson."

"What *now*?"

"Can you come over?"

"Oh Carson, I'm tired. Can't it wait?"

"Um. I don't think so. It's Raven."

"Raven! What, did she come back and serenade you?"

"No. Palmer? She's dead."

Chapter Twelve

Rockabye baby in the treetop.
When the wind blows the cradle will rock,
When the bough breaks, the cradle will fall,
And down will come baby, cradle and all.

Carson's house, Thursday, May 25

"You found her, Mr. Hawk?"

"Yes."

"And you didn't touch anything?"

"I touched everything. This is my house. I had no idea she was there until it was too late."

Captain Thrasher indicated the bench opposite him at the picnic table. Carson sat. A policeman straddled the garage doorway. Palmer stood by the grill next to Sergeant Jaeger, who was taking notes. Thrasher nodded at him. "Ready, Ollie? Okay, Hawk. Start from the beginning."

Carson closed his eyes. "I was asleep."

"What time was this?"

"I don't know—sometime in the wee hours. I'd had a light supper and read for a while. It was about midnight when I turned out the light."

"And?"

"A crash woke me up. I lay in bed for a few minutes deciding whether to go run the pest off or let him eat the leftover chicken."

"You assumed it was a raccoon in the garbage."

"Or a coyote. The two species seem to be gearing up for a major battle over food scraps on the island."

Thrasher twirled a finger. "Go on."

"I don't know what piqued my interest—maybe it was *too* quiet outside. I expected some kind of snarling or yelping or that weird screechy noise raccoons make when they're fighting...Where was I?"

"You got up and went outside."

"Yes, and sure enough, the garbage can was overturned, but the top was still on and there was no sign of trash strewn about. That's when I noticed it."

"A raccoon?"

"No, that the overhead garage door was partially open. Since I keep my Bugatti in there, I'm always very careful to secure it when I go to bed." He looked at Palmer. "Would you mind grabbing me a water from the fridge, please?"

She complied, and he went on. "I left the rolling door where it was and opened the side door quietly. Nothing seemed disturbed, and I was about to leave when..." He stopped and rubbed his forehead. "I saw a hand."

"A hand."

"Yes. It was hanging out of the go-kart. I was sure it was Raven. She had been dying to see it and—" He glanced at Palmer, his expression miserable. "I had promised to let her drive it. She's—she was—just a child. I guess she couldn't wait and snuck in."

"What did you do next?"

"I stomped over to the kart, debating whether to call her father or give her a talking-to first. That's when

I realized the hand hadn't moved."

"You said you were careful to lock the garage. So why was the side door open?"

"She must have found the key. I keep it in a flower pot by the door." He looked at his hands. "Once inside, she manually rolled up the garage door to take the kart out."

Palmer had to know. "How did she die? Was it a heart attack? She's only thirteen!"

Thrasher checked his notebook. "Our preliminary examination indicates she was knocked unconscious by a blow to the head. She seems to have sustained another wound as well—there was more blood than the head wound indicated. We'll have to wait for the autopsy to be sure which was the primary cause of death. Whoever did it knew what he or she was doing."

"A professional?"

"Looks that way. So far we've found no prints and no trace of either intruder or weapon."

"How about on the side door?"

"That's only got yours and the dead girl's prints on it. And no prints on the inside knob." He checked his notes. "Salvaged some DNA from the garbage can, but I'm guessing it's the vic's. She collided with it in the dark."

Palmer was more perplexed than upset. "But who would want to kill a child?"

Thrasher looked from her to Carson. "There are two possibilities."

Carson observed, "I only see one. Someone mistook her for me. Maybe whoever left the death threats."

Thrasher went still, glanced at the sergeant, and

leaned forward. "Death threats?"

Palmer could tell Carson regretted the admission. "I…uh…"

"Mr. Hawk, any significant events during a homicide investigation must be reported. Please elaborate."

"That's just it, I can't. After Atticus's—Senator Wren's—death, I wrote a column about the lack of a thorough police investigation. I opined that Wren may have been murdered. After that I received a few emails and phone texts warning me to stop suggesting it was anything other than suicide."

"Who were they from?"

"I have no idea. There was no demand other than to back off…or else."

"Nothing explicit? Nothing to tip you off as to the identity of the writer?"

"Nope. And once I left DC, they stopped."

"Huh." The detective's expression was clear.

He doesn't believe Carson. Palmer brought the conversation back before his train of thought would lead Thrasher to the inevitable conclusion. "You mentioned two possibilities. What was the other one?"

"That Hawk killed her."

Damn. In the strained silence that succeeded this statement, Hardy's voice—pitched higher than ever—came from inside the house. Palmer said quickly, "That's Hardy Bantam, Raven's father."

"Where is she? Where's my daughter? Let me by!" He came crashing through the back door to the patio.

Thrasher nodded at the officer, who let Hardy into the garage. The others didn't wait for permission but trooped in after him. He reached the go-kart in three strides. For a long, painful minute he looked down at his dead daughter, then in one swift motion spun around and lunged at Carson, his fingers closing around the latter's neck. Ollie leapt between them. "Sir! Take your hands off him!"

Hardy's scream rose to a high C. "He murdered Raven! Arrest him. He—"

Thrasher spoke, his tone low and calm. "I'm glad you're here, Bantam. We need your help. Can you come with me?"

"No!" He tried to wrestle out of the sergeant's arms. "I have to take my daughter home. Let me go!"

At a signal from the captain, Ollie beckoned Palmer and Carson and together they went into the kitchen. Thrasher and the uniformed officer remained with Hardy. Even from across the yard, they could hear his cries and bellows. To Palmer, they seemed to last forever, but finally quiet descended. Watching out the window, she saw the two policemen escort Hardy out of the garage and put him in the back of the squad car. It reversed out of the driveway and drove off just as an ambulance arrived. Palmer turned to Ollie. "Where are they taking Mr. Bantam?"

"If I had to guess, home. Maybe to the police station if he wants to make a statement."

Carson put his head in his hands. "I feel responsible. If I hadn't encouraged Raven, she'd be alive."

Ollie looked interested. "Encouraged her how?"

"She was obsessed with go-karts and kart racing. I regaled her with my exploits racing Bertha."

"Bertha?"

"The Voodoo VR-1 in the garage. Where she…"

He put his head down again.

"Ah." Ollie nodded knowingly. "My nephew's into that stuff too. I think they've started a club in their middle school in Bradenton."

Palmer had been deliberating. *Do I ask or leave it alone?* She didn't want to cast more suspicion on Carson but... "Um, Carson? You only met Raven yesterday, and we were together the whole time. When exactly did you do this encouraging?"

Carson's jaw dropped. "Oh shit. I forgot to mention it to Thrasher. She called me last night."

Ollie straightened. "You're going to have to amend your statement then."

"I said I forgot." He glared at the sergeant, who took his notebook out again and clicked his pen. "It was about ten o'clock. She wanted to schedule a date to see Bertha."

"The Voodoo VR-1." Ollie wrote it down. "And how long did you talk?"

Carson bit his lip. "Maybe ten, twelve minutes."

"Ah, that will help in determining time of death. How far away does she live?"

"No clue."

Palmer said, "Hardy lives on Perico Island."

"That's between Anna Maria Sound and Palma Sola Bay. At that time of night, it would have been a twenty-minute drive."

Carson said heavily, "Except Raven was only thirteen."

"Oh. Well. So how did she get here?"

As they pondered this remark, a lanky, pale man in a jacket emblazoned with Sheriff—Crime Scene Unit knocked on the door. His face was vaguely familiar.

"Body's removed, Ollie. When we're finished in the garage, we'll need to go over the house."

"Okay. Thanks, Phil."

Phil—that's it. He was at the marine post when we brought Tipsy's body in.

Carson had been mumbling to himself. He held up a hand. "Phil? Did you happen to log the other vehicles in the garage?"

"Besides the go-kart? We're still dusting that. Lessee…" The agent turned over a page on his clipboard. "You have a slew of 'em." He read. "One Bugatti Chiron sports car, British racing green." He looked up. "Really kick-ass. And one Schwinn low-entry bicycle. Also, there's a shed behind the garage with a Harley-Davidson Sturgis motorcycle—also kick-ass—and a 1984 Peugeot 505 station wagon. Buttercup yellow."

"She came by bike."

Palmer was stunned at Carson's unambiguous response. "How do you know?"

"It's the only vehicle I don't own. It has to be hers."

Phil turned back toward the garage. "I'll swipe for DNA on the bike seat."

Ollie pulled the phone from his shoulder and called Thrasher. "What do you want me to do with Mr. Hawk?…Okay." He clicked off. "He asked me to bring you down to the station, but not for an hour. He wants to finish with Bantam first."

"That's fine. I'll just—"

"Um, sorry, but you can't stay here. Forensics still has to go over the house."

"Oh. Well…"

Palmer took Carson's hand. "I'll take him to my place."

"Okay. You're at 5854 Gulf of Mexico Drive?"

"Yes. Number 2B."

When they arrived at the Palapa, Carson went straight to the kitchen. "I'm starved. I only had a bowl of soup for dinner and no breakfast." He rummaged around in the refrigerator. "You got any cheese?"

"There's some Roquefort in the bin." Palmer arranged buttered, toasted muffins on a plate with red grapes and sliced pears. "Do you want something to drink?"

"Oh boy, yes. Whiskey?"

"It's ten o'clock in the morning!"

"All right. I'll have orange juice. *After* the whiskey."

She indicated the bottle on the counter. Carson filled a tumbler with ice and bourbon, poured two tall glasses of juice, and brought their drinks to the balcony table. The sun shone over their heads, bathing the gulf in a haze of apricot and peach.

Palmer sipped her juice. "You seem to have recouped awfully quickly."

Carson popped a grape in his mouth. "Well, to be fair, I didn't really know Raven. I do feel responsible, especially because it's pretty clear she was in the wrong place at the wrong time." He pursed his lips. "That does bolster my contention that someone is after me. Do you think it's the files I took?"

"You mean, the materials on the bill?"

"Yes. *Hmm*...or maybe not."

"What do you mean?"

"When Atticus gave me his briefcase for

safekeeping, he refused to tell me what was in it. I knew he'd been drinking, but he also seemed—how do I put it?—both scared and angry."

"Where did you hide it?"

"In the freezer." When she cocked an eye at him he said, "I never kept food in the apartment. The only thing in the freezer was a bottle of Stoli. There was plenty of room."

"I take it the murderer—if he was looking for it—didn't find it."

"Right, so I grabbed it when I left for Florida."

"And where is it now?"

He started to answer, then shut his mouth. "Maybe it's better you not know. Safer."

Palmer agreed wholeheartedly.

An hour later, Ollie honked the horn of his police cruiser. As he left, Carson said, "If I avoid incarceration, I shall return this evening."

"Okay." That sounded rather nonchalant, so she added, "Good luck."

Once they'd gone, Palmer felt at loose ends. She went out on the balcony and watched a family on the beach, the children running from the waves and the parents chatting under umbrellas. *Maybe I'll take a swim.*

She was picking out a bathing suit and looking for her water shoes when the doorbell rang. She opened it to a stranger. The woman was thin, sixtyish, with perfect makeup and natural-looking blonde hair. A ten-carat diamond sparkled on her left hand.

"May I help you?"

"I'm looking for Carson Hawk. I was told he was here." Her voice was carefully modulated, with a distinctive private school accent overlying a southern twang.

"May I ask who you are?"

"Joanna Wren."

Chapter Thirteen

It's raining, it's pouring, the old man is snoring
Bumped his head and he went to bed
And he didn't get up in the morning.

The Palapa Inn, Thursday, May 25

"Mrs. Wren! Do come in." Palmer led the way to the living room. "Would you like something to drink?"

"Yes, please. Chivas if you have it."

"Er…that's scotch, isn't it?" Palmer glanced at her watch. 11:30. *These people sure start early.*

The woman allowed an ironic smile to graze her lips. "Yes, but any whiskey will do. Except—obviously—Canadian."

Palmer had upon her arrival checked out the liquor stock in the condo and knew it contained an assortment of booze. The representative of the scotch family was half a bottle of something called Canadian Fog. "Obviously?"

The woman raised a chin that showed definite signs of chemical modification. "Only peasants and college co-eds drink the stuff." She seemed to take in her surroundings for the first time. "I'm so sorry; I didn't realize you were *renting*. I'll have a glass of whatever you have on hand." She gave Palmer what she must have believed was a roguish look.

"Coming right up." Palmer toyed with the idea of bringing Joanna a can of Pabst and decided to go for it. She handed her the beer. "Oh, let me pop the top for you."

She got herself a glass of seltzer and sat in the chair opposite the sofa. "Now, what can I do for you?"

For the first time, the woman lost some of her assurance. "Perhaps I should have asked this first. You are Palmer Lind, correct?"

"Yes."

"And you do know Carson Hawk?"

"Yes."

"How well?"

"I met him less than ten days ago."

"And yet I understand he's living here with you."

Vogel. "Not at all. He has his own house in—" She stopped, unsure whether it was a good idea to tell this woman where Carson lived. "He has his own place. You might say we were thrown together by circumstances beyond our control."

"Tipsy. Yes. Poor man. I heard he was drunk and fell out of a boat. It wouldn't be the first time." She was shockingly dismissive. "Is Carson coming here today?"

Palmer checked her watch. *I'm sure as heck not telling her he's with the police.* "He said he might stop by sometime this afternoon."

She sat on the edge of her chair. "What did he tell you about himself?"

The intensity of her gaze bewildered Palmer. *What is she getting at?* "That he's from DC. That he worked for your late husband."

"Did he mention he was there when Atticus committed suicide?"

Palmer's defenses went up. "He wasn't by his side, if that's what you heard. He was out getting food."

Joanna shrugged. "We only have his word for that." She paused. Palmer sensed she was working herself up to an unfamiliar emotion. "I'll regret to my dying day that I wasn't there for my husband. I"—here her voice cracked slightly—"I was out of town. By the time I returned, Carson had fled."

"You missed the funeral?" *Didn't Carson say he didn't go because he was avoiding Joanna?*

"Certainly not. The funeral was in Rockford, Illinois, Atticus's home town. I went straight there from New York to...er...make financial arrangements and deal with the will." She took a sip and hastily put the can down. "There were quite a few outstanding matters, since he died so...suddenly." She gave a little gulp.

I'm guessing she majored in drama. "What did you want with Carson?"

She took a deep breath and let it out slowly. "Miss Lind, I only...I only want to hear what Carson saw that night—if Atticus said anything about me. If he...blamed me." She raised eyes filled with liquid to Palmer. "He'd been moody for weeks, but I presumed it was because he was at odds with his best friend, Wilfred Vogel."

"Vogel was his best friend?" *Not his protégé?*

"Oh, yes. For years. Wil donated reams of money to Atticus's campaigns. They were in sync on almost every issue. Except one."

"S. 219."

She gave Palmer a shrewd look. "Oh, you know about the bill? Atticus was originally upset about Chinese purchases of US property, but then he learned

126

an anonymous buyer had been sucking up the undeveloped land around some of our larger cities. Wilfred admitted it was he, insisting that he intended to preserve the parcels for generations to come. Sadly"— her eyes dropped—"Atticus didn't trust him. He was sure Wilfred was going to build on the land—or sell it to the municipalities at an exorbitant price."

Palmer had an inspiration. "But you believed Vogel. Did you encourage your husband to withdraw S. 219?"

"I did everything I could to convince him the only way to save the land was to allow Wilfred to acquire it." She started to reach for the can but hesitated, then folded her hands in her lap. "I could never get Atticus to care for the environment the way he should. Republicans are perfectly willing to rape the pristine soil of our continent as long as it enriches *them*." Her eyes turned dreamy. "There's so much acreage around Atlanta, Dallas, Tampa, Chicago—land that's never been worked by man. It should be allowed to remain so. Wilfred would have ensured that happened."

Palmer kept to herself the acid remark that she was pretty sure there was zero ground around any of those cities as yet untrammeled by man. "How does Mr. Vogel plan to protect it?"

"He's going to make it off-limits to the depredations of humans, allowing it to revert to its natural state. No cattle churning up the soil, no tractors slicing through defenseless fields, no suburban tracts of Levittown hovels. Perfect." She stopped to catch her breath, her eyes aglow.

The woman's insane. "That sounds pretty extreme. Did Vogel tell anyone else of his plan besides you? Did he make it clear to Senator Wren?"

She shook her head. "Oh dear, no. That would have made the Republicans' heads explode. No, he sold them all a bill of goods about reserving the land for affordable housing." She looked like she wanted to spit. "What a disaster—whole shantytowns surrounding Chicago, full of rednecks and…and *you* know."

No, I don't know. "Was Senator Wren in favor of the affordable housing idea—if Mr. Vogel kept the price reasonable, that is?"

Joanna grew suddenly restive. Her eyes on the painting over Palmer's head, she murmured, "He was weighing it. He wasn't positive Wilfred would keep his end of the bargain. Atticus preferred to let the locals— not large benevolent organizations like Wilfred's— decide for themselves what to do with the land. Fool." She reached for the beer again but let her hand fall. "He trusted the working class—as though any of them know what's in the best interest of the planet." She bit off the words. "Humans are expendable—but once the earth is gone…" She left the horrors to Palmer's imagination.

"The night of his death Senator Wren told Carson he had decided to support the bill." *Let's see how she reacts to that tidbit.*

Her eyes flickered. "Oh? I wonder if that's because Atticus had received a tip that Wilfred was in fact acting for someone else."

"A straw buyer?"

"Yes. He didn't like that. They clashed over it. Wilfred denied it completely, but I'm afraid it put a chill in their relationship."

Palmer opened her mouth, but Joanna rose precipitously. "Oh my heavens, I didn't notice the time.

It looks like Carson isn't coming back any time soon. I'll take my leave then. Thanks for the…" She held up the can. "I'll let myself out."

She left. Palmer heard a car start up and went to the door. Through the peephole, she saw Joanna burn rubber out of the parking lot in a red convertible Porsche.

****

The Palapa Inn, Thursday evening

After a relaxing swim, Palmer was dialing Oma's Italian restaurant when Carson arrived. He flopped on the sofa. "What a day!" He noted the phone in her hand. "You ordering food, by any chance?"

"Pizza. Want some?"

"With anchovies?"

"It isn't pizza without anchovies."

He whistled. "Bless you! I feared you would insist on broccoli and kale, or"—he shivered—"chicken barbecue. Only godless people desecrate pizza that way."

She agreed. "Stomach turning." She gave her order and put the phone down. "What happened at the police station?"

He sat up. "I could use a beer."

"Oh, sorry, I gave the last one away."

He glowered. "Not to Hardy, I hope."

"No, and that's not very nice. He just lost his daughter."

"I don't want him looking to *you* for comfort."

There was so much wrong with that sentence that she refused to acknowledge it. "No, it wasn't Hardy."

"Oh. Well, do you have any wine? Whiskey? Absinthe?"

She uncorked the bottle of Santa Margherita pinot grigio she'd been saving for a rainy day and poured them both glasses. "Let's go out on the balcony."

Once they'd admired the sunset and watched the single-engine airplane fly by trailing a banner that proclaimed O'Leary's Tiki Bar and Grill Ladies' Night Every Night, she asked again, "So? What happened?"

"I signed my official statement about Raven. They've finished with my house but are still working on the garage."

"Have they found anything?"

"I don't know. They'll be sifting through the evidence back at the lab for a few days. Thrasher said he'd get back to me." He put down his glass. "There is some big news, though. As I was getting ready to leave, a detective came in. He'd discovered where Tipsy Swallow was when he was killed."

"He wasn't killed in the boat?"

"Yes…no. What I *mean* is, they've learned where he was *before* he got in the boat. He was at Tide Tables. It's a seafood place just across the bridge."

"The Cortez bridge? Is it that wooden shack in the middle of the mobile home park? The one with picnic tables outside?"

"That's the one. The bartender remembered Tipsy. It was the Friday before he floated into our lives, making it May 12. He'd arrived right after they opened, around eleven, and sat inside drinking Long Island iced tea."

"I thought you said he was a boozer."

"He is…was. Long Island iced tea doesn't have any tea in it—it's made with gin, vodka, tequila, rum, and cola. It was his go-to brunch beverage."

"Oh. So then what happened?"

"He seemed to be waiting for someone. An hour later, this guy shows up in a boat and yells at Tipsy to come on board."

"Could the bartender describe the man?"

"No, he never came inside. Tipsy paid his tab and went out to meet him."

"How about the wait staff?"

"One of the waiters saw them get in the boat, but the glare from the sun obscured the man's face. Also, he wore a sun hat with a wide brim."

Palmer put her wine down. "So all we really know is that Tipsy met someone at Tide Tables and left in a boat with him. He was killed once they got out in the channel."

"Uh-uh. Too open. He would have waited until they were across the Intracoastal, close to the keys. That way he could glide under the mangroves and dispose of the body without anybody seeing him."

"But if someone were nearby, they'd hear the shot, wouldn't they?"

"If he'd been killed with a gun, yes, but a crossbow is silent. That's why it's popular with snipers and terrorists."

Wait—snipers and terrorists. She took a chance. "You're an expert marksman. Were you a sniper?"

Carson was quiet. Finally, he mumbled, "Yes. Army. Did a tour of duty in Afghanistan. I don't like to talk about it."

"Well, at least you weren't a terrorist." She hoped he'd laugh but wasn't surprised that he didn't. *Quick—get back to the subject.* "I seem to recall Thrasher saying a crossbow isn't a close-quarters weapon. The two men were together in a small fishing boat."

"Good point. If it was rocking, it would have been difficult to shoot him. What are you getting at?"

"Tipsy could have been in the water when he was shot."

"*Hmm*. Then where would the blood in the boat come from?"

"Maybe the killer was hurt. Maybe they struggled, and Tipsy wounded him."

"With what?"

"I don't know—a pen knife?"

"Why didn't the police find it?"

"It fell out of his pocket when he was in the water."

"It's a thought. Perhaps we should be looking for a limping man." Carson gave her a weak grin.

"Oh, wait a minute—the lab tested the blood stain, didn't they? They said it matched the dead man's, who we now know was Tipsy."

"That settles that." Carson poured more wine. "In the meantime, what did you do this afternoon?"

She was glad she'd saved her news. "I already told you. I shared my last beer."

"But not with Hardy."

"No. With Joanna Wren."

Chapter Fourteen

Who caught his blood?
I, said the Fish,
With my little dish,
I caught his blood.

The Palapa Inn, Thursday, May 25

"Joanna! She's in Florida?" He tilted his head. "Huh."

Palmer would have liked his reaction to be slightly more dramatic. "Yes. Didn't you know?" She hoped her tone was sufficiently condescending.

"No. What did she want? And don't tell me she wanted a beer."

"Well, no, she wanted Chivas—that's a scotch."

He nodded impatiently. "Her drink of choice. She thinks it makes her look more cosmopolitan—deep down she's ashamed of her Alabama upbringing, even though her family traces its roots back to Jamestown. I know for a fact she sneaks sweet tea when no one's looking."

The doorbell rang. "That must be the pizza." Palmer paid the boy and put the box on the kitchen counter. Carson brought the bottle and their glasses inside. "Toppings?"

"The aforementioned anchovies. Plus jalapeno

slices and bacon. And don't start."

"Perfect. My favorite combination."

Palmer, charmed, kept her tender thoughts to herself.

Carson refilled their glasses. "So why did Joanna accost you?"

"Accost? On the contrary, she was quite gracious." Palmer took two plates from the cabinet. "She was looking for you. She wanted to hear all the particulars of Senator Wren's passing." She glanced at Carson. "Mrs. Wren was not convinced that you were away from the apartment when he died."

"That's absurd. If I were there, he wouldn't be dead today. I would have stopped him."

"Well…" Palmer faltered. "Her story did seem to mutate a little. At first she insinuated that you were responsible—"

Carson stiffened. "That b—"

"But then—" She interrupted hastily. "She suddenly morphed into this grief-stricken widow and talked about how her husband had been alternately morose and petulant. She asked if you felt she'd contributed to his suicide." Palmer sipped her wine. "Actually, I'm not sure whether *anything* she said was the truth. She's a bit loony."

"Oh, she got into the Mother Earth stuff, did she? She's had that bee in her bonnet for years."

"She said S. 219 would prevent Vogel from buying any land. That he and Wren had this explosive argument about it."

"Not on my watch. DC swamp-types rarely raise their voices; they save their breath for the backstab. But Wilfred and Atticus were truly friends. Like Reagan and Tip O'Neill, they never let their differences interfere with their drinking."

"That's what Mrs. Wren told me. I didn't believe her."

"Joanna—bless her heart—is capable of honesty when push comes to shove." Carson put down his glass. "Speaking of drinking, change of plans. Let's go out for dinner."

"What about the pizza?"

"Save it for a midnight snack. I'm suddenly in the mood for a fish bigger than an anchovy."

She gazed out at the bank of cinereal clouds lining the horizon. "Somewhere inside though."

They were seated by a window upstairs at Dry Dock when the storm ripped through. The winds roared and the rain smashed itself against the plate glass. Outside, the bay was a deep charcoal color, punctuated by towering whitecaps. A seagull bravely beat against the wind before giving up and diving for shelter.

"Oh, thank you, Elise." Palmer accepted the vodka gimlet from the waitress.

"You ready to order?"

"Give us a minute." Carson picked up the menu. "Something warm, I think." Lightning forked across the sky, cracking it like a mirror.

"It is mesmerizing, isn't it?" Palmer watched the scudding clouds.

"Yes. I love the way you allow just a few of those lustrous chestnut locks to trickle down a neck that by rights should be in a Fragonard painting. Or maybe Poussin."

"Huh?"

He ignored her. "Also mesmerizing: the

scintillating gold streaks in those expressive malachite eyes."

She sat back. "Go on."

He framed her face with his hands, but before he could continue, her phone went off. He sat back, his face sullen. "I'll wait."

She answered it. "Oh, hi, Hardy…Yes, definitely. We'll be there. Where is it?" She gestured for a pen and wrote something down on a paper napkin. "Got it. How are you holding up? I see. Well, if there's anything I can do…Oh? Sure. I have her number. Okay. See you then."

"Let me guess. Raven's funeral?"

She wiped a tear away. "It's so unfair."

"Yes," he said gently, "but when is it ever? So…time? Place?"

"Saturday morning. Christ Church on General Harris Street." She clicked her phone on. "I promised to call Hortense to make sure everyone knows the club picnic has been canceled. I'll be right back."

Palmer returned just as Elise arrived, pencil at the ready. "What'll you have?"

"The Longboat Key salad, please."

Elise turned her gaze to Carson.

"For me? Um…the lobster rolls. No, the grilled shrimp. *Hmm.*" He winked at her. "Tell me, what's the absolutely freshest seafood you have today? Something that came in in the last few hours?"

The waitress simpered. "Freshest? Besides you, Carson?" She tapped her lip. "As a matter of fact, Chef took the morning off to fish. He brought back some nice black grouper. I may be able to persuade him to grill some up for his favorite stone crab supplier."

"Sounds perfect." Carson handed back the menu while Palmer stared open-mouthed at him. "What?"

"I thought you'd only recently arrived here. My landlady told me crab trap tags were as precious as Superbowl tickets. How did you manage to snag one?"

"My cousin Albert has permits for a couple of prime spots. I was out in the gulf checking them when George—the chef here—puttered by fishing for snook. We hit it off."

Elise set a salad in front of Palmer, and a platter with a whole fillet, roast potatoes, and a mound of steamed baby spinach before Carson. Palmer cadged a bite of the grouper, which proved to indeed be fresh as a summer breeze in the mountains. She smacked her lips. "Next time I'll let you order for me."

Carson caught Elise's elbow. "Send our compliments to the chef, and tell him I have five pounds of frozen stone crabs if he's interested."

The chef appeared a minute later. To Palmer he looked exactly like the chef in the movie *Ratatouille*— round and jolly and short. The resemblance ended when he opened his mouth. In a thick New Jersey accent, he boomed, "I see your universe has expanded, Carson, my friend. Who is this lovely creature, and how did you prevail upon her to accompany a bum such as yourself to my humble establishment?"

"Hello, George. We met over a corpse. I rescued her from the vultures, and she followed me home."

His eyes widened, then crinkled. "I'm guessing the corpse was a dead fish?"

Carson just smiled.

The storm passed and, without actually discussing it, they drove back to Carson's house. If he had asked,

Palmer was prepared to say she wanted to try the water bed again to see if her dreams were wet.

****

Carson's house, Friday morning

Friday morning came with yet another early call, this time from the police. Carson grabbed the phone just before it went to voicemail. "Hello…Thrasher? You have the report?… I see. No, I have no idea.… Is it in decent shape? I might be able to identify it. Yes, I can come down. See you in an hour." Carson hung up.

"What was all that?"

"They found the rest of the crossbow that killed Tipsy."

"Where was it?"

"In my garage."

"In your—Oh! Do they think it's the same one that was stolen from your apartment?"

"Uh-huh."

"When did they find it? We were here all night. I didn't hear any sirens."

"They found it yesterday evening while we were at Dry Dock. Thrasher sent it to the lab to check for prints. He wants me to confirm it's mine."

Palmer didn't like the sound of that. "If it is, they could arrest you."

"Again. Yes, they could, but I *did* report the theft to the DC police, so they had the serial number and everything. Why would I kill Tipsy with it? That would immediately implicate me. And then I turn around and kill Raven and conveniently leave the bow next to her? I mean, they can't think I'm that stupid. No, it makes more sense that the crossbow thief is the killer."

"But what was he doing in your garage?"

"The sixty-four-thousand-dollar question. The only thing that's certain is that the same person who killed Swallow also killed Raven." He rubbed his chin. "So what do a K-Street lobbyist and a thirteen-year-old girl have in common?"

"You." Palmer's throat constricted. She gurgled, "All three of you were in Longboat Key. Swallow could only have come because you're here."

"To kill me? To warn me? Why? And if this is all about me, why was *he* murdered and not me?"

Palmer threw up her hands. "I don't *know*."

Carson's eyes were grim. "Despite my reporting the theft, it's still possible the police will decide I'm guilty."

"Oh dear. Maybe I should go with you."

"I was hoping you would. You can at least give me an alibi for Wednesday."

"The day we went to Oscar Scherer?"

"Yes."

"I could, but you were home alone when Raven was killed, weren't you?"

"Oh damn, I was. Well—" He threw the covers off. "Let's get this over with."

****

Longboat Key police station, Friday late morning

"You're sure it's yours."

"Pretty sure. See there—that's a partial serial number. If I recall correctly, it matches the last four digits on my sales receipt."

" 'Recall'? Don't you have the paperwork with you?"

"No," Carson said patiently. "As I told you, the receipt is in my safe back in Illinois."

Thrasher looked dubious. "But you kept the crossbow at your place in DC."

For the first time, Carson seemed uneasy. "You caught me. Yes, I brought it with me when Wren hired me for his Capitol Hill office. He was fascinated by medieval ordnance and wanted to see it up close." He looked at Thrasher seriously. "The crossbow is an antique. Your expert was correct: it's a Genoese weapon dating from the eleven hundreds. It's way too delicate to be used in competitions."

Thrasher grunted. "Tell that to the killer."

Palmer leaned forward. "You say it was in the garage. Where exactly?"

"In the go-kart. Under the girl. We only discovered it after they removed the body."

"*Under* her?" Carson was puzzled. "Do the CSI folks have any idea how long it had been there? Tipsy died at least two weeks ago."

Thrasher didn't immediately answer the question. "When was the last time you used the go-kart?"

"Here? Never. I had it transported to Florida with my other vehicles. It's been sitting in the garage since April."

Thrasher stared at Carson over the top of his glasses. "The girl's death wasn't the result of the head trauma. The killer knocked her out, yes, but then he finished her off with the crossbow. Which explains the excess blood we found pooled under the kart."

"What!"

Palmer fixed her gaze on Thrasher. "Hold on a minute. You just said the crossbow was found *under* Raven's body. If he used it to shoot her, why wouldn't he have taken it with him? Or at least disposed of it somewhere else?"

"CSI thinks she was killed elsewhere in the garage, and then the perpetrator tossed the crossbow into the kart and threw the body in on top of it."

"But—"

He waved her down and homed in on Carson. "The fact is, it's *your* crossbow that was found at both crime scenes."

Carson shook his head in disbelief. "How do you suppose it got to Florida?"

"You tell me."

"Someone must have hunted me down. The thief." His brow furrowed. "But, like Palmer says, why leave it in plain sight?"

Palmer said through bated breath, "To frame Carson?"

"*Or* you put it there yourself." When Carson didn't answer, Thrasher said, "Yes. Well. The thing is: we found your blood on it."

"My blood!"

"Also Raven's, a smudge of Swallow's, and a few specks of someone else's."

"You mean, on the part that was in my garage?"

"Yes."

"What about the piece we found near Tipsy's boat?"

"Clean. The water must have washed off any blood or fingerprints."

"But you *have* ascertained that the blood in the boat was Tipsy's?"

"Correct."

Palmer had been ruminating on the news. "The unidentified blood must belong to the killer."

"How would he have gotten hurt? There was no sign of a struggle. He whacked the girl from behind."

Palmer tried not to gag at the image. *Concentrate.* "The crossbow is broken and splintery. He may have cut himself on it when he threw it in the go-kart."

"Or—" Carson straightened. "When it broke apart after he killed Swallow."

"Either way, it has to belong to the killer. Don't you have, like, a DNA database to compare it to?" Palmer appealed to Thrasher.

"Thanks for reminding me," he said drily. "It's being checked now. While we wait, do you mind explaining how your blood could be on a crossbow last used by a murderer?"

Carson started to shake his head but paused. "Wait. I took it to the archery range a few days before Wren's death. I think I scratched my hand on the bolt."

Thrasher pounced. "You just told me it was too delicate for competition."

"It is. But it still works. Senator Wren was keen to see it in action, but I wanted to make sure it was in working order first." He peered at the detective. "How old is the stain?"

"That'll be on the report too."

Just then a man in a white lab coat came in. "Captain? We can't find a match for the fourth blood in any database."

"How old are the stains?"

"It's difficult to tell. While the bow wasn't wet—"

"That means it didn't sit in water for any length of time."

"Which *also* means," Palmer broke in, "that the killer couldn't find the piece that broke off when he killed Tipsy, but he took the rest of it with him."

The lab technician rolled his eyes. "If you'll let me finish. The wood must have been in a hot place for days—like the trunk of a car. That depleted the blood of some key factors."

Carson leapt to his feet. "Wait a minute. The crossbow in my garage *couldn't* be the murder weapon."

"Why not?"

"Because the crossbow couldn't have been fired without the part we found in the mangroves." His triumph was short-lived.

"We're working on that." Thrasher dropped the file on his desk. "Bottom line, you're still a suspect, Hawk. We've established the bow belongs to you. Until we have a better explanation for the crossbow in your garage, don't even think of going anywhere."

Chapter Fifteen

To market, to market to buy a fat pig,
Home again, home again, jiggedy-jig.

The Beach House, Friday, May 26

"What's this here on the menu? Wild boar? I don't recall driving through the African savannah to get here, Katie." Carson eyed the waitress.

Katie scoped out the nearby tables and lowered her voice. "It's pig, sir. Feral pigs are overrunning the fields east of here, so Mr. Chiles arranged with some guys— he calls them 'wranglers'—to capture and butcher them for the restaurant." She smiled proudly. "Mr. Chiles is big on farm-to-table stuff."

" 'Wranglers'? Well, well."

"Yes sir." She blushed pink. "It sounds so romantic, doesn't it?"

Carson wasn't in the mood to indulge her. "So what we're talking about here is gamey pork."

Katie's face fell. "Wild boar. Just like it says on the menu. Mr. Chiles says it's a delicacy."

Palmer stifled the snicker. "Does it come with an apple in its mouth?"

Katie turned on her with a look that said, "Et tu, Brute?" She barked, "May I take your order?"

"I'll have the salmon BLT, please. And a Jai-Lai

IPA."

Carson closed the menu. "All right, I'll give the pig a try. For your sake, Katie."

The waitress flounced off.

Palmer remarked, "It's true about the feral pigs. Hardy and I saw one at Myakka."

"Never mind that." He chewed on his lip. "Do you really think someone's trying to frame me? I swear the crossbow wasn't in my garage before Wednesday night."

"How can you be sure?"

"Like I told Thrasher, it was stolen from my apartment in DC the day after Atticus's death. Unless the thief brought it to Florida, I have no idea how it got here."

Palmer fiddled with a roll. "How well do you know your cousin?"

"Albert? He's a shoe salesman in Peoria."

"Is he a hunter too? Would he keep firearms in the Longbeach house?"

Carson snorted. "Albert is incapable of putting a worm on a hook, let alone bagging a four-point stag. The most lethal weapon in the place was a pair of cuticle scissors. I had to go out and buy a paring knife."

"All right. I was just trying to help. I mean, since he *is* your relative, his DNA would be a close match. It would get you off the hook, as it were."

"By ensnaring my cousin in this mess? My poor, gentle cousin whose car sports every hippie bumper sticker ever devised, including Visualize Whirled Peas?"

Their beers came. After Carson took a large swallow, he muttered, "And anyway, I'm sure they'll find the trace of my blood on the crossbow is weeks old."

Katie brought their orders. "Your pig, sir."

He looked at her quickly. "You didn't spit on it, did you, my dear?"

She laughed. "Then you wouldn't know what it really tasted like. Enjoy!"

They ate quietly for a while. Above them the fans slowly rotated under the canvas roof, keeping them cool. Beyond the restaurant patio, children screamed and chased the shore birds on the sand. Palmer pointed. "While that kid is off scaring the seagulls, a heron just made off with his sandwich."

"Circle of life. This boar is really quite good. Don't tell Katie."

"Are you going to the funeral tomorrow?"

"Yes. No matter how I feel about Hardy, Raven was a sweet, innocent girl who didn't deserve to die. I sent flowers."

"Good."

After lunch, Carson dropped Palmer off at her condo. "I've got some work to do. Want me to pick you up tomorrow?"

"No, I think I'll drive myself."

His mouth tightened. "Don't want Hardy to see us together?"

"That's absurd." But after he left, Palmer spent some time going through her wardrobe to look for the perfect dress.

****

Christ Church of Longboat Key, Saturday morning

The sanctuary of the church seemed very dark to Palmer. There were candles at the end of each pew, and chandeliers, but the high clerestories let in very little light. She supposed it was to mitigate the hot, humid Florida weather, but still found it depressing, adding as it did to the already depressing nature of a funeral for a young girl. She sat in a back pew and watched as the casket was trundled up to the chancel. Hardy walked behind it, staring straight ahead, his face rigid. He stumbled once, and the old lady at his side clutched his elbow. *She must be his mother.* A couple sat close to the front, whispering together. Palmer recognized Gareth and Hortense from the birding group.

She jerked at a tap on her shoulder. Carson whispered, "I see you're one of those parishioners who sit in the last pew so they can get the first slice of cake after the service."

"I didn't want to be too conspicuous."

He sat down next to her. "A lot of flowers."

"Which ones are yours?"

He indicated a large spray of lilies.

"Perfect."

"Get a load of that gigantic horseshoe. Somebody went all out. Or maybe the florist mistakenly sent it here instead of to the winner's circle at Tampa Bay Downs."

Palmer observed a wreath so big it had been attached to a tripod. Roses and chrysanthemums formed an O, surrounding the words RIP Raven. "Somewhat unseemly."

"Tasteless is the word you're looking for. Or indecent. I wonder who sent it?"

Palmer shushed him as the minister stepped up to the pulpit. An hour later, the same old lady supported a weeping Hardy down the aisle. She and Carson waited until the pews had emptied out. The reception was at a house across the street from the church, but Palmer turned her steps instead to the parking lot.

Carson touched her elbow. "You're not going to the reception?"

"I'd rather not. I'd feel out of place."

"Me too. Let's hit Mar Vista for some lunch. My car's next to yours." He started toward the Peugeot but stopped.

Palmer followed his gaze. A white limousine idled in front of the house. A man in a spiffy blue-and-white-striped seersucker suit got out of the rear and stood by the curb, fanning himself with a straw hat.

Carson said loudly, "That's Wilfred Vogel! What the hell is *he* doing here?"

Palmer stayed where she was while Carson strode across the street. "Wilfred!"

Vogel turned and saw him. He called something to the chauffeur, who was approaching from a side door of the church. The man took Vogel's hat and threw it into the limo. He slid onto the front seat and drove slowly away, leaving the two men standing on the sidewalk. Palmer forced her legs to move and headed toward them.

Wilfred was saying, "Hawk! I'm glad I caught you. So sorry I didn't make the funeral, but I wanted to pay my respects."

Carson reared back a step, and Palmer almost ran into him. "Why would *you* go to the funeral?"

Vogel took a less than successful stab at heartfelt sympathy. "I know I never had the pleasure of meeting your daughter, but I still wished to offer my condolences. I sent my chauffeur in to arrange to have the wreath taken to the cemetery. You saw it, of course?"

"Wha...what are you talking about?" Perspiration stood out on Carson's brow.

"Your daughter Raven. I read in the Tampa Bay *Bugle* that she was found dead at your house. I assumed she had come for a visit. How is Susan, by the way?"

Carson blinked twice. "Raven was not my daughter."

Vogel began to speak, but Palmer interrupted. "Carson doesn't have a daughter."

The man stared at her. "Miss Lind, isn't it? I admit I haven't kept up-to-date on Hawk's family affairs, but I'm fairly certain he and Susan produced a child. She would have been about twelve, I believe. Am I wrong, Carson?"

Carson didn't answer.

The other two faced him. After a long minute, Vogel repeated, "Carson?"

"Nestor is fifteen. She lives with Susan in Chicago."

"Ah. Oh, right." Vogel's tone held a touch of malice. "You were divorced, weren't you? It was rather...messy, as I recall." His mouth dropped open. "Oh dear, but that means... Who's the victim?"

Palmer *really* didn't like this man. She thrust herself in front of Carson and—her voice low and menacing—said, "Why don't you go retrieve your *horseshoe* and take it to the grand opening of some tire store?"

His body tensed. "It's not wise to insult me, young lady. You have no idea what I'm capable of." He spun on his heel. Like magic, the limousine appeared. He jumped in the rear, and the car sped up, turning the corner on two wheels.

Carson watched the dust settle. Finally he said quietly, "Vogel is right. It's dangerous to cross him. He's not only a billionaire; he's very vindictive. People much more powerful than you have regretted finding themselves in his bad graces."

"Tough. The man's scum. I'm small fry to a bully like him." She scowled. "How dare he needle you like that? Was that his idea of fun?"

"Maybe. I can't think of any other reason why he'd come to the funeral."

Funeral. Palmer's anger ebbed. "Didn't he try to warn you that you were in danger?"

"He thinks Joanna killed her husband and is after me too. Yes."

She made a serious effort to be positive. "Could he be hanging around to keep an eye on her? To shield you?"

"You're assuming everything he's told us is on the up-and-up."

"He may be a creep, but what other motivation could he have?"

Carson scoffed. "He has no special brief for me. And if he's so sure Joanna killed Atticus, why didn't he go to the police about it?"

Light finally dawned. *We've been looking at this the wrong way round.* "Carson, you should get out of here."

"Why? I thought we could grab some lunch and then—"

"Listen: Vogel may be keeping an eye on Joanna, but you're the one he's spying on."

"How do you know?"

"He came to my condo looking for *you*, not Joanna. He came to the funeral to see *you*, not Joanna."

"So what?"

Palmer held Carson's elbow. "Vogel doesn't consider you a target. He considers you an *accomplice* in Senator Wren's murder."

Carson pulled his arm free. "That's crazy. Why would I help Joanna do away with Atticus? And despite Wilfred's accusations, Joanna couldn't have wanted him dead. I can't see her objecting to S. 219."

"That's not true. She *wanted* the bill to fail. Vogel promised her if he could continue to procure land, he would preserve it, not build on it."

"And she *believed* him?"

Palmer recalled Joanna's earnest speech. "She sure seemed to. One way or another, somebody is after you. You should run away."

He shoved her in the direction of her car. "Sure. Okay. After lunch."

****

The Village, Saturday afternoon

"Ooh, that last daiquiri went right to my head."

"It's the heat. Maybe we shouldn't have indulged in rum before the sun dips over the yardarm. I'll take you home. We'll come back and get your car tomorrow."

Palmer snuggled as close as she could given the bucket seats. "Um...you don't have to." She tried to flutter her lashes but hiccuped instead.

He gazed down at her. "You know what? You're right. You'd better come with me. You're in no condition to be alone." He kissed the top of her head.

"I'll sleep in the guest room."

Palmer hoped he was joking. As they pulled into Carson's driveway, she roused enough to sit up. "You left a light on."

"It's automatic. Motion sensor." He checked out the street. "There's a car parked in my neighbor's driveway. Jake must be home."

"He's a—what do you call it?—a snowbird?"

"Yup. Left beginning of May. He should have shut everything up then. Maybe the property manager reported a problem. I'll go see if he needs help later." He waited for Palmer to get out of the car. "Come on."

As they walked into the living room, he flipped a switch, illuminating a table lamp. Through a door to the left Palmer noticed a pile of sheets and a folded blanket on the bureau. "You seem prepared. Did you know I was going to stay here?"

He frowned. "No. *Hmm.* They weren't there this morning. Someone's been in the house."

Now she was wide awake.

Carson walked slowly around the room peering out the windows. "Whoever it is, he can't have gone far. I'll check the garage."

"Should you? Shouldn't we just run? What if it's Joanna?"

He looked at her. "Why on earth would she be here? And can you see Joanna Wren making her own bed? No, we have us a squatter. This house was empty for months before I came." He rubbed his chin. "Or maybe Jake had to crash here."

"Why?"

"He might have a roof leak, or a broken appliance, and has to get out of the house while the repairs are being made. I don't know. I'll go try his door."

Palmer was vacillating between going after him or hiding in the station wagon when the back door opened. A young girl walked in. Slim, on the cusp of womanhood, her braided hair was of the same dusty blond as Carson's. She wore a microscopic purple bikini.

While they were staring at each other, Carson came through the front door. "Jakes's not home. I'll—" He halted abruptly. "Nestor!"

Chapter Sixteen

Did you ever see a lassie, a lassie, a lassie?
Did you ever see a lassie, go this way and that?
Go this way and that way,
Go this way and that way.
Did you ever see a lassie go this way and that?

Carson's house, Saturday, May 27

Palmer suddenly remembered the thing she'd wanted to talk to Carson about. *His daughter.*

"Dad! *There* you are. Where have you *been*?"

Palmer was impressed. *It takes a special talent to put a choleric parent on the defensive with a single phrase.*

Carson's jaw remained hanging open.

Finally Palmer stepped in. "You must be Carson's daughter. I'm a friend, Palmer Lind. How do you do?"

The girl looked her up and down. "Hello. I'm Nestor. Are you his girlfriend?"

"No! I mean, no. We just met. We've…uh…come from a funeral."

She didn't ask the obvious question but instead stepped tentatively toward her father. "Daddy? Aren't you…are you glad to see me?" She suddenly went from independent young lady to little girl, her face on the verge of crumpling into tears.

Carson was jolted into action. He picked Nestor up and gave her a bear hug. "Happy to see you? Are you kidding?"

Her face crimson, she cried, "Daddy! I'm in a *bathing suit*. Sheesh."

He set her down. "When did you get here? What are you doing here? *Why* are you here? And since when did Mom allow you to wear a bikini?"

She grinned. "Let me get out of this wet suit, and I'll tell you everything." She cast a glance at Palmer. "She can stay."

The two adults sat in stupefied silence while the girl ran into Carson's guest room and closed the door. She traipsed out a few minutes later in shorts and a T-shirt, and plopped on the easy chair. "Okay, what do you want to know?"

"How about you start at the beginning?"

She let her tongue loll. "First, do you have any soda?"

"No. Sorry."

Palmer piped up. "I believe I saw some orange juice in the refrigerator. Would that do?"

"That would be great, thanks. I'll get it myself." She got up and was loping toward the kitchen when she halted and swung around. "Anyone else want a drink?"

"No, thanks."

Carson sat on the couch, his head in his hands. Palmer ached to rub his shoulders, but was afraid Nestor would misinterpret her gesture. *Well, maybe misinterpret isn't exactly accurate.*

The girl appeared, took a big drag of the juice, and started in. "See, it's spring break and—"

"No, it's not."

She seemed startled, then a little wary. "Um. I didn't think you kept up with the school calendar."

"Of course I do."

She rallied. "Well, it *is* Memorial Day weekend, so I have Monday off school. I left Midway on a red-eye at three a.m.—"

"You flew?"

"Sure." She said plaintively, "Just because you won't take me up in Queenie doesn't mean I haven't been in a plane. I've flown lots of times. I went out to Portland to see Auntie Dina, and with my class to Montreal, and—"

He held up a hand. "Got it! Go on."

"And then—" Her eyes lit up. "This was *so* neat. Bobby Pipit got me this fake ID, and I used it to rent a car at the airport." She ignored Carson's shudder. "I drove out here all by myself!" She turned to Palmer and stated with sublime complacency, "I have a learner's permit."

Carson's voice was hoarse with suppressed emotion. "Setting aside—*for now*—the dangers of your little junket, as well as all the laws you've broken, why are you here?"

Nestor's eyes grew moist. "Mama and me—we had a humongous fight."

"Over Bobby Pipit?"

"Uh-huh. He wrote me this letter with"—her blush went to the roots of her hair and floated toward the ceiling in hot pink waves—"some dirty words in it, and she found it."

Carson said nothing, but Palmer shivered at the look in his eyes.

"It wasn't my *fault*! *He* wrote it. I didn't even

encourage him. He's just a boy. He doesn't know any better. You know boys." She gazed at her father with conviction, as though she had no doubt he agreed.

Palmer smothered the laugh.

Carson got up and pulled his phone from his pocket. Nestor gulped. "You're not going to call her, are you?"

"What did you think I would do?" His finger was poised over the keypad when the doorbell rang.

Palmer answered it. She swung around to the pair inside. "It's the police."

****

Longboat Key police station, Sunday morning

"All right, you've smoothed it over with the girl's mother?" Captain Thrasher looked from Carson to Nestor to Palmer.

Carson grimaced. "We're still working it out. At least Susan no longer wants to press charges for kidnapping."

Thrasher grunted. "They would have been overridden by the murder charge anyway."

"M…m…murder?" Nestor's eyes widened.

Thrasher looked at Carson. "She doesn't know?"

"We didn't get much chance to talk yesterday, what with the brownshirts storming in and busting me."

Thrasher pretended to peruse his notes. "I'll leave that to you, Mr. Hawk, shall I?"

"Thanks." Carson's tone was dry. "Am I free to go?"

"Not quite yet." The detective contemplated Nestor. "Now, young lady, we have some options."

Nestor, dressed in a demure baby-blue shift Palmer had lent her, cast her eyes down.

"Fortunately, the car rental agency has agreed to transfer the rental to your father's name. We can still charge you with a misdemeanor for the fake ID. You'd have a court date a week from now." He turned a page. "Uh-oh, Judge Turnstone is presiding that day." He shook his head. "He's a real hardliner. Sends most kids straight to juvie."

Nestor began to tremble. "But Mr. Thrasher—"

"That's Captain Thrasher." He bore down on the hapless child. "He might, on the other hand, give you probation—maybe a hundred hours of community service. That's only if he's in a good mood, which generally he's not. *Or*—"

Father and daughter tilted forward. "Or?"

"I could remand you to your father, who will return you to your mother in Chicago."

This was greeted with a chorus of "Sounds good!" and "Great idea!"

"Well, then." Thrasher closed the file. "I'm counting on you to accompany your daughter all the way to Chicago, Hawk."

Carson squeezed Nestor's hand. "You better believe it."

"And come back to Longboat Key immediately after you've delivered her."

Carson grinned. "No problem!"

Five minutes later, they were on the sidewalk in front of the station. Carson laid a hand on Nestor's shoulder. "Let's go home, and I'll make the reservations."

"Can't we take Queenie?"

"Captain Thrasher insists we fly commercial— easier to track us." He put a hand on each of her arms.

"Now, when we get to Chicago, you, Nestor, will make a formal apology to your mother." He kissed her cheek. "Next time, face the music; don't dance away to Pop. It only gets us both in trouble." He started toward his car. Palmer turned north and began to walk to her condo.

Nestor called, "Where are you going?"

She looked over her shoulder. "Back to my place."

The girl stared at her. "Don't you live with Daddy?"

"Heavens no, dear. I told you, we've known each other less than two weeks."

"Oh." She seemed disappointed. "Well, can you come with us now? I need a woman to support me while Daddy and I talk."

She looked so sweet and childlike that Palmer gave in. "My pleasure."

Carson took Nestor's hand. "We can pick up your car on the way, Palmer. You left it at Mar Vista yesterday."

Palmer reddened. "Oh, right. I'd forgotten."

When they reached his house, Carson went off to his study to arrange the trip. Nestor made Palmer sit next to her. "Now tell me about this murder."

"Don't you want your dad to explain it?"

"Nah. He'll get all upset and hide crucial facts from me, thinking he's protecting me. You'll tell me everything. I'm old enough to hear bad stuff." She sat up straight.

"Okay." Palmer told her about finding Tipsy Swallow and about Raven's death. She hoped Nestor wouldn't guess that the girl's murder was most likely a mistake. *She may think she's a tough cookie, but finding out someone is after her father is a lot to handle.* "You know your dad worked for a senator who died, right? That's why he's here."

"Senator Wren. Uh-huh. He committed suicide, didn't he? I wasn't sure why Daddy left DC. It wasn't his fault, after all."

She might as well know. "We're not totally convinced it was suicide, Nestor. Your father received some…threats. He thought it prudent to leave Washington."

"He's hiding out?" Her eyes sparkled.

"It's nothing to be concerned about. It—"

"Oh, it's so *fire!* My father—a fugitive! Just like the movie." She recited, "The hero is innocent of the crime, and he's sworn an oath to bring the real killer to justice." She dimpled at Palmer. "*And* there's a policeman after him, dogging his steps. That's Mr. Thrasher." She wrinkled her pretty nose. "He's not very photogenic, is he? Mr. Thrasher, I mean."

Palmer thought of the middle-aged man with heavy, black-rimmed glasses and the vestiges of a gradual hair-dye product clinging desperately to his thinning locks. She couldn't deny it.

Nestor had already moved on. "But Daddy is always one step ahead of him. And then—"

So much for sparing her feelings. "Um, Nestor? This isn't a movie."

She sobered. "I know, but it *is* exciting." She stared into Palmer's eyes. "You sure you don't love Daddy?"

Palmer gulped. "Sweetie, I don't know him well enough to know how I feel about him."

She folded her hands with an air of inevitability. "It doesn't take that long, you know. My father is so handsome. And smart too. Prolly by the end of the week it'll all be clear."

Palmer was amused. "If you say so. How would you feel about that?"

"Oh, I think it would be swell! See, my parents were married right after college. They divorced when I was two. Mama says they were both too young. Then a couple of years ago, Mama met someone else." She said confidentially, "I call him Uncle Toby even though they're married now. He's real nice to me. And to her. Daddy needs to find someone like Uncle Toby." She stopped and giggled. "I mean a *girl*, not a guy." Before Palmer could come up with a suitably equivocal reply, Nestor whispered, "You'll take care of him after I go back home, won't you? Promise?"

Palmer melted. "Cross my heart."

Carson came in. "It's all set. The flight leaves from Sarasota-Bradenton Airport tomorrow at ten. It's a nonstop to O'Hare. Now, shall I grill something for us?"

"Oh yes, Daddy. I'm positively ravenous!" Nestor turned to Palmer. "Daddy's the *best* cook!"

Palmer could not but agree.

"Okay, I'll see what I can rustle up. You guys want to take a swim while I work?"

"It's kind of a trek from here to the gulf." Palmer patted her dress. "And I don't have a suit."

"Not to worry. Jake—my neighbor—lets us use his pool." He ran his eyes over her figure. "Maybe Nestor has—"

"I'll just keep an eye on Nestor while she swims."

The girl held up a key. "It's fenced in, but I found this hanging by the gate."

An hour later, they sat down to grilled jerk chicken,

black beans and rice, and fried plaintains. "Just like we had on our trip to Jamaica, Daddy."

"*Mm-hmm.* I got the recipe for the jerk spices from that old man who ran the roadside barbecue." He patted his daughter's hand. "And I only had to pledge Nestor to his firstborn son to get it."

****

The Palapa Inn, Monday morning

"We're about to board. I'll call you when we land."

"Okay." Palmer rather liked the casual way Carson said it. *Like we're an old couple. I might as well play along.* "When are you coming home?"

"Susan won't want me to stay long, so I'll try to hop a flight back tomorrow. I want to make sure Nestor is squared away. Plus I'll have to endure the requisite impugning of my character."

She really didn't want to say it but felt she had to. "Maybe you *should* stay there awhile longer—you'll be safer there than here."

"You mean from the diabolical Thrasher? I believe the police have the means to track fugitives down anywhere in the country."

There's that word fugitive again. "No, I mean from whoever may be trying to kill you."

"Oh, that. I'm betting the danger has passed. The new chairman of the committee has decided to reintroduce Atticus's bill. They're holding a hearing next week. If someone thought they'd stop it by killing its sponsor, they failed."

"I hope you're right."

"Oops, Nestor's beckoning me. Looks like our zone's been called. Talk to you soon."

Palmer clicked off the phone and walked out to her

balcony. The holiday had brought out hordes of sun lovers. Kids frolicked in the waves, their fathers heedlessly casting fishing lines into their midst. Mothers in swimsuits better suited for their teenage daughters lolled on the sand. Palmer was thankful no one on Longboat Key brought boom boxes to the beach. *At least I can hear the surf.* Far out a pair of dolphins circled a school of fish, breaching and diving. *Playing with their food.*

There was a knock on the door. She opened it to Joanna Wren. She pushed past Palmer and stopped in the middle of the living room. "Where is he?"

"Carson? He's out of town."

"Carson Hawk? Who cares about him? I mean Wilfred Vogel. I saw his limo—he always rents a white stretch limousine, the ass. You've been seeing him, haven't you?"

Chapter Seventeen

Peter Peter pumpkin eater
Had a wife and couldn't keep her.
Put her in a pumpkin shell
And there he kept her very well.

The Palapa Inn, Monday, May 29

Joanna whirled around and advanced toward Palmer, her cheeks flaming and her teeth bared.

Palmer fell back a step. "I beg your pardon?"

"You heard me, you…you floozy. Keep your smutty hands off Wilfred!"

Palmer was too astonished to respond, but the thought gamboled through her head that jealous rage was hardly a suitable look for a bereaved widow. She was weighing options for escape when Joanna toppled into a chair.

"Oh Miss Lind, I'm so sorry. You must think I'm a crazy person. My emotions are all over the place." To prove it, she burst into tears.

Palmer gave her a box of tissues and went for a glass of water. When she returned, Joanna had regained her composure. "Thank you." She sniffed. "I suppose I should explain my behavior."

That would be nice. "If you like."

"You see, Atticus and I had what you'd call a

political marriage. We did love each other in the beginning, but after a few years, the unabating hostility from my relatives…" She broke off and sipped the water. "You see, my family has lived in Mobile, Alabama, for over two hundred years. We've *always* been Democrats…well, for as long as there's been a Democrat party, that is. Atticus was not only from the Midwest"—she said it with a moue of distaste—"but he was a Republican. Two colossal strikes against him in the view of my grandmother Rose, the matriarch of the clan. She turned everyone against him, shunned him. At least, until he was elected senator." She gave a resentful snort. "Even then they barely acknowledged him at family gatherings. I got tired of defending him all the time, and we drifted apart, but the demands of the job meant we had to pretend we were the idyllic power couple."

That's how Carson described them. Palmer had trouble feeling sorry for her but could hardly interrupt the flow. "Go on."

"Last year we were at Davos—that's an annual economic forum in Switzerland. Everybody who's anybody in the financial and political worlds goes. Atticus was giving an interview to Forbes, and I took to the slopes for an afternoon's skiing."

The lives of the rich and famous…

"I was on my last run and visibility was poor. I took a spill, and suddenly Wilfred appeared out of the gloom. He helped me up and escorted me back to the lodge. We had tea together and…and one thing led to another." She raised damp eyes to Palmer. "Do you hate me?"

"Me? Why would I hate you? It's nothing to do

with me."

"Even though I'm a rival for his affections?"

"What on earth are you talking about?"

"He came here to see you, didn't he? Why would he do that unless he was attracted to you?" She produced a tiny hiccup. "He's left me, you see."

Palmer wasn't sure what to say. *I'm sorry your adulterous lover booted you out? How about: then you're hardly my rival for his affections, are you?*

Joanna wiped her eyes with a lace handkerchief and stuffed it into a tiny leather purse that undoubtedly cost more than a house. "How did you meet him? Did he sweep you off your feet? He can be so romantic when he wants to be." Her mouth drooped.

"Nothing of the sort. He showed up one day looking for Carson Hawk."

"Carson? Why… Oh, I see…" Her expression turned crafty. "So Wilfred's after Carson? The police think he killed my husband, you know. Carson, that is. I assume Willy's trying to help them bring him to justice. The rule of law is very important to him."

The nice lady has a rich fantasy life.

"But he didn't." Joanna allowed herself a satisfied smile.

"Who didn't what?"

"Carson didn't kill my husband. Atticus committed suicide. He had been depressed for a long while. We hid it as well as we could. He just couldn't deal with his problems anymore." She said the words in a mechanical manner, as though she'd said them many times before. Which she probably had.

Palmer rose. "At any rate, I am barely acquainted with Mr. Vogel. It's none of my business what you do or don't do with him. May I show you out?"

Joanna rose gracefully. In a silky voice she said, "I'm so glad we had this little chat. It's cleared the air, hasn't it?" She smiled coldly. "I shall be returning to Washington, so I'm afraid this is goodbye. Do give my regards to Carson." At the door, she turned. "Oh, and please tell him that if he needs anything—anything at all—he should get in touch. I still have many connections."

Palmer watched her red Porsche turn onto Gulf of Mexico Drive. She recalled Carson's comment of a few days ago—that maybe Wren's death was triggered by a personal and not a business affair. *Hmm.*

A white limousine pulled into the lane behind the Porsche. She pursed her lips. "The man tails everyone. He's like a stray cat."

****

The Palapa Inn, Monday afternoon

Palmer was eating lunch when Carson called. "All is well. Susan has forgiven me, and Nestor has been grounded. No more solo plane rides. She says she forgot to give you back the dress she borrowed, and do you want her to mail it or can she keep it?" He chuckled. "She's very persuasive."

"Well, the color is better on her than on me. Tell her she's welcome to it. When are you coming back?"

"I forgot this is Memorial Day weekend. I was lucky to get seats on the Chicago leg, but I couldn't get a return flight until tomorrow. It lands at Tampa International at four p.m." He paused.

"I can pick you up."

"That would be sweet, although I can always take an Uber..." He left the sentence hanging.

"Nonsense. You can repay me by making dinner."

"Again? I'm fast becoming your personal chef."

"Well, if you don't want to…"

"Of course I want to, but I insist on a toque."

"You are not allowed to smoke weed in my kitchen."

"What? Oh, you think… No, a *toque*—the white balloon hat. Silly girl."

"Ah. In that case, I'll try to dig one up. Do you need anything else?"

"Yes. Go to the Star Fish Market. Ask if they have grouper cheeks. If not, then buy whatever's freshest."

"Star Fish Market?"

"It's in Cortez village. Cross the bridge and turn down 123rd Street. The market's at the end of the road next to A. P. Bell and the Coast Guard station."

"Okay. Sounds like an adventure. Do you think they'll carry stone crabs? I have yet to try them."

"Sorry, the season's over for them. After this, I'll have to bribe George with snapper…or maybe alligator meat. I wonder if that's still verboten? Better check…" He petered out. "Where was I?"

"You were telling me what you needed."

"Oh, right. I'll need a mango, and chutney, lemons, and…let's see…limes? No, I think I have some in the hanging basket. Look, I'll email you a list, shall I?"

She said drily, "That would be helpful."

"Done." His voice faded. "Be right there, hon." He came back to the phone. "Nestor says we're going to dinner with *Uncle Toby*—it appears he only frequents the Magnificent Mile. I'm lobbying for the Billy Goat Tavern."

"What's that?"

"Only the greatest bar in Chicago. It's under the L—that's the Loop train tracks—and its regulars are the best reporters and sports writers in the world. A real dive."

"I love dives."

He was quiet for a minute. "Maybe someday I'll take you there."

Before she could answer, he hung up. She stared at the phone. *If he'd given me the chance, what would I have said?*

****

Tampa airport, Tuesday afternoon

Palmer waited impatiently in the line of cars by the baggage claim entrance. Carson had texted her that the plane had landed, and she hoped she wouldn't be waved on by the airport police before he appeared. There were several doors he could emerge from, so she was kept busy checking up and down the long terminal sidewalk. Which is why she didn't immediately see the white limousine pull in behind her.

As her eyes swiveled to the rear, she caught a glimpse of a stocky, uniformed man with a pencil-thin black moustache and light brown skin. He was helping a short, balding man out of the car. *Vogel!* Joanna said he always rented a limo. The driver must be a temporary hire then, and not an employee. Just then Vogel handed the man a plane ticket. *Huh.*

She left off wondering about the two men when a familiar red Porsche shoehorned into the space in front of her. Joanna shot out of it. She thrust a handful of bills toward the young man at the wheel. *So the Porsche is also a rental.* She waited to see if Joanna and Vogel noticed each other, but they marched in through separate doors and disappeared.

"Miss me?"

She jumped. "Oh, Carson. Did you see Joanna? She must have passed you on the way in."

He looked over his shoulder. "No. I came out way up there." He pointed to the taxi stand sign. "I forgot to tell you I changed airlines."

"Oh. Well, Joanna just went inside…and so did Vogel."

"Together?"

"It didn't look like it."

"*Hmm.*"

Palmer decided to save her news of Joanna's visit till they got home. "Let's get going before rush hour hits."

As they drove, Carson kept her cackling over stories of Chicagoland bars he'd been thrown out of. "Uncle Toby turned out to be a good sport with a knack for picking up quirky characters. We did a little barhopping after we left the ladies."

"I'm glad. Your ex-wife is happy?"

"Yes. He's perfect for her." He patted her hand. "Nestor tells me she advised you of our botched attempt at marriage in our twenties. Breaking up was for the best."

She didn't answer, occupied with trying to squelch the question that kept bubbling up. *Are you ready now*?

He looked out the window at the parasailers shooting the breeze in the bay. "At least we produced one good thing."

"Nestor."

"Yes."

Palmer thought of the girl with the sparkling eyes

and effervescent attitude. "She's a remarkable child."

They arrived at Carson's house as his phone tinkled to life. "That must be Susan checking on my arrival." He listened. "Wilfred? How did you find out? Who? Oh. Thanks, I guess." He hung up. "No reason to unpack. Can you drive me back to the airport right now?"

"To Tampa? Why?"

"Because, according to Wilfred Vogel, who learned it from his chauffeur, the Longboat Key police are heading here to arrest me for the murder of Raven Bantam."

Chapter Eighteen

Little Robin Redbreast sat upon a tree,
Up went Pussycat and down went he,
Down came Pussycat, away Robin ran,
Says little Robin Redbreast, "Catch me if you can."

Carson's house, Tuesday, May 30

"Arrest you! But how—" Palmer was about to protest that Carson should stay and defend himself, when he spun around.

"No, wait. He's bound to have officers at the airport. I'll take the Cessna. I'd better grab my pilot's license." Carson ran inside. "You were right. I should have stayed in Illinois!"

Palmer's throat constricted. "Where are you going?"

"Back to DC. I've got to retrieve Wren's briefcase."

"It's in DC? I thought you brought it with you when you came to Florida."

Carson shook his head. "I left it there—in what I thought was a safe hiding place. Now, I'm not so sure. I'd better stash it somewhere more secure."

"No! You should stay here. You can't evade the police." She summoned up Nestor's breathless words. "You don't want to be on the run the rest of your life."

"I don't intend to be. I just want to get hold of the contents. Senator Wren intimated they contained proof of a major fraud being perpetrated on the American people."

"What! Why didn't you tell me that before?"

"I didn't want you involved."

She put her hands on her hips. "Like I'm not *now*?"

Her sarcasm was lost on him. "You've only brushed the fringes. This thing may be a lot bigger—and therefore a lot more dangerous—than I originally thought. I need to have evidence to show the cops." He took hold of her arms. "But I do need you to do something."

She gulped. "What?" *I don't think I'm up to barricading the door or blocking Detective Thrasher with my body.*

"Stall the police as long as you can."

Damn. "How?"

"Tell them I haven't called you. You've been waiting here, but I've sent no word since yesterday. That you're afraid I've dumped you."

"Dumped me! We're not even an item." Palmer sputtered furiously. "Dumped me, indeed."

Carson grinned and kissed her. "Okay, how about this? I'm still in Chicago. That's more credible."

She was still fretting. "What am I supposed to do with all those groceries?"

"Put them with the pizza. With any luck we'll get this sorted out and I'll be back before the fish stinks."

Palmer wasn't in the mood to argue. "All right, but if you're not going to Tampa, how do you plan to get to Washington?"

"My plane's at Hidden River airport."

"Your plane? Oh right, the Cessna." She essayed a joke. "You only have the one plane? Sad!"

"Queenie's for short flights. The Citation IV jet is parked at National Airport for my North American trips."

Sigh. "And where is this Hidden River?"

"It's a private airport on Myakka Road, about forty miles east of here. A friend arranged for me to store Queenie there." He shouldered his duffel bag and tucked a folder in his inside jacket pocket. "Just tell Thrasher that Nestor had a school project or something, and she asked me to stay for it. I'll be back as soon as I can." He kissed her again.

As he roared out of the garage on his Harley, it occurred to Palmer that she hadn't asked the most important question. *How did Vogel's chauffeur know the police were going to arrest him?*

****

The Palapa Inn, Tuesday evening

Palmer drove back to the Palapa. She tried to eat a cookie, but it tasted dry and powdery. She didn't feel like a drink. *Maybe a short snooze.* The tension forced her up after only a few minutes. *I need to burn off some of this nervous energy. A brisk walk on the beach should do it.*

A three-mile hike later, she returned to find Captain Thrasher sitting in his squad car in the back lot. Behind her, the sun dipped below the horizon, its brilliant rays emitting a final, silent, agonized shriek as it gave up its hold on the west. He got out when he saw her climb her stairs to the condo and followed her to her door.

He waited, mute, while she washed the sand off her

feet. He stood patiently in the hall while she went to her bedroom and donned a fresh sundress. He didn't say a word when she got a bottle of water from the refrigerator. Finally she relented. "May I help you?"

"I'm looking for Carson Hawk. He's not at his house."

Since her story was a simple one she told it easily. "He's still in Chicago."

"Did he call you?"

"No…he texted me that he was staying a few more days."

"May I?" She nodded and he sat down. "Funny, his ex-wife says she saw him off at O'Hare this morning."

Ulp. She hadn't thought of that. "I don't know what to tell you. Maybe he decided to stay at the airport. Maybe the flight was delayed. Could be anything," she finished lamely.

"I see. Well, we'll keep an eye on his house."

"What do you want with him?"

His eyes flickered. "We have more evidence in the Swallow murder and want to run it by him."

"Swallow! Not Raven Bantam?"

He gawked at her. "The dead girl? No, there's been no progress on her murder. Why did you—"

Hmm. *Was Vogel lying? Or is Thrasher?* She said quickly, "What kind of evidence?"

"A possible witness."

"A witness! Who is it?"

He scratched his head. "Not something we're ready to divulge, Miss Lind." He rose. "If Hawk gets in touch with you, tell him we'd like to talk to him."

"Sure thing," she said brightly.

When the detective had gone, she collapsed in a

chair. So it wasn't about Raven? *Why would Vogel say they were going to arrest Carson for her murder? Where would he get that idea?* On the other hand, Thrasher may have made up the story about Swallow to conceal his real purpose. Vogel certainly had good sources. Still, what reason could the *police* have to lie to her?

Swallow had met someone at Tide Tables. A waiter had seen the man but couldn't identify him, so they must have located someone who could. A customer? Another waiter? *What time of day was he there?* She cast her mind back. Tipsy had been at the bar from eleven on. *According to the detective, that was five days before we discovered his body. So where was Carson the day Tipsy was killed? I've no idea.* Her heart sank.

Thrasher wants to talk to Carson. They have a witness. If that witness was at Tide Tables, it means…it means…the man Swallow was meeting had to be…Carson.

****

The Palapa Inn, Wednesday, 1:00 a.m.

The ringing of the telephone next to her bed woke Palmer up. She picked up the receiver and asked groggily, "Who is it?"

"Who else would call you at one in the morning?"

She rubbed her eyes. "Well, the police seem to have me on speed dial."

"Huh?"

"They were here again. Carson, they have a witness to Tipsy's murder."

"They do? That's splendid news!"

"Thrasher didn't exactly say so, but it looks like he fingered you."

"Me! That's ridiculous. I didn't even know Tipsy was in Florida. And anyway, why would I want to kill him?"

"Don't ask me. Ask the good detective."

"Did he say anything about Raven?"

"Only that they had nothing new. That is strange, isn't it? Why would Vogel tell you Thrasher was going to arrest you for her murder?"

"I don't know." Carson was silent for a minute. "I wonder if Wilfred has an alternate agenda."

"Like what?"

"Well, what did I do when he told me about the impending arrest?"

"You scarpered."

"Precisely. Perhaps that was his plan."

"All right, but does he want you *out* of Florida, or *in* DC?"

"I'll find out tomorrow. He's back here. I have to get hold of the think-tank folks—see where they are in their investigation. I'm hoping they can help."

"Why are they interested in Senator Wren's death?"

"They specialize in environmental issues. Two-nineteen was on their radar."

I wonder... "Carson? What's the name of the group?"

"Extended Earth Solutions."

Oh dear. "Carson, please don't—" She heard a voice in the background say something unintelligible. "Who's that?"

"Joanna. I'm hiding out here."

Oh no, that's even worse! "Do you think that's wise?"

"Better than staying in my own apartment. The police won't look for me here. Joanna's offered her lawyer and any defense I need. She's a good friend."

Is she? "All the same, be careful. What do you want me to tell Thrasher when he shows up again?"

"Nothing. You haven't heard from me." Joanna's voice sounded again. "Okay! Be right there…Gotta go. Miss you!"

Palmer had fallen back on the pillows when it came to her. *I forgot to tell him about Joanna's and Vogel's affair! Again!* She hoped it wouldn't come back to haunt them.

****

The Palapa Inn, Wednesday, 5:00 a.m.

Doesn't anyone call during banking hours anymore? Palmer felt for the phone in the dark. "Hello?"

"It's me again." Carson was whispering.

"I know."

"I'm at the Greyhound terminal in Union Station. Bus leaves for Nashville in twenty minutes. Just wanted to let you know."

"Nashville? What's in Nashville?"

"I don't know. Why do you ask?"

"Um…because you're going there?"

"Oh, I see." He lowered his voice even more. "It's the first bus out of here. I had to cut and run."

"Again?"

"You don't sound very sympathetic."

"Not at five a.m., no."

"Then I guess I won't tell you why."

Sigh. "All right, shoot."

He waited a few moments, presumably to allow the guilt to really set in. "Joanna is not my friend."

Duh. "What makes you say that?"

"Before I left town, I hid the briefcase at her house in Maryland without telling her. As I was carrying it out of the guest room, she tried to steal it from me."

"Is there a chance she thought *you* had stolen it from *her*?"

There was a pause. "*Hmm.* Hadn't thought of that. She went berserk. I lost my head and made a run for it. I'm wondering now if I was too hasty."

"Berserk?"

"That may be a tad hyperbolic, but she did turn this freakish shade of puce and her voice went higher than Franklin's kite."

"What did she say?"

"It's not what she said—mostly a lot of cant phrases—it's the way she said it."

Patience. "Did she want you to give her the briefcase?"

"Yes, but when I balked, she began to ramble about it having sentimental value. She claimed she gave it to Atticus on their honeymoon."

"Kind of an unromantic gift."

"That's what I thought. When that didn't work, she started in on Atticus's work for the environment. I made the mistake of laughing."

"Why?"

"Because Atticus's idea of conservation was replacing the divots on the polo field. His excuse for dropping his cigar ash on the lawn was that it made good fertilizer."

Palmer remembered the woman's lecture about pristine wilderness and the joys of back-to-nature. "How did she react?"

"She made the absurd claim that the case contained legislation making west Texas a national wilderness. When I still refused to give it to her, she started screeching at me again. I swear, Palmer, her eyes were bulging."

"And that's when you left."

"I hightailed it out of her house back to DC. I couldn't go to my own apartment, so I wandered downtown for a few hours, then made my way to the bus station. Oh, I've got another call coming in. I'll try and phone you from Nashville."

"Wait, what about—"

Click.

As she lay back on the pillow, the phone rang again. She picked it up. "Carson, if you—"

"Is he there?" Joanna's frantic voice filled her ear.

Oh shit. "Who?"

"You know very well. Carson Hawk. He tore out of here and…and he took something of mine. I called the police. They're watching all the airports."

"Airports?" Apparently it didn't occur to Joanna that people actually took buses. *No reason to disabuse her.* "Well, he's not here." *And that's the truth.*

Joanna kept babbling, oblivious to Palmer's response. "I asked them to arrest him, but I wish I hadn't now. Miss Lind? They're also going to charge him with my husband's murder."

Chapter Nineteen

Snail, snail, come put out your horn,
Tomorrow is the day to shear the corn.

The Palapa Inn, Wednesday, May 31

"The police want to charge Carson with Senator Wren's murder? They told you that?" Palmer gulped.

"Yes." Joanna's voice rose. "If he shows up, you *must* warn him."

"Warn him? I don't understand. Do you or don't you want him arrested?"

"Not for murder! Lord, that would make a huge mess. Atticus killed himself. I don't want a lot of mud dredged up by some stupid homicide investigation. You of all people should be with me on this—you worked inside the Beltway."

"How did you know?"

"Carson told me. He seems to have taken a fancy to you. *Hmm.*"

Palmer could almost hear the synapses clicking over in the woman's head.

"Look, I know he'll get in touch with you. Tell him…tell him I won't press charges if he gives me back the briefcase."

"It won't make any difference if the police are intent on holding him for murder."

"Oh, that." She sniffed. "Come to think of it, I rather think Wilfred's ginning them up. I'll straighten him out."

Palmer was beginning to wonder if she was in a movie or some kind of candid camera prank. Joanna seemed to imagine she could turn an official criminal inquiry on and off at will. *Well, that* is *how the DC elite rumble.* She considered asking her why Vogel believed Carson had killed Wren, but thought better of it. "If I hear from Carson, I'll pass along your message."

"What? Oh, thanks." Joanna hung up without saying goodbye.

Palmer gave up on getting any more sleep. She made coffee and went to sit on the balcony. Rosy sunbeams shot through the window in the hall, washing her tile floor and walls with color. She contemplated this new set of accusations against Carson. Vogel said the police were after him for Raven's murder, but Joanna claimed it was for Wren's. *Did Carson tell Joanna why he showed up at her door?* She hadn't mentioned Raven, but that could be because she didn't know about her—or merely didn't care. The image of a grave face rose before her. Thrasher. He had hinted they suspected Carson played some kind of role in Tipsy Swallow's death. *That's three.* Three murders all connected intimately to Carson Hawk. A horrible thought passed through her fevered brain. *Could he actually be guilty?*

She forced her mind to shut down. The sun was fully up, but the beach was still swathed in a fine mist. Through it a lone woman wandered the shore, her eyes trained on the sand. She wore a long, flowing robe of white. Every once in a while she'd bend down, pick up a shell, and put it in a small bag. Palmer was always tickled by the obsession people had for finding shells. *There's this whole vast, exquisite gulf spread out to her left, and she only has eyes for the ground.* A pod of humpback whales could swim by, or an albatross wing slowly over the bounding main, and the beachgoer would stay glued to the thin line of calcareous fragments strewn at the tide line.

Suddenly the woman opened her bag and pitched the shells out into the water. Then she gathered up her skirts and began to gallop down the beach. Even from her balcony, Palmer could hear her whooping with joy. *Well, I'll be.*

As she was heading to the kitchen, the phone rang again. She leapt to pick it up. "Hello? Hello?"

"You sound winded. Did I catch you at a bad time?"

She shut her eyes and rammed her heart back down her throat. "Hi, Hardy. No, I...uh, got up too fast. How are you holding up?"

There was a catch in his voice when he answered. "Fine. I'm, *um*, fine. I'm calling because the club is going to the Celery Fields today for a spot of birding. Would you care to join us?"

"What or where are the Celery Fields?"

"Oh dear, I keep forgetting that you're a stranger in these parts. It's a 400-acre preserve just east of 75 and one of the best spots for sighting birds in south central Florida. Last time I checked the total count was almost 250 species."

"Why is it called the Celery Fields?"

"Because it was originally a celery farm, part of a parcel of 140,000 acres that Bertha Palmer purchased in

1910 during the heyday of Sarasota's Gilded Age."

"Bertha Palmer... Was she collaborating with John Ringling? I read that he was active in developing this part of Florida."

"No. They had separate spheres of interest. Ringling bought property on the coast and the keys for tourism development, but Bertha went inland. She inherited a lot of money from Potter Palmer of Chicago and decided to use it to modernize farming in Florida."

"When did the farm become a preserve?"

"Sarasota County bought it in 1995 for storm mitigation and then worked with the Audubon Society to turn it into a park." He chuckled. "They killed two birds with one stone."

"Ha-ha." One word in Hardy's recitation stuck in her mind. *Chicago. That does it. Now I'll sit around all day and stew over Carson. Not gonna happen.* She snapped her fingers. "All right, when are you leaving?"

"I can pick you up at ten. It's supposed to be overcast today, so hopefully we can stay cool. The area is very exposed."

Palmer ate a quick breakfast, collected her binoculars and bird guide, and was downstairs when Hardy pulled up. "The others are meeting us there."

It took about an hour to get off the island and through the endless strip malls, retirement communities, and medical centers. Once past Route 75—the main north-south interstate in western Florida—it was a short distance to the entrance of the park.

It was not what Palmer expected. She'd been to many preserves in Florida by now, most of which consisted of either mangrove wetlands or dry pine woods and prairies. The principal feature of the Celery

Fields was a high promontory that looked exactly like a grass-covered dirt mound left over from some major construction project. At its feet lay a grungy, swampy area of black water and even blacker mud.

"Isn't it swell? The county erected the hill as a flood buffer, but it's proven to draw all kinds of passerines." They were standing in the parking lot when Hortense and Gareth pulled into the slot next to Hardy's van.

Gareth waved. "Hi, Palmer. Hardy."

Hortense's face slipped from enthusiastic to sorrowful the instant she saw Hardy. "I'm so glad you're getting out, Hardy." Her chin wobbled.

Gareth chirped, "Opal couldn't make it—she's babysitting her great-grandchild."

"All right." Hardy slung his binoculars around his neck. "Let's head up to the top, and then we can decide which path to take."

They climbed the steep, rough track to the flat, mesa-like top. The sun—already hot—went behind a merciful cloud. Gareth pointed. "There—isn't that a northern shrike?"

Four sets of binoculars swung up and trained on a sabal palm. "It is!"

"Gorgeous."

"Thrilling!"

Palmer swept the area with her glasses, then looked down the hill to the marsh. Spots of pink dotted the mud. "Roseate spoonbills!"

Hardy touched her elbow. "And over there: see the red crowns on those large white birds? It's a mated pair of sandhill cranes. Ooh, and they have a baby!"

Palmer made out a ball of golden fluff pecking at

the ground between the two adults. Her mood lifted. "Let's head down!"

Just as they reached the marsh, a flock of glossy ibis flushed, leaving in their wake a moorhen flustered and squeaking like a frightened mouse. A red-winged blackbird dive-bombed them, chattering angrily at the trespassers.

Hardy bent down and picked something up. "Get a load of this fella." He held a snail the size of an ostrich egg in his hands.

Palmer surveyed the bank. "Oh my gosh. There are *hundreds* of them."

"They must love the sludge."

She hefted one. "I wonder why no one is scooping them up and cooking them."

Hortense gasped. "You're kidding! Yuck!"

Palmer grinned. "No, really. You place them in an aquarium and give them fresh water and lettuce or bran for a week or so to purge the gunk from their system. Boil them, then stuff 'em back into the shell with garlic and butter and parsley and broil." She smacked her lips. "Yum." She wondered if Carson would consent to make them for her. *If I ever see him again.*

Hortense held a hand over her lips. Hardy looked queasy.

Palmer laughed. "That's just me, I guess. I have—shall we say—an *open-minded* palate. I've been known to rate flora and fauna according to their gastronomic potential." She smiled reminiscently. "On my first date with my future husband, we went to a zoo. We were feeding the waterfowl, and I said, '*Mmm.* I'm in the mood for Peking duck.' "

"If the date was with me, I would have had second

thoughts." Hardy softened the statement with a smile.

"Oh, once Peter got over his initial, some might say knee-jerk, objection"—she didn't look at Hardy—"he decided to be enchanted. We were married a month later." For once, the memory didn't revive the grief. *Is the cloud lifting?*

"Well, I, for one, agree wholeheartedly with Palmer," said Gareth. "There's nothing more ambrosial than a morsel of escargot, glistening with butter and redolent of garlic. That is, unless it's sopping up the juices with a tranche of baguette." He rubbed his stomach.

They strolled the boardwalk that encircled the marsh, then backtracked, skirting the hill to return to their cars. Hortense and Gareth produced water bottles, and the group went over their harvest of sightings. "The shrike was a life bird for me." Hortense beamed.

"I wish I'd gotten a better look at that wading bird. I'm sure it was an American bittern." The bittern—shy, solitary, a master of concealment—was the prize that had so far eluded Palmer.

Gareth held up a muddy plastic bag filled with snails. "As for me, I'm going to experiment with Palmer's system." He grinned at her.

Hardy cringed. "Better you than me."

Hortense nodded vigorously in agreement.

Palmer wasn't sure if it was the right time to bring up the club picnic, but before she could say anything, Hortense said cautiously, "Let us know if you'd like to reschedule the picnic, Hardy." When his smile froze, she said hastily, "Never mind! We'll discuss it at our next meeting, shall we? See you next week!" She and Gareth got in her minivan and took off.

Hardy opened the car door for Palmer. "Shall we take a different route home?"

She was amenable. They drove north on the highway, exiting at the Fifty-Third Street interchange. In between the cattle ranches and fruit farms sprouted brand-new, high-end developments.

Hardy griped, "They say some two thousand people a day are moving to Florida. Pretty soon there won't be a blade of grass between here and Tampa."

They passed a high gate. Hardy slowed. "That's the IMG Academy—it's a sports and school complex. Raven was enrolled for next year. She played soccer. Striker. Her coach said she had a real future." His hands gripped the steering wheel.

Palmer couldn't think of anything to say except, "I'm so sorry, Hardy."

He shook himself. "Say, how about a spot of lunch? We're early enough to nab a seat at Tide Tables. It's on the way home."

Tide Tables! Where Tipsy Swallow was last seen alive. *It might be worthwhile to have a look around.* "Okay."

They went around the circle to Seventy-Fifth Street, passing through broad tomato fields on either side, and took a left on Cortez Road. Traffic was light through Cortez village. Just before the bridge, Hardy turned into a parking lot before a funky, beach-style shanty.

Palmer slid onto a picnic bench outside, while Hardy went in to order. She gazed across the water at Anna Maria Island. A long pier struck out into the bay, with porch swings under an open-sided shelter at the end. To her left, she could just make out the tip of

Leffis Key. She tried to calculate how long it would take for a jon boat to get there from Tide Tables. *Was it choppy the day we found him? No, it was very calm.* Not too long then. *Wait. He died five days earlier. Huh, then maybe—*

"Fried mullet for you, chips, and a PBR coming up!" Hardy sat on the bench across from her.

"Mullet. You know, when I first arrived, a fisherman told me that it wasn't palatable, but that's not true." She remembered with fondness Carson's delectable smoked fish, and her lips twitched into a smile.

"I wouldn't know."

"Oh, that's right—you're a vegetarian. What are you going to have?"

"I ordered a bowl of gazpacho. That'll do me."

She gazed at the boats tied up at the dock, and her thoughts turned again to Carson. Had he made it to Nashville? Was he really fleeing Joanna...or the law? *Has he been lying to me all this time? Did he in fact kill Tipsy?* One of the waiters had seen the man who met Swallow but couldn't identify him because a hat hid his face. Was Carson wearing a hat when they met over the corpse? She couldn't remember. And what about Thrasher's mystery witness?

The waiter brought out a fish fillet and potato chips in a plastic basket and a bowl of gazpacho. He set them down along with two cans. "Your beers."

"Thanks." She scrutinized the waiter, wondering if she should ask him what he'd told the police. Out of the corner of her eye, she glimpsed Hardy's glum face. *Nah.* She waved a hand over the water. "The Intracoastal Waterway is an amazing piece of engineering, isn't it?"

Hardy, his mouth filled with soup, could only nod.

As a sailboat idled in front of them, waiting for the drawbridge to open, a little outboard cruised past the yacht and pulled into the marina next to the restaurant. A man dressed in slacks and a button-down shirt and wearing a Panama hat jumped over the gunwale onto the dock and tied the boat to a cleat. Palmer examined him. Stocky build. Shiny black hair. He turned for a moment to face the bridge and pushed the wide brim of the hat up on his forehead. She recognized the sallow complexion and thin moustache of Vogel's chauffeur. *Didn't Vogel give him a plane ticket at the Tampa airport? I wonder when he came back?*

Hardy rose. "I've got to get back to my office. Do you mind if I drop you?"

She shouldered her purse. "Not at all. Say, I don't think you ever told me what you do for a living."

"I'm a lawyer. And no lawyer jokes, please. I worked for a trial firm in Tampa for a few years before coming down to Bradenton to hang out my shingle. My office is right next to the county courthouse, so I draw quite a lot of business."

"Criminal law?"

"Not anymore. Now I stick to less sensational stuff. I do whatever comes my way—wills, trusts, small claim mediation."

"Ah. Do you like being on your own?"

"Well enough. I'll never be rich, but I can go birding whenever I'm so inclined." He grinned.

He left her in her parking lot, turned around, and headed back toward Bradenton.

Palmer trudged up her steps. Lounging against the

door was her old pal Detective Thrasher.

"Why, if it isn't the fuzz." She was too tired to be nervous. "What do you want?"

"I want to know where Carson Hawk is. And I think you have the answer."

Chapter Twenty

Run, run, run as fast as you can.
You'll never catch me, I'm the gingerbread man.

The Palapa Inn, Wednesday, May 31

Palmer flopped on the sofa. "I have no idea where Carson is, Detective." *And it's the honest truth...for once.* "Why would you believe he'd keep me in the loop?"

The question seemed to baffle Thrasher. "He's your boyfriend, isn't he?"

"Carson Hawk? Not on your life. I shared a couple of dinners and a dead body with him. That's all."

He seemed stuck on the one topic. "So he hasn't contacted you? He's been off the grid since yesterday." He seemed to think this made a difference.

Word it carefully. "I told you yesterday. The last time I saw him was the night before he took his daughter back to Chicago."

"I have information that he went to the Washington metro area after he left Chicago. The police have an APB out on him for theft."

"Oh?" *Single word answers, Palmer. Don't give anything away.*

"Yes. A woman named Joanna Wren—the widow of the senator who committed suicide—says he broke into her house and stole a briefcase."

Broke in? The bitch. She stood up. "Look, I've already had a long day, and I'd like to rest." *Well, actually, it was a long night, but let's not quibble.* "Can I see you out?"

Thrasher's lips pressed tightly together. "All right, but I expect you to notify me if he calls you." His eyelids fluttered. "I...uh...don't necessarily have to work with the Maryland cops, you know." She almost expected him to add, "Wink, wink. Nudge, nudge." "There's enough on my plate right here on Longboat Key."

Even though she understood he was offering a deal, she felt a "thank you" might spoil the secret, so she settled for a discreet "Uh-huh."

When he was gone, she went to the bedroom, lay down, pulled a pillow over her head, and was out along with the light.

****

The Palapa Inn, Wednesday night
Ringgg.

Why do I even bother to try to sleep? She felt around on the night table for the telephone and picked up the receiver. "Hello?"

"Palmer?"

"Yes, Carson."

"I'm...um...in Nashville."

"I know, Carson."

"But not for long. Did...did anyone call about me?"

"Oh, yes. The NFL called to say you're the number-one draft pick. And Publishers Clearing House came to your house, but since no one was there, the million-dollar prize went to your neighbor."

"Anyone else? Joanna?"

"Yes, she called too. Said the police want to charge you with Senator Wren's murder but seems to think she can talk them out of it. She believes Vogel is trying to frame you." *Don't forget this time—hit him with the juicy bit.* "Did I mention she and Vogel had an affair?"

"Affair? Sure, everybody in Washington knew about it. Even Atticus. But why would Wilfred try to frame me? Unless he did it."

Palmer was beginning to tire of the game. *It's like Peyton Place, only the people aren't as pretty.* "Frankly, I don't care." When he didn't respond, she ventured, "And Captain Thrasher dropped by for a chat."

"A chat? What about?"

"The fact that the Maryland police are looking for you and so is he."

"That's not good. If they catch me, will you at least visit me in the Big House?"

"Every other Tuesday. Now was there something you wanted?"

"Um, yes. I was expecting a package when I was forced to decamp."

"A package?"

"A small one. It should be delivered today or tomorrow. Can you go by my house and pick it up?"

"I suppose. You want me to forward it? If so, where?"

"I'll let you know. Best bet is Chicago." He hung up.

Without so much as a kiss my foot or have an apple. She sighed, took the phone off the hook, and went back to bed.

****

Carson's house, Thursday, early morning

Carson's house looked even more derelict than the last time she'd been there. A box marked Amazon lay on the mat. She picked it up and opened the front door, to be met with suspicious scurrying sounds. *Rats?* At least there weren't any alligators on Longboat Key. Something about them not liking to cross salt water. Small comfort when she knew the island was still infested with snakes and poisonous treefrogs and fire ants. As far as she was concerned, Florida was like Australia: teeming with dangerous creatures. She took a step over the threshold and something skittered away. A brown anole. Harmless. A spider web had already been spun across one window. As she watched, the spider deftly wrapped a fly into a silky bundle of filaments.

Palmer carried the box to the kitchen. *Should I open it? What if it's the briefcase? If Thrasher interrogates me, I'd have to tell him I'd seen it.* She put it down.

Dirty dishes were piled in the sink. She found some dish soap and cleaned up the mess. *While I'm at it, I'll sweep the floor. Looks like the lizards have been here awhile.*

An hour later, she put the vacuum back in the closet and dropped into an easy chair. The living room and kitchen were clean. *I'll take five, then tackle the grill.*

She was rooting around in the garage for a grill brush when she heard scratching. *Please don't let it be a snake.* Would a raccoon be preferable? She was reaching for the light switch when a hand folded over hers and squeezed.

She screamed.

"*Shh.* Quiet! It's me."

"Carson!"

He turned on a penlight. "I don't want anyone to know I'm here."

"I thought you were in Nashville…or on the way to Chicago."

"Yes, that's what I wanted them to hear."

"Them?"

"I think your phone is bugged."

"Balderdash. How can they bug a cell phone? And besides, I've had it with me the whole time."

"You forget: I called the land line. I heard a distinct click before you picked up."

"Oh." She gathered her wits. "Did you take the bus here?"

"No. I suspected they were watching the terminals, so I flew the Cessna back."

"From Nashville?"

"From Gaithersburg. I left it at the Montgomery County general aviation airport. It was the closest to Joanna's home." He grimaced. "I never actually went to Nashville."

"I see. So the plane's back at that airport. Hidden something."

"Uh-huh. Hidden River."

"What are you planning to do now?" She looked around the garage. "Your supply of transportation is rapidly diminishing. I don't see the Harley. The plane's gone. The pickup's not working. How about the Bugatti?"

"I haven't put the new plates on yet."

"I see. The station wagon?"

"It's being serviced in Bradenton."

"Raven's bike?"

"Really?"

"I guess you could use the kayak."

"Not where I'm going."

"You'll be reduced to the go-kart pretty soon. It doesn't have a great range. Where *are* you going anyway?"

"I haven't decided. That's why I came to get the camper. They may be watching airports and railway stations, but I doubt they're looking for a vintage 1954 Airstream Cruiser."

"An Airstream!" She visualized Carson's outbuildings. "I don't think I noticed a shiny silver mothership. Where is it?"

"It was parked in a mobile home community until I brought it here last night."

She decided to skip over the next twelve questions. "How are you going to haul it?"

"Lenny. I installed the new distributor cap, so we're good to go."

"Lenny? The truck?"

"Yeah." He went to the garage side door and looked out. "I have to get some stuff together."

The Amazon box. "Were you waiting for the package?"

He blinked. "Package?"

"The package on your doorstep. The one you asked me to fetch."

"Oh, that." He wouldn't look at her. "It was the only way I could think of to get you here."

"Why did you want me here?"

"To kiss you goodbye. Is it inside?"

"The package? It's on the kitchen table."

He zipped through the back door of the house. She was about to confront him when he brayed, "You'd better skedaddle."

There was nothing Palmer wished to do more than skedaddle. *I just want to look for birds. Please let me wave a lighthearted goodbye and get on with my life.* "I'm coming with you."

"No, you're not."

"Yes, I am." Before he could respond, she said firmly, "I promised Nestor I'd look after you."

"Oh, really?" His tone was dry. "And when was that?"

"When I was explaining about the death threats. Face it, Carson, you can't do this on your own. Everybody's after you. Besides..." She gestured at the clean dishes stacked next to the sink. "You need a minesweeper." She did a double take. "Oh my God—the place was clean when you lit out for the airport, wasn't it? Have you been here the whole time?"

"Certainly not. I was at Joanna's...until yesterday." He regarded the dishes with chagrin. "I had to leave everything when I heard you come in. Fudgie would kill me if she knew I didn't clean up after myself."

"Fudgie?"

"Our old cook. She was a tyrant in the kitchen."

That explains his abnormal cleanliness habit.

Carson flicked his hands at her. "So, shoo. You can't come with me. What about your birding tour?"

"Oh that. I planned to head west..." She stopped. "That's it. They'll be searching for you in Chicago. But Arizona..."

"Arizona?" He looked mildly alarmed. "Why Arizona?"

She ignored him. "Did you know there is only one species of hummingbird in the entire eastern United States? The ruby-throated. But in one small area of southeast Arizona up to eighteen species have been spotted."

"Well, bust my buttons!"

"A camper's just the ticket. We head out tonight. I have a great guide to state and county parks." She pushed him aside and walked toward the front door. "You hook up the camper. I'm going home to pack."

"What about Thrasher? What if he shows up here?"

"He won't. I'm going to call him."

"And rat on me?"

"Absolutely. You've treated me shabbily. You sent me a text—a cold, unfeeling text—that you'd taken up with a floozy who lives in...let's see. Chicago?"

"How about Nova Scotia? Send him in the totally opposite direction."

"Ah, but how did you meet said floozy?"

"Okay. Nashville? Lots of floozies there."

"All right. And it has the advantage of being partly true."

He gave her a big smack on the lips. "No, it doesn't. Besides, I only have eyes for you."

"Yes, well. I'll be back when it's dark."

****

Carson's house, Thursday night

Palmer wasn't sure if Captain Thrasher believed her tale of woe, but he couldn't very well accuse her of lying. She told him she was leaving town for a few weeks to continue her bird tour and nurse her broken heart.

"Where next?"

"*Hmm*. I think maybe New Orleans."

"And will you be coming back to Longboat Key?"

"Oh yes, but…er…I haven't decided when." She warbled, "I'm sure you will have solved all your mysteries by then."

"I appreciate your optimism." His gloomy tone belied the words.

She packed a couple of bags, left a note for the cleaning lady, and drove to Carson's.

The Airstream cruiser was hidden behind his neighbor's garage. It gleamed in the glow of a floodlight. Carson opened the door and let down the folding steps. Palmer climbed into the main compartment and paused, awestruck. "It sure doesn't look vintage inside." She brushed a hand across the granite countertop. "This is pretty snazzy."

"That's because the guys who bought it at auction retrofitted it with all new appliances and furniture. It's 1954 on the outside, and 2020 on the inside."

Palmer didn't want to admit how relieved she was. She'd expected to have to pee on the side of the road and sleep standing up.

In the dark of a moonless night, a red Ford 150 truck towing a silver, bullet-shaped trailer with a Harley motorcycle tied to its rear bumper passed quietly out of the Village, crossed Longboat Pass, and headed north.

About three hours later they were driving through a lightly populated part of northwest Florida when they heard a bang. The truck limped to a halt. "Great. Flat tire."

Chapter Twenty-One

Way down upon the Suwannee River,
Far, far away,
There's where my heart is turning ever,
There's where the old folks stay.

White Springs, Thursday, June 1

"Where are we?"

"Let me check the map." Palmer clicked the roof light on and consulted her phone. "Oops. Looks like we missed the exit to Route 10."

"We were supposed to take it to New Orleans?"

"Yes. We're only about a mile past it."

"Well, we're hardly in a condition to backtrack now. What's the closest town? One big enough to have a service station."

"There's nothing showing on the map." She looked out the window. Only two or three lights twinkled in the inky darkness. "Wait a minute. Up there. Isn't that a sign advertising a Motel Five? It doesn't look too far. Let's see if they have a room."

"Okay. I'll put the spare tire on, and we'll head there."

"Why don't we take the bike?"

"We can't leave the camper on the highway."

Once back on the road, they used the neon light to

guide them to the motel. They rousted up the clerk and soon found themselves in a grey-carpeted, grey-walled room with a small double bed and a big TV. Palmer felt the mattress. "This is nice." She tittered. "At least it doesn't jiggle like yours."

Carson's response was to make it jiggle.

A panting Palmer came up for air half an hour later. "I spoke too soon."

Carson slipped on his jeans and shirt and held up a bucket. "I'm going to fill this with ice and scout out a snack machine."

"Isn't there any food in the Airstream?"

"I didn't have time to stock it." A few minutes later Carson returned with ice and candy bars. "It's all they had."

She plucked one of the bars from his hand and munched on it while he filled two plastic glasses the size of medicine cups with bourbon. He held his up. "To the open road."

"May it not rise to meet us." She drained the cup and picked up her toiletry bag. "I'm going to freshen up." She sidled into the minuscule bathroom. Once the door was shut, Palmer stared at her face in the cloudy mirror. It hadn't crossed her mind when she insisted on accompanying Carson in his flight that there would be extracurricular activities involved. She'd been consumed by the need to protect him and hadn't really thought it through. She winked at the mirror. *The extracurricular part's not the real problem, though, is it?*

She sighed. It was the whole escaping-the-police bit she was unsure of. To be on the lam with a fugitive from the law was a new experience for her. And these things rarely ended well. *Am I prepared for this? Is he just using me?* No—he hadn't wanted her to come at all. The tune to "Me and Bobby McGee" ran through her head. The only words she could remember were "took us all the way to New Orleans." *If we* do *get to New Orleans, will he leave me there and disappear? Will I want him to?*

Carson knocked softly on the door. "You about finished? I need to pee."

"I'm going to take a shower. Come in when you hear the water running." She chuckled at her own shyness. *It's not like he didn't just see me in my birthday suit.*

She almost laughed to find him in bed with the covers up to his chin when she came out of the bathroom. If she hadn't been so tired, she would have torn the blanket off and had her way with him. *Maybe tomorrow.*

****

White Springs, Friday morning

Palmer woke to the soft cooing of a mourning dove. She carefully untangled herself from Carson's limbs and went to the window. Their camper sat next to a spindly tree on which the dove perched. The rest of the view consisted of an empty parking lot. The roar of traffic on Route 10 almost drowned out the bird.

Carson's arms slid around her waist and squeezed. "Shall we sally forth to find some breakfast? I'm betting Motel Five has discontinued its once lavish buffet."

"I'll get dressed." She turned around and kissed him. "I'm famished."

The desk clerk directed them into town. "Parky's is

on the main drag. It does a good fry-up. Try the biscuits and gravy. Taylor's Garage is right across from them. He'll fix you up with a new tire."

It would have been hard to miss the only two establishments in the village that weren't boarded up. "Looks like White Springs has seen better days," observed Carson.

They consumed a breakfast that would keep their stomachs occupied for at least four hours and crossed the road to the service station.

Freddie Taylor, proprietor of Taylor's Garage, advised them that he'd have to order the tire from Live Oak. "Come back around noon, and I'll put it on for you."

The thought of checking back into the motel did not appeal. Carson turned to Freddie. "Any sights within walking distance around here?"

"Ha. Used ta be. Used ta be White Springs was *the* place to go for the waters."

"Waters?"

"Yup. Out by the Stephen Foster center there's these sulfur springs. Bathing in 'em's supposed to be good fer yer joints. They built a spa back a hunnerd, hunnerd fifty years ago. The old bath house is still there." He pinched his nose. "Stinks to high heaven, but city folks—well, they'll pay for anythin' so long as it's billed as a wonder cure."

"Worth a visit. Can you give us directions?"

"Too far to walk."

Palmer looked at Carson. "Let's take the Harley."

Freddie perked up. "That there hog's an awesome machine. I noticed its tires are low, though. Want me to check it out while it's here?"

He looked so hopeful that Carson relented. "Sure, but how do we get to the springs, then?"

"Take my truck. She could use the exercise." He led them to an antique blue pickup, polished to a high shine. He patted the door proudly. "This here's a 1955 Chevy 3100. My grandfather bought it new. All original interior, but had to replace the transmission last year."

Carson ran a hand over the hood. "Man, you've kept it in fantastic shape. It would be an honor to drive it."

Freddie waved them off. As they turned onto the main road, Palmer looked in the rearview mirror. The man was already eyeing the Harley, an anticipatory grin plastered on his face.

A long asphalt drive led them to the Stephen Foster Folk Culture Center State Park. On one side, the dusky Suwanee River flowed, curtained in Spanish moss-draped live oaks. Gravel paths meandered among the small white buildings that dotted the broad green space. Dominating the center was an imposing antebellum mansion. "That must be the main attraction."

A little old lady wearing a tag that read Gladys ~ Volunteer sold them tickets for a self-guided tour of the interior. Stephen Foster's life was depicted in displays of miniature dollhouse figures and furniture. Palmer nudged Carson. "I haven't seen a diorama since the one I made of the gunfight at the OK corral in third grade."

Carson read the first plaque and broke into a belly laugh. "Guess what? Foster never actually lived here. He spent most of his life in upstate New York."

Palmer raised her arms to take in the vast room. "Then what's this all about?"

"Says here the design reflects how the Stephen

Foster fan club thought he would expect a southern plantation house to look."

"It's like something out of *Gone with the Wind*."

Carson continued to read. "There's more. Foster was stuck on a song he was writing and called a friend. He asked for the name of a southern river with two syllables." In a mock falsetto voice he sang, "Way down upon the *Swaaanee* River. "

"I'm guessing his friend had a drawl."

Once back outside, a sign directed them to a quiet river pool surrounded by tall cypress. Palmer admired the somnolent black depths. "At least the Suwanee River is real."

A few feet away a jam of flotsam blocked the channel, churning up eddies and small whirlpools. Carson twirled a stick in one and suddenly jumped back from the bank. "That's not a log—it's an alligator!"

Palmer bit off the snicker. "Don't panic. I have it on good authority that alligators only feed at night."

He checked his watch. "Yeah…well…what say we head back to Taylor's garage?"

****

On the road, Friday afternoon

They picked up the newly shod F-150 and hitched it up to the Airstream. Carson paid fifty dollars for the tire and ten dollars to gas up Freddie's pickup. The mechanic gave the Harley a final swish of his rag. "Real beauty you got there. I changed her oil and pumped up the tires."

Carson reciprocated with effusive compliments about the Chevy truck, and the two men parted as old friends.

Palmer joined Carson in the cab of the truck. "Back

to Route 10?"

"Uh-huh." He revved the engine and accelerated up the ramp going west. "New Orleans is about halfway to Arizona. We should be able to make it by tonight."

Palmer felt a stab of worry. "Oh dear. I told Captain Thrasher I was going to New Orleans. I hope he doesn't put a tail on us."

"He doesn't know I'm with you, does he?"

"No. He thinks you dropped me for someone in Nashville and I'm drowning my sorrows in road dust."

"Good." Carson pulled into the middle lane. "What about the Airstream? Does he think you own it? If he knows it's mine…"

"The subject didn't come up."

"That's okay, then. We won't stay in New Orleans long anyway."

They had been driving a while when Palmer asked, "Did you bring the briefcase with you?"

Carson jerked. "Why do you ask?"

"Just wondered. Is that a yes?"

"No. When I took it from Joanna's guest room, I stashed it where no one would suspect."

"Did you look inside it?"

"I shouldn't have, but curiosity got the better of me and I took a quick peek."

"Was there anything in there worth dying for?"

He blew his cheeks out. "I really can't say. I only skimmed the contents. Besides the files on S. 219, there were a couple of receipts for large amounts of money made out to Wren and some to Vogel. Wren's were taken on his campaign account. That might or might not be legal, depending on what he was using it for. The Vogel documents all looked like bank transfers."

"Did you make copies of them?"

"Copies? No. First off, I didn't have time. And second…well, truth be told, I didn't think of it. Damn."

He passed a flatbed truck filled with chickens in cages. Palmer gagged. "Pee-you."

"Why couldn't it be a truckful of sparrows? Wild bird poop doesn't smell as bad." Carson opened the window vents. "Love these. You can get some air without having rain and"—he swerved to avoid flying excrement—"other substances flung in your face."

When the stench had dissipated, Palmer asked, "What were the bank transfers?"

"They involved several institutions—some US-based, like Republic and the Bank of the States, plus a bank in China and one in Singapore. Not unusual on its face. Vogel *is* a global investor."

"That's right—he has offices in Switzerland, doesn't he? Could they be for land purchases?"

"As far as I know, the foreign banks don't invest in property—just cryptocurrency and telecommunications. Nothing in the papers indicated land sales."

"*Hmm.* Anything else in the briefcase?"

"Ah, that's where it gets more interesting. Evidently Atticus was initiating divorce proceedings against Joanna."

"Really?" Palmer thought back. "I don't think she knows it."

"It was only a preliminary form, but he'd signed it."

"Maybe that's why she wanted the briefcase."

"It hardly matters now."

Palmer rubbed her chin. "Still, she wouldn't want anyone to know it was even in the works, would she?"

Carson shrugged. "There was one more item that caught my eye. A coupon for ten free lessons at an archery range in Fairfax County. With two holes punched."

"Was it yours?" Before he could answer, Palmer's phone buzzed.

A squeaky voice came out loud and clear. "Palmer? Where's Daddy?"

Oh my God. "Nestor? Is that you?"

"Yes! He's not answering his phone. Where is he?"

Carson nudged Palmer and whispered, "I turned it off."

"Is anything wrong, sweetie?"

"The police were just here. They're looking for Daddy."

Chapter Twenty-Two

Eh là bas, eh là bas, eh là bas chérie
Comment ça va
Mon cher cousin, ma chère cousine
J'aime la cuisine,
Je mange beaucoup, je bois du vin
Et ça ne me coûte rien.

Route 10, Friday, June 2

Carson grabbed the phone from Palmer. "Nestor, honey? It's me, Daddy. What did the police say?"

Palmer pinched him. "Put it on speaker."

Nestor's voice was high-pitched, reminding Palmer that she was still a little girl. "Daddy? Where are you? I've been so worried—and so is Mama."

"I'm…I'm in Nashville. On business."

"But Daddy, what do they want with you? Is it about that girl who died in the garage?"

Carson sucked in a breath. "How do you know about her?"

"The detective mentioned it, and Palmer told me all about her. It's very sad. She was so young."

Palmer reflected that the parallels were lost on Nestor—probably because she was so young.

"Er, yes. I'm sure they just have a few questions. I…uh…thought they were finished with me and left on this business trip, but I guess they need more information. Nothing to worry about, Nessie. Look, I have to go. Will you tell your mother I'll take care of it?"

"Sure. Daddy? When are you coming back to Chicago?"

"I don't know. Don't worry, sweetheart. I'll be in touch." He handed the phone back.

They were entering the outskirts of New Orleans. Traffic was heavy. When Carson barely missed sideswiping a passing car, he said, "No way we can drive this thing through the city—is there a beltway we can use?"

Palmer searched on her phone. "Route 61 is a four-lane highway that curves south. Turn left here."

"Got it. How about a campground? We need to find a place to stop."

"There's a KOA campground on the west side. It's on the way." Even the highway was slow going, with many lights. Twilight was coming on when Palmer said, "Okay, turn right here." She pointed. "There it is."

Carson went into the office and registered. He returned and swung into the driver's seat. "We're lucky. I snagged the last site." He backed the camper in and connected all the lines. They settled in just as the sun went down.

Palmer sat on the fold-down steps and gazed at the lights of the city in the distance. "New Orleans is supposed to be such a magical place. Could we at least go into the French Quarter and walk around?"

Carson chuckled. "Haven't been there since I was in college. I wonder if it's changed?"

"Come on, please? Let's take an Uber in."

The driver dropped them at Jackson Square, and they made their way to Bourbon Street. Hordes of young people crowded the sidewalks, dancing and chittering, their drinks sloshing from large plastic cups. Carson shook his head. "I swear to God, it's exactly the same as it was twenty years ago—the air still smells like stale beer and the sidewalks are still sticky."

"Oh, but it has such a festive air!" Palmer was exhilarated. "Look—there's Preservation Hall!" The strains of Dixieland jazz issued from the venerable old concert venue out into the street. Next to it was a noisy bar. "Pat O'Brien's? That's where they invented the Hurricane! Come on!"

She drew a reluctant Carson inside. Over his objections she ordered the famous cocktail. As they sat sipping from the twelve-inch-high, hourglass-shaped glasses, Palmer watched the passing carnival. She started. "Huh, that's queer. I'm pretty sure that was Vogel's chauffeur. Did I mention I saw him at Tide Tables the other day? He must not be Vogel's employee." At that moment, the man she was looking at turned so she could see his face. "Never mind. That's not him."

She pivoted back to the bar, but a commotion at the entrance made her swing round again. A man shoved his way toward them. Palmer dropped her straw. "Oh my God, it's Hardy!"

Hardy made a beeline for them. "Palmer! I can't believe I found you."

Palmer looked around at the milling revelers. "I can't either. What are you doing here?"

Hardy must have caught sight of Carson, for he stopped, his mouth hanging open. "Is *he* with you?"

Oh shit. "I…uh…"

Carson interrupted and said glibly, "No, no. I'm here on business. I bumped into Palmer in Jackson Square. Small world, isn't it? Buy you a drink?"

Hardy didn't seem entirely satisfied with the explanation but accepted a small Pernod.

Palmer let him take a sip, then asked, "Why are you looking for me?"

"Captain Thrasher told me you were going to New Orleans. By the way, he has a new theory about Raven's death."

"Oh, really?" *Was Vogel right after all?*

"He said you, Hawk, have a daughter, and that she turned up right after Raven was…was killed."

"That's right. She only stayed a day. I took her back to her mother in Chicago."

"Yes, but she's about the same age, right?"

"She's fifteen. What are you getting at?"

"What does she look like? Hair? Build?"

Palmer answered. "She's about medium height and has dark blonde hair."

"Is it short? Long?"

Carson grunted. "Her mother insists she keep it in braids. Personally, I think she's too old for them."

Hardy put down his drink. "Raven was only thirteen, but tall for her age. And she was wearing braids the night she…she…"

The three were silent. Finally, Carson said roughly, "Are you suggesting—"

Hardy put his hand to his chest. "Not *me*. The detective."

"All right. *Thrasher* is suggesting that the murderer meant to kill my daughter and not yours?"

A frightening thought crossed Palmer's mind. *Is that the real reason the police were at Nestor's house?*

"Well, he had already been going on the presumption that the killer thought it was you in the garage."

"So did I." Carson rubbed his chin. "This sheds a whole new light on the situation. Perhaps I'd better warn Susan."

Raven... Nestor... "Hardy, your news concerns Carson, not me. You didn't know Carson and I...er... I mean, how did you know Carson was in New Orleans as well?"

"I didn't." Hardy finished his drink. "Actually, I'm here to take a deposition. Thrasher mentioned you were heading to New Orleans. I took a chance I'd run across you here in the French Quarter. Now that I've found you, may I squire you to dinner? I have a reservation at Galatoire's."

"I...uh."

Carson beckoned the bartender. "That's a great idea. I have a conference call in fifteen minutes, so I'll take my leave." He brandished an invisible hat. "It was a pleasure sharing a taste of *le bon temps* with you." He lowered his brows at Palmer. "If you need to get in touch, I'm staying at the Hotel Monteleone. It's just down the street on Royal."

She took the hint. "Oh, really? What a coincidence! I'm staying there too. That must be why we ran into each other." She tossed Hardy a vivacious smile.

Hardy glared at Carson. "We'll be off then. Thanks for the drink, Hawk."

Galatoire's was a tribute to turn-of-the-century New Orleans, with waiters in crisp white shirts and black pants spiraling between the tables almost as though they were on skates. The mirrored walls and old-fashioned tile floor gave the illusion of great space.

Palmer chose the paté maison with bacon. Hardy, after hemming and hawing and some twisting of lips, opted for the avocado and crab salad—"But could you hold the crab? Thanks."

"Oh, right, you're a vegetarian. I forgot." Giving in to an uncharitable urge to provoke him, Palmer ordered redfish—"Caught this morning by our own fishing crew." It came with crawfish and lemon beurre blanc. She was tempted to request a side of steak.

Hardy asked for the wine list. In perfect French he said, *"Une bouteille d'Au Pied du Mont Chauve Puligny-Montrachet Premier Cru La Garenne, 2018, s'il vous plaît."* Both the waiter and Palmer were impressed. He explained with exaggerated modesty, "I spent my summers from the age of sixteen at my aunt's in Dordogne. She had a small vineyard and taught me about wine."

They rounded out the meal with coffee and black bottom pecan pie with whiskey caramel sauce. Hardy asked for a scoop of vanilla ice cream on the side.

At least he doesn't turn his nose up at sweets. Or wine.

Hardy made no mention of Raven or Nestor or Carson throughout the meal, which was a relief. They talked birds. "What's your itinerary?"

"I'm heading to Arizona for the hummingbirds."

"Oh yes. That southeastern region is an amazing place. The desert is so different from Florida." He seemed wistful.

Palmer cocked her head. "Where are you from

originally, Hardy?"

"Me? Nevada. Boulder City. I hated it growing up—the average temperature in the summer is over a hundred degrees, and the drought is year-round. Our garden consisted of tumbleweeds. My mother used to laugh and say they were the only plants that flourished and she might as well invent some recipes for them."

"So Florida must be a refreshing change."

He shook his head. "Nevada's a dry heat. When it's ninety percent humidity at six o'clock in the morning in Florida, I miss those parched lips and hair that crackles with static electricity." He put down his fork and laid a palm on her hand. "I just had a thought. How about if I come with you to Arizona?" He flushed. "Would you like that?"

Oh my God, no! Quick, Palmer. "Um, don't you have a law practice to attend to?"

"Like I told you, I'm on my own. I can make my own hours." He smirked. "And days."

"What about the deposition?"

"Deposition? What deposition?"

"The one you came to New Orleans for?"

"Oh, that one." He seemed slightly flustered. "I…uh…took it this morning. No, I'm free…as a bird." He grinned.

Palmer thought desperately. *How do I put him off? This is nuts!* She put her napkin on the table. "Um, I'm awfully tired. Thanks so much for dinner. I'll just catch a taxi back to the…hotel."

"Nonsense. I'll walk you back."

Ack! Luckily she remembered seeing the grandiose entrance to the hotel on their way to Jackson Square. "All right. It's this way."

As they walked, Palmer considered her options. *I could desert him in the lobby, but if I'm not at the hotel tomorrow he'll deduce I fibbed—or worse, that I'm with Carson.* When they reached the door, Palmer turned to Hardy. "Thanks so much for the escort and the lovely meal."

"Shall I meet you for breakfast tomorrow?"

"Tomorrow? Oh, darn. I forgot entirely. I'm meeting an old friend from Virginia. She's moved down to Louisiana and is feeling homesick. I promised to spend the day with her. I may end up staying at her house." *Brilliant!*

"I see. Then day after tomorrow? When are you heading to Arizona?"

"I'm…um…on the waiting list for a tour. I don't know what my schedule will be."

"But—"

"So, bye-bye! Maybe I'll see you back in Florida!" She waved gaily and lurched through the revolving door. To forestall his tagging along, she went straight to the ladies' room in the lobby.

She was still cowering in the stall when she heard tapping. She didn't respond. A familiar voice whispered, "I can offer slightly more luxurious accommodations, unless you prefer to perform your toilette in the toilet."

She swung the door open. Carson stood on the threshold of the ladies' room. She looked around warily. "Is he gone?"

"Hardy? Yes. He loitered around the front for a few minutes but then stomped off. I do believe he's frustrated."

She washed her hands and dried them. "Carson?

He wants to go to Arizona with me."

"Well, that's not acceptable. If you let him, he'll definitely get the wrong idea."

"Ya think? I told him I didn't know when I was leaving." She pushed past him into the lobby. The room was empty except for a bored bellhop flicking at his phone.

Carson steered Palmer toward the hotel entrance. "I've been thinking. That song and dance about a deposition was at best an excuse and at worst, a lie. He's here because of you."

Palmer thought the same thing but wasn't about to agree. It would only fan the flames. *Next he'll be accusing Hardy of Wren's murder just to get rid of his rival.*

Once on the street, he took her arm. "He's going to come back here tomorrow, you know."

"Oh, I took care of that." *I hope.*

****

KOA campground, Friday night

Palmer found Carson sitting at the picnic table when she came back from the camp showers. A lantern cast a warm yellow glow on his face. A face that wore a frown. "What's the matter?"

"I've been mulling over Hardy's news. Could it be true that Nestor was the real quarry? If so, why?"

She dithered over whether to say it out loud. "She was travelling alone. She may have caught the attention of a…of a…"

"A sex trafficker? Possible. And he was trying to abduct her?"

"Maybe. He might have shadowed her from the airport to Longboat Key. He hides in the bushes waiting for her to show herself, sees a young girl with braids arrive on a bicycle. She goes into your garage. He assumes it's the one he's been trailing, and sneaks in behind her."

Carson pursed his lips. "But if he wanted to sell her, why kill her? By mistake?"

"I have no idea."

"No, wait. The medical examiner said she died from the crossbow shot. That couldn't have been accidental." He went inside the RV and returned with a bottle. Without asking, he poured bourbon into two dixie cups. "The sex-trafficker thing doesn't jibe."

"Why not?"

"Because of the timing. Raven was killed early Thursday morning. My daughter didn't arrive until Saturday."

"Huh. True. So Raven *must* have been the target." She had a frightening thought. "Unless, that is, Nestor arrived earlier than Saturday. It was a long weekend, after all."

"She couldn't have. I spent Friday night at my house. I'd have noticed if she were there."

Palmer thought back to when Nestor borrowed her shift. That was Sunday. She'd noticed a big pile of dirty laundry beside the girl's suitcase. "Nestor didn't exactly tell us when she arrived in Florida. She might have stayed elsewhere for a night or two before coming to your house."

"Why would she do that?" He drained his cup and immediately refilled it.

"You could ask her."

"Ah. Okay. So how do you propose I contact her without alerting the authorities?"

"Use my phone." She pulled it from her pocket.

"All right." He took it and dialed. "Susan? It's me... That's not important. I have a question. When did Nestor actually leave home? Was it Saturday?... Really? What did she do before she got to my house?... I see. Okay. What? No, it's probably nothing. Thanks. I'll call you later." He clicked off. "She got to Tampa in the wee hours on Thursday and crashed at Jake's house. Then, when she saw all the police activity in the morning, she decided to lie low until she could figure out what was going on."

"She may have feared they were looking for her." Palmer tapped a lip. "I wonder why she didn't announce her arrival when it quieted down?"

Carson flushed. "Were we...you and I...uh..."

Palmer flushed too. "Yes, we were. She must have been too embarrassed to intrude. What did you do Friday?"

"Remember? We spent some quality time with Captain Thrasher. Then, after the pig lunch, I popped up to the Anna Maria public library to do some research. I had a meal at Mar Vista and went home about eight." His brow furrowed. "I was exhausted after all the excitement and went straight to bed. Then I was up early Saturday and left the house by nine."

"So Nestor was left to her own devices until we returned on Saturday. What did she do with her rental car between Thursday and Saturday?"

"She put it in Jake's garage. After I left for the funeral on Saturday morning, she parked it in the driveway. She...uh...wanted to surprise me." He gazed at Palmer, his eyes fearful. "So she could have been the intended victim after all."

Chapter Twenty-Three

Doctor Foster went to Gloucester
In a shower of rain.
He stepped in a puddle
Right up to his middle
And never went there again.

KOA campground, New Orleans, Friday, June 2

Palmer sat down at the camp table next to Carson. "Nestor's perfectly safe now that she's home with her mother and Uncle Toby. She was only vulnerable when she was alone."

"Still, they should take precautions." He put his hands on his knees and stood up. "We're going to Chicago."

Palmer had been looking forward to the birding excursion and felt let down, but a look at Carson's face told her there was no use arguing. "Okay."

"We'll get an early start in the morning."

****

New Orleans, Saturday morning

"Okay, the app says it'll take us thirteen hours to get to Chicago. Best route is I-55 to just south of Cape Girardeau, Missouri, where we pick up I-57 north to Chicago." She perused the map. "Where do Susan and Nestor live? A suburb?"

"No, they live in Andersonville—it's a Swedish American enclave in north Chicago."

"I didn't know there were Swedes in Chicago."

"Oh, yes—some fifteen thousand. They were the immigrants who decided city life was preferable to farming the plains of Iowa and Nebraska." He followed the signs to the interstate, threading his way through the bustling rush hour traffic. "It's a congenial little community. There's a museum that chronicles the history of Scandinavians in America, plus shops where you can buy Swedish horses and Swedish coffee bread." He smacked his lips. "Yum."

"How did you end up there?"

"Susan's great-grandmother emigrated from Sweden. After the Great Chicago Fire of 1871, Swedes moved north, settling in the neighborhood around Clark Street. When we married, Susan insisted we move from Hyde Park on the south side to a safer area."

Palmer felt a nebulous little pang and sought to pinpoint its origin. Jealousy? *Nah.* "Well, we'd better get going."

"Batten down the hatches, boys." Carson pressed the accelerator, and the truck lumbered up the ramp to the highway, the camper tootling along behind like a Lionel caboose. When they'd reached its cruising speed of sixty miles per hour, he relaxed. "I have a feeling it'll be more like twenty-four hours with this baby in tow."

"I'll check for campgrounds."

Eight hours later, they pulled into a spot in Happy Camper Land on the outskirts of Monkey's Eyebrow, Kentucky, and hooked the Airstream up to the water and power lines. The campground was adjacent to the

Ballard Wildlife Management Area and overlooked a pleasant little oxbow lake.

Carson unfolded the map and laid it on the picnic table. "We made good time. We're about halfway there."

Palmer pointed at the red circle Carson had drawn around their position. "So what's the story behind the name?"

"Monkey's Eyebrow? Notice how this bulbous part of Kentucky pokes its nose between Tennessee and Illinois? The guy in the office said people think it resembles a monkey face."

She examined the map. "I don't see it."

"Perhaps I can find a better explanation." Carson keyed in the name on his phone. "*Hmm.* Says here no one really knows, although one version has it that a monkey escaped from a riverboat." He pointed west. "The Ohio River's just beyond that clump of trees." He scrolled down. "I like this one. A farmer got his wagon stuck in the mud, and when he went for help, they asked him how high up on the wheels the mud came. He answered, "As high as a monkey's eyebrow.""

Palmer checked the contents of the mini refrigerator, then dropped onto the bench next to Carson. "Zero to none chance Monkey's Eyebrow has a restaurant. We'll have to make do with the leftovers from lunch."

Carson put his arm around her and squeezed. "I bet never in your wildest dreams did you expect to be lounging in a palace like this, popping cold chicken nuggets into your mouth and sucking whiskey through a straw, eh?"

"Oh, no. One look at you and I knew I was going

somewhere."

He dropped his arm. "When I figure out what that means, I'll come up with a zinger of a retort. Actually, I have a treat for you."

"What?"

"I happen to know how to turn chicken nuggets into a gourmet delight."

"Have at it. I'll walk over to the park while you perform your magic."

"Git along wit' ya."

A narrow boardwalk wended its way alongside the lake. Palmer pulled out her bird guide. "Oh gosh, Monkey's Eyebrow is right on the Central Flyway. What luck!" She wandered down the path peering into the brush. "That's a wood duck hiding under the bank." A familiar woo-hoo made her raise her binoculars. "A barred owl! Oh, and what's that dabbler?" She was scrabbling through the book when her phone dinged. Without thinking, she answered it.

"Palmer? This is Hardy. Where are you?"

Quick. "I, uh, got the call for the tour out of the blue and they wanted me to get to Phoenix by tomorrow, so I had to rush off. Sorry!"

"Oh. Huh." She couldn't tell from his tone whether he was angry or disappointed. When he spoke again, he sounded upbeat. "Well, I wrapped up my business in New Orleans. Why don't I toddle over to Phoenix? There's a regional flight from here to Sky Harbor airport. Where will you be staying?"

Damn damn damn. I can't tell him I'm not going because he'll suspect I'm with Carson, and then Thrasher will pick up our trail... "Hardy? I'd really rather you didn't."

There was a pause. "I see."

"Hardy, I'm sorry. I'm still not quite ready to date after Peter's death. I like you. It's just—"

"Say no more. I understand." He chuckled. "But if you see me standing on the corner in Winslow, Arizona, don't be upset."

"Ha-ha. Thanks for understanding, Hardy."

When Palmer arrived back at the camp, she found Carson holding a newspaper. "Picked it up at the office. It's a couple of weeks old." He opened it to an inside page. "You might be interested in this."

She was about to tell him of her conversation with Hardy when she saw what his finger pointed at. Under *Farm Sales* was this item:

Estate of Hoyt Family to W. Vogel: 100 acres, Chesterfield, MO, $800,000.

Underneath it was another:

John Jones to W. Vogel: 250 acres, Wildwood, MO, $1,000,000.

She looked at Carson. " 'W. Vogel' is *our* Vogel?"

"Yes."

"But what are you implying? Where are these parcels?"

"Both are in the suburbs of St. Louis." He typed in some words on his phone. "Aha. He's also bought land outside Indianapolis and Chicago."

She was lost. "And this is significant how?"

"It could mean affordable housing is in fact his purpose, but I have a gut feeling it's connected to Wren's bill."

"S. 219? It only prohibited foreign investors from buying up US property. Vogel is an American citizen."

"It would also restrict international conglomerates.

Up to now Vogel Enterprises handled the deals." He pointed at the paper. "He's found a way around S. 219 by acting in an individual capacity."

She considered this. "Joanna believes Vogel lied to Wren, that he's actually planning to take land out of production and to return it to a state of nature." She looked up at Carson. "What if Senator Wren discovered the plot? Could that be why he was killed?"

Carson clicked his phone off. "I don't see it. Vogel has every right to buy whatever land he can afford, and do whatever he wants with it—as a private citizen. The bill wouldn't apply to him." He got up and went over to the grill. "Can't do anything about it now. I'll check into it when we get to Chicago."

Oops. Hardy. "Oh, by the way, Hardy called. He wanted to meet me in Arizona."

Carson whirled around, a lethal-looking barbecue fork in his hand. Palmer flinched. For a second he puffed, his exhalations mingling with the steam rising from the grill. "*Did you say Hardy?*"

His displeasure only made her cross. "Yes, I did. What's wrong with that? The last thing I told him was I was headed to Arizona—*alone*—to hunt for hummingbirds. You can forgive him if he believed I wouldn't make it up."

Carson took a deep breath and turned back to the grill. His voice muffled, he said, "What did you tell him?"

"Well, I certainly wasn't going to tell him the truth." She paused as the irony of her words struck her. "I mean, he can't know we're going to Chicago together. So I merely said it was too soon to date after Peter." *Ulp. Is that double irony? Or double jeopardy?*

Mercifully, Carson didn't respond. After a minute, she said meekly, "You were going to whip something up for supper?"

"Yes, indeed. It'll just take a sec to plate the food." He went inside the camper and a minute later brought out a tray. He handed her a paper plate topped with small chicken pieces in a yellow sauce drizzled with red ribbons.

"What is it?"

"Chicken nuggets reimagined—in a tangy mango sriracha sauce." He set down a plastic bowl. "I paired it with cucumbers marinated in vinegar and sugar, topped with a sprinkle of wild mint I found near the office." With a flourish, he pulled two bottles of beer from his pockets. "From the Hawk cellars, our finest lager."

She held up her fork. "You, sir, have your moments."

****

Route I-57, Illinois, Sunday morning

Carson woke Palmer at dawn. "Let's get a few hours driving in before we stop for breakfast."

They had reached the outer suburbs of Chicago when Carson slowed. "There's a Denny's at this exit." As he changed lanes, they heard a bang and the truck started to wobble. He steered it into the turnoff lane and stopped. "Damn it, another flat tire!"

"Did Mr. Taylor give you back your spare?"

"I forgot to ask for it." He got out and started to unhook the motorcycle. "You stay here; I'll go for help."

At that moment, a siren started up. An Illinois State Police sedan passed them and pulled over in front. The trooper—unexpectedly short and chubby—sauntered back to them. "You folks need a tow?"

"No, thank you, sir—I'm off to find a spare." Carson put a hand on the bike's seat.

The trooper looked the two over, then walked slowly around the camper. "You from Florida?"

"Yes, sir. On a road trip with my bride." Carson draped an arm over Palmer's shoulder.

"Uh-huh. I'll call the garage for you. Sit tight." He went back to his squad car.

"Now what?"

Carson watched the back of the policeman's head. "I don't like this. I swear he recognized me. Or maybe Thrasher sent out a notice on the license plate. Wait here." He climbed into the camper. A minute later he came out stuffing something into a backpack. He edged back to the Harley, keeping an eye on the officer.

She whispered, "Are you going to make a run for it?"

"Yeah. If I don't cruise, I'll lose."

"What about me?"

"He's got nothing on you. Just stay mum. Keep safe. I'll be back for you." He swung onto the bike and roared off.

The trooper jumped out of his car. "Hey!" He ran up to Palmer. "Where the hell is he going?"

She hoped she sounded more casual than she felt. "He...Bill...said he knows where a tire store is. He wanted to save you the trouble. Bill. We'll...we'll be all right, Officer."

"Did he tell you his name was Bill?"

"Uh, yes."

"Well, his real name is Carson Hawk." The policeman scrutinized her face. "But I'm guessing you knew that."

"Me? Um…" She was at a loss.

The policeman stood very still. Slowly he tapped his radio. "Suspect has absconded. He's heading down I57 on a Harley-Davidson motorcycle." He listened to the tinny voice. "Okay, then. I'll bring in his female companion."

Palmer gulped. "What…what do you mean, 'bring in'?"

He clapped handcuffs on her. "I am arresting you for aiding and abetting the flight of a wanted man. You have the right to remain silent. Any…"

The rest of the words melted together in an unholy mess. *Arrested!* She let the trooper put her in the back seat of the cruiser and watched the landscape whizz by. They reached the station a few minutes later. A large plaque by the front door said Kankakee Sheriff's Office. She was taken to a desk, where another officer took her particulars. Through the haze, she remembered to ask about the Airstream. "It's stuck on the highway."

The policeman was unconcerned. "Right."

"Is someone going to change the tire on the truck?"

He looked at her, amusement vying with annoyance. "Nah. It's not like it needs to go anywhere." At her gasp, he said, "They've both been towed to the impoundment lot. Now, Miss Lind, you have one phone call."

"Huh? Call? Who should I call?"

He said gently, "It's customary to call a lawyer. Would you like me to get a name for you?"

A lawyer? "No. I have one. I know one. May I use my phone?" He handed it to her. She looked up the number in her contacts and dialed. "Hi, Hardy. It's me. Palmer."

Chapter Twenty-Four

Oh, where have you been, Billy Boy, Billy Boy,
Oh, where have you been, charming Billy?
I have been to seek a wife, she's the joy of my life,
She's a young thing and cannot leave her mother.

Kankakee, IL, Sheriff's office, Sunday, June 4

"Palmer! Where are you! Are you in trouble?"

"Actually, a bit, yes, Hardy. I would have called sooner, but they took away my cell phone."

"Then how were you able to call me?"

This is not going well. "The sergeant gave it back to me."

There was a pause. "Sergeant?"

She took a stab at perky. "Sergeant Scoter! He's guiding me through the process."

"Process?"

"I'm...er...being booked. He said I could call my lawyer. That's you." She hoped she sounded so confident he couldn't contradict her.

Hardy's voice was not reassuring. "I repeat: where are you?"

"I'm in Kankakee. It's about fifty miles south of Chicago."

"Chicago? Last I checked, that isn't on the way to Arizona."

"No, it isn't." *Bite the bullet.* "I wasn't exactly honest before. Well, I was, but my plans changed. Car—Mr. Hawk called Saturday morning. He had reflected on what you said about Nestor and Raven looking alike and decided Nestor was in danger. He…uh…asked me to accompany him to Illinois."

He whistled. "So Thrasher was right. Nestor was the real target of the killer? Not my Raven?"

"I've no idea. We don't know who's committing these crimes." Palmer caught Sergeant Scoter watching her. "But it's not Mr. Hawk."

"Then why are you under arrest?"

She wailed, "I don't *know*. Captain Thrasher only wanted to ask Carson some questions, but these cops are calling him a fugitive. They won't tell me from what."

Hardy said soothingly, "He may be a person of interest, that's all. He just needs to turn himself in. I'm sure it will all work out."

"But he can't turn himself in now. He has to get to Chicago. His daughter may be in mortal danger."

His voice turned slightly huffy. "But why does he need *you* along?"

She thought fast. "Her mother is out of town. He—Carson—believed the presence of a woman would help."

"What about your car?"

"Car?"

"Did you leave it in New Orleans?"

Ulp. "Um…no. I…uh…took the bus. I…uh…don't like to drive alone." *Will he buy it?*

Hardy seemed to accept her excuse, for he said, "*Hmm.* Well, I'm sorry, I can't represent you. I'm not a member of the Illinois bar." Palmer tried to stifle the sob, but he must have heard it, for he said hurriedly, "Look, I have some contacts in the legal establishment in Chicago. I'll get in touch with them and see what I can do. Hang in there. I'll call you back as soon as I have something."

"Oh, Hardy." Suddenly Palmer felt very alone and scared. "I…I don't think you can call me back. I…"

"How about if I come up? At least I can lend moral support—and bail you out if necessary."

"Oh, yes. Could you?"

"Let me talk to the sergeant."

Sergeant Scoter took the phone. He gave Hardy directions and hung up. He turned to Palmer. "Mr. Bantam says he'll be on the next plane. Closest airport is Greater Kankakee. I'll let you know when he arrives. Now, permit me to show you to your quarters." He grinned.

He took her to a building labeled Jerome Combs Detention Center, signed her in, and led her to a cell. She flopped on the cot. *Damn Carson! I can't believe he just left me here. What a coward.* He should have known they'd arrest her. He should have stayed to take the heat. So what if he had to get to Nestor? *What about me?*

Her anger and grief ran in an endless loop through her brain until finally she fell into an exhausted sleep.

****

Kankakee jail, Monday morning

"Palmer?"

She opened her eyes and for a minute wondered why the sunlight was broken up into vertical stripes.

"Palmer? Are you awake?"

She struggled up, blinked, and looked around. *Oh my God, this is a jail cell! I'm in jail!* It all came back to her. *Carson!*

"Palmer!"

The voice finally penetrated. Standing on the other side of the cell door was Hardy. Palmer opened her mouth, but no sound came out. Her throat was dry as a bone. She stumbled to a small sink attached to the cell wall and cupped her hands under the trickle of water. *At least it's cool.* She slurped up enough to moisten her lips, then tried again. "Hardy?"

"Good, you're okay." Hardy indicated a police officer with a ring of keys. "Sergeant Redpoll's going to release you." He smiled at her.

She stretched and shuffled to the door. Hardy took her hand and led her down the hall. "Do you want to…er…?"

"What? Oh. Yes." She went through the door marked Ladies and made the mistake of looking at herself in the mirror. "Ulp!" Her hair was a wild mess. Her mascara had smeared one cheek, and there was a gob of mango stuck in her teeth from her last meal. *Mango? Oh dear, that was thirty-six hours ago!* She stuck her head out the door. "Can you get me my purse, Hardy? I think they confiscated it."

He handed it in to her. She did the best she could, then trudged out. "Did you post bail for me?"

"Sure did. And I reserved a hotel room for you. Once you're checked in, we'll get the ball rolling."

She heaved a great sigh. "Thank you, Hardy. Hardy? Have they heard from Carson?"

He gave her a little shove. "We can talk about that later. Let's go." He led her to a waiting taxi. "Hilton

Garden Inn, please." When he dropped her off at the lobby, he handed her a paper bag. "I thought you might need some necessities." He grinned.

She opened it. Inside she found a comb, toothbrush and paste, and a pack of underwear. "Oh, bless you! You are so sweet."

"I'll come back and take you to lunch."

She remembered the fairly empty countryside they'd been passing through before the disaster. "Where are you staying?"

"I have a room here, but I have to return to the airport to pay for the jet I chartered. Turns out the closest airfield is for general aviation only. Oh, and I've drummed up a lawyer for you. His name's Roger Merlin, but he can't see you until tomorrow."

"That's okay." She felt herself nodding off. "Right now, I just need some rest."

Palmer took a long shower, then fell on the bed. The hotel phone woke her. "Hello! It's your friendly neighborhood alarm clock. Are you decent?"

"Give me a minute." She shook out her dress. It had been fresh Sunday morning and thankfully wasn't too rank.

"You must be hungry. The deputy said you were sleeping when he brought your dinner."

The last thing she remembered eating was the gob of mango. "Hungry doesn't cover the half of it."

"Oh dear." He clicked his teeth. "There's an Indian place down the street. The concierge recommended their sambar. It's a lentil and tamarind stew."

Her stomach rumbled. *I need solid food.* "Hardy, would you mind awfully if we went somewhere that serves plain old American?"

He was quiet for a minute, then said gruffly, "Yeah, okay."

He didn't say a word in the cab. It dropped them off in front of an Italian place that looked like it had been there since the 1930s. Red leather banquettes lined the walls and the windows were covered with dark velvet drapes. The menu was handwritten and consisted almost entirely of pasta dishes. Hardy's lips were set in a tight line. "Give us a minute, would you, Romeo?"

The waiter raised a Latin eyebrow and said in a thick accent, "My name is Giuseppe."

"Oh. Sorry."

Giuseppe started to leave, but Palmer cleared her throat. "May I have a martini?"

He smiled at her. "With pleasure. Any special brand of gin?"

"Tanqueray if you have it."

He wrote it down. "And for you, signore?"

"Let's see. Why not? We're not going anywhere this afternoon. How about a…um…Manhattan?" He turned to Palmer. "I know wine, but I'm lost when it comes to mixed drinks."

Once she had the cocktail in hand, Palmer felt restored enough to start asking questions. "What happens next?"

"I gather the priority for the police is to get hold of Hawk, and therefore they may be using you as bait. I don't think they intend to charge you. That is, unless it's the only way to lure him back."

"But Carson wasn't running away—he had to get to Nestor. He hasn't done anything wrong, Hardy."

"Where is she?"

"She lives with Carson's ex-wife Susan in

Chicago. I don't have the address."

"Could we find it in the phone book?"

She tried to remember. "She's remarried. Nestor calls her stepfather Uncle Toby, but no one mentioned his surname."

"Well, then, why don't we leave it in the hands of the authorities? I'm no detective." Hardy tasted his drink. His nose scrunched. "Um…Giuseppe? Could you bring us a carafe of red wine?"

"Certainly, sir. Would you like to see a wine list?"

He shook his head. "Your best chianti would be fine." When the waiter had gone, he whispered, "I doubt they have much to offer."

Giuseppe returned with a carafe. Hardy waved him off. "I'll pour, thanks." He filled his glass. "Palmer? I have a confession too."

Great. "What is it?"

"I did track you to New Orleans—at the behest of Captain Thrasher."

"You're an informer?"

He grimaced. "That's not exactly how I'd put it. He knew we were seeing each other…socially"—he blinked twice—"and asked if I'd report any contact you had with Hawk to him."

"I don't understand. I told him Carson and I had broken up."

"Broken up? You *were* seeing each other?" Hardy wore the expression of one whose suspicions had been confirmed and who wasn't too pleased about it.

Might as well stick with the script. "No. I just made that up. To cover for Carson."

"I see." Hardy's expression went from dubious to exasperated to hopeful. "Well, Thrasher didn't believe you anyway. So"—he paused to sip his wine—"you aren't together?"

Palmer took a long drink, stalling for time. *What do I say? Does it matter? Will Hardy refuse to help me if he knows the truth?* Her mind suddenly cleared. "Nope." *I'm not lying—he's in Chicago.* She looked up at Hardy. "What are you going to tell Thrasher?"

He rubbed his chin. "I don't know. I guess it depends on what you do. I'm pretty sure they'll let me take you back to Florida, if..." He petered out.

"If I cut off communications with Carson? Or do you mean if I turn him in?"

"You've just told me you don't have his address, so you can't do the latter. Will you promise me you'll do the former?"

She regarded him. "You seem to have a lot of sway with the Longboat police."

"I've done some legal work for them in the past. Thrasher trusts me."

"I'll have to think it over."

Giuseppe brought spaghetti and meatballs for Palmer and dropped a plate of plain boiled broccoli in front of Hardy. He clipped his words. "As requested, no butter."

Hardy stuck a fork in a broccoli floret and held it up. "Well, bon appétit!"

They talked birds for the rest of the meal. Twilight was coming on when her sleepless night began to take its toll, and Palmer's eyelids drooped. "It's been a really long couple of days, Hardy. I'd like to go back to my room if you don't mind."

"No problem." He signaled for the check. "I'll call your room in the morning, and we'll go together to the lawyer."

Back at the hotel, Palmer sat on her balcony and gazed out over the fields. A grain thresher sat alone in the middle of a row of wheat. *I guess farmers keep strict hours—when the sun goes down, the work day's over no matter where you are.* She sighed. *I sure wish my whole* week *were over.* What to do about Carson? Would he be safer if she obeyed instructions and let him go? Did he need her at all? Hardy seemed to have a little more authority over the police than he admitted to. *Is he an undercover cop?* If so, could he protect her?

Too many questions. *I guess I'll brush my teeth.* As she ripped open the package Hardy had given her, her cell phone dinged. "Hello?"

A voice whispered, "Palmer? Do you happen to know why Susan's house is surrounded by a SWAT team?"

Chapter Twenty-Five

The wheels on the bus go round and round
Round and round, round and round
The wheels on the bus go round and round
All through the town.

Hilton Garden Inn, Kankakee, IL, Monday, June 5

"Carson! I'm not supposed to talk to you."

"You're not? Why not? Where are you?"

"I'm in Kankakee, at a hotel. The state trooper arrested me after you zoomed off. I spent the night in jail."

"Oh my God, that's ridiculous." He was quiet. "I suppose he did recognize me. Damn. I'm sorry."

Palmer griped, "Not much of an apology."

"What's that?"

"I said, why didn't you come back for me?"

"I didn't think I had to. I reckoned the trooper would change the tire and you'd be on my trail in an hour or so. I didn't want to risk reappearing before he let you go."

"When did you figure out I *wasn't* on your trail?"

She gave it all the sarcasm she had, but it didn't seem to register. He continued as though she hadn't spoken. "I waited at a rest stop until dark, then decided you must have missed me and hightailed it to

240

Andersonville. You knew where I was headed."

"Are you saying Andersonville consists of a single house—Susan's?"

This time the sarcasm hit its mark. "Oops, sorry. Well, I'm sure if Susan came across you wandering the neighborhood, she'd take you in. It didn't occur to me you'd let yourself be harpooned by the constabulary." He mumbled something.

"Excuse me?"

"I thought you'd be spared since I removed the...er...weapon."

"Weapon?" Palmer's voice rose. "You had a weapon in the camper? That's what you took out, isn't it? When you abandoned me."

"Uh...yes. I thought we might need some er...insurance for the trip."

"Oh, you did." She took the fire down to a slow boil. "What is it?"

"A crossbow."

Her heart flip-flopped. "You're kidding. A *crossbow*? Do you *want* to look as guilty as possible?"

"It's just a mini-bow. An Ace 80. Only weighs a pound, and it's plastic so it doesn't set off metal detectors."

"Yeah, okay. Now I feel *much* better." She thought of something. "That's what was in the Amazon package, wasn't it?"

He didn't answer for a minute, then said playfully, "Come to think of it, how come you're not still in jail? Did you break out?"

Ha. "No need to. Hardy came to my rescue."

"Oh, he did." The words felt chilly.

"Well, *someone* had to. He found a lawyer for me

in Chicago, arranged for my hotel, and took me to lunch. Carson, he's working with Thrasher. He...he asked me not to communicate with you anymore. He says it's the only way he can get them to drop the charges. He's offered to take me back to Florida."

"Tommyrot. He tried to accompany you to Arizona, didn't he? He wants you for himself."

Over his inarticulate grumbling, she said crisply, "This is hardly the moment to be territorial."

"Oh yes it is. Transparency is healthy. Hardy's only trying to scare you. They're not going to hold you. For one thing, exactly which crime have you aided and abetted? I'm only a person of interest. Which brings me full circle to my original question: why are the police staking out Susan's house?"

"I have no idea." She cast her mind back to the conversation at the restaurant. "Hardy said the police would find out where she lived. They must have succeeded."

"Blast. I'll have to think of another way to get in touch with her."

"Hey, here's a thought. Why don't you turn yourself in?"

"Why? Because I'm afraid they'll hold me while they investigate all these other allegations. If they don't hit me with Tipsy, they'll try Raven, or Senator Wren. Who will keep Nestor safe? This is all part of a plan—someone wants me off the streets."

"Count Joanna in that number. She has accused you of stealing the briefcase."

"She has? She's got some nerve, considering she tried to steal it from *me. Hmm.*"

"She told me if you return it, she'll rescind her

complaint."

"Is that so? She must want that briefcase desperately. I wonder why?" He was silent. "I'll bet that's what this is all about. She's at the center of all this. If they had anything on me, I would have been arrested by now for one of the other…er…incidents."

"I don't understand. How is she at the center? And what do you mean by 'all this'?"

He didn't answer. Instead he said ruminatively, "You know, this could work in my favor. I'll return the briefcase and prevail on her to pluck the gendarmes off my back."

"And just how are you going to get it to her? She's in Maryland, and you're in Chicago… Wait a minute. You said you'd stashed it somewhere no one would look for it. Where is it?"

"It's still at her house. I circled around after I ran out and hid it under her back porch. I figured it wouldn't occur to her that I wouldn't take it with me, but I'll have to convince her I don't know what's inside."

"You can't expect her to believe you haven't gone through the contents."

"I've got it. I'll pretend I stashed it in a locker in Nashville. That I never opened it."

"So how did it find its way back to Maryland? She'll see right through that."

"Okay… Aha. I'll tell her I didn't look inside because I already knew what it contained—materials on some other bill and nothing else. Something innocuous, like naming a post office." His eyes lit up. "Or maybe a Texas wilderness bill—that should thoroughly confuse her. I'll say Wren left it with me because he needed a floor statement."

"You won't mention the divorce papers?"

"Oops. Forgot about those. Maybe that's what she's after. Interesting." She could hear tapping through the phone. "I have to call the think-tank folks."

"The think tank? That judicial watchdog?" Palmer felt a tremor. "Who did you say they were?"

"Extended Earth Solutions. They've uncovered more evidence in Atticus's death. Their text said—and I quote—it was 'worrisome.' "

"EES! Carson, you need to know something about them—"

He interrupted her. "As for you, you go back to Florida."

"But—"

"No buts. You'll be safe there. I'm sure *Hardy*"—he said the name with a sneer—"will watch over you. Until I get there, that is, and then..." He left his intentions clear.

She gave up. "What about the Airstream? They impounded it."

"I'll be back to get it once I settle things with Joanna."

****

Hilton Garden Inn, Kankakee, Monday night

"And so, Hardy, I thought it over, and I think you're right. I'm washing my hands of Carson Hawk. And his daughter. It's his problem, not mine."

"Very sensible. I'll pick you up tomorrow at ten. I've hired a limo to take us to Midway Airport. There's a nonstop flight to Tampa at two."

"What about the lawyer?"

"I've already squared it with him and the police.

They were happy to remand you into my custody to return to Longboat Key."

Palmer slept fitfully that night. At dawn she sat on the bed, fully dressed, staring at the muted television. *So that's that.* She'd return with Hardy to Florida. Carson's plans didn't seem to include her anyway. *He told me to go back to Florida too.* In fact *everyone* was telling her to go back to Florida. *The question is why?* Carson was going to give Joanna the briefcase. Okay. If Joanna was true to her word, the SWAT team would back off and Carson would be able to see Susan and Nestor. He'd probably stay there. *And where does that leave me? Hanging out with Hardy forever?* She made a snap decision.

She picked up the phone. "Front desk? Can you get me a taxi? Yes, I'm checking out."

An hour later, she was standing in the police impoundment lot watching a mechanic replace the tire on the truck. She had called Hardy and told him her change in plans.

"The police released the camper?"

"Uh-huh."

"And after all this you're still going to Arizona?"

"Yes. There's no reason for me to return to Florida, at least not right away. Thrasher only wants Carson. This way I don't risk running into him. I might as well resume my birding tour."

"I see. I'll cancel your flight reservation and tell Thrasher of your decision. You will be coming back through Longboat Key though, right?" His tone stopped just short of entreaty.

"I surely will. I'll keep you posted. And Hardy, thank you for everything."

He was quiet for a minute. "I hope you know what you're doing."

She sighed. "I just want all this behind me. Please try to understand."

"I...guess I do. Keep in touch, will you?" He forced a chuckle. "I'll expect to hear the roster of hummingbird species you've identified."

"Will do."

The mechanic tossed his tools back into his bag. "All set to go, miss. That'll be thirty-five dollars."

Palmer spent a precious half hour trying to figure out the controls on the pickup but finally got back out on the highway and headed south. Four hours later, she was pumping gas at a rest stop when Carson called.

"I presume you're safe on Longboat Key by now."

"Er...no."

His voice rose. "Why not? You didn't stay in Illinois, did you? Are the police still holding you? Is Bantam with you? I won't have it!"

When he'd simmered down, she said quietly, "I'm on my way to Phoenix."

"I'm sorry—what did you say?"

"I decided to commandeer your camper and take it for a spin." She climbed back in the cab and started the engine. The radio blasted Willie Nelson singing "On the Road Again." She hummed along.

"I see. Well, I know you were on pins and needles, so I'll tell you the news. You do not need to rescue me after all. Joanna has her briefcase and has dropped the burglary accusation. I'm a free man. You may continue on your journey of discovery without concerning yourself with my welfare."

"So Joanna's not mad at you anymore?"

"It appears not. She was making noises about returning to Chicago when I hung up."

"What for?"

"It's her home. At least, the family manse is there."

"Did she buy your version of the contents?"

"Joanna isn't the brightest bulb. So yes, she did." He paused. "At least she seemed to. When I said the papers were on another bill and not 219, she gasped, and then went very quiet."

"Did you tell her about the divorce application?"

"No. I didn't see any reason to upset her just when she was easing up on me."

"Then how do you find out if that's why she wanted the briefcase?"

"It's pretty unlikely. Atticus had only signed a preliminary form. I don't think it counts until she signs it too. She would have said something if she was aware of it."

Palmer wondered fleetingly if Joanna would be surprised or not when she saw the form. *She did say the romance had gone out of their marriage.* Would she be relieved? Or sad? "What about you? Are you staying in Chicago?"

"Yes, for the nonce. Nestor's stalker could still be out there."

"Well, um, I guess I'll see you when I see you."

"You have to give me back my Airstream some time. Not to mention Lenny."

"Yes."

She was weighing where to stop for a midafternoon break when the news came on. A male voice trumpeted the headline. "Tragedy in Tampa. Well-known DC socialite dies in hotel. Stay tuned."

She took the last exit before St. Louis, found a diner, and parked in the space marked for tractor trailers. As she walked in, the waitress was changing the channel on the TV. Palmer ordered coffee and sat on a stool.

"The wife of a prominent US Senator was found dead this morning in a hotel near Tampa airport."

A photo appeared on the screen. *Oh my God, it's Joanna!*

"Police suspect foul play. Our reporter, Alphonso Alvarez, is on the spot. Alphonso?"

A pudgy young man with a thick Spanish accent yelled over the mob of reporters. "We haven't been able to get near the hotel, Leroy. The police have the entire block cordoned off. All we know so far is that the deceased is Joanna Wren, an elderly woman from Chevy Chase, Maryland."

"Elderly"? Ooh, she won't like that.

"She was alone. Wren is the widow of Senator Atticus Wren of Illinois, who committed suicide on April fourteenth. The police are just beginning their investigation, but they did disclose one detail. She was shot with…are you ready, Leroy? A crossbow."

Palmer dropped her coffee mug. The waitress came over. "You okay?"

"Uh, yeah. Just…staggered at the news. Did I hear the reporter right? She was shot with a crossbow?"

"Yeah." The woman grunted. "What the heck's a crossbow anyway? Sounds like some medieval torture instrument."

"It's a kind of mechanical bow—you know, for hunting." Palmer tried and failed to realign her jaw. "Do you have a road map? I need to find the quickest way to Tampa."

"You mixed up in this?"

"No! I mean, no, but I...er...am acquainted with the lady—Mrs. Wren. I...I just want to see if there's anything I can do to help."

The waitress handed her a folded map. Palmer opened it, tracing the route with her finger. "Looks like 64 East is the quickest route. Then I pick up 57 south again to Interstate 24. Damn, backtracking means it'll take me fourteen hours. I wish I could ditch the camper and fly."

The woman clucked. "Me and hubby have an old pop-up. Been to twenty states. Best way to travel." She reached up to switch channels. "It's gonna be wall-to-wall coverage for days. Nothin' but murder 24/7. Let's see what's happening on *Days of Our Lives*."

"They didn't precisely say it was murder, did they?"

"Doesn't matter. These media joes are all hype. They'll make up all kinds of stuff, and then when the facts come out, it's buried. Nothin' to see here, folks." She shook her head.

Palmer paid for the coffee and went outside. She plugged her route into the GPS. *I can get to Nashville by seven or eight if I push it*. On the other hand, what was she rushing for? Carson was in Chicago. He couldn't have anything to do with Joanna's death. *Could he?* They said she was killed by a crossbow. *Shit.* She put the truck in gear and headed south.

****

On the road, Tuesday

The waitress was right: the tragedy was hashed and rehashed on every radio station Palmer tuned into. At first, the police theorized she was dead by her own hand, grief-stricken at the loss of her husband. *With a crossbow? Come on!* One reporter dredged up interviews Joanna had given when the senator's body was discovered. She had played the distraught widow to the hilt. In one scene, she actually passed through the five stages of grief in the space of an hour. She had hand-wringing and tearful gulps down to an art.

Maybe, just maybe, Joanna wasn't as broken up as she pretended to be. Which ruled out her suicide, even absent the crossbow. *What about Wren's intent to divorce her?* According to Carson, she didn't know about it...but she might have suspected. And she would have found the application in the briefcase. Palmer wondered if the Wrens had had a prenuptial agreement. If Joanna wouldn't get anything in the event of a divorce, could she have killed her husband for money? *Then what about her own murder? In whose interest would that be?*

The top-of-the-hour news report came on. "Police now feel that Joanna Wren's death was due to a robbery gone bad. There have been several incidents in hotels near the airport in recent weeks. Also, it has been pointed out that it would have been virtually impossible for her to shoot herself with the crossbow."

Nothing gets past these pros.

"Mrs. Wren was a very wealthy woman but a bit eccentric. She liked to travel with her jewels and always refused to put them in the hotel safe. A search turned up a pearl-and-sapphire necklace in her bathroom, but the box that held the rest of her collection was empty. Both her purse and a briefcase she'd been seen carrying into the hotel were gone. Police have an all-points bulletin out for a man in a black coat seen in the vicinity."

Pearls and sapphires? *Sounds like Joanna didn't have to worry about money—at least not enough to kill for.*

Chapter Twenty-Six

Pat-a-cake, pat-a-cake, baker's man.
Bake me a cake as fast as you can;
Pat it and prick it and mark it with a B,
And put it in the oven for baby and me.

On the road, Tuesday, June 6

Palmer made it to Nashville by dinner time and was on the road at dawn the next day. She wished she had time to stop at the many preserves and parks she passed. *All those birds gone unseen and unchecked-off. Pity.* She wasn't sure why she felt such urgency. She hadn't heard from Carson—or Hardy for that matter. *No one knows where I am.* Her gut told her Carson was in trouble—*Well, isn't he always?* It was the crossbow. She knew Thrasher would immediately fix on Carson. *And if the police find him with yet* another *crossbow...* The question was, did Carson know about Joanna?

The radio blared, "No further news on the Wren tragedy, but the Hillsborough County sheriff's office has announced a press conference at twelve thirty."

If he doesn't know about Joanna by now, he's been hiding in a cave. A distinct possibility. She drove on.

****

Longboat Key, Wednesday evening

Palmer reached Anna Maria Island as the sun went

252

down. Beachgoers straggled across the parking lots lugging chairs and wet towels. Cars snaked along the two-lane road on their way home to the mainland, or to the beach for the sunset. She marveled at the crowds. *I guess all those New Yorkers and New Jerseyites moving to Florida to get away from the urban sprawl are creating their own right here.* Still, that vast Gulf out there, tangerine and coral sunbeams striping its surface, was indisputably alluring. She sighed.

She unlocked her door and turned on the light. The hall was empty. *Thank God, for once no unexpected visitors.* She walked to the living room. Also empty. A sudden swishing, followed by a squawk, jolted her. *What the—?*

The sliding door to the balcony was open an inch. A juvenile ibis—patchy brown and skittish—perched on the railing. As she watched, a white adult landed next to it and nudged it away. *Whew.* She swung around to the kitchen.

"Beer or wine?"

While Palmer was occupied with slowing her heart rate down, Carson uncorked a bottle. "It's been a long trip. A nice glass of pinot noir should help you unwind."

"Carson, I'm going to kill you."

"Well, add your name to my dance card. It's filling up rapidly."

She accepted the glass, drained it, and held it out for more. "Your Airstream is outside."

"Oh, it made it? No more flat tires? How was the mileage? I could only get maybe ten miles per gallon with that thing hooked up to Lenny."

"The point is, you can be sure Thrasher is watching

this house, and he'll recognize the camper."

"Oh, I don't know about that. One Airstream looks pretty much like another."

"But this one is in my lot."

"Touché. *Hmm*. Perhaps we should move it. Give me the keys. I'll do a food run, then stash it."

He loped down the stairs. Palmer toyed with the idea of locking the door after him, but if it hadn't deterred him before, it wouldn't now.

Forty minutes later, he set the keys and a grocery bag on the counter. "There. Thrasher will never find it in the police lot."

"With any luck, they won't notice when you take it out again either. Now, spill."

"Spill? You in the mood to clean something up?"

Palmer waited.

"Okay, Nestor and Susan are sequestered with Toby's parents on a lake in Minnesota. I heard about Joanna and came galumphing back."

"By the way, what was she doing in Tampa?"

"No clue. When I last talked to her, she was going to Chicago."

"So we have no idea what drew her to Tampa instead?"

"Not at present." Carson unpacked the bag. "I hope you like Mediterranean. Tonight we are featuring shish kebabs and Persian rice. Perhaps a little taramasalata to dip our pita into. Do you have any olives? A grill?"

"Yes and yes—there's a grill insert for the stove." Palmer eyed him. "Did you hear what Joanna was killed with?"

He was glum. "Yes. That's why I've been keeping my distance from the saintly Thrasher. Methinks he will hold me responsible."

"Speaking of, what did you do with the mini crossbow?"

For a minute, she thought he would duck the question, but he finally blurted, "Susan made me leave it behind."

"She kept it?"

"No, she's going to put it in the safe at my house. I didn't want to be spotted there, so she took it."

"Good."

He poured more wine. "Anyway, it's not as though I'm the only archer in the entire state of Florida."

"Granted, but you're the only one with ties to three crossbow deaths in the space of a few weeks."

"Not true. The killer also has ties to the deaths."

"Oh? And have you figured out who it is?"

"No, but it's got to have something to do with Senator Wren's briefcase."

"Why?"

"Atticus gave it to me for safekeeping—that means it's dangerous to someone. Joanna set the cops on me to get it back, so it's of value to her. When Joanna is found dead, some jewelry—but not all—is missing. The murder weapon—which unfortunately happens to be a crossbow—is left at the scene, *but*"—he finished dramatically—"the briefcase is gone."

"Remind me what was in it."

"Background papers on S. 219, bank documents about payment transfers, some with Vogel's name, some with Wren's. A ticket to an archery range. Divorce papers."

"We're still not sure if Joanna would have been upset to find out about the divorce."

"How does that get *her* killed?"

"She was in an adulterous relationship with Vogel."

"So? Like I said, everyone knew about that. Even Atticus knew. And may I remind you he died *before* she did."

"This is too complicated. Can't we forget the whole thing?"

"That would be my choice. But it's not my choice. In Thrasher's eyes, I'm suspect number one."

She stood. "The only thing for it is to find the killer or killers ourselves."

"Now?"

"No. *Now* you're going to whip up something to eat. I'm going to take a shower and put on some clean clothes."

He sniffed loudly. "Excellent idea."

Palmer "accidentally" stepped on his foot on her way to the bathroom.

****

The Palapa Inn, Thursday morning

"Are you still here?"

Carson rolled over and kissed Palmer. "You wouldn't let me go home, remember?"

"No, I don't." But she smiled to herself. It had been a very nice night.

He sat up. "I've been thinking."

"That's not very romantic."

"Well, it just happened. What can I say?" He rose and pulled his pants on. "The briefcase."

"What about it?"

"The bank statements. I think we should reexamine them."

"We don't have any copies though."

He said moodily, "No."

"And you gave the case to Joanna."

"Yes, and I wonder who has it now."

"Task number one."

He scratched the top of his head. "If she *did* go to Chicago before she flew to Tampa, it could be there."

"I am not—I repeat, not—driving back to Chicago. And besides, according to the news reports, she was seen with a briefcase in Tampa."

"That's right, but the police didn't find one in her hotel room."

Palmer threw off the covers. "Aha. The killer stole it."

"Well, it wasn't the maid."

"If Senator Wren was killed for it, maybe so was Joanna."

Carson emitted a low whistle. "And we're back to the briefcase being the lynch pin. I propose—"

"Not anytime soon, I hope. I hardly know you."

He kissed her nose. "Later, then. For now: breakfast. We'll think better on full stomachs."

"Speak for yourself." But she rose and went to her closet.

When Palmer arrived in the kitchen, Carson was putting the finishing touches on a platter of fruit and cheese. "I located a packet of prosciutto in your mostly empty refrigerator." He turned to the stove. "I believe properly sauteed prosciutto is even better than bacon."

"Blasphemy!"

"I'm incapable of blasphemy, at least when it comes to food." He put a tub of butter on the counter. "Found just one lonely egg, but"—he held up a hand at her cry of protest—"fortune shone upon us. Your cabinet is stocked with a few staples, so I was able to whip up a honey cake."

Palmer was aware she would have limited time to eat in peace and strung it out as long as she could. When Carson's knuckle-cracking began to interfere with her appetite, she asked, "So what's the plan?"

"The briefcase. We have to find it."

"I've been pondering our predicament. We should beard the lion in his den."

"Which lion would that be?"

"Thrasher. He's been after you for weeks. He even sent Hardy after me."

"Oh yeah? So—as I said all along—he wasn't in New Orleans to take a deposition?" He huffed happily, vindicated.

"Thrasher asked him to keep an eye on me in case I contacted you."

"A snitch." He was even more gratified.

"I think he'd prefer the term 'informant.' He claimed it was an excuse to be near me." She chuckled. "I'm inclined to believe him."

"Huh. Well, if it will keep the Bantam at bay, we might as well go straight to the big boss."

"Thrasher?"

"Thrasher."

****

Longboat Key police station, Thursday afternoon
"*Bonjour, mon capitaine.*"

Thrasher dropped his pencil. "Hawk!"

"The one and only. And may I present your hook." Carson stepped aside to reveal Palmer.

The detective didn't miss a beat. "So, my pretties, I

have you at last."

Palmer was game. "Are you going to clap us in irons? Chain us to the dungeon wall?"

"We don't do that anymore. Or at least we don't report it. Sit down."

They sat. No one said anything for a while. Finally Palmer ventured, "Are we waiting for something?"

The detective started. "Why, yes. I had sent out a bulletin asking to be notified if a certain briefcase was recovered. A briefcase which Joanna Wren—presently deceased—recently reported as stolen by Mr. Carson Hawk. The Tampa police called a couple of hours ago. They obtained an item of interest from a dumpster behind the hotel where her body was found. It's being couriered to me." He lapsed into silence again.

Carson said quietly, "You know I never stole it, right? Senator Wren gave it to me the night he died."

Thrasher opened his eyes wide. "I didn't until now." He made a note on his pad. "Did you check the contents?"

"Yes."

Palmer jumped up. "And there's evidence in it that will exonerate Carson!"

"Really?"

She looked at Carson, whose face was a mask. "He found a ticket for lessons at an archery club near Washington—with two holes punched. Someone else was learning how to use a crossbow."

This didn't stump the detective for long. "Was there a name on the ticket?"

"N…no."

"So how do we know it wasn't yours?" While Carson and Palmer were occupied with concocting an incontrovertible response, the sergeant tapped on the glass door. "Come in, Ollie. Is that it?"

"Just arrived." The officer held up a brown leather briefcase, somewhat the worse for wear. One of the buckles was missing, and from where she was sitting, Palmer could make out a smudge of what looked like banana. Ollie dropped it on Thrasher's desk. "Outside's been checked for prints, but we didn't open it."

The detective pulled on latex gloves and gingerly pulled up the flap. He shook the contents out onto the desk top. Setting aside a file marked S. 219, he rummaged through the receipts and forms. He held up a piece of paper torn from a spiral notebook. "What's this?"

They all looked. Carson remarked, "It appears to be a note in Chinese."

The detective gazed at Carson. "You know Chinese?"

"No, but don't they look like Chinese characters to you?"

"Yes. Or they could be Japanese. Or Korean. We'll have to find someone to translate it." He beetled his brows at Carson. "Did you know this note was in the briefcase?"

Carson shook his head. "I didn't notice it when I skimmed through the contents. I couldn't tell you if it was there or not."

Thrasher set the note aside and started flipping through the documents. "They all appear to be financial transactions."

"Yes, some for Wren, and some for Vogel."

"Wilfred Vogel? The hedge fund investor?"

"Yes. He and Senator Wren were close friends."

"*Hmph.* We may be looking at bribes or insider trading or something. You say Wren gave the case to you?"

"Yes. He had it with him when he came to my apartment the night he died. He asked me to hide it for him."

"Why would his wife be so anxious to get hold of it?"

"That's the question of the moment."

Palmer touched one of the papers. "She may have wanted to see the divorce application."

Thrasher sat forward. "To destroy it? Do we know what their prenuptial arrangements were?"

Carson shrugged. "I believe Joanna was wealthy in her own right. The question of divorce is moot now, anyway."

Palmer added, "It wouldn't explain why she wanted the briefcase even after his death."

"*Hmm.*" Thrasher continued to thumb through the papers. "How long was it in her possession?"

"I gave it to her last Monday. May I?" Carson picked up the empty briefcase and jiggled it. "It's pretty heavy. I wonder if it has a built-in charger."

The detective wrinkled his nose. "I doubt it. It looks like one of those high fashion-low efficiency bags—fine-tooled leather and not enough pockets."

Carson opened the flap and felt around the interior. "Huh, I feel something. I think there's a hidden section in the lining." He unzipped it. A piece of metal about fourteen inches long landed with a clang on the desk.

Thrasher picked it up and examined it. It was shiny aluminum with feathery plastic fletchings at one end.

"Correct me if I'm wrong, but isn't this a bolt for a crossbow?"

Chapter Twenty-Seven

Humpty Dumpty sat on a wall,
Humpty Dumpty had a great fall;
All the king's horses and all the king's men
Couldn't put Humpty together again.

Longboat Key police station, Thursday, June 8

Carson's answer to Thrasher's question was drowned out by a racket that erupted in the hallway. The door burst open. Wilfred Vogel—Sergeant Jaeger in hot pursuit—skidded to a stop in front of Thrasher. His eyes took in the papers and briefcase. He started to speak, then apparently noticed Palmer and Carson for the first time. "Whoa, you're not going to arrest Hawk, are you?"

Thrasher took a minute to allow the angry sparks in his eyes to die down. He said calmly, "What's it to you, sir?"

"I'm Wilfred Vogel."

Thrasher hid the shock well. "And?"

"I want to turn myself in. I killed Joanna Wren."

Dead silence reigned. Finally Thrasher managed, "Are you prepared to make a statement?"

"What do you mean? I just did. I killed Joanna Wren. What more do you want?"

"Perhaps you would like to contact your lawyer

before we go any further."

Vogel's eyes wavered for a mere instant. "He's on his way, but I already told him what I was going to do. We don't have to wait for him."

"Still, I think we should err on the side of caution." The detective indicated the one empty chair. He lifted his chin at the sergeant. "Officer Jaeger, please read Mr. Vogel his Miranda rights." After Vogel acknowledged the declaration with an exasperated scowl, Thrasher went on. "The officer will take down your statement now. First, please provide your full name for the record."

"Wilfred Percival Adonis Vogel."

Palmer started to laugh but, at a gesture from Carson, suppressed it.

Ollie's jaw dropped. He gulped a weak, "Could you spell that for me?"

When Vogel had done so, Thrasher steepled his fingers. "Okay. Why don't you start from the beginning."

With a glance at Carson, Vogel muttered, "I was in Tampa on business and ran into Joanna at the airport."

Carson said sharply, "She said she was going to Chicago. What was she doing in Tampa?"

When Vogel didn't respond, Thrasher said gruffly, "Please answer Mr. Hawk's question."

He pursed his lips. "She didn't say. We agreed to meet at her hotel for an early lunch. All was fine until something set her off." He paused.

"What was it?"

"I really couldn't tell you. Joanna... Well, she has—had—been behaving rather erratically recently—"

"After the death of her husband?"

"Actually, before that. She's never been entirely stable. She has this mania about returning everything to its wild state—prehuman, you might say. She won't prune her trees—stuff like that." He chortled, a harsh sound in the somber atmosphere. "That's how they lost the roof on their house in Illinois. Dead tree fell on it."

"Go on."

"Well, she'd been pressuring Atticus—Senator Wren—to designate lands in every state as wilderness. Even suburban areas."

Carson recited, " 'Wilderness: an area where the earth and its community of life are untrammeled by man, where man himself is a visitor who does not remain.' The Wilderness Act of 1964. I always considered it curious that the authors of the bill excluded humans from the 'community of life.' "

"Yes. In Joanna's mind, people only muddy up the world and should be removed from as much territory as feasible. She thought if you simply *claim* a plot of land is 'pristine,' ipso facto it is." Vogel shook his head.

"You said something set her off." Thrasher was growing impatient.

"Yes. See, one of my…affiliates has been acquiring property around the country."

Palmer caught Carson's eye. *Affiliates?*

"I…uh…plan to build affordable housing in undeveloped areas bordering thriving cities. As the urban areas expand, lower-income people are squeezed out of the housing market." He bent his head and inspected his fingernails. "My…purchases would ensure there was adequate living space for them. Joanna knew I was working with Atticus Wren on legislation that would affect the properties—"

Palmer nudged Carson, who put a finger to his lips.

"—and she had been pressing me to use my influence with him to make at least some of the land off-limits to builders. I opined that, if she—his own wife—couldn't win him over, how was I supposed to."

Thrasher nodded as though this made perfect sense.

Wilfred eyed the detective with some mistrust. "Anyway, after Atticus's death she became, if possible, even more aggressive. She buttonholed every member of the committee. No dice. She turned to me as her last resort. Get this"—he raised a sardonic eyebrow—"she expected me to shut off all access to perfectly good land in prime locations."

Carson said abruptly, "Is any of this land in Florida?"

Vogel's eyes closed to slits, then suddenly his face cleared. "Yes. There are some great deals around Tampa and Jacksonville."

"And are you also picking up parcels outside Chicago? St. Louis?"

Vogel gave him a speculative look. "Why do you ask?"

"Just wondering."

Thrasher cleared his throat. "You were saying, Vogel?"

He shifted on his seat. "She—Joanna—brought the subject up again while we were eating lunch. I tried to stay on neutral ground, but she grew increasingly irate as the meal went on. I thought I'd calmed her down and took her back to her hotel room. She called me half an hour later and apologized. Asked me to come back to the hotel." He pulled out a handkerchief and wiped his forehead. "When I got there, she attacked me."

"Attacked you? She hit you?"

"Not exactly. She picked up this contraption—looks like a bow but more lethal, and tried to poke me with it."

"It's a crossbow." Thrasher looked directly at Carson as he said it.

"Oh? Oh, yeah, I've heard of those. Anyway, I grabbed it from her, and when she tried to take it back, the arrow—it looks like a big nail—was released. Hit her smack in her stomach." He bowed his head.

"Why didn't you call 9-1-1?"

"I did!"

"But you didn't identify yourself."

Vogel squirmed. "I…uh…I'm an important man, Detective. It could have been interpreted—even though it was perfectly innocent—as…er…compromising. If word were to get out that I was in Joanna's hotel room…" His puppy dog expression fooled no one.

Palmer said gently, "Everyone knows about the affair, Mr. Vogel."

Vogel's face shut down. "Affair? I don't know what you're talking about, Miss Lind."

Carson snapped, "Oh come on, Wil."

Thrasher gave an irritated shrug. "Whatever hanky-panky you and Mrs. Wren were engaged in has no bearing on our case. You say you called 9-1-1, but you didn't stick around. Why not? If you were worried about publicity, you could have given a false name."

Vogel didn't answer for a minute, then hissed, "She wasn't dead."

Carson spluttered, "You thought having a fourteen-inch metal bolt stuck in her abdomen was *survivable*?"

"I had no idea!" Vogel hunched his shoulders

defensively. "To be precise, the nail or bullet or whatever it is didn't actually perforate her stomach. It hit her, yes, but then it slanted off to the side. I didn't look too closely… I mean"—he shut his eyes tightly—"it was pretty gruesome, but it did appear to be only a flesh wound." He straightened. "I felt I could leave it in the capable hands of the EMTs. I didn't want to be in the way." Vogel put a hand to his chest. "I swear she was still breathing when I left."

Carson pounced. "How did you know she died?"

"I heard the radio report. That's when I decided to come here and make a clean breast of it."

Thrasher grunted. "You say you hightailed it out of Tampa. Why did you come down to Longboat Key? And what made you come to me?"

"I had…business here. And when I heard that the police were focusing on Carson, I thought I'd better come forward." He gazed fixedly over Thrasher's shoulder.

The other three stared at him, dumbfounded. Finally Thrasher said, "You haven't cleared anything up, Mr. Vogel. Two bolts were released from the bow. One was found stuck in the fabric of her blazer. The bolt that killed Mrs. Wren went straight through her body and lodged in the wall behind her. If your account is true, someone else took the fatal shot." The detective switched his attention to Carson. He picked up the bolt from his desk. "This was in the briefcase. How do you suppose it got there, Hawk?"

Carson had no answer.

Palmer jumped in. "Carson told me there were only papers in the briefcase. If he was trying to hide the bolt, he wouldn't have checked the pocket in front of you."

"Are you saying Mrs. Wren put it there?"

"She was furious with Carson. She hid it inside the case to frame him."

"For what? The senator's death? He hanged himself. And anyway, how would she know about Carson's hobby?"

Carson found his voice. "Lots of people knew about it. It wasn't a secret. My question is: how and where did she get *herself* a crossbow?"

Thrasher smiled grimly. "From you."

Carson's jaw dropped. "The only crossbow I reported stolen was the antique. As far as I know, the two pieces of it are in your evidence locker."

"You said yourself you're a collector. Plus you're a competitor. I'll hazard a guess you use a modern crossbow in the events."

"Was the crossbow that killed Joanna a new model?"

"Yes." He picked up the bolt. "As is this."

"May I see it?"

Thrasher laughed delightedly. "Not on your life! It'll be bagged for evidence. You'll be given an opportunity to confirm or deny ownership at the trial."

Carson said angrily, "That's not fair. You're assuming it's mine without giving me a chance to examine it."

Palmer broke in. "Wait a minute. How could she put the bolt in the briefcase *after* she was killed with it?"

Thrasher had his answer ready. "It was a spare bolt."

"What do you mean, spare?"

"Hawk saw Mrs. Wren put the bolt in the briefcase,

realized she planned to incriminate him, and killed her."

"With the crossbow which he just happened to have with him?"

Carson said indignantly, "I am not prone to wander around hotels with a deadly weapon."

Palmer prayed desperately that Thrasher didn't know about the mini crossbow. *What did Carson say he did with it?*

Vogel's voice rose above the hubbub. "Um, the crossbow was there when I arrived. Carson couldn't have brought it after I left."

Thrasher shot back, "Maybe Hawk had been in the room earlier and left the crossbow behind. When he came back, he found Joanna wounded on the floor and decided to finish her off. Either way, he's guilty."

Palmer said, "Carson was in Chicago. He didn't get to Tampa until yesterday."

"That's what he told *you*. Do you have corroboration?"

Palmer shut her mouth. *Oh dear. I don't, do I?*

Carson huffed. "Why would I leave my crossbow behind? I'd have to know you'd immediately zero in on me."

"We haven't established title yet."

"What does that mean?"

The staring match was interrupted by a cough. Vogel raised his hand. "Excuse me? I'm the one confessing to homicide—or would it be manslaughter? At any rate, accidental death. I've been going over the scene in my mind, and I think Joanna may have been bleeding out. If he wanted her dead, Carson wouldn't have needed to do anything."

Thrasher swung on him. "You! Why are you

covering for Hawk?"

"Me? I hardly know the man." His face was impassive.

Palmer wondered if he sensed an escape route. *He's insinuating that Carson had a reason to kill her. Why?*

"So are you retracting your confession?"

"On the contrary. I freely admit I shot Joanna Wren by accident in self-defense. I understand you have a stand-your-ground law in Florida. I believe it applies here."

Thrasher considered this. Finally, he called his sergeant in. "Ollie, please book Mr. Vogel here on charges of involuntary manslaughter."

Ollie helped Vogel up and took him through the door. As he left, Wilfred said, "You're doing the right thing, Captain."

Thrasher said wryly, "Am I?"

Chapter Twenty-Eight

Rub-a-dub-dub, three men in a tub.
And who do you think they be?
The butcher,
The baker,
The candlestick-maker,
And all of them going to sea!

Longboat Key police station, Thursday, June 8

When Vogel had gone, Thrasher turned to the two remaining. "I suppose you expect me to let you go?"

"Well, under the circumstances, yes."

"When I figure all this out, I'm coming for you, Hawk. All four victims are linked to you. I just have to find the key."

Carson grinned. "Yes, Sheriff." He took Palmer's elbow. "You can find me hiding out with the Hole in the Wall gang."

Out on the sidewalk, Palmer hung back. "What now?"

"Dinner. I'm starved."

"Mar Vista?"

"Too crowded. Let's go to Dry Dock."

"Too crowded. How about that place with the chicken livers?" She smacked her lips.

"The Bridge Tender. Sounds good."

****

Bridge Tender Inn, Thursday evening

Provided with the requisite drinks, they watched the sailboats and cabin cruisers float by as the sky turned from blue to yellow to red. Carson cleared his throat. "Time to reconnoiter."

"Or rather, to recap."

"Yes. What *do* we know, and what *don't* we know?"

Palmer put her drink down. "We know that both Wrens are dead, as is Mr. Tipsy Swallow. Two were killed by crossbow; one hanged himself."

"We don't know that last for sure. And don't forget Raven."

"Oops. That makes three shot with a crossbow. However, let's leave her aside for now."

"Why?"

"Because she was a case of mistaken identity."

Carson was grim. "The killer mistook her for me. Or Nestor."

"Not Nestor." She held up a hand to forestall his objection. "It's just too much of a stretch. Nobody knew Nestor was in Florida, and nobody in Florida knew her. Ergo, the target had to be you."

"I guess so," he said grudgingly. "Susan thought as much, and Nestor scolded me for even hinting that she didn't have enough street smarts to know when someone was stalking her."

"And you're linked to the whole bunch, as Thrasher so graciously pointed out."

"Let's order." He waved at the waitress, who ambled over, wiping her hands on the scrap of apron that barely covered her cut-offs.

"Hi, guys! What'll it be?"

"Fred's livers for me, Ivy."

"Me too. And a salad to split, please."

When Ivy had gone, Carson put his hands, palms down, on the table. "All right, what else do we know? One, Vogel told us in Thrasher's office that he planned to set aside some of the land he was buying for affordable housing."

"Yeah, but you said yourself that Vogel tells different people different things. He promised Joanna he would close off the land to development."

"He claims he refused her pleas. That's why she blew a gasket."

"*Hmm.*" Palmer tapped her glass. "Was it the same land? I mean, did Joanna want to preserve the same plots that Vogel was purchasing?"

"That's a very good question. Not easy to ascertain, since we know Wilfred used a variety of entities to secure the properties—sometimes in his own name and sometimes with shell corporations."

"How about Joanna?"

"She is—was—such a bobblehead, I'd be surprised if she had any specific preferences. It's more likely she just wanted what Vogel had."

"Agreed." Palmer contemplated a grackle begging for crumbs at her feet. She tossed it a pinch of bread.

Carson gulped down his drink. "How about this? They were *all* in cahoots."

"You mean, Atticus, Joanna, and Wilfred? I don't see how. They each had a different goal."

"Yes, but if they all had designs on the same chunk of land…"

"That would make them competitors, not

conspirators." Palmer hoped that was the end of the discussion. She was hungry.

"Okay, but what about Tipsy?"

"Tipsy! I keep forgetting him." She gazed at Carson. "Is it possible his death had nothing to do with any of this? A drug deal gone bad—or gambling debts?"

Carson was skeptical. "Murder by crossbow is hardly a common occurrence. And don't forget, he was killed with the same bow that was used on Raven. No, there's got to be a connection. We'll just have to work it out through reverse engineering."

Palmer licked the salt off her margarita glass. "Crossbows... There were *two* crossbows used. One old and one new." She stopped short. "Tell me the modern one wasn't your mini bow?"

"I told you, Susan put it in my safe the day *before* Joanna was killed."

"So perhaps her murder constitutes a whole separate crime."

"That's a little far-fetched. Besides, since I haven't seen the second crossbow, I don't have any idea if it belongs to me or not."

"True, but as you say, three crossbow murders can't be a coincidence."

Carson accepted the plate from Ivy. "Can I get a beer, please?"

"Sure. Bottle or draft?"

"Whatever's on draft." The waitress crossed the road back to the bar.

"Vogel declared Joanna was unstable."

Carson shook his head. "I knew Joanna pretty well. She was flighty and slightly off-the-wall, but I don't think she was mentally ill."

"Why would Vogel insinuate that she was?"

"So he could use the stand-your-ground defense?"

"Because?"

"Because he actually did murder her."

****

The Palapa Inn, Friday morning

Despite the gloomy dinner conversation, Palmer and Carson managed to cheer up enough for a rousing session of lovemaking. For breakfast Carson whipped up *oeufs en cocotte*. They scooped out the warm, runny egg with pumpernickel toast points. Palmer pronounced it passable and had three helpings. "Where did you learn to cook anyway?"

"Mrs. Fudge."

She sipped her coffee. "You mentioned her before. Who was she?"

"Our cook. Mrs. Fudge was not your typical round lump of rosy-cheeked woman in a mob cap. Oh, no. She was in her twenties and had studied at the Culinary Institute of America. After a stint as head chef at a French restaurant on Michigan Avenue, she decided she preferred the low-stress environment of a single family." He chuckled. "Since there were five of us kids and my father was a diplomat, the social life was still pretty frenetic, but Fudgie never complained."

Palmer waded through the field of facts and latched onto one. "Diplomat? You're not American?"

"I am. I was born here, and my mother's American. My father was the Canadian consul general in Chicago."

"Impressive. So what were his duties?"

"He was responsible for looking after Canadian

interests in Illinois, Missouri, Wisconsin, parts of Indiana, and Kansas City. Needless to say, he was a busy man."

"Was?"

"Yes, he died five years ago. But"—he grinned— "Fudgie lives on, catering to his children and grandchildren. She taught me everything I know."

Palmer licked the last wash of egg off her spoon. "Which is a lot."

Carson's phone buzzed. "Wilfred? Where are you?" He mouthed to Palmer, "He's free on bond." He listened. "Oh, you do. All right, I'll meet you at that lunch place in Whitney Plaza. The newer one. You know it? Good. One o'clock? Okay." He hung up.

"What does he want?"

"He wants to talk about the briefcase."

"Huh."

"Huh indeed." Carson rose. "I've got to get back to my house. Can you give me a ride to the Airstream?"

"You expect the police to let you have it?"

"I know a back gate that's easily jimmied. That's how I got inside in the first place."

Palmer looked at him with new eyes. "Do you have any other felonious skills?"

"I prefer not to trot them out until they're required. More fun that way. Coming?"

"Yes, and I want to go with you when you meet Vogel."

"I expected no less."

Palmer left Carson fiddling with the combination lock on the gate and went home to take a dip in the pool.

****

Whitney's, Friday, 1:00 p.m.

A toot told her Carson had arrived. Today he was in the Bugatti. "Your chariot awaits, Mistress Lind."

She surveyed the low-slung, dark green sports car. "Is it okay to take it on the road?"

"Yup. Finally got around to attaching the new plates while I was waiting for you to come back."

"How did you know I was coming back?"

He chuckled. "I knew you wouldn't be able to resist once you heard about Joanna."

Am I an open book? "Why didn't you bring the RV?"

"I thought you might need a break from her. Is this not to your liking? You prefer more legroom?"

She slithered into the car and lay back on the soft leather seat. "This'll do for now."

Vogel wasn't there when they arrived. They ordered hamburgers and iced tea. Palmer was watching out the window when a limousine stopped outside. Vogel got out, and the car drove out of sight. Today he was nattily attired in a blue chambray suit and polka-dot bow tie.

Once inside the sleek dining room—fitted out in retro chrome stools and white tile walls—he peered around. His face lit up when he saw them. "Ah, there you are." He beamed at Palmer, although she detected a glimmer of uncertainty in his expression. "I didn't expect *you*, my dear. What a pleasant addition to our little tête-à-tête." He shook Carson's hand. "Thanks for coming. I'm sorry I'm late. I had to zip up to Tampa to pick up clean clothes. Orange does *not* suit me." He smiled but not with his eyes.

Carson said quietly, "So they let you go."

"I bailed myself out." He contrived to look cherubic. "I persuaded the judge that I wasn't a flight risk."

"And then proceeded to drive to Tampa."

He sat down abruptly. "You know, it never occurred to me that I shouldn't. I guess only men who've been ensnared in the judicial system are familiar with the protocol." He winked at Palmer.

"When's the arraignment?"

"No idea. My lawyer's taking care of everything." He said airily, "Malcolm says I won't even have to be present."

In order to muzzle Carson's expletive, Palmer asked, "Did you really kill Joanna?"

He stiffened. "I told you. I didn't mean to. She was like a wildcat, kicking and scratching. Before the accident, I tried to call 9-1-1, but she snatched the phone from my hand and stomped on it." His eyes shot from face to unbelieving face.

"That's not what you told Thrasher."

"Oh? Well, it hardly matters since, according to the good detective, she wasn't actually dead when I left. You were there. You heard him."

"So you never called 9-1-1. Huh."

His remorse was patently artificial. "No, but I informed the concierge on the way out that a guest required medical attention."

This was met with stunned silence. Finally Palmer found her voice. "Why was Joanna so angry?"

Carson interrupted. "And don't tell us she was sore because you wouldn't help her designate land that's been farmed and ranched and lived on for generations as wilderness."

Wilfred beckoned the waitress. "Linda, is it? I'll have a white wine spritzer." He looked at the others' plates. "Anything on the menu besides hamburgers?"

"We have a nice Caesar salad."

He sighed. "All right—and a bowl of chowder."

"Haddock okay?"

He sighed again. "It'll have to do, won't it? Oh, and a cup of coffee with the salad."

When the spritzer had been delivered, Carson fixed an eye on Vogel. "Palmer asked you a question. What was she pissed about?"

"Worse than pissed; I'd call her infuriated. Like I said, I think Joanna had been slipping into the deep end of the pool for a while. Atticus's death just propelled her over the edge."

"Really? Even though he was divorcing her?"

Chapter Twenty-Nine

Star light, star bright, first star I see tonight,
Wish I may, wish I might, have the wish I wish tonight.

Whitney's, Friday, June 9

Vogel reared back. "Atticus wanted to divorce Joanna? He never told me."

Carson said drily, "Perhaps because you were cuckolding him with his wife."

"Me?" He pretended to innocence, but only for an instant. "It's true, we had a...a dalliance—more of a fling, really. It lasted a couple of weekends. So it was common knowledge? I guess I shouldn't be shocked. DC is such a swamp." He paused to let Linda place his salad before him. "She was dynamite in bed, though."

The waitress dropped her tray with a clatter and held a palm to her mouth. "Oh, I'm so sorry." She backed away.

Vogel was amused. "I imagine these southern folk aren't used to the ways of the big city."

Carson stirred. "You haven't said why you wanted to see me, Wilfred."

The man sipped his coffee, made a face, and put two spoonfuls of sugar in the cup. "I want to hear about the papers. The ones in the briefcase."

"I don't have them. Thrasher does."

"I know, but you went through the briefcase. What was in it?"

Carson gazed at him speculatively. "Why do you care? It held documents that belonged to Senator Wren."

Vogel's face was a mask of disbelief. "You're saying it contained *nothing* pertaining to my affairs?"

"No. Just some financial papers of his, and of course the bolt."

"That crossbow arrow?"

"Yes."

Vogel seemed dissatisfied. "You're sure?"

"Absolutely."

Palmer watched Carson. *Why is he lying? Does he think Vogel will give something away by mistake?*

The man spent another hour probing unsuccessfully and finally took his leave. "I've got to get back to my hotel in Tampa."

"You'd better check in with Thrasher before you go."

Vogel grinned. "By all means. I don't want to find myself in bad odor with The Law."

Palmer watched him walk to the corner of Broadway and Gulf of Mexico Drive. The white limo appeared like magic, and he jumped in. "He must have a secret signal that brings his car to him. Dog whistle?"

"Smart watch." Carson paid for their lunches. "What did you think of that little display?"

"I think he's afraid that Wren had dirt on him."

"Me too."

"Why didn't you tell him about the bank transactions?"

"I'm hoping to put him off the scent for the nonce.

He doesn't fully trust me, but he won't dare demand that Thrasher let him see the documents. *Hmm.* I think I shall have a word with the good detective."

"And I think I'll spend some quality time on the beach. I haven't seen the water in weeks."

"Okay. See you later."

Palmer spent the afternoon sunbathing, shelling, and scanning the gulf for passing dolphins. When her skin began to sting—a sure sign she was about to burn—she gathered her things and went home. She'd had a shower and was plunking ice in a tumbler preparatory to a splash of whiskey when Carson knocked. He looked pointedly at the glass in her hand. "I hope that's for me."

Sigh. She filled the glass and handed it to him, then got herself one. "Let's go out on the balcony."

"Lead on."

She set her drink on the railing. "So how was your day?"

"Fruitful. I was able to tear down the notice of an Airstream missing from the police lot without repercussion."

"Where is it now?"

"The camper? At my place."

"How did you get it out of the lot?"

His eyes twinkled. "Turns out *ingress* is tough, but *egress* is a piece of cake."

"All right, how did you get *here*?"

"Nellie. At present all my other vehicles are in their proper berths."

"Even the plane?"

"Queenie is tucked up in her hangar with her blankie. The only item deleted from the inventory is the go-kart."

"Oh?" Palmer thought of poor Raven. To be murdered was bad enough; to be mistaken for someone else smacked of bad karma. "What did you do with it?"

"To be honest, I couldn't bear to look at it. I donated it to Camp Lackanookie—that's a boys' summer camp on Lake Okeechobee."

"So there's a vacancy in your garage."

"Not anymore. I filled it with a dune buggy, or if you prefer the more manly term, ORV."

Palmer watched a laughing gull try to sniggle the fish from a little boy's rod. The standoff took longer than expected and only ended when the boy's father shook a palm frond at the gull, who stalked disdainfully away. "So liberating a camper constituted your day?"

"No, that was just the start. I had quite a jolly encounter with Captain Thrasher."

"Surely you jest."

"I do not. I mentioned Vogel's request. He was intrigued."

"Does he also believe Vogel is afraid there's something incriminating in the briefcase?"

"Indeed. It could be the bolt. It could be those financial transactions with his name in bold. Thrasher called in an accountant."

"Ah." She got up and retrieved the whiskey bottle. After topping up their glasses, she sat down. "What was the accountant's opinion?"

"That Vogel appeared to be acting as an agent for several other entities, but it's not clear what they're buying. If it's land, and they are foreigners, passage of Senator Wren's bill would halt the activity."

"But it's not illegal now."

"Right, so he doesn't really have to worry about it."

"Then why is he in such a sweat?"

Carson shrugged. "No clue. The accountant was looking at the Wren papers when I left. There may be something there. Maybe Atticus wanted me to hide his own illicit dealings."

"Oh dear. Do you have any reason to believe Senator Wren was crooked?"

"Not me. Although I've been hornswoggled before by members who purport to be noble, upstanding citizens, and when they leave office, you discover they own five houses, a golf course, and an island in the Caribbean."

"Which they couldn't have afforded on their congressional salaries."

"Exactly." Carson pointed out to sea. "What are those ripples in the water? Rays?"

Palmer made out a vee of triangular black bodies undulating just under the surface. "Yes! They're manta rays. I was just reading about them. They don't sting like other rays. Aren't they graceful?"

"Reminds me of an underwater cohort of kites."

They watched them out of sight. Carson said, "Oh, there's one new item to add to our pile. You remember that note in Chinese? Turns out the accountant knows Mandarin. Go figure."

"Could he read it?"

"Well, he said it was almost indecipherable—I guess there are Chinese with just as execrable penmanship as American doctors—but he identified names and a few of the words. He said it seemed to be an introduction to someone named Li Bai and mentioned a Fletcher Avery. It said, 'He can help you.' "

"Who can help whom? Was Wren dallying with the Chinese?"

"Maybe that's what he wanted to hide. Remember that senator from California? Turns out her chauffeur of some twenty-five years was a Chinese agent." He sipped his whiskey. "But that's not the weirdest part."

"Oh?"

"Yes. The accountant said he knew of only one Li Bai. He was a famous communist spy."

Palmer gasped. "Oh dear, could Senator Wren have been mixed up in an espionage plot?"

"I don't see how. I looked Li Bai up. He's been dead for twenty years."

Palmer put her drink down. "Maybe it's merely a recommendation to read his biography."

"But why would it be in Atticus's briefcase? And why in Mandarin? I'll bet a dollar Atticus wasn't familiar with the language."

Palmer was at a loss. "Could the note have already been in the briefcase, left there by a previous owner?"

"Joanna told me she gave that case to Atticus as a wedding present. It was a Vicenza—premium Italian leather."

"Then I'm plumb out of ideas."

Carson rose. "I propose we have a nice dinner and talk about politics and religion instead of crime. Then tomorrow we'll go fishing."

"Works for me."

****

Sister Keys, Saturday afternoon

"Hold on." Carson slid the long-handled net into

the water and lifted the fish out along with Palmer's line. "Ooh, you hooked a good one."

"Is it a snapper?"

"Black drum. Must weigh two, three pounds." He dropped the wiggling fish in the bucket and took a beer from the cooler. "That's entrée number one."

"Is it good eating?"

"The small ones like this are. When they get big they carry worms. It has to be prepared very simply. Dust on a little flour, squeeze some lemon, pan sauté." He smacked his lips. "Okay, my turn."

Their fishing rods were set in downriggers, the lines trailing from the stern. Carson took one pole out and tossed his line expertly into the shallows. "Like I told you, lures work better than bait, since you're drifting past the coves where the predator fish are lurking."

Palmer lolled on the cushion as the bass boat putt-putted through the mangroves. She leaned forward and pointed. "Carson, look!"

He peered into the jungle. "What?"

She sat back. "Never mind. I thought I saw a coyote, but it was just somebody's white jacket stuck on a branch. Must be storm debris." She chuckled. "Or perhaps we have a Floridian Robinson Crusoe."

Carson—occupied with fighting what turned out to be a giant mangrove snapper—didn't reply. When he landed it, he fell back onto the captain's chair. "Whew! That's one for George." He threw the line in again.

An hour later—two coolers bursting with fish—they motored back to Carson's house. Carson carried one of the coolers to the station wagon. "I'll take these babies down to Dry Dock. This should guarantee free dessert for the rest of the summer."

Palmer handed him the other cooler. "Could we ask George to cook up my drum for me? I don't think I can wait until you get home. I'm famished."

"Sure. He's a sucker for a pretty fin."

They marched in the back door of the restaurant pushing the coolers stacked on a dolly. "Where's George? There you are, my good man. Where would you like us to put our contribution to the potlatch?"

The chef peered into the first cooler and did a little jig. "Look at the size of that snapper!" He whirled around and yelled, "Hey, Nick! Guess what the special is?"

The maître d' eyed their offering. "I'll write it up."

George opened his arms wide. "And find a table for my favorite customers. I shall make you a feast!"

The chef outdid himself, and they left fat and happy.

Later that evening, they went down to the deserted beach. Only a sliver of moon shone, and clouds colored the night sky gray. Carson almost tripped over a beach chaise emerging from the gloom. "Want to sit?"

"No, let's wade." Palmer dipped a toe in the water, then impulsively drew her dress over her head and sat down on the sand. Carson sat down behind her, his legs hugging hers. They let the waves wash over them. A slightly bigger wave smacked Palmer in the face, and she convulsed in giggles.

He whispered, "You're funny."

"I can't help it." Another wave hit her, and she giggled again.

He said nothing but kissed her shoulder.

She raised her head to the sky. The clouds scudded

away, revealing a milky wash of stars. "Isn't it marvelous?" She pointed. "Look, there's Orion. Oh, and the Big Dipper." An explosion of lights like a Fourth of July sparkler spread across the darkness. "That must be a meteor shower!" She felt him sigh. "Are you okay?"

He murmured, "I just wish…I wish we didn't have these murders hanging over our heads. I wish we could just enjoy…"

"Enjoy what?"

"Each other. Palmer—"

Another voice intruded. "Mind if I move this chair? It's turtle nesting season, you know. Have to take all the beach paraphernalia off the sand."

A man stood behind them, his face veiled in darkness.

"Oh, oh sure. It belongs to the resort I'm staying in. I'll return it when we go back up."

"Great. Thanks." The man disappeared down the beach.

As they trudged up the stairs to her apartment, Palmer brooded.

"What's the matter?"

"That guy's voice was familiar. Now who?" It suddenly came to her. "That was Hardy!"

"Bantam? Why didn't he identify himself?"

"Why indeed?"

Chapter Thirty

The more we get together, together, together,
The more we get together, the happier we'll be,
'Cause your friends are my friends
And my friends are your friends.
The more we get together, the happier we'll be!

The Palapa Inn, Monday, June 12

Palmer didn't receive an answer to her question until Monday morning. Carson had gone home Sunday to work on his menagerie of vehicles—"My babies need constant care. I may have to take Nellie down to Port Charlotte for a tune-up."

She was studying her book on Florida birds when there was a knock. She opened the door. "Hardy! When did you get back?"

His grin was lopsided. "Sorry I haven't been in touch. I returned three days ago."

"You were the one on the beach Saturday night, weren't you? Why didn't you say something?"

"Oh, that." He tried to sound casual. "I didn't realize it was you...and Hawk...until I'd spoken. Then I was too embarrassed to identify myself." He dropped his eyes. "I didn't want to intrude. So...you're dating him now?"

"Yes." *See, that wasn't so hard.* "Did you need

something?"

He looked over her shoulder. "Are you alone? May I come in?"

"Yes, and yes. Come and sit down. Would you like some coffee?"

"No, thanks." Once they were settled on chairs in the living room, he began. "When I told you Detective Thrasher asked me to keep an eye on you in case you contacted Hawk, it wasn't entirely true."

"I am so sorry if I led you on or gave you the wrong impression, Hardy. I only—"

"That's not it either, although—" He leaned forward and gave her hand a squeeze. "I admit I hoped I could win you away. No, I'm actually a private detective."

Is everyone *after Carson?* "What do you want with me…or is it with Carson?"

"Neither…at least originally. I was hired by Atticus Wren to surveil Joanna Wren. Carson being in the sphere of influence, I kept tabs on him. After she came to visit you, I included you on my list."

"Me? I only met her once or twice—and that was after the senator was dead. She accused me"—she couldn't hide the smirk—"of having amorous designs on Wilfred Vogel."

Hardy didn't laugh. "She didn't say anything to you about Senator Wren's suicide?"

Palmer recalled the canned speech Joanna had recited. "Nothing new." She cocked her head at Hardy. "Why were you monitoring her? Because she was having an extramarital affair?"

"No. Wren knew all about that. Theirs was a marriage of convenience. What really perturbed him was her involvement with some extremely radical people."

Palmer thought of Joanna's rant about wilderness. "You mean environmentalists? Sure, they can be obdurate in their approach to safeguarding nature, but I haven't heard of them resorting to violence."

"Generally they stick with lawfare, yes, but there is a cadre that believes humans are the cause of all ills. To save the earth, the population must be reduced to a fraction of what it is now. They call themselves Enders. It's short for End Human Hegemony Now." He paused and closed his eyes. "They started with minor actions like tree spiking and plugging factory smokestacks, then graduated to knocking down power poles and poisoning poultry before it gets to market."

"Oh, my. I've never heard of tree spiking. What is it?"

"The activist finds a tree marked for cutting and drives a metal spike into it. When the lumberjack's chainsaw bites into the tree, it hits the spike, which sends it flying back in his face, causing horrendous injuries."

Her hand flew to her mouth. "But that's depraved!"

"Yes. However, it's nearly impossible to trace the culprit. Everything the Enders do is both lethal and secret—nothing overt or public. They don't announce themselves like other activist groups do. The objective is not fame or notoriety; it's to make the human activities that interfere with nature too costly to carry on."

Palmer went to the kitchen and came back with two water bottles. Hardy accepted one gratefully. "We're definitely into summer now."

She sat across from him. "So the senator worried that Joanna was in league with this Ender bunch?"

"Uh-huh. He found some of their literature in her bedroom. He wanted me to find out how far the infection had spread, since he was about to introduce a bill making farmland sales off-limits for any purpose other than agriculture."

"That's not what S. 219 says. It just bars sales to foreign entities and international corporations."

"That's in S. 219, yes, but this was a separate bill. Once Senator Wren decided to back S. 219, he learned that there were also American investors who planned to take farmland out of cultivation."

Vogel? But he said he resisted Joanna's demands. "Why?" At Hardy's baffled expression, she clarified. "Why would an American do that to his own country?"

"It's part of an agenda that goes back several decades. A few very wealthy, powerful men were convinced that the human population was going to explode and overwhelm the earth's resources."

"Right. Paul Erlich's *The Population Bomb*. I thought his theories were completely debunked."

Hardy smiled wanly. "Not entirely. Anyway, this group of businessmen decided the only way to prevent catastrophe was to cap the number of people allowed to live."

"How did they propose to accomplish that?"

He took a long drink of water. "Through forced sterilization."

"That's monstrous!"

"Maybe." He produced a half-hearted snigger. "You have to agree there are quite a few folks the world would be better off without."

Before she could protest, he said, "There's evidence that a portion of the current crop of US-based investors adhere to the dogma, but they want to speed up the process by decreasing the amount of land that's farmed, thus reducing the food supply. The population will be thinned in record time."

"And what role do the Enders play in this?"

"They see themselves as natural allies of the investors."

Palmer hung on to the only lifeline in the nightmare. "Senator Wren saw the danger."

"Yes. Hence the second bill, which would have blocked their scheme."

"What did Joanna have to do with all this?"

"Joanna was looking for financial backers to take as much land as possible out of production. Senator Wren was petrified the Enders would commit some act of domestic terrorism to further that aim and that Joanna would be entangled in it."

"Is the FBI aware of them?"

"Yes, but it's a low priority. They're obsessed by an utterly fictitious army of domestic terrorists." He grunted. "They seriously believe whole herds of white supremacists are hiding in flyover country, conspiring to overthrow the same country they're fiercely defending."

"Poppycock."

"Anyway, the feds don't have any interest in investigating some wild-eyed leftist group that wants to eliminate a billion people."

Palmer sipped her water, digesting Hardy's words. "Are you hinting that this group killed Senator Wren?"

"Not at all, but I do think he was murdered. I had

spoken to him in his office the night he died. There was nothing in his demeanor or voice to make me suspect he wanted to kill himself."

She had to ask. "Do you think Carson killed him?"

He hesitated. "Honestly? I'm not sure. Wren told me he planned to entrust Hawk with some information he'd found—proof, he called it, of a criminal enterprise. He didn't specify what it was—perhaps it was something on Joanna and the Enders."

"Did he say it was in the briefcase?"

"He implied it, but Captain Thrasher allowed me to look at the contents." He made a wry face. "I saw nothing relating to land sequestration or a terrorist plot. I'm at a loss." He put down the bottle. "That's why I'm here. I need your help."

"My help to do what?"

"I want to find Wren's killer."

She rose. "You don't need my help. You need Carson's. Let's call him."

She half expected Hardy to quibble, but he jumped up. "Yes! That would be great!"

"Better yet: let's go see him. You can explain to him what you've been doing."

Hardy's initial buoyancy faded. "I suppose. Can't you just call him and tell him to meet us at the police station?"

Palmer's suspicions flooded back. "You're trying to trap him, aren't you? You do believe Carson killed Wren." She went to the door and opened it. "Get out."

He drew back. "Wait! No! I'm sure Atticus Wren was murdered; I just don't know who did it." When she didn't move away from the door, he said, "All right, we'll go see Carson first. We'll put our heads together.

There has to be some piece of the puzzle we're missing."

"Welcome to our world."

****

Carson's house, Monday noon

Pounding on Carson's door brought no answer. Palmer went round the side of the building. "I'll check the shed. He was going to take Nellie to Port Charlotte. If she's here, he's back."

"Nellie? He has a horse?"

"No. Well, not that I know of. Nellie is his motorcycle." They crowded into the galvanized metal building. The station wagon and the motorcycle sat side by side. "Okay, so he must have returned yesterday." *That's odd. Surely he would have called or come over. At least by this morning.* "His pickup wasn't in the driveway. Maybe he's off on an errand."

Hardy looked out the dusty window. "There's a red Ford 150 parked in back. Is that his?"

She looked. "Yes. *Hmm.* Let's try the garage."

Hardy pulled the lever to open the overhead door, but it wouldn't budge. "Must be locked."

"The side door may be open." It was also locked. She peered through the grimy panes. The Bugatti and the dune buggy sat in their usual places. Beginning to feel a little desperate, she said, "Maybe he took the bass boat out to fish."

The bass boat was tied up at the dock. The kayak lay on its side on the grass. Palmer whirled around. "I'm going in the house. This is starting to freak me out."

"Why?"

"Carson owns every type of vehicle known to man.

296

I can't see him walking anywhere."

"The house will be locked as well, won't it?"

"He usually leaves keys to all the doors in that flower pot."

Hardy gave her an eloquent look.

Sheesh, Hardy. At this point it shouldn't come as a shock that I'm familiar with his habits. Palmer went through the screened back porch into the kitchen, Hardy trailing her. A dish with a half-eaten omelet sat on the table and dirty pots covered the range. "This isn't like Carson. He would never leave this mess." *Fudgie would hit the roof.*

Hardy looked around, perplexed. "Mess?"

"Let's try the living room."

The big room was tidy. Hardy went to the telephone. He picked it up and listened. "No dial tone."

Palmer remembered all the thrillers she'd read in high school. Her eyes wide with dread, she turned to Hardy. "The line's been cut!"

Hardy sniffed. "*Or* he was tired of solicitation calls. If you leave the receiver off the hook long enough, the dial tone eventually stops."

"Oh." She opened the front door. Her eyes swept the porch. Something lay on the mat. She picked it up and held it out to Hardy. Her words coming in staccato gasps, she said, "It's…Carson's…wallet."

Chapter Thirty-One

Lucy Locket lost her pocket,
Kitty Fisher found it.
Not a penny was there in it,
Only ribbon round it.

Longboat Key police station, Monday, June 12

"Captain Thrasher!" Palmer barged in ahead of Hardy. "He's been kidnapped!"

The policeman looked up from his desk. "Who's been kidnapped?"

"Carson Hawk."

"Are you sure an alert citizen didn't nab him for us? I wouldn't mind having a little chat with him myself."

Palmer said crossly, "If that were true, Carson would be here, wouldn't he?"

Thrasher chuckled. "Right you are. Well, then, who did you have in mind to play the perpetrator?"

She didn't appreciate his lukewarm reaction and spat out, "Isn't that *your* job?"

"We do generally rely on the public to report missing persons, but I must advise you there's a forty-eight-hour waiting period before we take action." He peered from Palmer to Hardy. "What makes you think he's been abducted?"

She exclaimed, "There were dirty dishes in the sink!"

Thrasher nodded wisely. "I see. A palpable clue."

"No, you don't understand. He—"

Hardy pulled her elbow back. "Why don't you tell him what we discussed?"

She spun on him, mouth open. "Discussed?"

He cocked his head. "You know."

Palmer thought wildly. *Enviro fanatics? Joanna's affair? Oh!* "Mr. Bantam here worked for Senator Wren. He thinks Wren was murdered."

"Oh, he does, does he?" Thrasher turned to the man standing beside Palmer. "Funny you didn't mention that before."

"You didn't ask. You only asked me to stay close to Palmer in order to keep an eye on Hawk."

Palmer added, "He's a private investigator. He works—worked—for Wren."

Thrasher eyed Hardy. "You're just full of secrets, aren't you? You told me you were a lawyer."

"I am. I can wear two hats, you know. Senator Wren hired me to confirm or disprove his wife's infidelity."

Palmer jerked. "No, he didn't. Everyone knew that Joanna was unfaithful. Even Wren. According to Carson, at least." *Wait a minute... Could he have been lying about that?*

She woke up to hear Hardy reluctantly muttering, "All right, I'll come clean. Actually, the senator was concerned that Mrs. Wren may have been secretly funding a radical environmental group."

"Was she?"

"I never found out. When Wren died, I was no

longer employed and I had to terminate my operation."

"I see. And Joanna Wren's death put the final kibosh on it."

"Yes."

Radical... The Enders... Have we been approaching this from the wrong angle? "The radical group you told me about, Hardy—the Enders. Could they have killed both Wrens?"

Hardy made a noise between a squeak and a guffaw. "That's a ridiculous idea."

"No, it isn't." Palmer was on a roll. This new solution would get Carson off the hook. *And it has the added bonus of sounding reasonable.* "You said the Enders are willing to use violence. If they'll spike trees, murder isn't that much of a leap."

Hardy said helplessly, "But why would they kill Joanna? If the senator was right, she was one of their loudest cheerleaders."

Palmer had the answer to that. "Maybe she betrayed them to Vogel."

Thrasher cleared his throat. "Hello? You two are here because Carson Hawk has disappeared, correct?"

"Yes… Oh! I almost forgot. I found his wallet."

"Was it empty?"

She fumbled in her pocket. "Here it is. I…we…didn't look inside."

Thrasher riffled through the sections. "Seems to have every item a normal healthy man carries." He held up a condom. "I'm betting this has been there since the seventh grade. Where did you find it? The wallet, I mean."

"On the doormat at his front door. He must have dropped it as a clue."

"Or it happened to fall out of his pocket." Hardy had apparently decided not to be helpful. At her glare, he shrugged. "Either way, he must have left in a hurry."

Palmer gazed at the detective. "And we have to find him before...before..."

Thrasher handed back the billfold. "Okay, I'll send out an APB, but if it turns out he's at the dentist or the dollar store, I'm charging you for the police time."

"He can't be." Palmer was increasingly nervous. "It wasn't just his wallet that was at the house. All his means of transportation are there." Something niggled at her. *Wait—the plane. I wonder...* She opened her mouth to mention it and immediately thought better of it. *Carson might not want me to divulge the plane's location. Please let him be there. And safe.*

"I'll let you know if we hear anything." Thrasher began flipping through papers on his desk.

Seeing they were dismissed, Palmer and Hardy left the station. They were standing on the sidewalk when the lights on the fire engine housed across from the police station flashed on. Horn blaring, it passed them and turned left onto Gulf of Mexico Drive. "I wonder what's going on?"

"I don't know. Do you think...?" She let the possibility hang in the taut air.

"Worth a try."

They jumped into Palmer's car and blew out of the entrance.

Palmer shaded her eyes. "It's slowing down. Is it turning into Windward Bay? No, that's not it. There's a car in front of it." She slapped the steering wheel. "Why don't these people pull to the curb when an emergency vehicle's behind them? Idiots."

When the car finally turned off at the entrance to the Zota resort, Palmer caught a glimpse. *A white limousine*. "It's Vogel!"

"Vogel! You mentioned him just now at the police station. Isn't he the one who admitted to killing Joanna Wren?"

"Yes." She eyed him. "How do you know about that?"

"Thrasher told me. He's a big-time investor, isn't he?"

"Uh-huh." Palmer watched the limo pull up to the hotel entrance. "He might know where Carson is."

Hardy nodded. "Let's go."

Palmer left her car in the visitors' lot and together they went to the desk. The clerk had no one registered under the name of Vogel.

Palmer didn't give up. "Stylish fellow? Given to seersucker and bow ties?"

"You mean like Tom Wolfe?"

Hardy slapped his knee. "*That's* who he reminded me of."

"I thought you didn't know him."

"I don't. His booking photo was on Thrasher's desk. I noticed it because he was so well-dressed. Unusual for a man who's just been arrested."

The clerk closed his ledger. "The only guest we have currently is a gentleman from Hong Kong."

Palmer had been surveying the lobby. A familiar figure stood at the bar in the next room. "There he is!" She ran over and touched him on the shoulder. "Wilfred?"

His eyebrows shot up. "Why, Palmer Lind. What are *you* doing here?"

"I could ask you the same question. Weren't you going back to Tampa?"

"I did. Carson called me. I agreed to meet him here."

"But you're not registered here."

"Not anymore. I checked out, but my associate, Li Bai, remained. Carson asked to use his room for our...conversation."

Li Bai? Why is that name familiar? Palmer was confused. "What does he want to talk about?"

"Carson?" He turned to sign the bill on the bar. "I don't know yet. I'm heading up to the room now."

Palmer's earlier panic evaporated, leaving her with a sort of befuddled trepidation. *Vogel doesn't sound guilty, but...let's see how he reacts to this.* "Can I come?"

He recoiled. "That would not be appropriate."

"Why not?"

His face went rigid. In a voice that set her teeth on edge, he rasped, "Miss Lind, I am a private businessman. I do not discuss my affairs in public."

She backed off.

Vogel went towards the elevator. Hardy joined Palmer. "Does he know where Carson is?"

"Yes, he's upstairs. Hardy? He says Carson called him."

"Oh, that's all right then."

"No, it isn't. Carson wouldn't leave dirty dishes on the table."

"You keep saying that. Is it supposed to be significant?"

"Yes." She headed back out to the concierge desk. "Hi there, I've just learned that Mr. Vogel is visiting a guest here. A Mr. Li Bai?"

"Ah, the Chinese gentleman."

"He—Mr. Vogel—asked us to join him there, but I'm afraid I didn't write down the room number."

The clerk checked his monitor. "Room two-three-five." He picked up the receiver. "Shall I call and tell them you're on your way up?"

"No, no, that won't be necessary. He's expecting us."

She grabbed Hardy's elbow and marched to the elevator. "Second floor."

They walked down the hall. "Here it is." She pressed her ear to the door. "I hear voices."

"Are they raised in anger?"

"No."

"Hey, here's an idea. Why don't we knock?"

"Vogel said he didn't want us here. I want to know why." She put her ear against the door again. "I can't make out the words, but the voices are getting louder."

"Palmer—"

At that moment, they heard a crash and a howl. Hardy put a shoulder to the door and shoved. Nothing happened. Suddenly it flew open from the inside. Hardy struggled to maintain his balance, pivoting to face Palmer. She caught his arms and steadied him.

Carson stood there. "What are *you* two doing here?"

Palmer thrust Hardy aside. "What happened? Did he hurt you? Why didn't you call me? Where—"

He seemed bewildered. "What are you talking about?" He gestured behind him. "Wilfred broke the vodka bottle and cut himself. I was coming out to find some more towels. He's bleeding like a stuck pig."

"Carson? *How did you get here?*"

"Me? I took the bike." He caught sight of Hardy. "Sorry, Bantam. The police left it at my house. I was in a hurry, and it was next to the front door. I just grabbed it. I'll be glad to return it if you'll give me your address."

Palmer brushed past him. Vogel sat on a chair holding a towel to his wrist. A tall Chinese man stood by the sliding door to the balcony. His dour features gave nothing away. She looked him over. He looked somehow familiar. "You don't seem very upset by Mr. Vogel's injury."

The man did not react. Hardy entered, took in the scene, and stepped toward the sliding door. He stared at the Chinese man. "I know you."

The man turned his back and walked out to the balcony.

Hardy called after him, "You're Li Bai."

Palmer nudged him. "Yes, the clerk told us."

"No. I mean...what I mean is, he's *Li Bai*. The Chinese spy. He's on the FBI's most wanted list. Number four."

Chapter Thirty-Two

Round and round the mulberry bush
The monkey chased the weasel
The monkey thought 'twas all in fun
POP! Goes the weasel.

Zota Beach Resort, Monday, June 12

"Li Bai a spy? Don't be absurd." Vogel dropped the towel. Blood spattered on the floor. He picked it up and pressed it back on his wrist. "Mr. Li is a respected businessman from Hong Kong."

"But—"

He cut Hardy off. "Who are you and what are you doing trespassing on a closed-door meeting?"

Palmer spoke for Hardy. "His name is Hardy Bantam. He's a detective hired by Senator Wren to keep an eye on Joanna."

Vogel snorted. "Well, he didn't do a very good job, did he?"

Hardy retorted, "Wren hardly expected his wife's lover to murder her."

Vogel didn't take the bait. "That's a pretty nasty accusation, Mr. Bantam. I defended myself when she attacked me. In fact, it turns out I didn't kill her after all. Someone else did."

Hardy gaped at him. Just then Carson returned with

a roll of toilet paper. "This is all I could scrounge up. How's the cut?"

Vogel removed the wadded towel from his wrist. "It looks like it's stopped bleeding." He threw the towel onto the bathroom floor. "Thanks anyway, Hawk."

Palmer took the opportunity to return to the subject foremost on her mind. She addressed Vogel. "You say Mr....Bai? Li?"

"Mr. Li."

"You say Mr. Li is not a spy. Okay, then. What is he doing here? Why did Carson ask to meet with you?"

Carson, about to take a gulp from a water bottle, gagged. "Me...ask to meet *him*?"

Vogel said smoothly, "Palmer must have misheard me. I said when I spoke with you about Li, you expressed a desire to join us."

Carson spluttered. "I did nothing of the sort. Yes, you called me about meeting a prospective employer, and I said I'd consider it. But right after that I got another call. My contacts in DC reported that a man who was staying at the Zota had news about Joanna's death. I came roaring down. I found Li and Wilfred here together. I didn't know what to think."

Palmer looked from Carson to Vogel. "Does Mr. Li have information on Mrs. Wren's death or not?"

Vogel cast a quick glance at the man on the balcony. "How would I know? The subject never came up."

"Then why is he here?"

"He's come to the States to invest in property."

Carson's brow creased. "Property? You told me he wanted to partner with you in a startup tech company. That he was in need of a communications person."

Evidently nothing rattled Vogel. He said unctuously, "Yes, that's why I thought of you, Hawk. You're out of a job, what with…well, you know."

"So, what kind of property does he need for a cloud network?"

"The company has to have a brick-and-mortar headquarters, after all. We're seeking at least five and up to ten acres for a campus. I've been scoping out the area around Tampa for him."

Li Bai returned from the balcony but remained standing by the doors. Palmer noticed he kept his hands at his sides.

Carson was still cogitating. "What about S. 219? If that passes, Li won't be allowed to buy US land."

"Ah, but it hasn't passed yet, has it? So far no one's stepped up to champion it now that Wren's gone. And Chairman Bunting opposes it."

"It's on the committee agenda."

"A mere formality. He is slow-walking it to avoid a dustup with supporters."

Palmer had been watching Hardy, who seemed to have tuned out. *Well, if he's not going to mention it, I will.* "What about the other bill Senator Wren was working on? The one that would proscribe any use other than agriculture for farmland?"

The room went still. Finally, Vogel cleared his throat. "Atticus had another bill?"

Carson was staring at Palmer. "Where did you hear that?"

Before she could reply, Hardy said, "The senator told me about it in confidence. He had only sketched the idea out. He hadn't run it by his staff yet." He swung on Vogel. "But that wouldn't interfere with *your* project, would it?"

Vogel shifted in his seat. "Certainly not. We're only interested in a small lot—a few acres at most. For the headquarters. Like I said." He peered at Carson. "If you—his speechwriter—were unaware of this second bill, I don't think we need be alarmed."

Carson blinked. "I'll have to think about this."

"What's the matter? A minute ago you were gung ho, if you'll pardon the expression"—Wilfred winked at Li Bai—"to come in with us."

Hardy started. "You, Hawk? You've accepted the job?"

"Wilfred is getting ahead of himself. No, I haven't. I need more details…but let's not allow ourselves to be sidetracked." He turned to Vogel. "You knew Wren had no co-sponsors for S. 219. He was the only one standing in your way. You killed him."

"That's ridiculous. He was my friend. Besides, he hanged himself. Look at me. Do I look strong enough to string someone up? Atticus had some eight inches on me, and a hundred pounds." Vogel certainly did appear too delicate to overpower a large, wriggling man fighting for his life.

Still, Palmer was puzzled by his sangfroid, considering he'd just been accused of murder. *He's virtually unflappable.*

"Enough." The Chinese man stood in the middle of the room. Palmer was astonished at how silently and swiftly he had moved. "Enough talk. You, Vogel, are no longer useful to my plans."

"What are you talking about, Li? You can't get the land without me."

"I have what I need." He produced a wicked-looking Beretta. Palmer realized that he'd been standing in that peculiar manner to hide the bulge in his pocket. "All of you, drop your cell phones on the floor and go into the bathroom."

They did as they were told and crowded into the four-foot-square room. Hardy was the last to go in. He tried to shoulder Li Bai out of the way, mouthing something.

The man's eyes opened wide, then he faced the others. "We should have divested ourselves of superfluous elements long ago. Now it is not so convenient. You, however"—he pointed the gun at Vogel—"should be put out of your misery." He shot him in the knee. Vogel yelped and grabbed his leg. As the others went to his aid, Li Bai took hold of Hardy and pulled him out of the bathroom. "You I take with me." He slammed the door on them.

Palmer whispered, "Are we locked in?"

Carson twisted the knob. "Yes." He cocked an ear. "Give Li Bai a couple of minutes to leave, then I think I can get us out. Anyone have a hat pin?"

Palmer didn't know whether to laugh or cry. Vogel, sitting on the edge of the bathtub, wheezed, "I have a Swiss army knife in my inside pocket."

Carson yanked it out, eliciting another yelp from Vogel, and sprung a needle from one of the slots. He fiddled with the tiny hole next to the knob. It clicked and he opened the door. "Voilà! Or is it eureka?"

Palmer ran to the hotel phone and picked it up. "Front desk? We need an ambulance! Stat!…What? Oh, room two-three-five. Did you see Mr. Li leaving with another man? No? He must have gone right past you! Oh, I see." She slammed the phone down. "The desk clerk was—get this—*indisposed*, and didn't see anyone leave."

"Damn." Carson helped Vogel to a chair. The older man was very pale. "Are you in pain?"

He opened his eyes. "What do you think?"

Carson barked at Palmer. "Call the desk again. Ask to be patched through to Thrasher." He picked up the bloody towel from the floor and applied it to Vogel's knee.

When Thrasher came on, Palmer explained about Li Bai and his hostage. She hung up. "He's mobilizing all the police departments, including TSA at the airports."

Distant sirens broke the stillness. Carson sat across from Vogel. "Now, before they arrive, you'd better fess up. You're buying a lot more than ten acres, aren't you?"

Vogel nodded.

"You want to monopolize the land around cities and then sell it back to the municipal governments at an inflated price, don't you?"

Vogel nodded again and pressed his lips tightly together.

"Did you in fact kill Senator Wren?"

"No! I told you I didn't. We—Li Bai and I—thought we'd worked out a deal with him. He'd vote for the bill but would grandfather us in. In exchange, we'd set aside a portion of our purchases for affordable housing. We were at his house the night he died. He was getting ready to head to your apartment when we left. That was the last time I saw him."

Palmer asked, "Do you think Li Bai killed him?"

"He couldn't have. He was with me the whole

night." Vogel seemed to be weighing his thoughts. "Joanna was there too."

Palmer started. "She wasn't out of town?"

"No." Vogel gave Palmer a quizzical look. "What made you think that?"

"That's what she told me. *Hmm*."

"No, she walked in just as we were concluding our meeting." He looked at Carson. "She might have been eavesdropping on us."

"What difference would that make?"

He looked chagrined. "I had enlisted her help with Atticus, but I fear I misled her somewhat. I promised her if the bill was defeated, I would buy the land and make it off-limits to any commercial development—or any development at all."

"That's not what you told Thrasher."

"Well, I was hardly going to tell him the truth, now was I?"

Palmer could think of no polite response to that.

Carson growled, "In other words, you pledged to return the land 'to its pristine state'?" He made air quotes around the phrase.

"Well, you know and I know it's absurd, but you can't—couldn't—reason with her." He pursed his lips. "If she overheard us talking about the affordable housing agreement, she…er…might have been ticked off."

"And in her heightened emotional state—"

Vogel said, his voice lugubrious, "I wouldn't put it past her to strike out."

Palmer conjured up the perfectly coiffed woman. "Do you think she meant to kill him?"

Vogel closed his eyes. "Where's that ambulance?

I'm losing a lot of blood."

Carson didn't move. "Wilfred? Answer the question."

"I honestly don't know. It could have been an accident."

Carson scoffed, "It's pretty hard to hang a man by *accident*."

Palmer wasn't buying it. "And why did she go after her husband? I mean, you were the one who deceived her."

Vogel allowed himself a small smile. "She did love me, you know. It's a shame, really. She was a lot of woman, but…well, she was nuts."

Carson said heavily, "All right, let's grant she had a hand in Atticus's death. How do we prove it?"

"I've no idea." He gave Carson a sidelong look. "I do know one thing for sure. It was Li Bai who killed the little girl."

"By mistake, right? He mistook her for me?"

"Actually, no. He went to your house to look for the briefcase. He was searching the garage when she came in unexpectedly. He hit her with a shovel."

"And then shot her with a crossbow and left it in the go-kart with the body. Why?"

Vogel sprang up from the chair and almost fell over. "What did you say?"

Palmer answered. "Raven—Hardy's daughter—was knocked out, yes, but the fatal blow came from a crossbow."

"Really?" Vogel's eyes swiveled to Carson. He didn't need to ask the question.

"Yes, it was my crossbow. And no, I didn't kill her."

Vogel frowned. "That's strange. Li Bai admitted to me just this morning that he bashed her head in. Maybe he didn't feel the need to mention the bow."

"The question remains: why would he leave it there?"

The older man contemplated Carson. "To frame you?"

Palmer wasn't going to let him shift the blame. "At your request?"

"Certainly not. He knew I'd disapprove." He shook his head in disgust. "The man's obviously trigger-happy."

"Why didn't you go to the police?"

"I haven't had much chance to, have I? As I said, Li was with me the night of Atticus's death." His eyes narrowed. "He did go down to Sarasota alone."

"Why?"

"I asked him to go when I learned Tipsy was headed here."

Carson was surprised. "You told me *you* sent Tipsy after me."

Vogel held a hand to his breast. "Me? No, sir. You, uh, must have misunderstood. I had fired him."

Maybe that's why he was dressed so shabbily. Huh. "On what grounds?"

Vogel pressed his lips together. "That's personal."

Carson huffed. "If he was no longer in your employ, what difference did it make where Tipsy went?"

Vogel grimaced in pain. "Can we talk about this later? Where the hell is that ambulance?"

Palmer knew once Vogel was taken to the hospital they'd forfeit the opportunity to pry any more information out of him. "You claim you sent Li Bai after Tipsy. Was it in fact Li's idea? He sure seemed to be the one in charge."

Vogel winced. "He did, didn't he? That caught me off guard. I thought I was dealing with a lackey—a subordinate of the big chiefs. He was represented to me as a go-between."

Palmer bore down on Vogel. "Out with it. Was Hardy right? Is he a spy?"

Vogel didn't answer.

Carson sniffed. "I don't see how he could be. Li Bai the secret agent has been dead for twenty years."

Palmer objected. "Maybe he's a descendant of the first Li Bai. Hardy said he was on the FBI's most wanted list."

Carson eyed her. "So he did. I've been wondering how he knew that."

"I...That's it! I remember where I've seen him before!" Palmer pointed a finger at Vogel. "Li Bai was your limo driver!"

Chapter Thirty-Three

Eenie meenie miney mo
Catch a tiger by his toe
If he hollers let him go
Eenie meenie miney mo.

Zota Beach Resort, Monday, June 12

"I'm surprised you didn't recognize Li Bai sooner, Palmer. The chauffeur disguise was his idea. He said he wanted to remain in the background." Vogel groaned and rubbed his leg. "So you can understand how I assumed he was an underling."

Carson looked out the window. Over his shoulder, Palmer could see lights flashing. "At some point, he took archery lessons." He turned to Palmer. "Where was the range? Do you remember?"

"I think it was somewhere in Virginia. Fairfax?"

Vogel looked dazed. "Archery lessons? Li Bai?"

"Yes. He stole my crossbow. It's difficult to handle, and he would have needed some training."

Vogel seemed unpersuaded. "Are you saying Tipsy's and Raven's deaths were premeditated and not spur of the moment?"

Palmer nodded. "He may be the one who came in after you and killed Joanna as well."

"Huh. How did you know about the lessons?"

"The ticket stub was in the briefcase. It had two holes punched in it. Two lessons."

"Whaddya know." Vogel seemed more bemused than anything.

Palmer felt her gorge rise. "May I remind you that three people died at your *lackey*'s hands."

"I haven't forgotten, missy. I feel terrible. But"— he pressed the towel to his knee—"I didn't exactly get off scot-free."

Carson gazed at him speculatively. "If you didn't know what was in the briefcase, why were you so keen to get your hands on it?"

"Atticus told me the land exchange papers were in it. I wanted to keep them from Joanna. If she saw them, she'd know I was working with the Chinese and had lied to her."

"You sure it wasn't to retrieve the note about Li Bai?"

"What note?"

"There's also a note written in Mandarin introducing Li Bai."

He shrugged. "I don't know anything about it. I never saw a note." He looked suddenly sly. "So how did Li Bai's stuff get in Atticus's briefcase anyway?"

The question brought them both up short. Before either Palmer or Carson could answer, the siren outside went up an octave, then died.

Palmer said with relief, "Here's your ride. After they fix you up, you can confess all to Father Thrasher."

"What have I got to confess to?"

"To being a scumbag."

****

Carson's house, Tuesday morning

Palmer found Carson in the kitchen. "What's for breakfast?"

"It's amazing how much better pancakes taste when you have all the ingredients. Sit yourself down while I whip up a few."

She poured juice, then plopped on a stool. "Did you call the hospital?"

"Uh-huh. Wilfred could be released as early as this afternoon. The bullet only grazed his kneecap. They patched him up, but he can't put weight on the leg for a week."

"Why didn't Li Bai just kill him?"

"Why indeed? Why didn't he knock us all off, for that matter? He didn't seem to hesitate before when someone got in his way."

Palmer got up and started opening cabinets. "Syrup?"

"Top left." As she rummaged around on the shelves, he mused, "Maybe the crossbow is his weapon of choice. The gun made a lot of noise."

"True. Do you think he used it at Zota because he knew there were no other guests?"

"It doesn't matter how crowded it was. Lugging a crossbow through the lobby would definitely draw more attention than a single pop from a pistol."

She set the syrup on the table. "Come to think of it, Li Bai only confessed to Raven's murder. Do we have any solid evidence that he was involved in Tipsy's and Joanna's deaths?"

"No." Carson flipped a pancake expertly onto Palmer's plate. "I suppose he's fled the country."

"If so, he'd have to have done it within hours of

leaving the hotel with Hardy, since Thrasher had all the airports under surveillance before we'd even delivered Wilfred to the hospital."

Carson filled his own plate and sat down. "If he's still here, he's well hidden. I'm sure the Chinese have a whole network of spies and safe houses. They've infiltrated almost every industry and university in this country."

Palmer agreed. "How many people are blissfully ignorant that their entire life is an open book to the Chinese communists."

"Gives new meaning to the term Nanny State, doesn't it?"

Palmer tasted the pancake. "Yum. What's that flavor?"

"It's fig. I mashed some fresh ones into the batter. You like?"

"I love it!" She finished it off.

"Then you'll adore the mango." He dropped a second cake on her plate and drizzled red sauce over it. "Try this instead of the syrup."

"What is it?"

"Red currant jelly. I melted it and swirled in a dollop of pineapple juice."

She took a bite and closed her eyes. "*Mmm*. One for the books."

"I'll write it down then." He returned to his seat. "Li Bai has another problem: what to do with the little Bantam."

Palmer clucked her tongue. "Oh my, I forgot all about Hardy." When Carson smirked, she said irritably, "It's not funny. He's in danger."

"Yes. Yes, he is." When she choked on her juice,

he said hastily, "I'm sure the police will do everything they can to protect him. They know how to deal with hostage situations."

Her lower lip trembled. "If they find them in time."

"In time?"

She gazed at Carson. "If he wants to leave the country, Li Bai may need to…shed…his encumbrance."

Carson didn't respond. After a minute, he said, "By the way, how *did* you trace me to the Zota?"

"We saw Vogel's limo turn into the resort. We followed him."

"Why?"

"Well, when we found your wallet, we took it to the police station, but—"

"My wallet?" He slapped his back pocket. "You found it? I had no idea where I lost it."

"It was on your front door mat." She pulled it from her purse. "Here. The captain gave it back to me."

"Huh." He peered at her. "You were at my house?"

"We—Hardy and I—were looking for you. You hadn't called or texted, and I was worried. So we came over. You didn't answer the bell, but all the cars were there and"—she goggled at Carson—"there were dirty dishes on the table!"

"Dirty dishes?" He looked mystified. "So what?"

"You *never* leave the kitchen in disorder. I told Hardy… I was scared. I thought you'd been"—she hoped he wouldn't laugh—"kidnapped."

Carson threw back his head and roared. "Oh God, I can't believe the way your mind works. It's like you get this one clue and wind it around and around itself until it's this enormous mishmash of tendrils and red herrings." He kissed the top of her head. "My excuse is

I was in a hurry. When the think-tank folks called, they said their contact would only be at Zota for an hour. I didn't anticipate an unannounced inspection from the sanitation police."

"I'm sorry. It just felt like something wasn't right."

"Well, you weren't far off. Fudgie drilled it into me: always clean as you go. It was a wrench to leave the kitchen that way." He ate a forkful of pancake. "By the way, what did Thrasher do when you handed him my wallet?"

"He put out an APB on you." She clapped a hand to her mouth. "Oh dear, I never got around to telling him we found you!"

Carson said drily, "I imagine he's given the stand-down order by now."

She finished her pancakes. "Maybe we should contact him anyway—see if there's been any news about Hardy."

Before Carson could answer, the phone rang. Palmer picked it up. "Hello? Hardy? Where are you? Are you safe? What about Li Bai?... Okay, I'll slow down. How did... Oh, okay. Do you need anything? All right, yes. I'll tell him." Palmer clicked the phone off. "Hardy's escaped."

"Bantam's free? How did he swing that?" Carson's forehead creased. "Li Bai struck me as extremely professional. He's unlikely to let a wimpy guy like Hardy slip through his clutches."

"He didn't provide any details, other than he's a little banged up. He called from the hospital."

"I suppose you want to go see him."

Palmer surprised even herself by saying, "Not really. He'll be fine. To tell the truth, I don't feel like it."

"Okay." Carson leered at her. "How about a little post-prandial whoopie to perk you up?"

She put her dish and mug in the sink. "Lead the way."

****

The Palapa Inn, Tuesday afternoon

Palmer was returning to her condo when Captain Thrasher called. "I thought you'd like to know the latest."

"Hang on, let me park the car." She pulled into the lot and walked up the stairs holding the cell to her ear. "Shoot."

"Oops, while I was on hold we had further developments. I'll have to call you back." He hung up.

"Well, I like that." Palmer stood in her living room, hands on hips.

"Like what?" Vogel, on crutches, shuffled in behind her.

Palmer was no longer dismayed to find uninvited strangers making themselves at home. She sighed. "How did *you* get in here?"

"Your door was open."

I don't think so, but at this point who cares? "The hospital let you out?"

He grimaced. "It took some serious bribery, but yes." He held up a crutch. "Doctor says I have to depend on these things for another week. Speaking of, may I sit down?" He indicated the sofa.

She nodded and took the chair opposite him. "All right, what are you here for?"

"To tell you I made a clean breast of it to the police. I thought you'd like to know." He smiled wanly.

322

"Also, they caught Li Bai. He had hitched a ride in an eighteen-wheeler headed to Canada. They arrested him at the border."

"For the murders?"

"No, no. At least not yet. They picked him up for taking Hardy Bantam prisoner. Thrasher says once they've gathered more evidence, they'll charge him with Raven's death, and likely Tipsy's as well."

"That's good. But what about your land deals? Or was that all fake too?"

He looked furtive. "Not at all. At least, I made them in good faith. How was I to know that Li Bai was an agent of the CCP?"

"So it's true? Li Bai *is* on the most wanted list?"

Vogel seemed to waffle. "Well, Thrasher didn't say so in so many words, but after Hardy said…"

"So what will you do now?"

"I'm not sure when or how the sales will go through. I only communicated with the buyers through Li."

"Did you know *they* were CCP?"

He suddenly evinced an avid interest in the view of the Gulf. He shaded his eyes. "Is that a pelican? *Hmm…*"

Someone pounded on the door. "FBI. Open up!"

Vogel whirled around. "What the hell do *they* want?" He tried to sound annoyed, but the tense intake of breath gave him away. "I'll just wait in your bedroom while you deal with them, okay?" He limped down the hall.

She let him go and opened the door.

"Ms. Lind? Ms. Palmer Lind?"

"Yes."

"FBI, ma'am. I'm Agent Crake and this is Agent Siskin." They displayed their badges. "We're looking for Wilfred Vogel."

She gestured at the bedroom door. "He's in there."

Agent Crake gave her a wary look. "Thanks." He called, "Mr. Vogel, would you please come out?"

Wilfred opened the door a crack. "Oh… Sorry! I didn't know Palmer had visitors." He shuffled out to the hall, his smile a thin line. "What can I do for you gentlemen?"

"Will you come with us?"

He held up his crutch. "As you can see, I'm recuperating from a gunshot wound. My…er…former colleague, Li Bai, shot me while I was attempting to defend my friends."

Palmer grunted. "Really, Wilfred?"

He ignored her. "Yes, and I also want to congratulate you fellows on the collar. Quick work."

Agent Crake stood stolidly through Vogel's speech. "Yes, sir. Thank you, sir. Now, will you come with us, please?"

"On what charge?"

"Acting as an unregistered foreign agent."

"Excuse me? What are you talking about?" Vogel's glance darted from Crake to Siskin to Palmer.

"We have received confidential information that you have been representing the Chinese company Greenbelt Group, which is affiliated with the Chinese Communist Party. As such, you are required to inform the Justice Department. You did not do so."

"Who told you that?"

"I am not at liberty to tell you more than it was a whistleblower in your employ."

"Tipsy." Wilfred spat the name out.

Palmer was stunned at the venom infusing Vogel's tone. *Tipsy Swallow was a whistleblower. So that's why Vogel fired him!*

When neither agent responded, Vogel made a valiant effort to rein in his temper. "All right, I'm happy to make amends. Who do I contact to obtain the proper forms?"

"Unfortunately, sir, you have exceeded the grace period for retroactive registration by...let's just say, a *lot*. Our evidence indicates that you knowingly and willfully violated the act, and therefore the Department of Justice is considering filing criminal charges."

" 'Knowingly'? Oh my heavens, no! I had no idea I was supposed to inform anyone. This is purely a misunderstanding. Let me get in touch with my staff, and we'll straighten this out in no time."

Siskin leveled a somber gaze at the little man. "Sir, we have reason to believe you were acting as an individual when you dealt with Greenbelt. That makes you—not your corporation—liable. However, at this time we would simply like to interview you. We are not arresting you...yet. I repeat, will you please come with us?"

Palmer half expected that Vogel would try to make a break for it, which under the circumstances would be a short flight.

As he hobbled toward the door, it opened, revealing Carson and behind him Detective Thrasher and Sergeant Jaeger. Carson took in the little group. "Leaving so soon?"

Chapter Thirty-Four

Mary Mary quite contrary,
How does your garden grow?
With silver bells and cockle shells
And pretty maids all in a row

The Palapa Inn, Tuesday, June 13

Agent Crake nodded to Thrasher. "We'll be taking Mr. Vogel along now."

"Better you than me." Thrasher made a little bow and stepped aside. The three men went down the stairs. Palmer watched a dark sedan leave the parking lot, then turned to the newcomers. "And to what do I owe the pleasure of your company?"

Thrasher spoke. "We weren't sure the G-men would arrive in time, so we hot-footed it over here to catch Vogel before he beat a discreet retreat."

"Wilfred wasn't going anywhere—fast, at least."

Carson grinned. "Especially without the limousine and chauffeur at his disposal."

She tried to keep the resignation out of her voice. "You might as well come in." The two men trailed her to the living room. "Wilfred says he didn't know he was doing anything illegal."

"Oh yeah? A high-flying financial guy like that not cognizant of the laws pertaining to foreign agents, not to mention working with the CCP?"

"Well, all he was doing was buying land around cities to build affordable housing."

"Is that what he told you?" The captain looked askance.

Do I go into all the other versions? No. "Yes. Why?"

"The Chinese plan—through this Greenbelt group—was to buy up as much land as they could in the United States, and then take it out of production entirely. No building, no farming, just empty wastes. We have some evidence they considered literally poisoning the soil. Like the Soviets with Ukraine, their aim was to starve us into submission."

Where have I heard this before? Oh right, the American investors Hardy talked about. He didn't name Vogel specifically. She eyed Thrasher. *Did he tell Hardy about the Chinese connection?*

Carson continued. "That's why Senator Wren introduced S. 219. He had discovered what the Chinese were up to—and what Vogel was embroiled in. The law would prohibit them from acquiring any US land."

Palmer added, "And also why he was writing the second bill, the one that would keep farmland as farmland."

"Right." Carson said slowly, "Joanna played right into their hands. She wanted to take the land out of production as well."

"But at least, in her script, it wouldn't have been poisoned."

Carson walked over to the glass door and stared out at the Gulf. "When I told her the briefcase contained materials on a different bill, she reacted oddly. She must have thought I meant the farmland bill. Here I was trying to put her off the scent, and instead gave her even more incentive to get hold of the case." He snapped his fingers. "I bet Vogel cozied up to her to help him schmooze—or is it bamboozle?—Senator Wren."

"He lied to her too." Thrasher was grim. "He lied to everyone. Let's hope the feds lock him up for a long time."

Even though Palmer disliked Vogel, it was difficult to accept that he would betray his country. "Do we have any proof that he was aware of Greenbelt's secret mission?"

"Not yet."

Carson came back and sat down on the sofa. "It's possible Atticus told him the night he died."

Palmer caught her breath. "Wilfred admitted he and Li Bai were with the senator that night."

"At his house in Maryland, not at my apartment."

"That was the same night the senator gave you his briefcase for safekeeping. He must have wanted to conceal the papers from Vogel."

"You're making an assumption there, Palmer. He didn't tell me *why* he wanted me to hide the case—or from whom." Carson slapped his thigh. "The note."

"Note?"

"The note in Mandarin. That must be what tipped Atticus off that the Chinese were involved. Maybe he planned to warn Vogel about Greenbelt before it went too far."

"And if Vogel didn't agree to pull out of the deal, Atticus threatened to take the evidence to the police?"

Thrasher dropped down on the easy chair. "If Vogel felt he was compromised, and needed to silence

Wren, that's a motive for murder."

Carson seemed inclined to agree. "Wilfred suspected that Joanna overheard him talking with Wren. That made her a liability as well."

Palmer hated hearing her recent thoughts echoed. *Could Wilfred Vogel be responsible for the murders?* Palmer coughed. "Are we now blaming Wilfred Vogel for the deaths of both Wrens?"

"No." Thrasher shook his head. "He only grazed Mrs. Wren. The medical examiner said the first blow went off to the side, just as Vogel described."

"That's still attempted murder."

"Unless his self-defense plea holds up."

Carson was thoughtful. "It took a second shot—through the stomach—to do the trick. I'm betting Li Bai was there with Wilfred and dealt the death blow."

"And Wilfred took the fall, assuming he'd get off under Florida's stand-your-ground law." She appealed to the policeman.

"And Li Bai wouldn't, because he's not an American citizen?" Thrasher wrinkled his nose. "It's kind of a gray area, law-wise."

"Well, Vogel's no lawyer." Carson stood up. The others followed suit. "Come to think of it, the only person who wasn't killed by a crossbow was…Atticus Wren."

Thrasher gawked at him. "You think he actually *did* commit suicide?"

"No. Look, Detective, could you have the DC police search Joanna Wren's house?"

"DC police? Wasn't she killed in Tampa?"

"Yes, but there might be proof of my theory in her home. It's in Chevy Chase." He ripped a sheet of paper from the pad on Palmer's kitchen counter and jotted something down. "Here's her address."

Thrasher took the paper. "This is in Maryland."

"Yes, Chevy Chase is a suburb of the District of Columbia."

"Then this has to go to the Maryland state police." He looked up at Carson. "To get a warrant, they'll need probable cause."

"I have a strong suspicion you'll find proof there that Joanna Wren murdered her husband."

****

Longboat Key police station, Wednesday afternoon

"Congratulations, Hawk. That was a lucky guess."

Carson and Palmer sat in Thrasher's office. Carson brightened. "The Maryland cops found something?"

"Uh-huh. The Florida state police hadn't expanded the investigation beyond Tampa yet, but their plan had been to coordinate with Illinois next. They wouldn't have gotten to the Maryland house for a while."

"What did they find?"

"It doesn't get any better than this. A written confession."

"From Joanna?"

"Yes. She was definitely unhinged. On the slippery slope to total lunacy. The letter was six pages long, full of rambling rants about *Homo sapiens* and Gaia and stuff like that." He paused and wiped his forehead. "She really hated humans."

Carson nodded. "That's why I asked you to check her house. People with that kind of derangement usually feel compelled to make a statement. Did she admit to killing her husband?"

"Yup. She says—in upwards of twelve hundred

words—that she overheard him, Li Bai, and Vogel discussing the bill. She went to Hawk's apartment to have it out with Wren. When she got there he was alone. They had an argument. She pulled the scarf from her neck and strangled him."

"That must have taken some strength." Palmer had trouble believing the oh-so-chic lady who only drank Chivas Regal was capable of anything more physical than a gentle slap across the cheek.

Carson disagreed. "Atticus had been drinking—a lot, I think. He was not in any shape to fend off an assault—especially one from his wife."

Thrasher went back to his notes. "She says she then took his belt and some twine and hanged him from the chandelier. She set a chair on its side under him so it looked as though he'd kicked it over."

"No penitence? No expression of guilt?"

"Zero. She even continued to scribble for a few more pages, raving about how justice had been served and the earth would now have a chance to heal. She extolled that group you mentioned, Palmer. They're called"—he ran a finger down the page—"Enders. I looked them up. Super-radical enviros—you know, nature is better off without us revolting hoomans. She said she'd contacted them with the good news."

"Of Wren's death?"

"Yeah." He stared directly at Carson. "She also wrote she overheard Vogel say Tipsy had betrayed him."

Palmer interrupted. "It's true. Vogel believes Tipsy sold him out."

"Tipsy? A rat?" Carson gaped at her.

"Uh-huh. I forgot to tell you. When the FBI agents

arrested Wilfred, they told him they'd received inside information that he hadn't registered as a foreign agent. He was furious. He uttered one word. 'Tipsy.' "

Carson turned to Thrasher. "Vogel told us he'd sent Li Bai after Swallow. We can infer he ordered Li Bai to kill him."

Palmer demurred. "He did claim that Li Bai had gone rogue."

Carson wasn't having it. "Li Bai was technically under Wilfred's supervision."

She held up a palm. "In that case, how come Li Bai shot Wilfred? No, even if Vogel ordered him to kill Tipsy, there's no reason to think he would do it."

The room fell silent. Finally, Carson sighed, "So we have no clear suspect for Swallow's murder?"

Thrasher clipped his words. "The only one with a halfway solid motive would be Vogel, but he was in DC when the murder took place."

"Do we have proof?"

"An airplane manifest listing him as a passenger on American flight 9210 from San Francisco to Dulles May 11, plus a bill from the Hotel Washington for four nights from May 11 to May 15. Swallow was last seen May 12."

"Damn."

Thrasher turned a page. "By the way, the Maryland guys went through Mrs. Wren's computer. In a file marked Atticus/60 there was an eBay invoice from a guy named—ready? Slugger McWhip." He read aloud. "Sold to Ms. Joanna Wren, April 10: one Barnett Whitetail Hunter crossbow, a three-pack of Barnett HyperFlite bolts, a set of strobe-lighted nocks, and something called a rope cocking device."

"The crossbow she was killed with?"

"Yup. So"—Thrasher busied himself with a paperweight—"you're reprieved, at least for the second bow."

Palmer decided to go easy on him. "I wonder what she planned to do with it?"

"That's the question of the day."

Carson cracked his knuckles. "It begins to look as though the first two deaths—Swallow's and Wren's—were unrelated."

"Joanna flew into an uncontrolled rage and killed her husband. It wasn't planned."

"A crime of passion?"

"If you can call insanity passion."

"Amen." Carson rubbed his fingers and winced. "Remind me to stop cracking my knuckles."

"Stop cracking your knuckles." Thrasher thrummed his pen on the desk.

Palmer stirred. "If there's no suspect for Swallow, there's no suspect for Raven either."

"Why do you say that?"

"Li Bai was supposed to have dispatched both. If he didn't kill Tipsy, but he killed Raven, how did they both end up dead by the same crossbow?"

****

Carson's house, Thursday evening

"I suppose you want to hear of my adventures."

"Oh, Hardy, are you up to it?"

Hardy touched his arm and flinched. "I'm okay. Li Bai only shoved me around a little. He left some bruises, but nothing broken."

Palmer fussed over him for another minute, then uncapped the bottle of beer in her hand and took a swig.

"Ah, that's good stuff."

They were sitting in Carson's backyard. Carson stood as usual at the grill. "How do you like your burger, Hardy?"

"Impossible."

"I beg your pardon?"

"My little joke." He held up a box. "Impossible burger—plant-based protein. Didn't Palmer tell you?"

Palmer put the beer down. "I'm so sorry, Hardy. I forgot to mention you're a vegetarian."

"Actually, I'm vegan."

She blinked. "Really? Since when? You had ice cream at Galatoire's."

"True. I finally went full-bore a fortnight ago, but it's been coming on for a while." He grinned at Palmer. "Maybe it was those snails at the Celery Fields that did the trick. Plus, it breaks my heart to see those poor little fetal chickens turned into omelets." Palmer could have sworn a tear came to his eye. "And how anyone could drink milk after watching a farmer torturing cows is beyond me."

Before Palmer could say something infelicitous, Carson jumped in. "Funny, you don't look like E.T."

Hardy flushed. "I have every right—I can do what I—You can't insult me like that. I'm the one who wants to save this planet. You people are the ones who—"

Carson held up a hand. "Relax, Hardy. I was joking. Vegan, as in an alien from the planet Vega Prime."

"Oh. Huh. Ha-ha." He handed Carson the box. "Anyway, I was fairly confident you wouldn't have anything on hand, so I brought my own. It's soy."

Carson unwrapped a grayish-brown square that

resembled a roof shingle. "Can I grill it?"

"Sure." He watched as Carson dropped the patty on the grate. "Um...If you don't mind, could you keep it over there, separate from the meat?"

Carson held the long spoon up—perhaps tempted to spread the patty with beef fat?—but merely said, "Not a problem. Palmer? I'm making you a Black Angus burger." After a glance at Hardy's face, he added, "Premium chuck, brisket, and short rib. You want blue cheese on it?"

"Slather it on."

"Got it. Oh, say, could you pop behind the garage to the garden? Pick some parsley and chives—maybe a handful of pea shoots—for the salad."

She got up. "Do you have a pair of scissors I can use?"

"Here you go. You'd better take these too." He handed her earphones.

She took them, puzzled. "What for?"

His mouth twitched. "So you don't have to hear the wails of the little plants when you rip them from Mother Earth."

Palmer heard a gasp from Hardy, and, with her own face strictly under control, replied, "I won't behead them. I'll just snip off the arms...I mean, the leaves."

When she reached the garage, she turned to glimpse Hardy gazing into his glass, his face ashen.

When the food was ready and Carson had passed the salad around, Palmer looked at Hardy. "Okay, let's hear it. What happened with Li Bai?"

He put down his burger, a slight frown on his face. "First off, I don't know why the man took me with him in the first place."

"Didn't he want you as a hostage?"

"I suppose...but he didn't act like it. In fact, he didn't say a word to me until we got in the taxi."

"Why didn't you scream or tell the desk clerk he was holding you against your will?"

"There wasn't anyone around. Even if I'd seen someone I wouldn't have dared. You didn't see the expression on his face." He shivered. "That man is a cold-blooded killer. He kept the gun in my ribs the whole time. I've no doubt he would have shot me right there if I so much as peeped."

Carson took a bite of hamburger and wiped barbecue sauce off his chin. "Wilfred Vogel says Li Bai is a businessman from Hong Kong, but you identified him as a spy the minute you walked into the hotel room. Before he'd said a word."

Hardy gulped down his wine. "I get bulletins from the FBI all the time as part of my job. One came across my desk—I guess it was last week—with a photo of a Chinese agent. It looked so much like Li Bai that I just blurted it out." He shook his head in embarrassment. "I felt kind of silly once Vogel introduced him."

Palmer swirled a potato chip in the juices on her plate and licked them off. "So where did he take you?"

"The taxi driver went out Fruitville Road to the junction with Route 75, where he dropped us at a gas station. Li Bai let me use the john. When I came out, he was gone."

Chapter Thirty-Five

Tweedledum and Tweedledee
Agreed to have a battle.
For Tweedledum said Tweedledee
Had spoiled his nice new rattle.
Just then flew down a monstrous crow,
As black as a tar-barrel,
Which frightened both the heroes so,
They quite forgot their quarrel!

Carson's house, Thursday, June 15

"Gone!" Palmer dropped the potato chip. "Li Bai just dumped you at the gas station?"

"Yes. The cashier said a trucker picked him up. They took the ramp onto the interstate."

Carson asked, "How did you get home?"

"I had my phone, so I called another taxi. I picked up my car at your place, Palmer, then drove to the hospital."

It occurred to Palmer that she hadn't even noticed it was gone.

Hardy said diffidently, "I tapped on your door, but there wasn't any answer."

Carson stopped, a forkful of salad halfway to his mouth. "Wait a minute. You used your *cell* phone? Didn't you surrender it along with ours in the hotel?"

"No, it was in my back pocket."

"You'd think he'd have confiscated it when he grabbed you."

Hardy stabbed a slice of tomato with his fork and chewed it slowly before gulping it down. "Oh, he did. He took the phone and my wallet on the way down in the elevator, but I guess it didn't matter once he'd secured a means of escape."

"The truck."

"Yes. I found them on the asphalt next to the bathroom door."

"Huh. Well, I guess you got lucky. Current theory is he killed both Tipsy Swallow and your daughter."

"I know." Hardy seemed more resigned than sad. "Li Bai told me everything while we were in the taxi. He said he thought Raven was you, Carson. He was searching the garage for the briefcase, and she interrupted him. It was pitch black in there, but he shot her anyway."

Palmer laid a hand on his. "I'm so sorry, Hardy."

He shook her off and slammed a fist on the table. "If only she hadn't been so fascinated by go-karts. If only—" He stopped. The menacing look he gave Carson only lasted a second. "Well, er…" He looked at his watch. "I'd best be going. I've imposed long enough on you two." He began to rise.

"Wait!" Palmer gestured at him to sit. "We haven't finished giving you the latest. Vogel was detained by the FBI."

He sat back down. "Really? Why?"

"He was acting as an unregistered foreign agent. Facilitating Chinese acquisition of American land."

"Is that against the law?"

Carson answered. "He's supposed to register with the government if he represents a foreign entity here in the US. He claims he wasn't aware of the requirement."

"Huh." Hardy absorbed the news. "So is he in jail?"

"No—they said they only wanted to interview him for now, but he could be arrested at any moment."

Carson added, "If they believe he was merely a dupe of the Chinese he may get off with a light sentence."

"Ah."

"Especially if he can shed light on any other participants."

Hardy stopped with the glass halfway to his lips. " 'Participants'?"

"There have to be other operatives working with him. Vogel may be able to identify them."

"*Hmm*. They're probably a dangerous lot. I hope he's under police protection."

"That I don't know."

"Well, again, thanks for dinner." Hardy got up quickly. Palmer saw him out.

When she returned, she found Carson staring at his empty plate. "Still hungry?"

"What? No. I was just thinking."

"I'm glad. Beef up that tiny brain with some exercise."

"Right." Carson was distracted. "Hardy's story. A couple of things didn't quite square."

"What things?"

"First of all, motive. Why would Li Bai take him?"

"That's easy—he needed a hostage and Hardy was the last one standing."

"All right, but why would he let him go?"

Palmer shrugged. "He must have decided he was no longer useful."

Carson paid her no attention. He muttered, "And why would Li Bai open up to his prisoner? Especially—and this is the part I have the most trouble with—in a public place like a taxi?"

Palmer's stomach lurched. "Good questions. Now you say it out loud, it does seem strange."

"Let's stipulate Li Bai isn't stupid. He must have had a reason to abduct Hardy."

"Hardy said he didn't utter a word until they were in the taxi."

"And then he took responsibility for the murders."

"There's something else." Carson turned a troubled face to Palmer. "Hardy called Li Bai a Chinese spy."

"But then Wilfred set him straight. Where are you going with this?"

"Could Hardy have been right after all?"

****

Anna Maria Public Library, Friday afternoon

Palmer clicked Talk and whispered, "Who is it?"

"Did you find an answer?"

"Carson? *Shh.* I'm in the library. Let me go outside, and I'll call you back." When she reached the sidewalk, she dialed his number.

"Who is it?"

"You know damned well who it is."

"Ah. So?"

"I've drawn a total blank. There is nothing online about a Li Bai who is even *suspected* of being a spy."

"Huh. Perhaps I was wrong." To drown out Palmer's spontaneous applause, he said loudly, "Hardy said something about FBI reports—what do you suppose he meant by that?"

"Well, being a private investigator, I'm guessing he has access to information that's not in the public domain."

"He's a *what*?"

"Weren't you there when I told Vogel? Oh wait, you were out getting toilet paper. Senator Wren hired him to watch Joanna."

"Oh? Atticus never mentioned it, and he usually confided in me." He paused. "He must have done it on his own dime, or his campaign treasurer would have raised a stink. Was it to track her affair with Vogel?"

"No, he was spooked about her affiliation with the Enders."

"Enders?"

"You know—End Human Hegemony Now."

"Oh, right. Thrasher talked about them. *Hmm.* Could there be a connection between Li Bai and the tree huggers?"

"The Chinese aren't exactly noted for caring about the environment."

"Perhaps, but if Li and these Enders were cooperating, and Hardy had uncovered it during his investigations—"

"That could be the reason Li Bai snatched Hardy."

"Uh-huh. I still think there's something fishy in that whole confession thing. Li Bai didn't strike me as the type to squeal. He must have had some ulterior motive."

"Like what?"

"To send someone a message? He would expect Hardy to report their conversation to the cops." Carson made a rustling sound. "I think I'll go see if Thrasher has any ideas."

"You go ahead. Since I'm up here on Anna Maria, I'm going to drive up to Bean Point. I hear least terns are nesting there."

"I'll meet you at my place for dinner. George dropped off a pair of snook he caught yesterday."

"It's a date."

****

Carson's house, Friday, midnight

"What was that?"

"Would you kindly stop bouncing on the bed? I'm getting seasick."

"*Shh*." Carson sat straight up. "Someone is in the house." He reached an arm out toward the lamp. Palmer held her breath. She heard a footfall, then the door knob scraping as someone turned it. Just as it swung open, Carson clicked the light on.

Hardy stood blinking in the sudden illumination. Before he could move, Carson leapt out of bed and caught the arm that was holding a revolver. Hardy shook him off and kicked him hard in the groin. Carson collapsed.

Palmer held the blanket up over her breasts. "What do you want, Hardy?"

He didn't say a word but bent down and zip-tied Carson's wrists together. As Carson struggled to rise, grimacing in pain, Hardy smashed the butt of the gun against his temple. He went down in a heap.

"Hardy? *What the hell are you doing?*"

"I shouldn't have to tell you. If he hasn't already, Hawk will soon figure out who I am. It was only a matter of time before he took it to the police."

Thank God, he doesn't know Carson saw Thrasher this afternoon. Palmer wished now that she'd made him tell her what happened, but after dinner they'd been engaged in other, more entertaining, activities. "What do you mean, who you are?"

Hardy ignored her. "Li Bai was convinced I'd blown it. Fool. That's why we parted ways. I knew I couldn't trust him. Just a pawn. No real ideals."

"Ideals?" *A spy with ideals?* "What are you talking about?"

Hardy didn't seem to hear her but continued to talk to himself. "Sure, they were willing to buy the land for us. We shared the mutual goal of bringing America to its knees. *But*—and I warned Joanna over and over of this—would they keep their promise and transfer ownership to us?" He spit on the floor. "Fat chance. The Chinese are just as bad as Americans. They would have exploited that untouched, pristine soil, raped it with genetically modified seed, poured pesticides and toxic fertilizers into it..." He shook his head sadly. "I told Joanna not to trust him. But no..."

*Joanna? Had he heard about the letter? Were they...*Hmm. Keeping an eye on Carson—who was still out cold—Palmer slowly drew her robe up over her shoulders. "So...let me see if I have this straight. You and Joanna hatched a plan to secretly acquire US land—through a Chinese straw buyer—with the goal of leaving it fallow and unproductive."

He stared at her. " 'Unproductive'? *Nature* isn't unproductive. We'd allow the land to revert to its original condition, where native plants and insects and animals can thrive without the interfering hand of man. It will become what it once was: a truly symbiotic system."

"But without farms there would be famine. People will die!"

"Yes," he said with satisfaction. "Precisely."

Aha. "You're an Ender."

"Smart girl. Smarter than Joanna. Boy, did she leap off the proverbial cliff. She almost blew the entire operation."

"You were working with Li Bai?"

He nodded.

Palmer regarded him. "That didn't pan out, though, did it? Senator Wren picked up on what was going on. He wrote S. 219 to put severe restrictions on the sale of land. The Chinese would have been prevented from acquiring US property."

"Yeah, but that didn't stop us for long. We found Vogel. He was…*said* he was…willing to act as a front man."

Palmer's chest constricted. *Oh my God, they were all in the plot!* "So you were already acquainted with Li Bai and Wilfred when we walked in on them at the Zota. Why did Vogel pretend he hadn't met you?"

"He wasn't pretending. Vogel had never seen me. All our communications were via text on a burner phone."

"But when I introduced you?"

"The name Hardy Bantam meant nothing to him." His eyes twinkled with some secret joke.

"So how did you blow it?"

"I didn't. It was Joanna who set the whole cascade of disasters in motion."

"What did she do?"

"She lost it when hubby said he was going to

344

introduce both S. 219 and the other bill over her objections. Tried to kill him, then covered it up in the most incompetent manner possible."

"Wait. Did you say she *tried* to kill him?"

"You heard me." His voice dripped contempt. "She was damned lucky I was following her. When I got to Hawk's apartment, Wren was unconscious, with her ridiculous scarf wrapped around his neck. Like *that* would have done the trick. She was dithering about calling the police and turning herself in. I didn't know how long Hawk would be gone and couldn't risk him walking in and catching us. So I took care of it."

Chapter Thirty-Six

Little Boy Blue come blow your horn,
The sheep's in the meadow, the cow's in the corn.
But where's the boy who looks after the sheep?
He's under a haystack, fast asleep.
Will you wake him?
No, not I—for if I do, he's sure to cry.

Carson's house, Friday, June 16

Palmer had a sick feeling in the pit of her stomach. "You took care of it?"

Hardy spoke languidly, as though detached from the horror of his words. "Finished the job, then set it up to look like a suicide. Everything was fine until Joanna had this *crise de nerfs* and called Vogel. He tells her Wren stole his briefcase, which contained all kinds of dodgy material. He thought Wren was going to present it to the committee as proof that Vogel was a conduit between us and the Chinese. So we ransacked the apartment, but no briefcase."

"You're saying the briefcase wasn't Wren's? It belonged to *Vogel*? Huh. As I recall, there wasn't anything in it that appeared to be what you'd call dodgy."

He moved restlessly. "We didn't know that then." He prodded Carson with the toe of his shoe. "Must've hit him harder than I thought."

Palmer decided to take a different tack. "Did you kill Joanna too?"

"Had to. Loose cannon."

"But you were still in Illinois when she died. How did you manage it?"

He sniffed. "Really? You believed me? I was on a plane to Tampa the morning you left. I was at the airport hotel by one. She was dead by two." He looked inordinately proud of himself.

"How'd you do it?"

"Killed her with her own crossbow. Hoist by her own petard, as it were. The idiot brought it with her to Tampa—along with the briefcase." He chuckled. "She bought it on eBay—amazing, right? The pols are running around bawling about gun control. Meanwhile, a four-year-old can buy a bow that can take down a giant buck using Mommy's credit card without any ID at all."

Maybe he can solve one little mystery. "What did she bring it for?"

"She planned to threaten Vogel with it. I guess her way of reigniting the passion was to wave a lethal weapon in his face."

"She told you that?" *Wilfred was right: she was nuts.*

"Uh-huh. I had arrived a few minutes earlier. She was whining about her troubles when Vogel knocked. I hid in the bedroom. They proceeded to have this terrific row. I couldn't tell what it was about, but she was cursing about traitors and he kept gibbering about some affair. I opened the door a crack and saw her fly at him. He ripped the bow from her and shot wildly. It's astounding he hit her at all."

"What did he do then?"

"Hot-footed it out of there. Must've thought he'd killed her, but the arrow had passed right through that liposuctioned belly of hers. She lay there like a cartoon character with the blood spurting out of her side." He blinked. "You'd think she'd be yammering her head off, but she was dead quiet. Maybe she was in shock. I dunno." He shook his head. "Anyway, I was going to help her up, but then I thought, 'Do we really need her? I mean, she's the ultimate poster child for a ticking time bomb.' "

Palmer remembered Joanna's letter. *He doesn't know how right he is.*

"So I offed her." He flexed his fingers. "Man, those crossbows are a bitch to cock."

Steady, Palmer. Steady. "What about fingerprints? Yours would be on the bow too."

"Nope. I always carry a pair of gloves. Comes in handy when you're slashing the tires on a timber truck or sabotaging a coal mine." He shook his head regretfully. "If only I hadn't taken one off to… Well, it's water under the bridge." He trailed off.

"So you were the one who dealt the death blow. How did you get away?" Palmer couldn't believe it—he seemed willing to let all the cats out of the bag. *Hopefully he'll keep yapping until Carson wakes up.*

He grinned. "My timing was—as usual—perfect. When Vogel lurched out of the room, the maid was in the hall. He was a mess after the skirmish with Joanna, so she promptly started screeching bloody murder. I slipped out during the commotion." He smiled reminiscently. "The look on Joanna's face when I pointed the thing at her was priceless. It was even funnier when Vogel waltzed into the police station with that cockamamie canard about self-defense. Hilarious!"

"Why did you let Wilfred take the blame?"

"Because he lied to us. He went behind my—our— backs and made a secret deal with the Chinese." Hardy waved the revolver around. "Fucking capitalist wanted to corner the market on the land around the cities and then sell it back to the state for a bundle."

"So you had to regroup?"

Hardy nodded. "Li Bai had no qualms about cutting Vogel out, but he insisted we come up with another way to acquire the land. We were working on it when the effing Chinos got cold feet and recalled Li Bai." He scowled. "We were left high and dry. Had to go back to the drawing board."

Did Carson just move? She said quickly, "If Li Bai was recalled, why did he kidnap you?"

"He didn't. I arranged his escape."

"Escape! Why?"

"Had to get him out of the country before he compromised us. If the feds caught him, they might trace the scheme back to the Enders." He scratched his nose with the barrel of the gun. "It came to me as we walked in. Li Bai didn't know who I was—"

"Let me guess: you'd only communicated by text?"

"Right. So I spoke to him in Mandarin. Identified myself and whispered the plan to him."

"Mandarin!" She thought of the note in the briefcase. "You speak Chinese?" When he didn't answer, she asked, "What do you plan to do now?"

"You mean after I kill Carson? *Hmm.* Maybe I'll head to Arizona to look for hummingbirds." He laughed mirthlessly, then abruptly stopped. "You could come with me, you know." His cold eyes softened. "We'd make a good team, Palmer. Now Raven's gone, it's been...lonely." He put out a hand as if to caress her cheek, but at her expression he dropped it. "We could be happy living off the land, just the two of us."

She gazed at him. She wasn't really scared any more. It all seemed quite dreamlike. "Are you really a birder?"

"Absolutely. Although I'm not really a PI. I made that up. Sorry."

Palmer felt dizzy. Clutching at a shred of hope that Hardy wasn't a complete monster, she brought up his daughter. "You must have been furious that Li Bai killed Raven."

A spasm crossed his face. "He was just supposed to get the briefcase. What a buffoon. Couldn't believe it. This is what I get for hooking up with foreigners. Their heart isn't in the mission." He spread his hands. "Have you ever seen a lithium mine? One of the biggest in the world is in China. It's a goddamn open pit mine! I bet if they could, they'd try the same thing here. They need to be annihilated! All of them!" His voice spiraled up to a shriek.

Carson's eyelids fluttered. From the corner of her eye Palmer saw his leg move slightly. *How long has he been awake?* She prayed he'd heard most of Hardy's rant. She said loudly, "She was your daughter though, and you loved her, right?"

"Loved? I dunno about that. She was only my step-daughter, you know. Her mother left us when Raven was ten. Last I heard, Karen was a pole dancer in Reno."

"But surely her grandmother was upset!"

"Grandmother? She didn't have a grandmother—at least not that I ever met."

"Then who was the old lady at her funeral?"

Hardy looked blank for a minute. "Oh, you mean Ursula. She's my cleaning lady. I roped her into accompanying me." He beamed. "I put on quite a show, didn't I?"

Palmer's mouth opened and shut. *There's really nothing to say.*

Hardy was still droning on. "Besides, Raven wasn't ever going to be a good candidate for the Enders. No matter how many clear-cut forests and gutted whales I showed her, or the articles about the coming apocalypse I made her read, she only cared about her friends and her hobbies." He added glumly, "I'd have had to do something about her eventually anyway. I—" He stopped when Palmer gasped.

He must have misinterpreted her expression. "It wasn't just the go-kart thing. Do you know how much exhaust they spew out? No, she also wouldn't touch vegetables—only meat." His nose wrinkled. "Ghoulish, if you ask me. Get this: she wanted to be a butcher! She claimed it required real artistry. Can you believe it? Gawd."

Palmer was about to defend the child when she felt Carson's finger poke her. *Maybe I should humor him.* "Disgusting. I don't know how you put up with her."

He smirked. "I don't have to anymore, do I?"

Suddenly, Carson's leg swept out and hit Hardy's ankle, nearly toppling him. He quickly righted himself and backed a safe distance away. "Okay, that's my signal to get this over with." He aimed the revolver at

351

Carson's chest.

The door swung open behind him, knocking Hardy forward. He tripped over the prostrate form of Carson. The gun went flying, and he landed face first on the bed. Palmer looked from him to the door, where Thrasher stood, both arms raised, holding a service pistol stiffly in front of him. He said over his shoulder, "Ollie? Get the gun. Hardy Bantam, you're under arrest. The sergeant will read you your rights."

Chapter Thirty-Seven

For every evil under the sun
There is a remedy or there is none.
If there be one, seek till you find it;
If there be none, never mind it.

Longboat Key police station, Saturday, June 17

"It's sort of like a nursery rhyme, isn't it?" Carson paced the lobby while Palmer sipped coffee from a waxed cup.

"Little Miss Muffet sat on a tuffet?"

"No."

"Itsy bitsy spider?"

"You have a thing for spiders?"

"All right then, which rhyme?"

He stopped. "My choice? 'Who Killed Cock Robin.' 'I,' said the sparrow. / 'With my bow and arrow / I killed Cock Robin.' "

"Whatever." Palmer was pensive. "It's funny."

"My poem?"

"No. Every character in our play at one time attempted unsuccessfully to kill someone. Joanna failed to kill Wren; Vogel failed to kill Joanna—"

"And let us not forget that Hardy tried to kill *us*. I can't believe he spewed everything to you."

"You're just miffed because you missed it."

"True. Although I did get a much-needed forty winks while he droned on about mundane things like planned mass starvation and wholesale murder."

"You were out when he admitted he killed Joanna, weren't you?"

"Yes." Carson counted on his fingers. "That's twice Hardy stepped in to save the day."

Just then the door to Thrasher's office opened, and the detective beckoned them. "Glad you could stay. Did the nurse fix you up, Hawk?"

Carson touched his head gingerly. "She gave me some aspirin."

"Good." Thrasher didn't seem overly distressed.

Palmer said indignantly, "He could have been killed, you know."

"Yeah, sorry about that. We got there as quick as we could."

Palmer looked from Carson to the policeman. "By the way, how did you know to come to his house?"

Thrasher grinned. "Our little confab yesterday afternoon. We were actually worried that Bantam might be in danger."

"From whom?"

"Chinese operatives, allies of Li Bai tasked with eliminating him."

"But Li Bai is incarcerated. How could he communicate with them?"

"Hawk here posited that Li Bai took Hardy, presuming the police all-points bulletin would be picked up by his cronies. Li released him to allow them to deal with him anonymously. So I set a tail on Bantam."

"For his protection."

"Yes, and are we glad we did. Ollie followed him to the end of Hawk's street. When he saw Bantam step out of his car with a gun, he called it in."

Palmer turned accusing eyes to Carson. "And you didn't see fit to tell me any of this?"

Thrasher hastily intervened. "We had no reason to think Bantam would attack you—we were concerned for his safety. Anyway, he's squared away in a holding cell for now. I'm sure the G-men will want him." He sat down at his desk and picked up a pencil. "Now, do you have anything else for me?"

"We were just recapping the gory details."

Carson spoke first. "It all started with Atticus Wren stealing Vogel's briefcase."

"Wait. The briefcase belongs to Wilfred *Vogel*?"

Palmer answered. "Uh-huh. We believe the senator intended to take it to the committee as proof of Vogel's...improprieties."

"Huh. Well, well. Interesting that Mr. Vogel didn't alert us to that fact." Thrasher tapped his pencil on the desk.

"Actually, it was even earlier than that," Palmer said thoughtfully. "It began when Joanna hooked up with the Enders."

Carson said with relish, "And when, in the throes of passion, Wilfred whispered lasciviously into the dainty Joanna's ear that he was going to buy up land around major cities—"

"She took the information to her newfound friends, who came up with the splendid idea of returning the lion cub—aka the land—back to a state of nature."

Thrasher's pencil tapped even harder. "Did Mrs. Wren tell Vogel about the Enders?"

"Yes." Carson went to the window and looked out. Over his shoulder, Palmer could see a gaggle of ibis snacking on worms. "They brought him in as backup in case S. 219 went through and they couldn't deal with the Chinese directly. But Wilfred went behind their back and made his own pact with Li Bai." He sniffed. "I agree with Palmer. I choose to believe that Wil had no knowledge of the Greenbelt Group's true objective."

"Which was?"

"To salt the earth in order to reduce the US food supply."

Palmer added, "The plan being, in our weakened state, they could march in and take over."

Carson nodded sagely. "None of the players knew what the other players had in mind."

Thrasher grunted. "It didn't stop them from trying to kill each other." He cocked his head. "How did you learn all this?"

"Hardy told me. He's an Ender. I got the impression he's pretty high up in the order."

The detective stared, slack-jawed at Palmer. "He is? When did you find that out?"

She said calmly, "Last night."

Carson grinned. "Bantam—ostensibly operating under the misguided notion that murder is like catnip to the woman of his dreams—unleashed a flood of revelations on Palmer while I was indisposed."

Thrasher's pencil suddenly broke in half. He tossed the pieces in the wastebasket and dug another one out of his desk drawer. "I assigned one of my detectives to research the group. Their manifesto was penned by the same Fletcher Avery who's mentioned in the note in Mandarin, but it's been damned difficult to find out much more than that. What else did he tell you?"

With a sharp look at Carson, Palmer took over. "A lot. Joanna tried to throttle Atticus Wren with her scarf, but Hardy did the actual work of stringing him up."

The detective ticked a sentence off on his note pad. His voice studiously calm, he said, "Next."

"Let me see..." Palmer tried to assemble the facts in some order in her head. "Hardy sent Li Bai to Carson's house to look for the briefcase. Raven popped up without warning, and he killed her with the crossbow."

Thrasher looked up. "Is that what Bantam told you? Huh."

Something in his voice made Palmer pause. "Come to think of it, he didn't say that in so many words." She looked at the detective. "Do we know where he was the night Raven died?"

Carson interjected, "We all assumed he was home when she snuck out and bicycled over to my place." He turned to the detective. "Did you ask him?"

Thrasher busied himself with some object in his desk drawer. "Um. No."

When it was clear he wasn't going to offer an excuse, Carson picked up a photo from the evidence pile. "We still have the problem of the broken crossbow. Without the bowstave we found near the rented boat, the weapon couldn't have been fired a second time."

"Remind me what the bowstave is?"

"It's the part that's fixed transversely on the stock or barrel. It's made of a flexible material like ash or steel."

Thrasher slapped his forehead. "That may explain

those pieces of wood Forensics found in the go-kart."

"Pieces of wood?"

He nodded. "According to Edward Dunlin—the arms expert—the part that was in the garage was the stock. It matches the bowstave you found. They're both yew, but CSI also recovered some fragments of balsawood." He picked up a second photo and showed it to Carson.

Carson studied it. "Yup. The killer jury-rigged a bowstave."

"And who would know how to do that?"

Palmer prodded Carson. "Those archery lessons. Would the student have learned how to build a crossbow?"

Carson said reluctantly, "The beginner's course goes through the parts of the bow and the mechanics, yes."

"So, besides you—" Thrasher jerked, and she went on quickly. "The jury-rigger is the only one with any expertise in crossbows."

Carson set the photo down. "I suppose anyone could figure out that a cross*bow* needs a cross*piece*. Only an expert would be aware that balsawood is way too flimsy to take the high tension required for stringing the bow."

The detective said casually, his eyes on his pencil, "I suppose now would be a good time to mention that we identified the fourth blood sample from the crossbow in your garage."

"Li Bai's?"

"No. Hardy Bantam's."

"You mean...you mean..." Palmer choked back the sob. "He killed his own *daughter*?"

Carson said gently, "His stepdaughter." He rubbed his lip. "I'll amend my earlier statement. It now appears Hardy killed not two, but three people."

The room was silent, its occupants pondering the evil that humans are capable of committing in the name of ideology. Finally Carson observed, "That explains something that's been niggling at me. Hardy had dinner with us after Li Bai released him. When he was describing his ordeal, he said that Raven was *shot*. The preliminary police report published in the *Longboat Key Planet* said her head was smashed in. It didn't mention the crossbow."

"He could only have known it if he were there."

Palmer sat up. "One more thing. Hardy once told me he always wore gloves, except once."

"Right." Carson nodded his head sharply. "Remember, when he came into the garage and saw Raven in the cart, he went for my throat. I didn't think about it then, but he had a Band-Aid on one finger."

Palmer sniffed. "If Hardy murdered Raven, that means Li Bai—the one professional assassin of the bunch—only killed one person."

"Tipsy."

Carson stood. "We have to find out why."

Captain Thrasher waved Carson back to his seat. "Where do you think you're going?"

Carson opened his mouth and shut it again. "I…"

"I would remind you that Li Bai is in custody. The police can handle any interrogation."

"Yes, but I have contacts in DC—on Capitol Hill. I can send out feelers to my political and diplomatic sources, maybe get some dirt on him that they wouldn't blab to the coppers."

Thrasher raised a palm and said abruptly, "Okay, but I'm not finished with you two amateur sleuths yet."

Palmer had a cold feeling in the pit of her stomach. "What did we do now?"

He held up a large poster. "Luckily we made backup copies of the notice. The first one mysteriously disappeared from the board." In the center of the poster, they saw an enlarged photo of a 1954 Airstream Cruiser. Above it was written in bold letters:

Have You Seen This Camper?
It was stolen from the police impoundment lot
sometime between June 7 & 9
If you have any information pertaining to its
whereabouts, please call
941-555-8290. LBK Police
Reward offered.

"Any idea what happened to this Airstream?" He lowered his gaze to Carson, who sat demurely in his seat, a modest smile playing across his face. "In order to reclaim a vehicle that has been impounded, the owner must pay a fine of $500 plus rental fees for every day it sits in the lot."

Carson perused the photo. "That there's a dandy RV. A real classic." He looked up. "Not sure why anyone would turn it back in. Besides, it was only there two nights."

Thrasher swooped in. "And how do you know that?"

Carson put a finger on the poster. "Says so right here." He grinned at the detective.

Chapter Thirty-Eight

All the birds of the air
Fell a-sighing and a-sobbing,
When they heard the bell toll
For poor Cock Robin.

The Palapa Inn, Sunday, June 18

"No, Hortense, I don't know what will happen to the club. No, I haven't spoken to Hardy since he was arrested... Yes, I'm as flabbergasted as you are. Are you going to be all right?" Palmer listened to the overwrought prattling of the birding club treasurer. She'd suspected that Hortense had feelings for Hardy, and now she had proof. Abundant, tearful, wretched, hand-wringing proof. "I'm so sorry, Hortense. Perhaps you should give Gareth a call? I don't think I'm really the one to... Yes, certainly. When you've had a chance to commis...I mean, comfort him, we'll all get together." *For a good cry.* Poor Hortense. She hung up.

Carson came in from the patio, his phone stuck to his ear. "I'll talk to her, Susan. Put her on the phone... Nestor, honey? Yes, I'm fine. We had a little excitement, but it's over now. No, you never met him. No, I wasn't in any danger. The police took care of it... What?" He snorted. "Sorry, kid, I'm no longer a fugitive. We found culprits for every crime." He eyed

Palmer. "Well, almost every crime. My slate is clean… Okay, let me talk to Mom… Hi Susan, Nestor says you have something to tell me? Uh-huh. Uh-huh. When is it? I'll be there. She wants what? You're kidding. That's more expensive than a wedding dress!" He sighed. "Yes, I know she's worth it. Yes, I will. Just send me the bill. Okay. Bye."

His face a mask of despair, he stared at Palmer.

"Is something wrong? Is Nestor okay?" She hugged him.

"Oh, yeah. *She's* just fine. As for me, I have to make reservations for the poorhouse."

"Why?"

"Nestor and I shall be going to the father-daughter dance at her school in two weeks. I'm expected to be in black tie. And she expects to be in Ralph Lauren." At Palmer's expression, he said, "A knock-off, but painful nonetheless."

"She'll look beautiful."

****

Longboat Key police station, Monday afternoon

"Thanks for coming back in. Did you glean any more information on Tipsy you'd like to share?"

Both Carson and Palmer shook their heads gloomily. Carson said, "Nada. Li Bai was certainly a professional. He's like a ghost. At least my sources haven't come up with any evidence of his past activities. We're no closer to finding out why he killed Tipsy." Carson squinted at the detective. "Do *you* have news?"

"I've got good news and bad news." Thrasher waited.

Finally, Carson said, "We're not biting."

The detective gave up. "Here it is: we not only don't know the 'why' Swallow was killed; unfortunately we can't yet pin down the 'who.' " He held up a file. "I received this report over the weekend from the FBI. Li Bai has produced proof that he represents a Chinese development company. The company is tied to the CCP—"

"As is every single Chinese entity."

"It's a fact. And considering the way they do business, he *is* more or less a spy, but—" Here Thrasher put down the file. "Get this: Li Bai swears he didn't kill anyone. He says his duties do not extend to homicide."

"But he shot Wilfred Vogel in the knee!"

"He's only authorized to intimidate; not to kill."

Carson chuckled. "Not a double-0?"

"Huh?"

Palmer pursed her lips. "If Li Bai wasn't sent to kill Swallow, who stole the crossbow and how did it end up in Florida?"

"I—"

"That reminds me." Carson stood up. "That was a very rare twelfth-century Genoese crossbow. Priceless. Do I get any compensation for its loss?"

Thrasher looked over the top of his glasses. "Surely you don't think the police are liable? You can always check with your insurance company."

Carson glared at Thrasher long enough to establish that it made no difference whatsoever to the policeman. He settled back and devoted himself to grumbling.

Palmer went on. "It all comes back to the briefcase, doesn't it? Just like we said. Hardy was looking for the briefcase. Joanna was looking for the briefcase. Li Bai—also looking for it. As was Vogel."

Carson added, "We still don't know what was in it that was worth killing for."

"True." The detective nodded. "The transactions haven't proved to be unlawful. The archery lessons don't identify the student. And the letter in Chinese appears to be a simple introduction."

"Hardy speaks Mandarin."

The detective gaped. "He does?"

"Uh-huh. That's how he got Li Bai to take him along when he locked us in the bathroom at Zota."

"*Hmm.* Well, the note only mentions Fletcher Avery, the chief of the Enders. He's rumored to be former Irish Republican Army, hiding out somewhere in the Balkans." Thrasher tapped his lip. "Wish we could unearth more about him. The Enders have been linked to all kinds of domestic terror, but to date we haven't been able to track any individuals down."

Palmer wasn't satisfied. "Don't these activist groups always have a social media presence?"

He shook his head. "Even the data we have on their actual number is inconclusive."

"We seem to be at an impasse." She shouldered her purse. "We might as well go."

Thrasher rose. "I have paperwork to do anyway."

Carson and Palmer found themselves on the sidewalk. "I feel as though there's still unfinished business."

"Me too. This Tipsy Swallow thing is frustrating me." He turned to Palmer. "Was it just serendipity that he happened to be here? A drug deal gone bad like you originally proposed?"

"We may never find out." They headed north toward the Palapa. Suddenly, Palmer stopped short.

364

"Wait, I've got it."

"I'm listening."

"The Enders and the think tank—Extended Energy Solutions. Carson, I've been meaning to tell you—"

"Yeah, they're great. I get regular updates from them. They've been working their tails off to—"

"Carson, may I get a word in edgewise?"

"Sure."

"I had to deal with EES when I worked at Interior. They come in at the extreme end of the environmental movement. I doubt very much they were helping you."

"Extreme? As in Enders' extreme?"

"As in, the End Human Hegemony Now folks look like sissified pantywaists compared to EES." She mulled it over. "I'm betting they were keeping tabs on you for Hardy. He seemed to know where you were at all times."

"Huh. He did dog our footsteps, didn't he?"

"Do you think they were in on the land deal along with the Enders?"

"It's possible. I wonder if sending me on that wild goose chase to Zota was a setup."

Palmer sat down on a bench and put her chin in her hand. "There's another loose end we haven't discussed. Your death threats."

"I'm sure it was just a malicious prank."

"Do you think Joanna was behind them?"

"I wouldn't put it past her. She was adamant that I lay off the murder theory."

She sniffed. "Well, we know why."

"True." He pulled her up. "Doesn't matter now. Let's go home."

As they neared the Palapa, an unexpected sight

greeted them: a white stretch limousine. An unfamiliar man sat at the wheel. Carson frowned. "What the hell's Wilfred doing here?"

"Only one way to find out." She marched up the steps to her apartment. The door was ajar.

Vogel sat on the balcony, a drink at his elbow. He turned at the sound of Palmer's steps. "Oh, there you are. You left your door unlocked again." He held up the glass. "I took the liberty of borrowing this and some ice, but I did bring my own vodka."

Palmer stood staring at him until Carson gently pushed her aside. "Can we help you?"

"I was hoping you could apprise me of the latest developments. Is…is everybody in jail who should be in jail?"

Carson sat down next to him. "Was there any particular person you had in mind?"

"No… Um… So Li Bai is in custody? He didn't tell the police anything about me?"

"Nothing they didn't already know. Turns out Li Bai is not a spy—at least not officially. He was just into your run-of-the-mill industrial espionage."

Vogel clicked his teeth. "I knew that. I have no idea where Bantam came up with that ridiculous idea. Most wanted indeed. What rot!"

Palmer went to fix herself a drink. "You want one too, Carson?"

"Yes."

As she neared the kitchen, she noticed the front door was still ajar. She moved to close it, but it was forced open. "Hardy!"

Chapter Thirty-Nine

Who saw him die?
I, said the Fly,
With my little eye,
I saw him die.

The Palapa Inn, Monday, June 19

Hardy held up one hand and pointed. "Get back in the apartment, Palmer." She was going to protest when she caught sight of the pistol in his other hand. He gestured for her to sit next to the two men.

Carson, his voice gravelly with alarm, asked, "How did you get here, Hardy? They couldn't have let you out on bail."

He waved the gun. "Would I have this if they had? No, hick cops couldn't hold me for long. Can you believe it? The lock on the cell door was broken."

That's what you get when you spend all your grant money on fancy vests and night vision goggles.

He sneered. "And that fat sergeant left this Glock lying around where anyone could pick it up."

Carson asked the obvious. "What do you want?"

"I have a bone to pick with little Willy here."

Vogel shrank back. "You stay away from me, Bantam. You killed Atticus and Joanna. I'm sure the police are on your track. It's only a matter of time before they come here."

Why not? Everyone else does. Palmer tamped down her jitters.

Hardy grunted. "Maybe, but I'm not taking the Enders down with me."

Vogel's eyes went wide. "The Enders! What about them?"

"I want you to tell the police that we had nothing to do with your crooked schemes. That we're clean. Get the cops off our back."

Vogel's lower lip trembled. "Sure, Bantam. Sure. I can do that."

Hardy transferred his gaze to Carson. "Know what this prick did? He lied to me."

Well, take a number, buddy.

"You mean about his secret deal with the Chinese?" Carson's glance went from Vogel to Hardy.

He gave a short nod. "Once he'd negotiated that, he started bleating that he needed to back out of our project. When I accused him of double-crossing us, he made up this cock-and-bull story about having evidence that would bring the feds down on the Enders like an iron anvil. And that Wren had it."

Palmer recalled the conversation the last time Hardy held her at gunpoint. "You told me there wasn't anything dodgy in it."

"Right," he said grimly. "Like I said, he lied. The papers didn't mention the Enders. Vogel insinuated the note in Chinese would expose my identity, but it was addressed to Fletcher Avery. The rest of the contents had nothing to do with me or our arrangements."

Palmer opened her mouth, but he was still berating Wilfred. "You had me running around after everyone who had the briefcase. I'll bet you even put the EES jerks up to those anonymous threats."

Vogel exuded innocence. "Anonymous threats? I don't know what you're talking about."

"Oh, come *on*, Vogel." His lip curled. "It nearly screwed everything up. Carson got the wind up and disappeared with the bag."

Carson said through gritted teeth. "It was the think tank? Not Joanna?"

Hardy smacked his lips. "Idiots. Those guys in DC live in a bubble—they have no idea what goes on in the trenches. We Enders had everything under control, but no—they had to stick their noses in. After this, I'm going to recommend we cut ties with them entirely."

There was a short silence as the others considered the pros and cons of telling him that sooner rather than later he wasn't going to be in a position to recommend anything. Finally, Palmer ventured, "So you've been looking for the briefcase all this time?"

"Yeah. I was sure Wren brought it with him to Hawk's, so after I strung him up, I searched the apartment. No dice."

Carson mumbled, "It was in the freezer."

Hardy shook his head. "I never thought of that. Would've saved me killing all those people." His grin was blood-curdling.

"You did bring it down to Florida, though, didn't you, Carson? Just like I told Hardy." Vogel nodded vigorously, as though that would convince the man holding the gun. "You hid it in your house."

Carson shook his head. "The briefcase was never in Florida. I stashed it at Joanna's in Chevy Chase."

Vogel sucked in a breath. He looked accusingly at

Hardy. "So it wasn't in the garage after all."

Hardy glared at him. "Thanks to you, I knocked the girl off for nothing."

Palmer's heart sank. *He casually murders his daughter and now regrets it because it didn't do him any good?*

"And to top it off, I discover you were using me to save your own hide."

Carson looked from Vogel to Hardy. "What makes you think that? Anything in the briefcase to do with Wilfred appeared to be legal and above board."

Hardy scoffed. "He didn't tell you? Wren was divorcing his wife—"

"We knew that."

"Yes, but what you don't know is that the senator's grounds for divorce were adultery, and he named Wilfred Vogel as co-respondent." He gave the little man a mocking salute. "It would have been devastating to your business reputation, not to mention getting hit with a sizable judgment. So you concocted the baloney about the Enders being in jeopardy. You hoped I'd destroy everything in the case, including the divorce papers."

Well, now that's *a twist!* Palmer had an inspiration. "You told Captain Thrasher that Wren hired you to confirm Joanna's affair before admitting it was to monitor her activities with the Enders. But the confession was a lie, wasn't it? "

"Ha-ha, yeah. Everything was a lie. Pretty clever, eh? Muddy the waters… Had you going, didn't I?"

Carson murmured, "How did you discover Joanna had the briefcase with her in Tampa?"

"She called to tell me she'd brought it and did I

want a peek. Bad move on her part."

"You went to her hotel room."

He brandished the Glock, prompting the others to duck. "Goddamn bitch. She teased me with it. Dangled it over the balcony. Claimed it held something that would put me away for life. Really ticked me off." He lowered the gun, but at a movement from Carson swung it back up to aim at Palmer. "Cut it out, Hawk."

Palmer wanted to keep him talking. *Otherwise he'll start knocking us off one by one.* "You killed her to get hold of it."

He hunched his shoulders and spat out, "She gave me no choice."

Palmer would have laughed at his perverted reasoning if she hadn't been staring down the barrel of a gun.

"When I finally got a peep at the contents, I realized I'd been snookered. Tossed the damn thing in a dumpster and hightailed it back to Longboat Key."

Vogel squeaked.

"What are you on about, Willy?"

The little man quavered, "It's not my fault! I didn't know what was in the case either."

"Then who did?"

"Tipsy. Tipsy put all the documents in the case. He tried to blackmail me too, you know."

Hardy was still fuming. "You yellow-bellied dolt. We never should have brought you in. I don't think I need you after all." He raised the pistol.

Palmer said quickly, "Did you know Li Bai wasn't a spy?"

He rolled his eyes. "Man didn't know one end of a firearm from the other. He meant to kill you, Wilfred, but couldn't aim to save his own mother."

"Then what was the purpose of saying he was wanted by the FBI?"

"I figured if you all thought he was this dangerous operative, you wouldn't question it when we disappeared. Or suspect I was not exactly an unwilling hostage."

Carson said heavily, "So you were willing to throw even Li Bai under the bus."

His eyes widened. "On the contrary. As I told Palmer, I helped him get away."

She stirred. "You know he was arrested at the border."

"Oh? On what charge?"

Vogel said it with relish. "Kidnapping. And he'll soon be free since we now know it was a hoax and that you're responsible for the murders."

Palmer corrected him. "All of them except Tipsy. Li Bai hasn't been completely exonerated for that."

Hardy snickered. "Really? Too bad he didn't do it."

"What do you mean?"

"Wilfred told me Tipsy Swallow had given his briefcase to the senator. When Joanna went to Carson's apartment to have it out over the bill, I followed her, intending to get it back."

Carson said, "But you couldn't find it."

"If only I'd been hungry, eh?" He sniffed. "What we didn't know was that Tipsy was watching the house. He saw Carson leave, then Joanna and me go in. After we left, he entered the apartment, found Atticus dead, and stole the crossbow."

"Stole the crossbow?" Palmer started to stand up

but, when Hardy jerked his head, sat back down. "What on earth for?"

"So he could blackmail Carson."

"But Wren wasn't shot with a crossbow."

"Let me finish. When I arrived, Joanna was fiddling around with it and accidently shot an arrow into the sofa. If the police had done their job, they would have found it. I wiped the bow and left it near the body, hoping they would figure that Carson tried to shoot Wren first."

"You wanted to frame him." *Well, at least* one *person wanted to.*

"Yeah, and it would've worked if it weren't for Tipsy. While the newspapers were all over Carson's disappearance, none of them mentioned a crossbow. I began to suspect that Carson had somehow doped out my strategy and taken it with him. Then Vogel tipped me off that Swallow was on your trail, so I followed him."

"When did you find out Tipsy had the crossbow?"

"Got in touch with him once I got down here. He told me he was going to hold it over Carson's head—threaten to tell the police Hawk was responsible for Wren's death." He chortled. "He had no clue the bow wasn't the murder weapon."

Palmer put her hand over her mouth and whispered, "You killed Tipsy."

He pulled a box of mints from his pocket, opened it with one hand, and popped a candy in his mouth. "I would have in a New York minute—but no, it wasn't me."

It occurred to Palmer that Hardy would have no trouble laying claim to a fourth murder. *So what's he up to?*

Vogel blustered. "Don't be modest, Bantam. You cleared the field of everyone who blocked your path."

Hardy allowed himself a slow grin. "Every one…but Tipsy. Yeah, I ran him down in Florida. I hoped he'd lead me to the briefcase. I was there—in the bar—when you met him at Tide Tables."

Carson gasped. "It was *you*, Wilfred?"

Vogel pinched his lips together. "It was only eleven thirty in the morning, and the bum was already blotto. Sheesh. I'd been trying to get rid of him for years, but I owed his father."

"What for?"

"Teddy Senior had given me seed money for my first startup. I promised him I'd keep his son on the payroll." He shook his head. "Tipsy had been a dead weight for years."

"So you thought wasting him was more honorable than breaking a promise?" Carson was incredulous.

Vogel shifted in his seat and stared at the floor. "I didn't *mean* to. We'd arranged to meet and then take the boat to Carson's house. Tipsy was sure the briefcase was there and we could sneak in from the water side. Halfway across he started sniveling about scoring a piece of the action. He didn't know why I was so eager to get hold of the case, but he figured he could soak me for money too."

"Extort *both* you and Carson?"

"Uh-huh. When I told him I didn't believe he had the goods on Carson, he pulled the crossbow from his satchel. I tried to wrestle it away from him, and the damn thing went off. Struck him smack dab in the heart." Vogel's chest heaved, and he made a retching sound. "God, there was a lot of blood." His nose wrinkled. "He was clearly dead. I rowed to the closest mangrove island and dropped him overboard, then beached the boat and tossed the oars away."

"Why didn't you use the motor?"

"Too noisy."

Carson whistled. "How did you get back to Longboat? The Sister Keys are only accessible by water."

Palmer chimed in. "Who helped you, Wilfred? Who was your accomplice?"

"Accomplice? The last thing I needed was a witness. No, I stripped down to my skivvies and swam across the bayou. Fetched up at the end of Norton Street. Told a guy I'd flipped my kayak. He gave me a ride back to Cannons, where Li Bai met me in the limo."

The white jacket I saw hanging from a branch.

Carson was pensive. "The crossbow broke apart in the fight. Why did you take the stock with you? Why not dump it?"

He shrugged. "I was too upset to think rationally. I mean, it's not as though I'd planned any of this. Once I'd had time to consider, the smart thing to do seemed to be to follow through on Tipsy's plan and leave the crossbow at Carson's house."

And that's how it ended up in the go-kart.

"Wait—Captain Thrasher said they had documentary proof that you were in DC when Tipsy died. How did you wangle that?"

"Easy peasy. Simply missed the flight. They don't scrub the manifest unless you cancel. Then I gave a junior executive my credit card for a well-deserved weekend at a luxury hotel." He beamed. "My employees love me."

All Palmer could think to say was "Oh." That seemed to sum it up for the rest of them.

Hardy had been grousing throughout Vogel's recitation. "Are you done? If I may *continue*."

Whew, guess he resents anyone hogging the limelight. "Do go on, Hardy."

He said bitterly, "No thanks to little Willy, now I know the briefcase was a nothingburger. The Enders will be okay—there's zero evidence tying them to either Vogel or the Chinese."

"What about the memo in Mandarin naming Fletcher Avery? The police know he's the leader of the Enders."

He clucked his tongue. "Yes, Avery would have been an issue, but he's been deleted, so we're copacetic."

"Deleted? You killed him *too*?" Vogel's jaw dropped.

"Killed? Hee-hee, that's a good one. Fletcher Avery is yours truly. My alias. I simply removed him from the database."

"So…the Irish Republican Army? Hiding out in Europe? All a sham?"

"Pretty swashbuckling yarn, eh?" Hardy preened.

"So you're in the clear. Are you going to let us go then?" Carson's voice was uncharacteristically querulous.

"I haven't decided about you two. As for him—" He bore down on Vogel. "After all his dirty tricks, he deserves to die." He pointed the pistol at Wilfred's forehead.

Vogel gurgled, "No!"

In the century that passed while they waited for the shot, a flock of ravens broke out in loud caws. *They must be after a hawk.* An hysterical giggle rose unbidden. *Raven. Hawk. Ha ha...Am I going to die?* She closed her eyes and thus didn't catch Carson's quick movement. She did hear Hardy scream.

She opened them in time to see Carson holding him in a painful-looking half-nelson and the gun on the floor. Vogel was cowering in the corner. "Call 9-1-1, would you, dear?"

She ambled over to her phone, clicked Talk, and dialed. "Captain Thrasher? Are you perchance missing a prisoner?"

Chapter Forty

Daisy, Daisy,
Give me your answer, do.
I'm half crazy, all for the love of you!
It won't be a stylish marriage,
I can't afford a carriage
But you'll look sweet upon the seat
Of a bicycle built for two.

Longboat Key police station, Monday, June 19

"It's official. Li Bai is the feds' problem now." Captain Thrasher put down the phone. "Ollie, take Mr. Vogel back to his cell."

"Actually, Detective, I know the way." It didn't appear to Palmer that Wilfrid was joking.

"Nonetheless. I don't want to have to chase after you too. The foreign agent stuff is on hold for now, since you're facing a potential murder charge. At the very least, two counts of negligent homicide."

Palmer watched the sergeant and his prisoner leave. "Well, all our questions are answered at last. If Hardy hadn't broken out and come after Vogel, we might not have known the rest of the story." She avoided Thrasher's eyes.

"We've solved the mysteries of the Mandarin note, the financial papers, even the divorce form. What else was in the briefcase?" Carson tapped his lip. "Do you suppose it was Joanna who took the archery lessons?"

Palmer mulled this over. "She bought the bow April 10, didn't she? Four days before Atticus died…It could have been her."

"Yes, but how did the ticket get in the briefcase then?"

Thrasher cleared his throat. "I forgot to tell you. I had my detectives visit the shooting range in Fairfax County. Only one of our players appeared to have availed himself of the facilities."

" 'Himself?' So it wasn't Joanna?"

"No. It was Senator Atticus Wren."

"Atticus!"

"Uh-huh. The manager remembered him. He said Wren was very gracious—not at all like a politician, he said. He told them his wife was going to give him a crossbow for his birthday, and he wanted to be prepared."

"Joanna's crossbow."

"So the ticket stub had nothing to do with the Enders, or Vogel, or the Chinese. It must have been mixed in with the other papers he put in there."

"All right, but who put which papers in the briefcase?"

"Well, Tipsy stole the briefcase with Vogel's land purchase documents and the note about Li Bai in order to finger Wilfrid. Atticus added the divorce form and the rest." Carson grunted. "It's funny. For a while there, we thought there was a different perpetrator for every murder. No wonder we couldn't figure it out."

"Remember when we suspected Li Bai of offing them all?" Thrasher grinned. "He was the only one who *didn't* try to kill somebody."

Carson took Palmer's hand and stood up. "Ring around the rosy?"

****

Coquina Bay Walk, Friday, June 30, early evening

Palmer flipped through her bird book. "Yellow breast, yellow breast. Damn, I only caught a glimpse of it. I *hate* warblers." As she turned another page, she caught movement out of the corner of her eye. A large brown bird with a banded tail flitted from branch to branch in a gumbo limbo tree. It opened its beak and emitted a series of loud toots. She ran a finger down the index. *Yes! It's a mangrove cuckoo! What luck!* The bird disappeared into the underbrush.

As she started down the hill, a streaked and spotted set of wings flashed past her. *Let me see if I can get a little closer.* She inched down the dirt path to the bridge that crossed to the mangroves. The bird perched on the railing. *Juvenile red-shouldered hawk. Phooey.* They were a dime a dozen. She scanned the marsh below.

A black-crowned night heron hove into view, stepping daintily among the spider-like legs of the red mangroves. It moved gradually farther and farther away. She walked after it, her binoculars glued to her face. When she stumbled over a root, she lowered the glasses. The spot she found herself in was unfamiliar.

She took a few irresolute steps to her right, then to her left, the black mud squishing up through her sandals. *Yuck. Where's the water?* She hobbled toward a glint of blue. Suddenly the trees fell away, opening to sight a broad expanse of bay. She shaded her eyes.

A bass boat chugged around the point. The man in the stern cut the motor. "I thought I'd find you here.

Can I interest you in a lift to the Bridge Tender Inn for a nosh and a sip?"

She checked her watch. *Nearly six o'clock!* "Why certainly, sailor."

"I want to talk to you."

Uh oh. I don't like the sound of that.

Carson helped her in, wrinkling his nose at the smell. "Have you been wallowing in a pig sty? Excuse me—a wild boar sty?"

"I slipped in the mud."

"Cast your feet over the side and rinse your toes off in the water." She did as she was told, and he motored toward the restaurant at the Bridge Street pier.

The tide was receding, and they chose a table near the wet rocks. The setting sun cast purple beams over their heads, reflected in the dark gray water. Palmer didn't bother to look at the laminated menu. "Hi, Ivy. I want a gin and tonic first, and then Fred's chicken livers with a draft."

"Same here." Carson paused. "And a plate of celery sticks, please." When Palmer blanched, he grinned. "A salute to the absent Hardy."

"May he remain absent," she replied tersely.

"I'll bring your drinks right away." The waitress headed back into the building.

Carson was quiet. Palmer decided it was up to her to start the ball rolling. "So…did your friend report to you on the fortunes of S. 219?"

"He did. It passed out of committee and is on the agenda for a Floor vote next week."

"Senator Wren would be relieved."

"Yes. It will definitely put a crimp in the Chinese plans to take us over."

"What about Li Bai? What will happen to him?"

"He was deported. He may not have been a Chinese James Bond, but he's still a *persona non grata*."

"That's good." She gazed at a mullet skiff slowly making its way down the Intracoastal. A squad of seagulls clamored in its wake, scrambling for the chum the fishermen tossed in the water. They looked like paparazzi chasing after the latest Hollywood sensation. "And Vogel?"

Carson shook his head. "Thrasher says they need more evidence to try him for Tipsy's death."

"But he confessed to us!"

"Well, he did claim it was an accident. Anyway, he's lawyered up and is now fighting the charge on the grounds that the prosecution's main witness is a criminal who killed three people."

"Hardy."

"Uh-huh." Carson chuckled. "Even if he gets off, a band of his shareholders have filed a multimillion-dollar lawsuit against him for shirking his fiduciary duty. Wilfred will be a poor man soon." He lapsed into silence again.

Palmer watched him. *Was that his big news? Nothing about...well.* She didn't have much more time. The days were counting down until she had to leave. *All he said was he wanted to talk to me.* That could mean anything. *Palmer, you're working yourself into a tizzy for nothing. Tell him your news. Get it over with.* "Carson? I—"

"The drinks should be here soon."

"Um. Yes." She wiped her lips. "Boy, am I thirsty."

"Did you see any interesting birds on Leffis Key?"

"A mangrove cuckoo."

"That's good?"

"Yes, they're quite rare. Oh, and I think I saw a scissor-tailed flycatcher. That would be a life bird."

"But you're not sure."

"No."

He must be waiting until she had some alcohol in her to absorb the blow. *What's he going to say? That it's been fun, but now it's over?* She was trying to remember what song that line came from and didn't see the waitress approach. The sudden plunk of the glass in front of her made her jump, and she knocked both drinks over. "Oh dear, what a klutz I am!"

Ivy dropped her hand towel on the table and swept the liquid and ice off onto the sandy ground. "Not to worry, luv. I'll get two more."

Palmer looked at Carson. His whole front was wet. A slice of lime was stuck on his collar. His smile was wry. "Are you trying to tell me something?"

She picked up a wad of paper napkins and wiped at his shirt. "I was distracted. I'm so sorry."

He caught her hand. "Distracted? By what?"

"Oh, I…I was thinking about a song."

"Not a nursery rhyme? We seem to be living in them lately."

"No. Carson, what did you want to tell me?"

"Hang on." He stood up and carefully grasped the two new drinks from the waitress. Still standing, he set one in front of Palmer. "Take a sip."

She took more than a sip. She swallowed half the drink. "Okay."

"Ready?" He sat down. "First, Albert's coming

down to Longboat Key, and he wants his house back."

"You mean you have to find alternate lodgings?"

"Not just for me; for my ménage of vehicles."

She sniggered. "Why don't you just buy an airport hangar?"

"The thought occurred, but then something else came along." He peered at her. "I want you to be the first to know. I've landed a new job."

"Wonderful!" She didn't really mean it, though. *It means he's staying here and I'll never see him again.*

"I've been named communications director for the largest field archery association in the country. I'll still be writing speeches, but it pays a whole lot better than Senator Wren did."

"It sounds perfect for you." She meant it this time, even though her heart had dropped from its usual spot down to somewhere below her appendix.

"The thing is—" He gulped his drink. "The thing is, it's in DC."

Life took a sudden upswing. "Washington, DC? Why that's fantas—I mean, swell."

He fell back in his chair, his eyes boring into hers. "Why?"

Is he just curious or is that hurt in his eyes? "I was waiting to tell you. I took a job too. I don't know if I mentioned it, but I used to volunteer at the Atlantic Birding Association. I got a call from Mr. Pochard, the president. He's a sweetheart—eighty-five and still up at dawn leading expeditions. Anyway, he'd heard that I left Interior and offered me a position in the membership services office. I'll be working at their headquarters."

It was his turn to be cautious. "Oh, I see. Are they

based in Florida?"

"No." She couldn't keep the joy out of her voice. "It's in Virginia! Alexandria."

"Oh? Oh! Well, that's nice." His expression was unreadable. "When do you start?"

The joy deflated like an old air mattress. "Not for another couple of months." She said tentatively, "When we're—you're—settled, maybe we could get together some time. Up there. You know, for coffee."

"Sure, but…"

Ivy set plates of chicken livers in front of each. "You want those beers now?"

Carson looked up at her. "Do you have any champagne?"

"We got domestic. You want a bottle?"

"Depends."

"Depends on what?"

He turned his gaze to Palmer. "On what she says."

Ivy looked from one face to the other and smiled. "I'll put it on ice."

Palmer was confused. "Champagne? Oh, to celebrate our new gigs. That's a nice touch."

"Nah, you celebrate a new job with chicken livers. You celebrate a new life with champagne."

"What does that mean?"

He took her hand. "I don't have to start the job for another six weeks either. Before I head back to DC, I'm going to Chicago to escort my daughter to the father-daughter dance at her school. After that I plan to drive out to Arizona."

"Okay."

"And hunt up some hummingbirds."

"Hummingbirds! Oh, I should give you my book. I

told you there are at least eighteen species of them in the southern part of the state. Some of them are very rare." She looked wistful. "I wish I were going with you."

"You wouldn't mind sleeping in the Airstream?"

"Me?"

He ignored her and spoke to the air. "I hope your idea of a honeymoon includes sleeping on a cot and boiling your coffee. Of course you already know I'm a whiz at creating gourmet dishes out of odds and ends. You won't starve. And you can help me identify the native birds. The only one I know is the vulture, but that's because I watched endless westerns when I was a kid. We'll have to find a garage to keep the cars, but we can hook the Harley up to the back of the camper like we did before. Yes, I think it'll work."

Palmer took a breath for him. "I—"

At that moment, Ivy arrived holding a bottle. She stood looking at Palmer, her fingers around the head of the cork.

"I think it'll work too."

Pop.

A word about the author...

Librarian, anthropologist, Congressional aide, speechwriter—M. S. Spencer has lived or traveled in five of the seven continents. She holds a BA from Vassar College, a diploma in Arabic Studies from the American University in Cairo, and Masters in Anthropology and in Library Science from the University of Chicago. All of this tends to insinuate itself into her works.

Ms. Spencer has published sixteen romantic suspense and mystery novels. She currently divides her time between the Gulf Coast of Florida and a tiny village in Maine.

http://msspencertalespinner.blogspot.com